P9-CSC-811

THE
BLACK
BROOK

THE
BLACK
BROOK

TOM DRURY

HOUGHTON MIFFLIN COMPANY

BOSTON NEW YORK 1998

Copyright © 1998 by Tom Drury
All rights reserved

For information about permission to
reproduce selections from this book, write to
Permissions, Houghton Mifflin Company,
215 Park Avenue South,
New York, New York 10003.

Library of Congress Cataloging-in-Publication Data
Drury, Tom.
The black brook / Tom Drury.
p.   cm.
ISBN 0-395-70194-5
I. Title.
PS3554.R84B58   1998
813'.54 — dc21   98-12843
CIP

Printed in the United States of America

QUM 10 9 8 7 6 5 4 3 2 1

Book design by Melodie Wertelet

FOR

VERONICA GENG

1941–1997

My poor Captain! He's going where we are all going, and the only extraordinary thing is that he hasn't gone there sooner.

Jacques the Fatalist

I

RASPORAS

1

It was a hot dry dusty summer day in New Hampshire. Mary and Paul Emmons had just taken a booth in a diner called Happy's when Mary noticed a dog in a car in the parking lot with its head turned upside down.

"What's the matter with that dog?" she said.

"Where?" said Paul.

Mary touched the screen. Rust flakes fell to the windowsill. "Down there."

"I don't see it."

"I don't think it has enough air to breathe."

"I don't see a dog."

Paul and Mary were natives of the United States who had lived in Belgium for the past six years. Before that, they had owned a house in Providence, where Paul had been an accountant. Then he came under indictment and eventually testified in a well-publicized criminal trial, for which the federal government gave him a new identity.

When the trial was over, Mary and Paul moved to Spokane. But they did not like Spokane, things did not work out so well for them there, and after seven months in Spokane they got on a plane and flew to Belgium, where Mary had relatives whom she had visited during her childhood summers.

Mary and Paul ended up living and working in a modest hotel in the Ardennes. Mary managed the inn and Paul kept the books, and between them they had to perform every sort of hotel duty except fixing the electrical wiring. It felt like, and was, a life in exile. Paul had more guilty knowledge than Mary, but Mary had some too. She was not a CPA but she understood numbers.

They had been warned never to come back to New England, but this was the third time they had done so. The urge to return is great among protected witnesses, and the more Paul and Mary came back, the less threatened they felt. They drove past their old house in rented cars with their arms resting in open windows. It was a shame how the place had fallen apart, with tall scorched grass and sagging gutters. They visited Paul's family down in South County, neither making a show of their presence nor trying to hide. In movies it may seem that gangsters have nothing better to do all day than hunt down and shoot turncoat accountants, but in the Emmonses' experience the opposite was true.

During these rare visits to the States, however, Paul and Mary found it difficult to get along with Paul's family. His mother and father, and especially his aunts and uncles and cousins, seemed both jealous of Mary's Belgian relatives and hostile to Mary and Paul themselves. The truth is Paul's family had never been that wild about Mary, who even before her banishment among French speakers would lapse into French for no particular reason. And Paul had thrown a cloud over the family, first by conspiring to racketeer and then by informing on people who had once considered him, if not their friend, at least their associate.

After a week of visiting Paul's relatives in Rhode Island, Mary and Paul were always more than ready to drive up to New Hampshire, where they owned thirty-nine acres of maples and meadows and evergreens, not far from Carr Mountain and the Polar Caves.

A waitress in red shorts and a white sweatshirt brought laminated menus that felt sharp enough to cut paper, Paul and Mary ordered, and as the waitress walked away they could see the small flags of many nations printed on the back of her sweat-shirt.

Mary pressed her light thick hair back along the sides of her head, her eyes widened, and she stabbed Paul's hand with the prong of a barrette. "There that dog is," she said. "Look now. You can only see him when he's on this side of the car."

Paul looked. He saw a tan dog whose neck was twisted so that the bottom of the jaw pointed almost straight up. The dog seemed to be staggering in circles. It would climb onto the passenger seat again and again, only to stumble down onto the floorboard each time.

"He doesn't look very good," Paul conceded.

"He must be suffocating."

"Hard to say from this angle, Mary."

By the time the waitress in the flag sweatshirt brought food to the booth, other patrons had gathered at the windows, making the dog's predicament harder for Paul to dismiss. A thin man in a black baseball hat spoke up loudly to ask if the driver of the car — a gray Audi with a Princeton sticker in the back window — was in the diner. No answer.

"Some people," said a redhead who held a pack of cigarettes in one hand and a lighter in the other. "You don't leave a dog with the windows rolled up in heat like this."

"It's not right," agreed an old man whom some of the others had called Judge, although he did not necessarily look like a member of the judiciary.

"And they're from Princeton," said the man in the black hat. "You'd think they would know better."

"They have education, all right, but no common sense," said the woman who gripped her smoking materials like pistols.

"You know it, Bonnie," said the old man. "Some people have learned too much."

Mary put her fork down. "I'm not eating."

"Maybe it's unlocked," said Paul.

They walked out of the diner and down a flight of cement stairs to the gravel lot. Sun glinted on the closed windows of the Audi. They tried the handles but there was not even a click that would have suggested engagement with some opening mechanism.

The car had been washed not long ago, and its gleaming charcoal surface, dusted with fine sand, seemed especially closed to Paul and Mary. They stood watching the dog, who climbed and fell, climbed and fell, and whose left ear, they could now see, was turned inside out.

Paul said that the dog almost seemed drunk.

"Of course he seems drunk," said Mary. "Because what does liquor do? It cuts the flow of oxygen to the brain. He can't breathe. He can't breathe and now he's going to die."

"Wouldn't he just pass out?"

"He will if we stand here long enough," said Mary. "He'll pass out and then die."

Paul put his hands on his knees and made eye contact with the dog. It seemed like the usual dog, dealing with enclosure through meaningless repetitive motion, except that its head and ear were very strange. "There must be a tire iron in our car. That's what we're talking about, isn't it? Something heavy."

Mary ran off, her yellow dress swaying in the wavering heat. When she returned she carried a cruciform lug wrench that she handed to Paul. He hefted the wrench in his right hand and scanned the smooth curving glass. What would a sensible person do? A swing of the tire iron would either save the dog's life or simply break the window of an expensive car with a grotesque dog inside. Perhaps the dog had rabies and would jump out and bite them. Then they would have to get all those shots in the stomach, if that was still the treatment for rabies. Perhaps bits of glass would fly into the dog's eyes, adding blindness to its many other problems.

Mary tapped the glass, chewed her fingernail, placed her hands on her hips. "*Vogue la galère,*" she said.

"What if the dog has rabies?" said Paul.

"I can't see driving around casually with a rabid dog."

"All right. Probably they wouldn't," said Paul.

Just then a short stout man with a long white apron and a gray goatee came running down the stairs. "Wait," he said. "I'm Happy."

"Excuse me?" said Paul.

"They call me Happy. I run the diner."

"Oh, I got you."

"I have an idea where you can find the owners," said Happy. "They're probably down the street at L'Embarras du Choix. That's another restaurant — they serve French food — and their customers are not supposed to use this parking lot, but a lot of times they do anyway."

Happy's words made Paul happy, though he understood how keenly Mary had wanted to hear and see that breaking glass.

"Hurry," she said. "There isn't much time."

Paul loped down the street of the New Hampshire town, past young trees with broken branches, past a newspaper store with model airplanes in the window, past a souvenir shop called Not Just Unicorns. A brass plate bore the name of the French restaurant. Paul stood before two wooden doors with opaque windows, of frosted glass. He wiped the sweat from his eyes. He did not want to go in, because he knew what he would find: people with money. He had tried once upon a time to get money himself and instead had been relegated to a tumbledown inn in Belgium. Not long before this trip, in fact, he had experienced a strange moment of self-awareness at the inn. He had been pouring liquid drain opener into a sink, scratching his stomach and looking absently out at cows standing in the Ardennes rain. Suddenly he had the notion that he had been doing these things forever — pouring, scratching, looking — and that in arriving at this moment he had come at last to his essence. And now, on the verge of entering the restaurant, he felt as if the customers, when their heads turned in his direction, would not see a hero trying to save the life of a dog but someone frozen ludicrously in time with a bottle of drain opener in his hand.

Nonetheless, in he went. Cool air brushed his ears, brown velvet covered round tables, diners huddled over pale glasses, and candles burned with steady light.

"I'm very sorry," said a waiter, "but you can't come in here wearing tennis shoes."

"Won't be long," said Paul, moving to the center of the restaurant. "Excuse me, folks. There's an Audi parked down the street with Maryland plates and a dog inside. I need to find the owner."

Nothing happened at first. Then a man stood slowly at one of the tables. He wore a canvas jacket with a green suede patch on one shoulder and an expression of infinite patience. "I have an Audi, and I have a dog."

"It seems to be running out of air," said Paul.

"Yes," said the man. "That's what he's like."

"His head is upside down."

"Rusty has a problem with his head," said the man. "What of it?" He laughed quietly. A woman sitting at his table took a drink of wine and gazed mildly around the room. Now Paul heard condescending laughter from other tables as well. It was the very sort of class antagonism that he had anticipated.

"Well, I wouldn't presume to tell you about your own dog," said Paul. "But I can tell you this — there's a mob of people about to knock the windows out of your car."

The man extended his hand and introduced himself as Raymond Scovill, as if Paul had, through his persistence, passed some kind of test. They left the restaurant together and walked to the diner called Happy's. The sun beat down, but Raymond Scovill stopped to light a pipe and in general could not be hurried. Perhaps by now Mary had broken the window and discovered that the dog was not suffering from oxygen deprivation after all. Paul hoped the window was intact. He hoped that someone cautious had taken charge of the tire iron. He wondered what it would cost to replace the window and clean thousands of slivers of safety glass from the interior. Perhaps a special high-powered vacuum cleaner would be required.

"I don't mind explaining," said Raymond. "And it's a good thing, I expect, that people are concerned. But I can tell you, the dog is fine."

"You've got to leave some ventilation."

Raymond nodded with a mouthful of smoke. The pipe bobbed up and down. "No, you're right of course. But it's not as if the car is airtight. I drive around with the windows closed, and I seem to get along all right."

"It's different when the car is moving."

Raymond shrugged. "Point taken."

"What is wrong with the dog?"

"It's a condition of the inner ear. We believe there was an infection that went unchecked when he was a pup. It's a long story. We picked Rusty up at an animal shelter in Bethesda some years ago. He had arrived at the shelter in much the same shape as you see him in today. Smaller, of course, but functionally the same. The funny thing is that Rusty enjoys traveling. Although I admit he can be disturbing to watch. It's a problem for us. Many people want to know what's wrong, what's wrong with Rusty."

Crossing the parking lot of the diner with Raymond Scovill, Paul remembered walking up the courthouse steps with his lawyer back in 1991. Paul's lawyer wore a stiff blue suit with the jacket unbuttoned so that the sides opened like a cabinet, and he carried a briefcase as big as a suitcase. By that time Paul was so familiar with federal agents and their bad jokes that he had welcomed the uncertain prospect of beginning again, with a new name and no friends. The future lay open for him and Mary, as it had on their honeymoon. He held this thought in his mind all during testimony, and no one understood how he could rat on the other conspirators with such an untroubled face.

A dozen people had gathered in the parking lot to argue the merits of assaulting the car in order to save the dog. Calm now in her yellow summer dress, Mary seemed the still center of the commotion. Paul took her hand as Raymond made his way to the car. Everyone understood who he was, and a murmur of anticipation washed over the crowd. Raymond removed his jacket, took the keys from the pocket, folded the jacket inside out, and laid it carefully over the hood of the car. Then he opened the door, leashed Rusty, and led him down onto the pavement — all while continuing to smoke his pipe.

"So you see, he is all right," said Raymond. "Aren't you, Rusty? Rusty had the people worried for nothing."

The dog was friendly enough, and his deformities and falling seemed less grotesque when they were known not to be life-threatening. Yet the people were not satisfied. It was the wrong outcome. They almost wanted to go ahead and break the car windows anyway. The old man called Judge led the group into the diner, but he turned at the top of the stairs.

"Maybe there's no harm this time, but I tell you that it isn't right," he said.

Raymond Scovill walked Rusty aimlessly around the parking lot, opened a window an inch or two, and shut the dog inside again. His hand brushed the metal contours of the car.

"There's so much dust in the air," he said. "I washed the car yesterday, and while it appears to be clean, if you look closely, you'll see that the entire surface is coated with dust."

Paul and Mary drove away from the diner as Raymond crossed the street on his way back to L'Embarras du Choix. He gestured with the pipe, as if writing words in the air. They waved in return and headed for the motel where they were staying.

"How do you feel?" said Paul.

"Hungry," said Mary. "Hungry and tired."

They took showers and fell asleep with wet hair on a hard flat bed in a room with varnished wooden walls and a painting of a woman holding a bushel basket of cherries.

Between legal fees and fines, the trial had cost Paul and Mary their savings, their car, and the house in Providence. The land in

New Hampshire was all they had managed to keep. The title had been transferred to Paul's cousin Lane, who had committed suicide some years before by jumping from a bridge in California. He'd been jilted by someone. If this ghost transfer were ever found out — which it wouldn't be, thanks to the skillful way in which Paul had set it up and the laissez-faire attitude of the town clerk involved — they could lose the thirty-nine acres too. So they had the land but couldn't do much with it, just show up once every couple of years, get a motel room nearby, and wander through the trees and grass for a few days before flying back to Brussels.

Paul and Mary woke up and went for a drive as the sun lowered in the sky. They picked up hummus sandwiches and beers on the way out of town and ate hungrily and silently in the car with the crumbs falling in their laps. A quarter mile past an auction house where they had never seen anyone, let alone an auction, they turned onto a sand road that climbed through dark dense evergreens into the hills.

Blue shade covered the crest of the road. Paul pulled the car off in soft grass and they stepped out onto their land. A trail wound through evenly spaced trees, and after some distance the trees gave way to a high golden meadow from which mountains could be seen, miles away.

Once there had been a farm here. Now brittle grass grew, and wildflowers, and trees, and here and there you might find an iron ring or a scrap of machinery. The skeleton of a truck rested at the top of the meadow. Every part of the truck that was not metal had disappeared. The doors stood wide open — left that way sixty or seventy years ago, they had frozen in place. Paul and Mary spread a red motel blanket on the grass by the truck. They could feel the blades through the thin blanket. No matter how hot it became, a breeze always moved through this meadow.

Paul opened two bottles of beer and passed one to Mary. They drank deeply and looked at the mountains.

"You know what I'm thinking?" said Paul. Mary shut one eye and shook her head. "That dog could have gotten out of this truck without any trouble at all."

Mary smiled ruefully, her long legs stretched across the red blanket.

"Do you remember when you loved me?" she said.

"I love you now."

"Not like you did then."

2

Mary and Paul had met seventeen years before, when he was a junior in college and she was a young widow.

Paul had attended Sherwood University in Quebec, where it was accepted fact that your studies would come to nothing, that you would fail and go on unemployment, if you did not obtain some kind of internship. Any kind of internship would do. So Paul's Uncle Bernard, a captain of the Boston police, got him an internship.

Paul sublet an apartment in the city of Somerville, outside Boston. The apartment did not cost much, and Paul found that cleaning the sink with Lysol held the cockroaches at bay. He lived above a package store run by a woman in a wheelchair who was a student of Somerville history.

"There was plenty of opposition to the railroads at first," she would say. "People put up barricades. They could not stop the trains. Still, there is something I admire about it."

"What were the barricades made of?" said Paul.

"Does it matter?"

He worked downtown at night, on the fifteenth floor of a narrow building of light green stone near Boston Harbor. He would ride the Red Line across the Charles and climb the stairs from the subway stop under South Station, carrying a brown paper bag with his supper and a Foster's Lager inside.

He had come from a small town in Rhode Island, and the mere fact of getting around in the city made him feel worldly and competent in a jaded way. The setting sun dropped shadows on the streets. Taxicabs and Ryder trucks rattled along Atlantic Avenue. The wind came off the harbor and on some nights the elevator would scrape the shaft sides going up or down.

Paul typed the details of felony assaults on a keyboard hooked by ponderous wires to a cathode-ray tube. That was the sum of his internship. He worked by himself at a long metal table flanked by rows of shelves bearing Xeroxed crime records from seven cities in the greater Boston area. The seven cities had not wanted to make or consolidate these copies but had done so under the terms of a federal grant that they had used to buy new guns and undercover disguises. The orphaned records resided in damp cardboard boxes, and the shelves groaned and shifted ominously as Paul moved among them, pulling boxes down or putting them back.

The work went slowly, as the terminal that he had been given lagged, froze, and buzzed in threatening tones. The machine stored information by punching holes in rolls of mint-green paper. When a roll was full of holes, Paul took it off its spool and snapped a rubber band around it. Then he tossed the banded roll into a shoebox. He was in no hurry once he understood that nothing was required. The only trend he identified was the tendency of home assaults to take place in the kitchen.

A gaunt professor of criminology named M. Leonard Dalton came up to the fifteenth floor every once in a while to supervise Paul's internship. He wore a silver bracelet identifying himself as an organ donor, and carried a leather portfolio full of car magazines, for he had restored a Fiat convertible.

"There've been three more kitchen scenes tonight," Paul said. "One with a serving fork."

"Don't think about patterns," said the professor. He smoked emphatically, with the cigarette jammed down between his index and middle fingers. "Take any two researchers and provide them with the same material, and the chances are one will make fine, startling observations and the other one will end up with bland results. What accounts for the disparity? Well, in all likelihood the second one got entranced by the anecdotal. And as a result he can kiss his research money goodbye."

"Was one of those researchers you?" said Paul.

"I've lost funding. It's nothing to be ashamed of."

Paul typed furiously, then stopped. "The woman in the kitchen was named Cheryl," he said. "When the cops arrived she was standing by the electric range with a fork hanging out of her arm. I can't get over it."

"It is a wicked world."

"She said, 'It isn't what you think.'"

"I drove the Fiat tonight but it needs a new head."

Paul wondered about the proper response to this remark. "That's too bad," he said.

"I'm getting this white smoke, just a little touch of white smoke. I don't like driving the Fiat into Boston in the best of circumstances. The thing about a convertible is they can slice through the roof and tear out the radio in a heartbeat. But my wife has our other car."

Paul cracked his knuckles and stared at the glass screen. "You leave it on the street?"

"Oh Jesus, no. It's in a parking garage. And so in that respect you would think I could relax. But even in a garage someone could go ahead and slash through the roof in a matter of seconds."

"Do you have insurance?"

"I'm working on a comprehensive package."

"Listen to this one," said Paul. "'Subject states that he did not mean to hit complainant in face and states furthermore that he does not know what gets into him sometimes.'"

Dalton turned the pages of *Car & Driver* with his heels resting on Paul's table. "What's your major again?"

"Biology and economics."

"We never get criminology students. Year after year they throw in obscure majors like you just because your old man is some big deal down at the cop shop."

"My uncle."

"You prove my point. What school did you go to?"

"Sherwood University," said Paul. "It's in Quebec. Maybe I'm not the one for the job, but it all seems like some kind of joke."

"Well, that's right," said Dalton. "It is a joke. But even joke books have a serious chapter."

"I could type faster if I had a better terminal. I know that much."

"Everybody wants something. Why Quebec? Are you Canadian? Or should I say, Are you *a* Canadian?"

Paul shook his head. "I'm from Rhode Island."

"The little state."

"Sherwood gave me the best deal of all the colleges I applied to."

Dalton planted his feet on the floor and hunched forward to tear a coupon from his magazine. "I'll bet that was a spirited competition."

The internship left Paul's days free. He visited Revere Beach, the parks of the Emerald Necklace, and Harvard University. He was surprised to find that the Harvard students looked like students at all. He was surprised that you could just walk into the middle of the campus, that you could just walk into Widener Library, that you, anyone from anywhere, could sit down and read a book in the reading room of Widener Library; that you could then walk out of the reading room and gaze for twenty minutes, without anyone telling you to move along, at John Singer Sargent's mural of a World War I soldier in a death's embrace with a blond angel. Paul had expected gates that never opened, earthen embankments, a difference in elevation. He had expected to get so close and no closer. The forking sidewalks of Harvard Yard seemed to suggest the rich and intricate lives that lay ahead of the Harvard students, and once, when a woman in a blue dress asked Paul for the time as he crossed the campus, he thought that she must have taken him for a Harvard student. Paul considered his own school, on the Canadian shore of Lake Memphremagog: it was a scenic campus but no Harvard.

Paul had a black tin mailbox near the doorway of his apartment building, but almost all of the mail that came was addressed to the person from whom he was subletting. One day, though, while leaving for work, he encountered the mailman, who drew from his bag a long manila envelope and said, "Do you work for the City of Boston?"

"In a way."

"I'd like to know how you swung it. I truly would. You've got to know somebody to get that gig."

Then he handed Paul the envelope, which contained a letter saying that Professor M. Leonard Dalton had died in an automobile accident. The funeral service would be held at the Church of the Logical Assumption in Wellesley, with burial to follow at Hopp Hill Cemetery. Paul found this very hard to believe. If a line connected the sarcastic character who had visited the record room from time to time with the man herein claimed to no longer exist, it was a line he could not follow. He would have to go to the funeral to get to the bottom of this reckless claim.

Paul went to a clothing store on Summer Street in Boston to buy a tie for the funeral. The salesman was a thin and elderly gentleman with a faint accent from some other country.

"It's for a funeral," said Paul.

"I'm glad you told me thought," said the salesman. He went into the back of the store and returned holding in both hands a blue tie with small white dots. "A good pattern for a funeral — subdued, well meaning — and afterward it will retain its utility. Feel. That's one hundred percent silk."

"Are you from England?" said Paul.

"I come from a town in the Scottish Highlands," said the salesman. "It's a beautiful place, but my brother is there, and we don't get along."

"I thought you were from somewhere."

"He's not the only reason," said the salesman. "But if you met him, you would know what I mean."

On the day of the funeral, Paul retrieved his car from a storage lot in Somerville and drove to Wellesley. Logical Assumption stood at a crossroads, a brick church with a shallow peaked roof and bronze medallions set into the facade. The medallions were the size of manhole covers and had been embossed with religious scenes, and Paul examined one while waiting for the funeral to begin.

Jesus hung on the cross — actually, he seemed to float — and a ribbon of blood flowed from a cut under his ribs into an urn below his feet. Two deer with antlers like ferns drank from the urn while in the background a candle burned and a skeleton bent forward as if discouraged, with finger bones fanned over eye sockets. The image suggested victory over death but had been rendered with a lurid lack of subtlety.

As Paul read the inscription he heard two women talking on the steps of the church.

"They say there wasn't a mark on him," said one.

"And the car was a convertible."

"It's almost a miracle."

"Well — he is dead."

"It's unusual, at any rate."

"I just feel that the term 'miracle' gets used way too much these days," said the doubtful woman. "Every time you turn around, this or that is being called a miracle. People see a pattern of knotholes in a tree, it's a miracle. I don't buy it. I don't buy all these miracles."

"At least the Daltons have no children."

"That is good. Although, again, it's no miracle."

The church had a black-and-white-checkered carpet and a large mahogany altar. Paul waited in line and then looked into the open casket. He thought that dying would be easy compared with lying in a box for all the world to see this way. Then he realized something — that he and Dalton wore the same tie, blue with small white dots.

Leonard's friends took the pulpit one at a time. They said he liked the art of the Southwest, that he was a gifted mimic, and that he had a well-hidden generous side. Paul imagined a speech that he could give: "I did not know Leonard Dalton well, and yet I say to you that he loved cars and car parts."

The other drivers in the automotive caravan to the cemetery would not admit Paul's car until the end of the line, as if they suspected that Paul did not care about Professor Dalton the way that they did, if at all, and only wanted to see what the funeral would be like. Maybe they regarded his car as shabby, which it was, a 1969 Plymouth Fury, military green, with large tires, no hubcaps, and an anti-handgun sticker on the windshield that seemed somehow wrong for a funeral. The car rose and fell like a graceless boat as Paul floored it through red lights to keep up with the procession. He wrenched the dead man's tie from his collar and jammed it under the seat.

Wind gusted through the tall and airy trees of the cemetery. Paul stood across the grave from the criminologist's wife. She wore a long-sleeved black dress and a dark and dotted veil that kept getting pushed aside, revealing red lips and glazed eyes.

"The harvest is past, the summer is ended, and we are not saved," said the priest.

The casket was gunmetal blue and suspended on a motorized lift over the grave.

Two thirds of the cars dropped out of the procession when it was time to go back to the Daltons' place for supper and drinks. Mourners drifted through the house, past desert paintings, sand-colored and green, and rattlesnake bones on drift-wood bases, and lamps made of smooth stones. Leonard had been a Johnny Mathis fan, evidently, and his wife drank Tom Collinses, spun Mathis records, and rocked gently to the sound of the strings. She had discarded her veil, and Paul saw that her hair was golden and her eyes were round and dark and tranquil. "Take my hand," sang Johnny Mathis, "I'm a stranger in . . . paradise."

The afternoon wound down. Students from Leonard's summer classes sat staring gloomily into the empty stone fireplace. Low sunlight streamed over the garden and into the windows of the house. Paul finished his drink, walked over to the young widow, and kissed the top of her forehead, where her hair was drawn back in discrete furrows the color of straw.

"I'm sorry," he said. "It isn't fair."

She looked up. "Who are you?"

"Paul Nash," said Paul, for Nash was his family name, and it would be years before he had to change it. "I was one of your husband's students."

"So was I," she said. "But that was a while ago. I'm Mary Dalton."

Paul thought her very beautiful. "How long were you together?"

"Three years," said Mary. "Would you like to see my wedding dress?"

"Yes."

"You're looking at it." She still wore the black dress, with long sleeves that narrowed to the pulse points of her wrists. She lifted her arms. "Get it? This is my wedding dress."

"In a way," said Paul.

"Nobody gets it," said Mary. Her arms settled in her lap. "Why don't you come out to the kitchen with me?"

They left the living room, crossed the kitchen, climbed some back stairs with a drawing of a cow on the landing, and made their way to a sky-blue bedroom with clouds painted on the ceiling. Mary walked into a large closet while Paul inspected a row of small horses standing on top of a dresser. Little gold chains hung from the bridles.

After a few minutes Mary came out of the closet wearing a white dress. Embroidery covered the upper part, and the skirt was long and glossy and full. The modest neckline revealed the graceful curve of her shoulders.

"This is it really," she said.

"Did you like being married?"

"We were getting there. We were getting to like it. But you have to understand Len."

"I don't understand Len," said Paul. "I had no idea he collected paintings."

"Those are mine, actually. I painted them. I can paint in virtually any style, and the desert scenes are what he liked."

"They are excellent," said Paul. "It's a good house."

"We don't own it. We rent the house from the college. What happens next is your guess as well as mine."

She looked at him steadily as they talked. He was not used to her gaze, and heat rose to his face, although he could not tell whether she was looking at him any differently than she looked at anyone else.

"On our honeymoon we went to Lake Mead," said Mary. "That's in Nevada. You're blushing. Have you seen Hoover Dam? Overall, I didn't like Lake Mead that much, I'm not one for that dry heat, but I'm glad that I saw the dam. Len was very happy, as I recall, on our honeymoon."

The bed was low, and they sat side by side on it for some time without talking, but the quiet was not uncomfortable.

"When I was a girl," said Mary, "I spent time on a sheep farm in Europe. You should have seen the sheep when they were first born. They walked just like this." She demonstrated manually, with the fingers of her right hand mimicking the lambs' stumbling steps on the bedspread between them.

Paul worked no more on the study of assaults. No one supervised it and he did nothing requiring supervision. He spent his nights in the record room reading and drinking. He had switched from beer to wine, a transition that made him feel even more jaded than he felt on account of understanding the subways. He knocked over a glass of red wine, staining the pages of *Looking Backward,* a Utopian novel by Edward Bellamy, in which a doctor falls asleep in Boston and wakes up in a better world one hundred and thirteen years later. Paul lugged a television set up to the file room and watched *The Movie Loft* on Channel 38. Of all the shows he had seen that tried to create a sense of camaraderie between the host and the viewer, *The Movie Loft* succeeded the most.

One night he opened a file cabinet and found some cigarettes and car magazines. He brought them to the long table where he used to work and began reading about the new Corvette. The new Corvette looked flabby and obvious compared with the Sting Rays of his youth, and Paul thought the makers should call off the model before the proud name became a joke. The article asked who could resist the chance to drive around in an orange neon Corvette.

"I could resist that," said Paul idly. Then he called Mary and asked her to come into town for the magazines.

"Can they wait?" she said.

"They could," he said. "I want to see you."

"Give me an address."

Paul took the elevator to the lobby of the building. Rain streamed down dark, key-shaped windows. Mary arrived wearing sandals and jeans and a yellow slicker, and carrying a white canvas bag. Paul explained that she should not worry if the elevator hit the shaft walls, because it just did that occasionally, but it didn't happen this time. She took off her slicker and folded it over a chair in the file room. Underneath the slicker she wore a ribbed white sweater with short sleeves. Her arms were long and tanned with fine blond hair. She leaned over the computer terminal and turned it on.

"You don't see many of these," she said.

"It's junk," said Paul.

She began typing. "I work with computers. Did you know that? For a living. This terminal is primitive, but still it responds to the Basic language. What I'm doing right now is creating an infinite random pattern."

She stood back. A green helix caromed slowly around the screen. When it hit the edges it would break apart and begin again somewhere else.

"The way you looked at me at the funeral," said Paul. "I couldn't help thinking it meant something."

"It did, it does," she said.

"Look at the windows," said Paul. He turned off the lamp on his table and the city lights came up.

She pulled a folded Navajo blanket from the white cloth bag. Between the stacks they fell to their knees on the blanket. He kissed the side of her face near the ear and felt the buzz of the soft whorled hairs at the turn of her jaw. Her breath slowed and he could feel her eyes closing, could feel the hesitation of the falling lids. His hands held her sides through the sweater; his thumbs met beneath the sternum, where the hard bone gave way to banded muscle. Then she nudged his hands away and lifted the sweater. Her fists, holding cloth, rose on either side of her face. He smelled her skin, a warm sandy smell like pencil shavings.

"How old are you?" said Mary.

"Twenty-two."

"I'm twenty-six."

"What do we do now?"

"A cigarette is not out of the question."

"Hold on," said Paul.

They got dressed and sat on a windowsill to smoke. The rain continued to fall. Mary seemed lost in her thoughts, and ash from her cigarette fell on her sweater.

"Do you really think I'm a good painter?" she said, as blue pearls of fire raced up the fabric.

A key turned in the lock of the door.

"Mary, you're on fire."

"Jesus Christ."

She slid from the sill slapping her chest and shoulders. Paul pulled her close to smother the flame.

Light edged over the top of the stacks, and bitter smoke rose from Mary's sweater. Paul figured that someone from either the college or the police would soon discover that his assault research consisted of watching *The Movie Loft* and making love to the criminologist's widow.

Instead, it was two men, exchanging money.

"Here," said one.

"I never held in my hand a hundred and forty thousand dollars," said the other.

"You mean a hundred and thirty."

"Didn't we say a hundred and forty, Bud?"

"We sure didn't, Don."

"Well, I don't see how that could be. I told Tim a hundred and forty. That's what Tim's expecting."

"What you told Tim is between you and Tim."

"You could fix it," said the one called Don. "If you wanted to, you know you could."

"I don't want to."

"You're tough."

"I have to be."

"What's that smell?"

"I don't smell anything."

"What do they do in here?"

"Nothing anymore. They were doing research at night, but the guy died. You know — that professor who rolled his convertible."

"Maybe it was a chemical experiment."

"Nah," said Bud. "It was that smoking professor and that creepy scowling intern. They say he was thrown from the car. That always makes me wonder when they say that. It sounds like it wouldn't necessarily be so bad, you know? Sounds like you might bounce a couple times and then land on soft grass."

"They bounce all right."

"Now, how are we going to work this?" said Bud. "You want the money or do I go back and say, 'It now appears that Don, for reasons best known to himself . . .'?"

"No, no, no, no. But what you forget is by the time everybody gets their share, I'm left holding the minimum wage. Meanwhile, the addition to my house keeps fading farther and farther from reality. Do you have any idea where my kids sleep?"

"The basement."

"Well, that's right. Their room is in the basement."

"You already told me that once."

"How would you like to grow up in a room without windows? Would you prefer that? Wouldn't be much fun, would it? You should hear them. It's enough to break your heart, oh it really is. On a sunny morning, on a perfectly sunny day, they call up the stairs, 'Oh Daddy, can you tell us if it's raining? Should we wear our rain clothes or our sun clothes?' That's what they call them, sun clothes."

"You kill me, Don. I mean, really. What do I look like, Squirrel Nutkin? Is that how I honestly come across to you? Because say so if it is . . ."

Then Paul could not hear them, and soon they were gone. Paul and Mary had been pressed together and still for some time.

"What were they talking about?" said Mary. "Who were those people?"

"I have no idea. Do you think I scowl?"

"I wouldn't call it scowling exactly."

She pulled the sweater over her head and stared at it.

"You can forget about that one," he said. "Did you get burned, Mary?"

She pressed her hands to her chest, here and there, testing. "I've heard of ramie doing that, but I never really believed it."

〜

Paul's Uncle Bernard and Aunt Triphena lived in a red house with white trim and small rooms in Arlington, over the Somerville line, and Paul had supper there one evening in August. Afterward, he and Uncle Bernard walked in the back yard with glasses of beer. A silver rail fence divided the yard, and beyond the fence two plaster children in straw hats fished perpetually from a stream. A chain saw buzzed distantly over the neighborhood. Bernard Nash was a small man with inscrutable features and a black beret.

"I hope you were able to take something from being an intern," he said. "Although it's too bad about your supervisor."

"At least he went out driving."

"They say there wasn't a mark on him."

"That reminds me," said Paul, and without mentioning Mary, he explained what they had overheard on the night her sweater burned. He and Uncle Bernard sat on the silver fence with their heels hooked on a rail.

Bernard blinked his eyes now and then, snorted, took a drink of beer, and finally said, "Well, hell, Paul. No law in the world against putting an addition on your house."

"No. That's not what I mean."

"Let me tell you something," said Uncle Bernard. "I'm going to tell you something now."

"O.K."

"Your grandfather told me this in, well, it must have been 'thirty-one or 'thirty-two, somewhere around in there, but it is as true this year as it was the year when he said it, and what he said was 'Very easy —' Wait, how did it go? 'Very easy to get into trouble, very hard to get out.' And the reason he said this was because someone had fallen down the stairs, and I wanted to help him, and he didn't think that was such a good plan."

"Who fell?"

"A drunk named Hibby, if you want to know."

"It just seemed like I should tell someone."

"Well, you did. You told me. And now you don't have to tell anyone else."

"I was in the stacks. I couldn't see anything."

Uncle Bernard poured the last of his beer on the grass. "Of course you couldn't, and it's just as well. I'm trying to remember the other thing your grandfather would say. Oh yeah. 'Be careful what you accept, because that's what you get.'"

"What did he mean?" said Paul.

"Just that," said Bernard.

When the nights grew colder and the light fell rust-colored and sharp on the tall houses of Somerville, Paul packed his car for the trip back to college. He left the key to the apartment with the woman in the wheelchair. On the way out of town he stopped at a tavern in Union Square to have a farewell drink and write a letter to Mary. He sat at the bar with pen poised over paper. Beside the paper lay an envelope with a stamp. He wanted to say that he was on her side, that he knew she would be a good painter, that he knew she would get another house when the lease was up on the place in Wellesley. So he did say these things, he wrote them on the paper, but once they were written and he could see them in his own hand, they did not seem convincing. Letters always gave him trouble. He would imagine the person he was writing to reading between the lines and getting madder and madder.

3

Paul Nash drove back to Sherwood University with the customary mix of curiosity and uncertainty. He had made it through three years of college, but there was no guarantee of making it through the fourth. Perhaps this would be the year when it all broke down. This had been his mindset every fall for the past fourteen years.

The evening sky assumed ever-deeper shades of blue. Paul rejected the reputation of interstate highways as corrupt or unnatural. Driving north, he could see far into New Hampshire, the forests growing dark and the white houses and the isolated TV antennas bringing programs to the lonely. He could pass slow drivers as he wished, taking long and revealing glances into their vehicles. Near Tilton, he overtook a massive truck rocking along with a crane mounted on its bed and a man with a red beard riding in the cab of the crane facing backward. The man fixed his eyes on the distance, as if in embarrassment, and Paul wondered if he was being punished or ostracized for something. In Vermont (it was dark by then, with a lopsided moon bobbing in and out of the rear-view mirror), a beat-up station wagon displayed one of those bumper stickers claiming that no one would take away the driver's gun except by prying it from his COLD DEAD FINGERS, and this threat invigorated Paul with its self-pitying and asinine quality. In the laboratories of the coming socialist dictatorship, he thought, one of the first orders of business would be the invention of a posthumous finger relaxant — like Mentholatum, only stronger. A man with long hair and a complacent, harmless expression drove the vehicle, outlined dimly by dashboard lights; whether he was dead or alive, it seemed, it would be no great trick to pry open his fingers and take a gun from them, but who could say. And for that matter, maybe it wasn't his car. Paul pressed close to the wheel, for the change of posture, and considered the plight of people driving borrowed cars with hostile or stupid bumper stickers. The radio carried an obscure theological discourse: "The dead have gone to be with God. The living need love, and they need money." He crossed the border into Canada and passed a Volkswagen Jetta with Kentucky plates, driven by a young woman with nervous eyes and a big stuffed dog pinned between her and the steering wheel.

Paul raised his right hand, formed a circle with his thumb and forefinger, and extended the remaining three fingers, as if to assure the woman that everything would work out. She did not see him, and he fell to wondering about the origin of this common hand signal.

Sherwood University clung to ledges on the banks of Lake

Memphremagog. The moon lit the moving water as Paul drove along the eastern shore. The white walls of concrete buildings shifted and glittered in the green haze of a ribbon of street lamps. The campus had its problems, and there was in fact a monthly newsletter called *Campus Problems*. The buildings leaked when it rained. Ceilings sagged. The course offerings seemed to have been chosen by someone throwing darts at the catalogs of more comprehensive schools. Funding was high but implementation low, and the overall impression was of a campus that had been cut off from civilization by some violent stroke, leaving a dazed band of faculty and students to conduct a warped yet curiously moving caricature of university life, a brave lost campus where rescuers would arrive one day and weep on the grass. Ticks lived in the grass and fed on those walking through. Sherwood's star scholar was the Egyptologist Virginia Lovetree, who would leave eventually for a job at the University of Michigan. Today, when you read an article about ancient Egypt, it is not unusual to find a quote from Professor Virginia Lovetree of the University of Michigan and formerly of Sherwood University, in Bell Station, Quebec.

People held the lake to be haunted.

Paul passed the campus and motored into town, where he shared a house with two other students. The house rose narrow by the railroad tracks with lights burning in the windows. Paul got out of the car. His housemates stood at the edge of the yard looking down into the ravine through which the trains ran. Their names were Loom Hanover and Alice Miller. Loom was tall and had an animated frame, prematurely white hair, and a long and somewhat pointed chin. Sometimes, for a laugh, a student would press a drinking glass onto his or her chin and say, "Who am I?" As for Alice, everyone called her "Little Alice," for she was fine-boned, though of no little height, maybe five eight or five nine.

"You just missed it," said Loom.

"It's early," said Paul.

"Loom's motorcycle rolled down the hill," said Alice.

"Take a gander," said Loom.

"What do you know about that?" said Paul. On the rail bed next to the tracks, the motorcycle lay with its front wheel turned painfully under. It was a big blue-green Trident that Loom had left on the porch of the house all summer while serving an internship in California.

"We tried easing it down the steps," said Alice.

"You should have waited for me," said Paul.

Loom slouched over Paul, as was his habit with whomever he addressed. He would speak into the tops of people's heads as if into a microphone. "We know, Nash," he said.

They made their way stiff-legged, like horses, down the overgrown bank and dragged the motorcycle away from the tracks. They gathered pieces that had broken off — a mirror, the hollow rubber casing of a footpeg, the red shard of a taillight — and set them by the bike.

They lay on the ground with their backs to the hill, Loom and Paul on either side of Alice. "It's only a material thing," said Loom.

Loom Hanover would inherit a factory in Ashland, Connecticut, someday and had developed a melancholy style that went hand in hand with his wealth. He played guitar in a band called the Declining Prophets. Whatever he might accomplish would be discounted because of his advantages, and if he accomplished nothing at all, it would not matter. He had said this himself. He had found a quote in a book: "Sons of rich men, when they have anything worth while in them, go through periods of desperation, like other young men. They go to college and read books." He carried this observation around on a piece of paper in his emu-skin billfold. Small jagged holes pockmarked the clay-colored billfold — proof, said Loom, of the emus' frequent gouging for group dominance. Paul thought that Loom, with his sheltering wealth, longed for some version of the emus' experience, that of being alone in a harsh world with no help except one's own claws.

Now Loom used the detached motorcycle mirror as a serving

tray for three rough-cut and clouded pills, one for each of them. He had spent the summer pasting up a drug guide for a publishing company in La Jolla.

"I call these soliloquy pills," he said. "All you'll want to do is talk. We ought to lay down ground rules or else it'll just be a constant babble."

"What is it?" said Paul.

"The street name is 'harbor pilot,'" said Loom.

They swallowed the pills and watched a woodchuck lumber darkly along the opposite side of the ravine.

Loom spoke first, concerning the murderous overkill with which the police in a small California town had that summer captured the headquarters of a Maoist organization called the Little Red Schoolhouse. Once you claimed to be a revolutionary in America, said Loom, it didn't matter if you were the worst-armed fool in the world; the police would not rest until the atoms of your body were dispersed to the winds. This was to make sure that nothing so egalitarian, so opportunistic, and, really, so good as the revolution of 1776 could happen again. The Hanovers claimed to be descended from an obscure branch of the family of Nathan Hale, and Loom said that if Nathan Hale were alive today, the police would hunt him down and kill him without asking questions. Loom said the shells the police fired upon the Little Red Schoolhouse were so powerful that they smashed through walls, glass, steel, blood, bone, and appliances, and came out the other side. The police staggered their positions around the house so as not to catch each other's powerful shells. As Loom told it, some of those shells might still be going, drifting in the vacuum of space. He said the warlike ammunition proved that the police intended to kill and not merely subdue the Maoist community. He had visited the place days after the confrontation and found people who appeared to be firefighters sitting at a card table on the perimeter of the ashes and playing poker. If anyone asked, they were supposed to say they were making sure that the fire did not rekindle, but their actual job was keeping anyone from sifting through the burned house for evidence that might be used in civil lawsuits against the police.

"They told you that?" said Paul.

"They didn't have to," said Loom. "It was understood."

Alice leaned forward and tied her shoes with great fascination. She had long black hair and heavy, provocative eyebrows. Her father and mother owned a theater in Yankton, South Dakota, and she had been the last of the three students to occupy the house by the railroad tracks. Paul had invited her to move in after she came to a party at the house in their sophomore year and called him a poet. All he had done to earn the compliment was carry a fluorescent desk lamp into a room full of drinking people, set it on a stereo speaker, plug it in, and turn it on.

"Hey," said Alice, "you're a poet."

"I thought there was writing involved," said Paul.

"You're a poet of light," she said.

At the party she had worn dark red lipstick that smelled of tranquilizers, and she and Paul ended up sitting between the spindles of the staircase and talking for an hour. It turned out that they were in the same hermeneutics class and had both written papers about Jesus' edgy behavior at the wedding at Cana, when he spoke sternly to his mother as she seemed to be pressuring him to produce some wine.

Alice had fallen out with her roommate and needed somewhere to stay. Loom used the house's third bedroom to store leg weights, and Paul suggested that Alice could take that room. (According to Loom, Nathan Hale had been able to kick a ball very high, and whatever Nathan Hale could do, Loom wanted to do as well or better, and so he worked on his leg strength.) Alice accepted the offer, and Loom transferred the leg weights into his own room, and she moved in. Soon, however, Alice and Loom began sleeping together, at which point she moved into his room and the leg weights went back to the spare bedroom.

Now, watching Alice tying her shoes on the evening of his return to Bell Station, Paul remembered how much he hated Loom's leg weights, which consisted of six pale red canvas cuffs with metal plates sewn in. Loom began every morning by strapping the weights on and clanking them endlessly on the floorboards. While the exercises were going on, Paul would wish for Nathan Hale to rise from the dead and demonstrate his legendary kicking skills on Loom.

Alice had managed to tie her hair into her shoelaces, and laughing urgently with her face bound to her knees, she tugged at the knots. She freed her black hair, shook it back, and began her story:

"When I was a girl in South Dakota, I had some Barbie dolls. Not that many. Maybe I had six. I wasn't a fanatic the way some girls were, but I would give little parties, things like that, the usual, although none of them could stand up unless I was holding their legs, because their feet were tiny and bent, as if they'd been broken and not set right. People talk about the large breasts of Barbies, but I remember the feet more than the breasts — all these hobbled Barbies falling over their feet. But this isn't about the dolls so much as it's about the suitcase I had for their clothes. It was made of blue vinyl, with a brass clasp and an illustration of Barbie and Ken in evening wear on the lid. Barbie had white gloves going up past her elbows. The suitcase was nothing special, but I liked it, I really did. I liked it as much as I liked the dolls themselves, I think, and I kept it in my bedroom, full of dresses and slacks and tiny twisted shoes. This was not a big deal for me, it was one toy among many, but there it was. Well, one day when we were all at school, there was a tornado warning and the principal sent us home early. Our house was three blocks away and so I walked home like I always did with my brother, Frank. The storm was close, and we were scared. I don't know if you've ever been caught in tornado weather, but the sky turns olive green and there is a darkness in the clouds so forceful that the clouds seem to glow. And when you see this awful green sky, you know you'd better hurry home. The trees stretched flat in the howling wind and someone's lawn chair danced down the street with its aluminum legs opening and closing. My mother met us halfway home and she was yelling things that we couldn't hear and I think in retrospect we barely got in the house. The wind came through the doorjamb making a music like bagpipes. We went down into the basement and huddled by the deep freeze, playing cat-and-mouse with flashlights while the house shook and crashed. Then it began to rain. We could see the drops pelting the basement windows, and our mother said that if it's raining, then it's over. So we left the basement to see what had happened to the house. The first floor was all right but upstairs a box elder tree had fallen through the windows of my bedroom. Branches filled the room, and the floor was covered with broken glass and small stones. My mother and brother and I tried to clean up but it was useless with the tree and everything. But you could climb on the branches without touching the floor and it was while climbing in the branches that I saw the Barbie suitcase buried in the middle of the room. I pulled it from the wet green leaves and dragged it into the hallway where I opened the lid to make sure it still worked. And this is the thing: the clothes inside were all different. I had never seen any of them before. They didn't even seem manmade. The fabrics shone like fire. I told my mother and later I told my father, but they had no explanation; they were too glad the house hadn't fallen down to worry about doll clothes. They said I must have gotten the clothes as a present a long time ago and forgot about them. 'From who?' I said. 'Who would know where to get clothes like these? Look at them,' I said. 'Look at the way they're made.'"

Paul and Loom said nothing after Alice finished. They could have asked questions. It was not that they weren't listening. But the full force of the soliloquy pills had settled over them, making questions seem the product of bad nerves. They all stood together and stretched. Paul's shoulders felt good, and he smiled in the dark by the railroad tracks. He and Loom and Alice pushed the Trident up the hill through the briars. It was hard to say how badly it was damaged. The wheels turned, anyway, and whether they were bent or not was a matter of guesswork. A train came through, as one always did at a quarter to midnight. The whistle blared, and the silver cars swayed, and the three students faced the train, losing themselves in the shroud of the big racket.

The train rocked under a bridge and around a bend. Its last light blinked out of sight. "What about your story?" Alice said to Paul.

They went into the house, into the kitchen, where a light bulb swung gently on its frayed cord, and where yellowed tape held an orange and blue illustrated poster called "The Commune's Fish Pond" to the wall above the table. In the poster, the members of a commune hauled a net through water, and the net belled with fish. Paul got three bottles of beer from the refrigerator and sat down with Alice and Loom at the table.

"In high school I had a friend named Lars," said Paul. "Lars Lamb."

"I'll bet he was a hellion," said Alice.

"Why do you say that?"

"All your stories are about hellions."

"Lars was all right in person, but behind the wheel of a car he would scream at drivers who made the smallest infraction. This was in the town of Verona, Rhode Island. You would have thought he had been driving for years and had got tired of bad drivers. But the thing was, he was only seventeen. Something about being in his car just seemed to make him furious. It was a blue Firebird, a pretty car. He screamed at people who didn't use their turn signals, he screamed at people who slowed down to look at things along the road, and God help you if Lars saw you eating food in your car. He hated that the most — say, if you had a piece of cake behind the wheel. Well, that was Lars. He had big shoulders and had been on the wrestling team until a bunch of us got caught with a bottle of ouzo behind the shop building. It was too bad. He got kicked off the wrestling team, and I got kicked off the football team. For me it wasn't a big thing. I never played much, and the main thing I liked about being on the football team was being able to wear forearm pads and slam things with my forearms. Sometimes I would even take bites out of the pads. They were made of this dense spongy material that was good to bite. But Lars had wrestled at the top of his class, and I'm sure he missed it. Anyway, in our senior year he started wearing a plastic skull mask while he was driving. Not every time, but often enough. It was a Halloween mask with an elastic string that went around the back of his head. He wore glasses, and what he would do is put the glasses on over the mask, which for some reason heightened the illusion that a skeleton was driving the car. So one day we were leaving the Ann & Hope when Lars let the Firebird roll into the back of a Pinto. We always used to go to the Ann & Hope, steal shirts, and return them for cash. Lars had the mask on, and basically he wasn't watching where he was going. A woman got out of the Pinto to see what had happened. Lars didn't scream at her; he was too busy trying to get the mask off before she could see that she had been hit by some goon driving around in a Halloween costume. But his eyeglasses were tangled in the elastic string and he finally gave up. So the woman came over to the window and helped him off with the mask, because she could see the problem, whereas Lars couldn't see anything by this time. His eyes didn't even line up with the holes."

"Then what?" said Alice.

"They exchanged insurance papers."

"That's it?"

"Not exactly. The story shifts to a Saturday night some months later. Lars and I were driving around Newport in the Firebird when some of our enemies penned us in. They jumped out of their cars with chains and tire irons and went to work. Lars sat and listened to the smashing of his car as long as he could, and then he got out. But every time he tried to stop these kids from hitting his car, they threatened to hit him instead. So that was a standoff. Then I got out and began yelling. 'Go away,' I said. 'Go away.' This was an unexpected strategy, and believe it or not, they went away. I guess they had accomplished what they set out to do. The next day, I went over to Lars's place to see how the car looked in daylight, and as I was walking up the driveway, I heard the same sort of pounding as I had heard the night before. I pushed up the garage door and there was Lars hitting his own car with the flat side of an ax. There was a loan on the car, you see, so it was fully insured, and he wanted it totaled so he could get a jacked-up Duster he had his eye on. Lars looked like some figure from an American folktale. He gave a little cry every time he hit the car. Because, strange though he may have been, he did not find this easy."

Then the stories were over. Paul stood and turned out the kitchen light. When they reached the top of the stairs, Loom and Alice went one way, and Paul went the other.

Alice Miller and Loom Hanover got married the summer after they graduated from Sherwood University, in the Devil's Hat-rack Wilderness Area in Quebec, with music supplied by the Lac Brome Mandolin Orchestra. Loom had served as chairman of the Marxist-Leninist Steering Committee for two years at Sherwood, but now he seemed eager to marry and assume his place in the family business, which was the manufacture of fasteners. Loom's father was a member of a fraternal organization called the Saberians Guild, down in Connecticut, and he wore a saber to the wedding, but when he drew it during the rehearsal, a piece of the handle flew off, and so he left it sheathed during the ceremony, on a mossy heath surrounded by gnarled apple trees. The first mandolinist wore a blue stocking cap although the day was clear and warm. Paul served as best man and read from the Song of Solomon, for that was the year that everyone read from the Song of Solomon at weddings. "How beautiful are thy feet with shoes," Paul read. "Come, my beloved, let us go forth into the field; let us lodge in the villages. Let us get up early to the vineyards; let us see if the vine flourish, whether the tender grape appear . . ." The reading made Paul thirsty, and he drank too much at the reception, which took place in the wilderness area's Howard "Mark" Rafferty Bird Museum, and he danced with Alice, and he smoked cigars in red leather chairs with Loom's father, Gilbert, but the cigars were old, and dry tobacco spilled down their shirts.

"Too bad about your saber," said Paul.

Gilbert Hanover picked up the sword and scabbard. "Take a look," he said. He had soft white hair combed like feathers over the crest of his forehead. "It'll have to be welded."

"What kind of fasteners does your company make?" said Paul.

Gilbert massaged the bridge of his nose in contemplation. "It varies," he said. "We make everything from submarine fittings to the anchor pins for large plastic cows at steak restaurants."

"Are your workers happy?"

"About what?"

"I don't know, conditions?"

"Are you Red, kid?"

"I keep an open mind."

Gilbert laughed. "That won't get the job done."

Paul finished a glass of ale and set the glass on the floor. "To me," he said, "Charles Fourier was on to something with his idea of the phalanx."

"Yeah, well, Brook Farm burned down," said Gilbert.

"But it could have worked," said Paul.

"Ah, wait a while before you know everything."

Loom's mother, Evelyn, approached the club chairs wearing a deeply cut black dress with a silver chain around the waist. "Listen," she said, "the minister wants to get paid."

"Write him a check," said Gilbert.

"He says his bank won't take U.S. checks."

"Tell him to come see me."

"Oh, Gil, just pay the man," said Evelyn.

"How much is it?"

"Six hundred."

"Pay attention, Fidel," Gilbert said to Paul. "The revolution will not have the support of the clergy."

"Don't bait the children," said Evelyn. "Let's not ruin the beautiful evening."

"Tell him it was a grand ceremony."

"I will," she said, and walked away.

Paul examined the scabbard of the saber. It was made of leather with an etching of a girl falling from a flying ram. "Why say it was grand if you're mad at him?"

"Those are the rules."

"The rules," Paul said. "That's where I get lost."

"There are many rules," said Gilbert. "On Christmas Day, wear a gray sweater with a red tie and drink Bloody Marys. On Easter Sunday, wear a blue suit with an ocher tie, again drinking Bloody Marys, but interestingly, omitting the celery. If after visiting your mistress you feel remorse, and your mistress asks what's on your mind, say, 'You are on my mind.' When you answer the phone and the call is for someone else, do not clamp your hand over the mouthpiece while summoning the intended party. Look everyone in the eye at all times, and don't look first into the right eye, then the left, and so on, for this is disconcerting. On Arbor Day, drink gin. Keep an orderly toolbox, and do as much of the work around your home as possible, and when you hit your thumb with the hammer, it is considered perfectly acceptable to say, 'Goddamn it all to hell,' but beyond this you must not go. If your thumbnail proceeds to turn dark blue, wear a houndstooth suit and switch your wristwatch to the other hand, thus preventing your injury from calling immodest attention to your wristwatch."

Paul left the reception at one-thirty in the morning, and on the way back to the college he put his car in the ditch. He walked for several miles under the low dark sky before taking shelter in some sort of wooden feeding station in a pasture, where he fell asleep. In the morning, horses nosed him bluntly in the back, to get at the hay in the feeder. Ragged clouds sailed across the sky. Paul returned to his car and drove it up and out of the ditch. I could have driven out anytime but I just didn't realize it, he thought. His cummerbund was gone, and he drove to the bird museum to look for it because he had been told by the rental people that loss of any part of the tuxedo would be regarded as loss of the entire tuxedo. The doors swung open onto a deserted museum; glasses, streamers, and cigarette ashes littered the floor. Paul wandered past cases of stuffed birds and into a small room with oak paneling and large panes of glass beyond which lay a diorama. The exhibit had been installed long ago, judging by its faded colors, and replicated a small Pacific island that had been picked clean at the turn of the century. Paul pushed a button set into the paneling, and soon a deep recorded voice spoke over the sound of wind and gulls. The narrator explained that a guano farmer who lived alone on the island had imported rabbits to spice up his diet. In time, the rabbits ate all the vegetation on the island, stripped it to bedrock, and the birds died or flew away, leaving whole species extinct and the farmer a broke and broken man in a ruined landscape.

Paul graduated late, as he had to take a make-up exam in a bowling class. He barely scraped by, coming up with a spare in the tenth frame to reach a passing score.

Back at his parents' farm in Rhode Island, he tried to call Mary Dalton, but her phone had been disconnected.

4

Paul taught high school for two years in Providence, but one of his students overdosed, and around the same time he happened to read an article in *The Atlantic Monthly* called "Why Accounting Matters," and on an impulse he decided to quit teaching and become a CPA. He joined the firm of Clovis, Luken & Pitch, and took an apartment in a brick building on East Manning Street. The accounting firm, like all of adult life, proved stranger and more tenuous than he had expected. Every year at tax time, when the clients' returns were signed and sealed, the senior partners would shut themselves in a room with three glasses and a bottle of whiskey to see who could rig himself the biggest refund. Among these haunted figures was Paul's boss, Jack Chance, a soft-spoken man who seemed equally wary of the tax authorities and of his fellow senior partners.

Paul did pro bono work for an art gallery near Fox Point and as a result got invited to a party at a sculptor's house on Morris Avenue one Thursday night in the spring of 1984. The sculptor specialized in bronze insects, and Paul was making his way through a hallway lined with praying mantises when he saw Mary. They left the party together and wandered into a dark church on Hope Street. Paul detected a loose knob on the balustrade of a stairwell, wrenched it free, and flung it into vaulted space. Silence followed, as if time had stopped, and then the globe crashed loudly on other wood. From the church they went to Paul's apartment building, where low green lanterns lined the walk. Neither of them had protection, so they lay in bed bumping and pressing all night. It was like paradise, beautiful and tense, and the next morning they sat at Paul's cracked round kitchen table and ate pancakes.

Five years had passed since they first met, and Mary Dalton had changed careers too. She had given up electronics to concentrate on painting. After Wellesley she had moved to Framingham, and from there to Seekonk, where she now rented an apartment in a house behind a shoe repair shop. She worked these days on a series of paintings depicting towels on a clothesline.

"Let's go to the Cape," she said. "We'll rent a cabin. We can swim, although it will be pretty cold. Oh, let's go, Paul. Things haven't worked out so well for me here. If only I had gotten my insurance settlement, it would have been different."

"I thought Leonard had insurance," said Paul.

"He had a policy in the works when he died. Some of the papers had been signed, but not all of them, and so they declared that it wasn't valid. I had to get a loan just to cover the cost of the funeral, and if that isn't depressing, you tell me. I contacted a lawyer, and he was very enthusiastic at first, but his interest waned over time, and pretty soon he wouldn't answer my calls."

"What happened with the computers?"

"After Len died, my company was very patient but then it disbanded," said Mary. "The focus of the scene has shifted to California. Then I heard about something down here, in Seekonk, but it turned out to be a big disappointment. First off, they were writing software I wouldn't have published when I was in high school. They were trying to develop a system just for pet stores, and so they would sit around saying, 'All right, what are some of the different breeds?' It all seemed so makeshift. Then they decided I was too combative, whatever that means. So guess what I'm doing now. We agreed to a parting of the ways, and I'm working in a laundromat."

"How's that going?"

"Not as bad as I thought it would be. It's hot, but at least it's not a dry heat. If anything, it's damp."

Paul ran hot water over a dishrag and cleaned the lip of the syrup bottle. "You're not combative."

"I can be," said Mary. She lifted her chin and swept her brushy yellow hair behind her ears. "You don't know me that well, Paul. What did we have? A few evenings. You really don't know me so well at all. When I decide I want something, my attitude pretty much becomes one of, 'All right, hand it over.' An example would be when Lenny got the job at the college and we had a choice between buying a little house in Watertown or renting the big house in Wellesley. He wanted to buy, he said burglars feed on rented houses, but I loved that house in Wellesley. I sat in the garden on the day we looked at it and I knew that I wanted to keep sitting in that garden. And no one ever burglarized it either. In the long run, of course, it was a mistake, because if we had bought the little house in Water-town, I might be living in it today instead of breathing shoe polish fumes in Seekonk. But I want to look ahead and not fixate on the past. I can't see you as an accountant."

"All my life I've been interested in numbers," said Paul. "I guess it began in grade school when I was able to solve the riddle of Mr. Klopstock and the missing horse. Later I found that if you carry the nine-times table past twenty digits and then remove everything but the threes and sevens, the resulting pattern looks exactly like Stonehenge. At the same time, I knew I didn't have the patience to be a mathematician. So suddenly it all fell together. Most people think it's boring, and I admit it can be, but you meet all kinds of people, you travel, you have some laughs."

"I didn't know that accountants traveled."

"There's some travel," said Paul. "The other day I had to go north of Providence to interview the manager of a silk-screen company. This interested me because I had always thought of silk-screening as an art form, but evidently there are industrial applications too."

"Certainly," said Mary.

"Yeah. So I got to the address and it was an abandoned church that somebody was using to store washers and dryers. I assumed I must have the wrong place, but then a guy came up from the basement, and I asked him, 'I must be missing something. Where is the silk-screening done?' And he said, 'It's mostly subcontracted.' And then he laughed, and I laughed, and that broke the tension."

Paul and Mary drove that night to Cape Cod. Paul had never been there. Everyone knows that most Rhode Islanders do not like to drive far, that their limited travel ambitions reflect the narrow dimensions of their state, that people in Providence consider Boston to be as remote as Nome, although it is only thirty-seven miles away. But Paul's family was not like this. His father enjoyed driving long distances, and the family had always taken arduous vacations involving days and days spent with seven or eight of them jammed into a station wagon, speeding toward Helena, Houston, Winnipeg, or Juarez as if the hounds of hell were biting at the wheels. Six-hundred-mile days were not unusual, and the family would fall exhausted into motel rooms under cover of night, and by the fourth or fifth day bitter hatred colored the atmosphere of the station wagon and the kids would be punching each other viciously in the upper arms, so that at any given moment a child might be suffering either the turbulent remorse of the violent or the spiritual desolation that comes from having been punched sharply in the upper arm. So the Cape had been too close, too easy, and now, as Paul drove across the Taunton River bridge, a green steel span from which humble Fall River appeared to be a golden kingdom of light, he enjoyed having Mary next to him, and he felt far from those trapped days of childhood.

They stayed two nights in one of a series of silver-blue honeymoon cabins on the bay side of the Cape. They could see the water from their cabin and at night could hear the sound of the waves mixed with the occasional traffic on Route 6A. Rough, winter-scarred sand lay all around the outside of the cabin. It rained the first night, and they inventoried the contents of the place: a telescope, a rowing machine, a copy of the *Kama Sutra,* and a dusty cardboard box with an inflatable vinyl device inside called the Bridal Pillow.

Paul blew up the grooved and wedge-shaped pillow and put the stopper in. "What do you make of this?" he said.

Mary took the pillow in both hands, threw it in the air, and caught it. "I think it goes under the bride. It's a real fifties thing."

"What's wrong with a regular pillow?"

"That's for sleep use only."

In the morning the sun shone through soft blue haze, and white waves crested randomly. The green water turned abruptly purple farther out, and gulls glided backward on the wind and fell awkwardly into the ocean. Paul and Mary left the door unlocked and drove out to Provincetown, where the boxer Emil Bondurant was training and where the streets were as crowded and lively as the lanes of a country fair. That afternoon they took a whale watch cruise in a strong wind. They saw a fast, rubbery minke and a humpback whale that dove with its forked flukes held high and slapped the water in various ways that the marine biologist aboard said were unusual.

"You could go weeks waiting to see this," he said. "This has been a magical day."

Heading back to the harbor, Paul and Mary sat behind the bridge, sheltered from the wind, and watched the engine's high wake, which itself fanned like whale flukes. The sun lay mercury pools of light on the water. When they got back to the cabin on the beach they found the door open. Sand covered the floor and a large blue braided rug.

"I don't see how all this could have come through the door," said Mary.

"Maybe the windows too," said Paul. He dusted off the vinyl pillow. "Did you ever think how the marriage ceremony emphasizes the eventual death of the bride and groom?"

Mary picked up a pair of tennis shoes she had left in the kitchen and took them outside. "I don't see how you can say that to me," she said loudly from the porch.

Paul walked to the doorway. Mary slapped the shoes together. She wore an aquamarine Danskins top, tucked into loose khaki shorts. "What do you mean?"

"After what happened to Leonard," she said.

"Oh, sorry," he said. "I never thought of that."

"But I follow your thinking. The vows do have a morbid quality."

"'As long as we both shall live.' Come on. That in itself tells you more than you need to know."

She sat down on the porch and put the shoes on her bare feet. "It's supposed to last, that's all."

Paul brought the telescope out of the cabin. "Or think of nature shows on television," he said. "'The coyote mates for life.' What comes to mind? One coyote laid out on the forest floor and the other one shuffling around in disbelief."

"To your mind, perhaps," said Mary. She stood, shaded her eyes, and peered into the doorway of the cabin. "I hope we're not liable for sand damage."

"The cabin is on the beach," said Paul. "Sand cannot be considered damage."

"Where are you going with the telescope?"

"Looking for whales."

"Do they come in this close?"

"That's why I'm using the scope."

"You know, what I loved most about the whales is the sounds they made."

Paul pressed the horns of the tripod into the soft wooden floorboards. "The slapping and the breathing."

"Their voices," said Mary. "They had them on a videotape below decks. They make very haunting sounds."

Later Paul and Mary carried the braided rug outside and shook it. They tried to coordinate their motions, but each shake of the rug rattled their elbows.

They met another couple staying in the cabins that night and inhaled cocaine with them. The couple said they were from Ohio and had come east to drum up support for a new women's boxing league. They had been trying to get an audience with the boxer Emil Bondurant. The woman's name was Melissa, and she showed them her boxing steps on the sand. She wore a green canvas jumpsuit with a wide woven belt of red, yellow, and blue, and she punched Paul in the neck. He had to walk up and down the beach gasping to unknot the muscles.

"I'm walking in rhythm," said Melissa.

Her husband, Clive, caught Paul by the arm. "Don't mind Melissa," he said. "She's knocked me on the deck many times. Sometimes I wish that old cocaine would dry up and blow away."

Paul leaned down with his hands on his knees, looking back at the cabin. Melissa vaulted from foot to foot with the light at her back. Mary came out and handed her a beer. Melissa drank and flung the bottle.

"Whoo," she cried.

Clive eventually dragged her back to their cabin. She was one of those people who do not want the night to end. Mary and Paul turned off their outside light and walked down to the bay. They kissed for some time with their feet at the edge of the water.

In New Bedford they stopped at a pay phone, flipped through the Yellow Pages, and found an advertisement, illustrated with church bells, for a justice of the peace whose house was within walking distance of the lobster museum. He produced a bottle of Freixenet champagne, performed the wedding ceremony, and showed Paul and Mary the tropical fish he kept in murmuring tanks in his basement. "I'm told I have the largest raspora collection in southeastern Massachusetts," he said. "These little bright fish are cousin to the carp. These are scissortails; these are redfins; these are harlequins."

Besides being a justice of the peace, the man said, he was a bounty hunter.

"Let's say you find some big guy who doesn't want to go," said Paul.

The justice of the peace led them upstairs to a bureau in the hallway. He opened a drawer and took out a sap that he handed to Paul. Cracks ran like veins through the chocolate leather. "I hit him in the knees with this," he said. "Then you're dealing with someone a lot shorter."

They moved into a new apartment on Siren Street — three rooms above a dentist's office. Sometimes they could hear the drill's high whine, and if they showered midmorning, the water dripped through the floor and onto the dentist's plants and patients. Every day the carpeting in their living room grew a crop of nylon snags that every night they harvested with a straw broom. Mary's paints and paintings filled the apartment, smelling of oranges. She had metal shelves and mason jars of brushes and an easel that they had to saw the top off of to make it fit. She had colored powders, tinted liquids, canvas stretchers, and delicate knives, like miniature trowels. In the evenings they played a game in which they took turns being dead weight that the other would be required to drag from the living room into the bedroom and somehow haul up onto the bed. This led always to wild laughter, followed by desperate sex.

They fought a lot too. Two months into their marriage, Mary began to think he would abandon her. And she objected to his singing. Paul had this tuneless manner of singing old folksongs. His parents had smoked Old Gold cigarettes, and when Paul was eleven years old he acquired, through an Old Gold promotion, a fat paperback called *Folk Song U.S.A.*, put together by the folklorists John and Alan Lomax. Paul had memorized many of the songs, and singing them provided a link to his past. But the lyrics often had to do with couples breaking up or with lovers who, given their descriptions, could not be Mary ("Black is the color of my true love's hair / Her lips are like some rosy fair"), and Mary would argue that by singing these lines he was subconsciously expressing his desire to replace her with another. She would even react to songs on the radio, as if Paul's secret mind dictated the playlists of FM stations in Providence and Boston.

"Man, there's your theme song," she would say.

"Hmm?"

"I know you want a pair of brown eyes," she said. "Don't you think I'm wise to what you're all about?"

"What color are your eyes?"

"You have no idea."

"Blue."

"They're violet, for all you care."

"Blue is close."

"You go to hell."

Sometimes these arguments ended in brittle silence, and

sometimes Mary curled on the carpet, writhing among the nylon blooms, crying out that he obviously wanted a divorce and why didn't he just say it.

Paul hated to hear her get that way and thought such stark emotionality could not be doing them any favors. The current wisdom regarding emotions was that they should all be expressed, or "brought to the surface," no matter their content, but he did not buy this. Sometimes he would respond by taking the broom and sweeping around her, as if to say, "This isn't happening, nothing is happening, nobody here but us sweepers." Once he got down on the carpet and tried to hold her still, but they only ended up wrestling, his face inches from hers, both of them breathing harshly, with taut jaw muscles and viselike grips on each other's arms. Really angry, no fooling around. He could not believe their fresh relationship had warped so soon. He seemed to have failed her in some fundamental way that it was too early for her to know about. It brought to mind the gyroscopes of his youth, how his father would buy gyroscopes every now and then and demonstrate their stable spinning for the kids. But the kids could never get the gyroscopes to work, and after a few tries would have them bent or tangled in their strings, and their father would say, "I can't believe it, the kids wrecked another gyroscope."

5

The silk-screening company that Paul had spoken of was suffering from an inexplicable surplus of cash, and it was this mysterious money that drew Paul to the illegal side of accounting. He did not give the transition the careful consideration that it undoubtedly called for. It seemed like a game to him, and he liked games. His whole family did.

So he took three suitcases full of money, converted the cash to traveler's checks, concealed the checks in a box of L. L. Bean fatwood, and shipped the kindling to a ski lodge in the Pennine Alps, where the checks were fished from the fatwood, picked up, and deposited in the account of a maker of circuit boards in Geneva, which then mailed to Paul's firm, Clovis, Luken & Pitch, backdated orders and corresponding checks equaling the amount conveyed in the L. L. Bean shipment, minus commission.

This maneuver proved elegant and unassailable, and it brought the money back to the United States so cleanly that the president of the parent company of Rain-Bow Silk-Screening invited Paul to have supper with him at a restaurant in the town of Madrid. The parent company was called New England Amusements, and the president was Carlo Record, also known as Carlo the Pliers, Carlo from Pawtucket, Pan-Store Carlo, the Shepherd, and Dr. Robert West. The reason he was called Carlo was because he had changed his name from Carl. The reason he was called the Pliers was because he had one real arm and one synthetic one, and on the end of the synthetic arm he had a metal hook.

Most everyone in Rhode Island knew about this and other aspects of Carlo Record's life. He was one of those crime figures whose actions and habits and sins were routinely reported in the newspapers but who never seemed to get arrested for anything. For thirty years he had run a criminal organization from a concrete-block bunker on the Providence waterfront. A large man called Ashtray Bob would sit out front and turn away those who did not show the secret ring. The ring ritual had faded out in the late sixties, as even the rackets became more democratic. Carlo the Pliers ruled his kingdom harshly — he was known for hitting his associates on the collarbone with his hook — but at the same time his life had been partly defined by his quietly enduring affair with the Boston scat singer Miriam Lentine. Articles about Carlo Record had scandalized his wife by including a discography of Miriam Lentine, including the albums *Against My Religion, Past My Bedtime* and *Who Are You and How Did I Get Here?* (Both are available from PolyGram.)

Powerful as the Record syndicate was, it did not have the city of Providence to itself. A rival gang existed on Federal Hill, but the relationship between them had grown to be symbiotic over the years, and the two gangs even cooperated on certain ventures, such as an annual picnic at Colt State Park, on the East Bay. In the touchy style of the modern criminal, many of Record's associates could not tolerate being called by their nicknames to their faces, but Record liked the sound of "Carlo the Pliers." He had lost his left arm in 1957, when his catboat sailed into a cove of Narragansett Bay and the mast touched a misplaced power line, but he did not become embittered. The catastrophe, in his view, added a jaunty nautical dimension to his image.

Record had the reputation of being the most conscientious of crime leaders. He insisted on the right of murder victims to have a last cigarette or a drink whenever feasible. He had decided early on to keep out of the drug trade, because it seemed especially immoral. Then he took a second look at the sharking of loans and decided that this, too, was a less than honorable way to make a living, preying as it did on character flaws and economic marginality. Next he ordered a moratorium on slayings (which raised obvious issues of due process) and announced that he was reconsidering the black-market dumping of radioactive sludge which might harm the ecology. It was around this time that Tommy "Mirage" Maynard, the Record Family subchieftain of Medford, Mass., and the handbag opener Duncan Priest held their infamous conversation, tape-recorded by the FBI:

MAYNARD: Pretty soon we'll be selling those things — going door to door — like human garbage . . .
PRIEST: I'm sorry? I wasn't listening.

MAYNARD: Those egg things — that you mix up [eggs with] . . .

PRIEST: Eggbeaters?

MAYNARD: Yeah — eggbeaters.

Eventually Tommy Maynard called for a sit-down at the Haunted Mortar and Pestle Inn on Martha's Vineyard (the so-called Haunted Mortar and Pestle Conference), where the various factions of the syndicate united to remind Carlo the Pliers that they were capitalists and not Jesuits, and that the uncertainty about whether the Records were serious about crime — whether they were in it for the long term — was hurting them with local distributors and had been partly to blame for the murder of the Record Family bludgeon worker Nicholas "Monkey Bars" Scoda while he was shopping for fall clothes in Stamford. In response, Carlo the Pliers revealed that he had become dependent on antihistamines and that this had shaded his judgment, and he renewed his commitment to making the Record syndicate the top crime family in New England. After that, everyone was visibly relieved and went down to the beach for gin and tonics.

Paul knew all these things, or he could have found them out by reading the newspapers, but still he agreed to have dinner with Carlo Record at a restaurant called the Terrapin down in Madrid. He made no excuses to himself — he was young enough, at twenty-seven, to believe that he could deal in crime as an existential experiment that would not be written against his name — but had he wanted to make excuses, he could have borrowed them from his associates at Clovis, Luken & Pitch, which had been the accounting firm for New England Amusements for many years. One of the excuses had three parts: (1) If Carlo Record was indicted, he would be regarded as innocent until proven guilty; (2) but Carlo had never been indicted; (3) therefore, Carlo must be regarded as extra-innocent. A second excuse took the form of the murderous-cousin analogy, which had been explained to Paul by the senior partner Jack Chance. He and Paul had gone walking one afternoon out by the hurricane barrier. Chance's feet moved slowly and his hands held a small silver cross inlaid with tablets of lapis lazuli. "Let's talk about that," he said. "Say some guy is planning to murder his cousin. He goes to his family doctor, says, 'Doc, you've got to help me. I need some poison to put in my cousin's soft drink.' What should the doctor do?"

"Call the cops?" said Paul.

"Of course," said Chance. "A child would say the same thing. But let's imagine a second scenario. Same guy goes into the doctor's, same plan to kill his cousin, but this time he doesn't mention it, because he's got a bad appendix and he's too sick to talk."

"You have to treat him just like you would anyone who is sick," said Paul.

"This is equally true," said Chance. "And for answering both questions correctly — not everyone does — you are rewarded." He held out the cross; it dangled on a black cord.

Paul drove down to Madrid, which was seventeen miles from his hometown. Along the way he encountered forests and lakes and hand-painted signs — LOP RABBITS FOR SALE — and vast sod farms offering flat vistas of endless green. Madrid was an inland village in a country of fire. Burned businesses lined the road: a tavern, an auto-body shop, an inn. The blackened timbers and fallen roofs and melted fixtures remained, they had not been bulldozed and carried away, and these charred artifacts in the gathering gloom seemed to underscore not only the failure of the Madrid Fire Department, if there was one, but also the bankruptcy of the dream of camaraderie associated with restaurants, taverns, and hotels.

Paul arrived at the Terrapin, a white plaster building with exposed framing painted brown. A neon sign glowed in the window. Fall was coming, and the air smelled of grass and the highway. Inside, red lanterns made islands of light, and a glazed slab over a wide doorway carried the inscription FATE CANNOT HARM ME FOR I HAVE DINED WELL. Paul took a table, the only customer. A ceramic bowl offered graham crackers with the image of a turtle baked into the surface.

A waiter came over. One of his ears was missing or deformed. "Mr. Record has called to say he will be late and that you should go ahead and order your dinner."

"Does he live nearby?"

"Mr. Record says go ahead and order."

"Where does he live?" said Paul.

The waiter laid heavy silverware on the wooden table. "You must mean his Nova Scotia house. He had it taken apart in Nova Scotia and shipped down here on trucks."

"Why?"

"Struck his fancy, I guess. The people didn't want to sell, but then they had a change of heart."

Paul ordered fried calamari, clear chowder, and red wine. The wine rose like leaf smoke in his head. Soon the season would change and the wind would blow, and what place was there in the ever-restoring world for fear of a criminal? And he liked restaurants that served clear chowders. Many restaurants skipped it in favor of the gluey white chowder or the unconvincing red chowder. All of Paul's cooking knowledge had to do with chowder. He knew, for example, that the first chowder recipe known to appear in North America consisted of a poem printed in the *Boston Evening Post* in the fall of 1751: "Parsley, Sweet-Marjoram, Savory and Thyme / Then Biscuit next which must be soak'd some Time."

Paul looked out the window. The sky was fading, and a pond glinted purple at the bottom of a hill. He punched songs into a satellite jukebox and ate the haywire tentacles of the calamari. Record arrived twenty minutes after Paul finished his supper. He sat down and rested on the table the artificial arm, which gave him an air of technical ingenuity. Then he picked up the wine bottle with his hook and read the label. Paul understood now why they called him the Pliers. What had seemed at first glance to be a single tubular hook was in fact two hooks that moved apart and together at Record's discretion.

"I've read about you," said Paul.

Record yawned. "I can't wake up tonight," he said. "A lot of what you hear is composed of half-truth and innuendo. The media toss around terms like 'stooge' and 'henchman' and 'mob connections.' I don't know any stooges. Are you a stooge?"

"No."

"Too bad," said Record. "Then I could see what one was."

"I read that you started out with a carnival game."

Record slung his hook over the back of the booth. "It was called Flash-A-Color," he said. "A ball rolled down a chute onto a table of colored squares, and the players bet on the color where the ball would land when it stopped rolling. That's all that happened in the whole game. It was just after the war, and people were in the mood for lighthearted entertainment. They wanted to have a good time with no bones about it. Everything I have today follows in one way or another from the game. Now, I say 'everything I have,' but I myself don't have much. New England Amusements is a privately owned holding company chartered in the state of Delaware and the British Virgin Islands. Its interests include shipping, feldspar, vineyards, trash compaction, sweaters, hydropower, miniature golf, circuit boards, oysters, clams, shad, flounder, rubber, and camping equipment. This restaurant is owned by Nonpareil Enterprises, which is a subsidiary of New England Amusements. Our chefs are named Mick and Nick."

"Food service looks easy to the novice investor, but you have to be canny to survive," said Paul.

"I've always been canny," said Record.

"I hope the place has insurance," said Paul. "There are a lot of fires down this way."

"It gets very dry."

A young man strolled into the Terrapin wearing tasseled leather shoes and a light blue linen suit.

"This is my son," said Record. "Carlo Junior."

"Call me Bobby," said Record's son. He turned a chair backward and sat down at the end of the booth. He had a cleanly shaven face and bright, unguarded eyes.

"That's his stage name," said Carlo.

"Are you an actor?" said Paul.

"I'm a dancer," said Bobby. "I've thought about acting, though. You're the second person to mention that lately."

"I always think that dancing must be pretty competitive," said Paul.

"That's your take on everything," said Carlo.

"My job is to have that take."

"He's right, though," said Bobby. "Especially when it comes to popular dance, which is what I do. It's a paradox. Popular means 'that which everybody likes,' right? But try to think of some venues where you've seen popular dance recently. See what I mean? There just aren't that many."

"Well," said Paul, "by 'popular dance,' you mean . . . not ballet, for example . . ."

"That's a good question," said Bobby. "Not ballet, not jazz, not folk, not square dance. But don't be misled, because it contains *elements* of them."

"When you call him and his girlfriend," Carlo said to Paul, "it always seems like they're either about to dance or else they've just stopped."

"What about tap dancing?"

Bobby nodded earnestly. "There's some tap."

"There's a good deal of tap, if you ask me," said Carlo. "But then he has a regular job too. He's in the contract department at New England Amusements."

"That's my day gig," said Bobby.

Carlo handed his son a graham cracker from the white ceramic bowl. "I always told him to chase his dream," he said. "I chased mine, so I know it can be done. And if this is his dream, then so be it. It may not be my first choice, but he works hard at it, I can tell you that. Show Paul that funny dance you do."

Bobby looked puzzled. "Which one?"

"That funny one you did the other night."

"Oh, O.K.," said Bobby.

Carlo Record put a quarter in the jukebox. Bobby removed his jacket, shoes, and socks. His feet emerged big and white from the cuffs of his blue slacks.

"It's all talk until you see him," said Record.

Vinyl crackled on the sound system, followed by the hammering chords of "Cinnamon Girl," and for the song's duration Bobby Record danced crazily around the restaurant. He slapped his knees, jumped on chairs, swung from ceiling beams. His bare feet thundered on the floorboards. The cooks and waiters stood watching from the door of the kitchen. "Hey, Junior's dancing," someone said. When the song ended Bobby froze with outstretched arms that rose and fell with his panting. Then he came back to the booth drying his brow with a handkerchief. Paul clapped and Record rapped his hook on the edge of the table.

"That is something else," said Paul.

"He used to go to dancing camp," said Record.

"But try," said Bobby, "just try . . . to get paid . . . for it . . . Somebody order me a beer . . ."

Carlo Record walked Paul to the door. Outside in the darkness the neon sign laid a green film on the parking lot. "When you run a restaurant you discover that nothing is simple. Now let me thank you for coming to see us." He reached into his shirt pocket with his hook and brought out a red ticket. "Please accept a coupon."

Paul raised his hands. "You don't have to."

"Of course not. Only from the heart. If you buy one entrée, the second is free." Paul put the ticket in his pocket.

"And one more thing," said Carlo. "I got a burlap sack laying around here somewhere. Here it is. You take this and come with me down to the pond."

"Why?"

"I've got turtle lines."

They walked together down the grassy hill in the moonlight. "When I catch turtle, the cooks make soup," said Record. "The customers love it. They love that turtle soup."

The little man walked around the edge of the pond, kneeling here and there to pluck lines with his fingers. He had something on one of the lines and began reeling it in — pulling on the filament with his good hand and stepping on the line before it could slide back into the water.

"What is it?" said Paul. "Is it a snag?"

"I don't think so," said Carlo.

A snapping turtle crawled from the black water, its horned tail tracing a furrow in the sand. Carlo dropped the line and knelt to wave the hook before the turtle's marbled eyes. The animal appeared to consider the metallic flash and then hit with terrible speed. The jaws clamped the hook with a leathery thud, and Carlo dragged the turtle up the bank. He wrestled the catch into the burlap sack and tied the neck with twine.

He worked very efficiently, and Paul could see how natural the hook was for him after all this time.

6

Paul left the Terrapin and drove over to his parents' place in Verona. Shining blacktop rose and fell between yellow lines and banks of trees. His parents lived outside of town on a former dairy farm. They had never farmed, but Paul's mother's parents had grown corn and raised cattle. Over the years, most of the farm had been sold off for subdivisions but ten acres had been retained in two parcels on either side of the house.

The yard light shone on Uncle Bernard's wide and sagging Buick in the driveway. Uncle Bernard had changed his life the year before, at the news of his son Lane's suicide in California; he had retired early from the Boston police and left his wife, Triphena, and now he visited Paul's parents despondently on weekends. Bernard carried letters from Lane in his beret, and he would stop in the middle of a conversation and take one out, unfold it — it would be folded very small — and read it silently. Then he would put the letter away and speak softly to himself. This sort of thing made everyone cringe, but of course no one would say anything.

Paul remembered Lane as an eccentric and sometimes cruel figure, but this is how he remembered all his cousins, and for that matter his brothers and sisters and his parents. So he had to wonder about his memory. Paul had visited Lane in Arlington once when they were both teenagers, and they had gone out after dark to hide behind a hedge and throw tomatoes at cars. Lane did this all the time, or said he did, and the drivers could never figure out what had hit them or from where. But on this night a man in a red Mustang slammed on the brakes, jumped out of his car, and made for the hedge where the boys were hiding. The man might have been as old as thirty, and Paul and Lane were thirteen, and they ran from him with the awful knowledge that he would kill them, break them in half, tear their heads off, if he caught them. Paul and Lane split up, and Paul jumped a fence into the yard of a house that happened to have an unlocked back door. In the kitchen he found a girl of ten or eleven, a girl with straight red hair and gently crossed eyes, who said, "Who are you?" A promotional clock for the Rival Dog Food company ticked on the wall by the refrigerator. Paul told her the truth. The girl listened carefully and then locked and bolted the doors of the house. She led Paul to a large sunken living room, where they sat on a couch and watched a television show about panthers in the wild as if they had been doing this all along. Soon the doorbell began ringing, and then the face of the man whose car had been hit with tomatoes appeared in the windows of the sunken room, looking so red and contorted that Paul thought it might burn up as old rags sometimes will in a barn. The girl walked to the windows — resourcefully, Paul thought — and closed the curtains.

Paul told Uncle Bernard and Aunt Triphena this story after Lane's suicide, giving the incident a carefree slant. Bernard said that it was easy to get in trouble and hard to get out.

Now Paul's father, Maurice, was trying to interest Bernard in short-wave radio. They sat together in a little room off the kitchen. Maurice Nash had worked for the Providence & Worcester Railroad until they closed the depot at Verona, and now in retirement he had become a ham operator. An antenna climbed the side of the house like a ladder, and whenever there was bad weather anywhere in the world, or even on the surface of the sun, Paul's father would be up late exchanging information with people in other countries. He had been a semiprofessional boxer earlier in his life, but this experience had not left him with an expert's wariness of using his hands on amateurs. Once when Paul was young his father had fought the mailman, and after that the family had to rent a box at the post office in the village.

"What should I say?" said Bernard, with earphones clamped over his beret.

"Say hello," said Paul's father. "Say whatever you feel like saying. That's the fun of it. Kotka speaks English. It's the international language of hams."

"Hello, Kotka," said Bernard. "What? . . . No . . . this is my brother's radio . . . my brother . . . Maurice . . . Maurice is my brother . . . I don't have a radio of my own . . . what? . . . well, that's what Maurice says, but it's hard for me to think of hobbies since my son died . . . my son . . . Lane . . . it's a family name . . . yes, exactly . . . you see, he moved to California and I believe that was his big mistake . . . well, it's all true from what I've seen . . . all they say and worse . . . I will despise that state until my dying day . . . I went out there and tried to persuade him to come home . . . everything so phony in California . . . we saw the Rose Parade but I could not talk to him, he would not listen . . ."

Paul said hello to his father, waved to Bernard, and went upstairs to find his mother, Diana. She sat at a dressing table in her room doing a jigsaw puzzle. Her shoulders bent to the table and her hair fell in gray waves over the pieces. "Did you see your father? This puzzle is the Tulip Festival in a place called Pella."

"Dad and Bern are messing around with the radio," said Paul.

"Poor Bernard. He stays up all night smoking, and in the morning I find his heaping ashtrays."

"I have something to tell you," said Paul. "I'm married now. I got married in New Bedford."

She looked up with a puzzle piece in her hand. "Why didn't you invite us?"

"It was a civil ceremony," said Paul. "Have you found the corner pieces?"

"I don't start with the corners," said Diana. "I know you do, but that's not my style."

"My wife's name is Mary."

"You should bring her to see us. I don't know anyone in the country." She stood and walked to the window. "The other night I heard the strangest noise in the trees. It must have been two or three in the morning."

"What kind of noise?"

"Full of despair," she said. "I think it may have been a raccoon." She turned to Paul and smiled. "But what does this have to do with your marriage? Nothing."

They went out to the hallway and climbed the stairs to the cold and raftered attic.

Diana's hand rested on a rocking chair with a cluster of dark grapes carved into the headpiece. "This belonged to my parents," she said. "The story goes that my mother's father carried this chair from Arcadia on his back. I've given something to all of you kids when you got married. Fred got a gate-leg table, Carmen got a hutch, and Lily got a footstool."

Mary and Paul could put up with the mild complaints of the dentist on the first floor about the drips from their shower, but then a neighbor moved in next door who said their phone rang too loudly, who banged with authoritarian vigor on the walls when they moved around their apartment at night, and who left notes on their door such as this one: "My boyfriend and I are professionals and we have to be in Boston every morning at eight o'clock on the nose with no excuses asked and none given and thus you can plainly see for yourself that . . ." and so on, in self-righteous backslanting handwriting. While Mary and Paul had a good time thinking up sarcastic replies to their neighbor's rambling notes, they wondered if it was time to buy a house. Clovis, Luken & Pitch had started giving Paul profit sharing, which arrived monthly in a brown envelope with cash inside. Jack Chance would give Paul the envelope and tell him not to count the money because it was bad luck.

At this time high interest rates plagued the country, allowing Mary and Paul to invest the profit sharing in certificates of deposit with rates between eighteen and twenty-one percent per year, and so when they found a small yellow house with red trim that they liked on Neptune Street in Providence, they were able to make a down payment. Carlo the Pliers did not cosign the mortgage, but he sent a letter of recommendation to the bank.

The house needed work, and they hired a college student who knew carpentry, charged a reasonable hourly rate, and had a girlfriend, Marcy, he could hire as his assistant. The student's name was Steve, and he had a habit of describing any smooth surface as "smooth as a bed sheet," and while Paul and Mary considered this a little odd, they did not give it much thought until they returned to the house one afternoon to find Steve and

Marcy asleep in the sheets of their bed. So they let the carpenters go and finished the work themselves. They scraped, steamed, caulked, and painted. Once they rolled primer on the walls of a room without opening the windows, and soon they were intoxicated and singing along with a radio so loudly that when they went outside to clear their heads, a man filling the oil tank of the house next door said, "I like that singing." Then they drove to the hardware store for an edger they needed and saw a dog trotting along the sidewalk with what appeared to be a woman's underpants in its mouth. At the hardware store they walked mystified among aisles of gleaming tools.

They did not have much furniture beyond the rocking chair, the cracked round table, two other chairs, and a wrought-iron floor lamp, and so they put the lamp by the windows in the living room and positioned chairs around it so that they could sit in the evening and read. Leaves pressed into the lampshade varied the light that fell on their books and magazines. At first they would trade passages back and forth from whatever they were reading. He spent weeks, for example, studying a book called *Corporate Suretyship* by G. W. Crist, Jr. ("The very foundation of society and of business is faith. Were it not for mutual confidence, for the demonstrable justification of our belief that things *are* as represented to us, that we may impose trust in the vast majority of our fellow men, all would be chaos . . ."), but after several months in the new house they did not read to each other as much.

Like many young couples in cities, they had few friends. They had gone out with Jack and Felicia Chance once, to a bar called Steeple Street, but Paul mentioned some news item he had read concerning religious people, and he made the mistake of calling them fanatics, and after the story was over, Chance said, "Actually, Paul, when it comes to Christ, I guess we are fanatics. Yeah, I guess that's probably what we are too."

Mary got involved in a project to put computers to classroom use, and although there were problems — in the time it took to make a picture or article appear on the computer screen, a student might have looked the information up in an encyclopedia, taken notes, and made a little clay sculpture in art class — she liked the work and it made her enjoy more than ever the evenings when they could sit by the leaf-shaded lamp and read. Sometimes they played backgammon, but Mary did not share Paul's fascination for the odds, and she got tired of his constant hints on what her next move should be.

One night the phone rang. Carlo Record happened to be in the neighborhood with Miriam Lentine, Bobby, and Bobby's girlfriend, Karen, and they wanted to bring some food over from the new Cambodian place in town. It would be a housewarming.

"What do they want to do that for?" Mary asked Paul after he had hung up.

"Oh Christ, I don't know," said Paul. He had been working hard, and the last thing he wanted was company.

They hurried into the kitchen and stared at the lime-green counters as if trays of food and drink would materialize on them at any moment.

"Well, they can come over if they want, but we have nothing to drink," said Mary.

"I'd better run out to the store."

Mary opened the refrigerator and leaned into it. "No drinks, no crackers, and no cheese. And I'm afraid that's how it's going to be."

"I'm running out now," said Paul. He sat down on a kitchen chair to put his shoes on. "I have no idea. Carlo said a housewarming. Don't ask me what it's all about."

"I don't like this," she said. "Work is work, and this I do not like."

"I'll be back."

Paul drove to the liquor store, where he bought a jug of red wine with a glass finger handle near the spout. "Taste this,

Paul," said Roger Oberon, the man who owned the liquor store. He held a water glass with orange liquid in the bottom. "It's some new vodka that's supposed to be flavored with cantaloupe."

Paul drank the vodka. "I'm not getting any cantaloupe out of that," he said.

"That's interesting, I didn't either."

"I have to run. A client of mine is dropping by on zero notice."

"Sometimes people call me on Sunday. I tell them, You know I can't open on Sunday even if I wanted to. Sure you can, they say. Give us a six-pack."

"This is Carlo Record."

"Well. He had my uncle's leg broken, you know."

"Why?"

Roger shook his head sadly. "My uncle was a piano teacher on Golden Hill in Central Falls, and the word came down that all the music teachers would have to pay up protection money from now on. Well, my uncle was a pretty feisty guy, and he said it wasn't fair because he worked out of his house and the rule had always been that if you worked out of your house, you didn't have to pay any protection money. This was, as I say, on Golden Hill, and music was very popular in that whole neighborhood, and my uncle I guess became a sort of test case. If he didn't pay, then nobody would have to pay. So anyway, they broke his leg."

"You would think his hands."

"That's what everybody says."

"Did he go to the police?"

"No, the hospital. Then he started paying. It wasn't even that much but just the principle of it."

Paul drove back to Neptune Street, where Carlo's black Crown Victoria sat in front of the house. Neptune was a narrow street, and whoever was driving the Crown Vic had pulled the passenger-side tires up on the grass to give other cars room to squeeze past. Paul drove into the driveway and walked across the yard. It was early summer. He could hear frogs and the thumping of a car stereo. Figures moved past the windows of the house, and even though he wished the Records had not showed up, he felt proud as he went inside. In the living room, Bobby's girlfriend was on the floor, going through their LPs.

"You have one good album," she said. "Janet Jackson. The rest you could throw away. Johnny Mathis! Hey, Bobby, didn't Johnny Mathis used to be on the Dean Martin show or something?"

"I don't think he was a regular," said Bobby. He sat by the leaf-shade lamp looking at the back cover of the book Paul had been reading. It concerned the latest theories on photon behavior, and Paul did not understand it, but he would sit in the bathtub reading it, and he had come to think of the sound of water running into the bathtub as the sound of his brain trying to understand what photons were and what they did.

Paul introduced himself to Karen.

"We brought spring rolls," she said.

"Karen's my girlfriend," said Bobby. He put the book down.

"Where's Carlo?" said Paul.

Karen examined a rich green album by the saxophonist Gato Barbieri. She had a straight red nose and a matter-of-fact set to her lips. "He and Miriam are in the kitchen with your lady."

Paul walked through the house carrying the wine in a paper bag. Carlo wore a black turtleneck and a medallion with a transparent stone in the center. The sleeves of his sweater were pushed up, revealing both his good arm and his putty-colored synthetic arm. He rummaged through the cupboard. "I'm going to show you how to make Cambodian food taste better than it does even in Cambodia," he said. "And that is cayenne."

"I couldn't vouch for the freshness of that," said Mary.

"Not to worry," said Carlo. He unscrewed the lid of the spice jar and tapped it gently over open white take-out boxes with the wire handles folded down. Then he shook it. "Tell Paul about the housewarming present."

"It's under the stove," said Miriam Lentine.

"You didn't need to do that," said Paul.

"Check under the stove," said Carlo.

Paul knelt. Six inches separated the bottom of the stove and the floor, and he could see only dust and darkness.

"It's a —" said Mary.

"Don't give it away, honey," said Miriam.

"I can't see anything," said Paul.

Carlo stirred the food with a wooden spoon. "Let's just tell him," he said. "Here we are, having fun, while Paul crawls on the floor."

"It's a cat," said Mary. She smiled helplessly. "They brought a cat for us, Paul."

"It's a kitten, really," said Miriam. "Not even six weeks old. Frankly, it's early to take it from its mother."

Paul stood and brushed off his knees. "Why is it under the stove?"

Miriam laughed, her arms full of plates. "Running under the stove is what cats do. You have a lot to learn. They're afraid and so they seek shelter."

They ate their food on the cracked table in the dining room. Carlo had added way too much cayenne to everything except the spring rolls, and their faces blanched and perspired.

"I think you overdid it, little man," said Miriam.

Carlo laughed but seemed to be suffering more than anyone. "I like mine spicy," he said, swiping at his eyes with a black handkerchief.

"Why did you do this to us, Dad?" said Bobby.

"Then don't eat it," said Carlo.

"It is too darned hot," said Karen.

"Then don't eat it."

Paul took a drink of water and asked where the cat had come from.

"Miriam and I got it from a place out in Foster," said Bobby. "We drove out there this afternoon. They had seven cross-eyed cats."

"It's because they're too young," said Miriam Lentine. "Their eye muscles aren't developed to where they should be."

Later they sat in the living room, where Carlo admired a picture that Mary had painted. It was a daunting copy of a portrait of Charles I by Anthony van Dyck of Antwerp. The heart of the painting seemed to emanate not from the English king but from his horse, bluish white with a bowed head, and from a man in the background who had his hand thrown over the horse's golden mane.

"Colorful," said Carlo. He rocked slowly in the chair with the grapes carved into the frame.

"And what of your style, Mary?" said Miriam. "Do you have a style of your own?"

"I really don't," said Mary.

"Sure she does," said Paul. "Sure you do."

"I used to be modest," said Bobby. "And then I asked myself, Why? What is there to be so modest about?"

"No reason in the world," said his father.

Paul led Mary and their guests to Mary's studio, a small room across from their bedroom upstairs. The easel stood in the corner and an open paintbox balanced on a wooden stool. The box was made of dark worn wood and contained a palette and brushes and twelve tubes of paint, crushed and rolled up to varying degrees. Paintings of apples covered the walls. Mary had long ago stopped painting towels and now worked exclusively on apples. There were sixty-three paintings on the walls, each on a piece of paper nine inches square. The apples seemed to look down like so many ripe eyes. Paul put his arm around Mary as if to protect her from the others' judgment.

"All this fruit makes me hungry," said Karen.

Miriam gestured toward the windows. "Do you have north light?" she said. "I guess you have to. That's what I understand."

Mary laughed. "I need overalls more than I need north light."

Carlo stood in the center of the room and turned slowly.

"Something occurs to me," he said. "I know a man who will buy any paintings of Arab subjects done at the turn of the century. Why don't you paint him some?"

"I copy to learn, not to sell," said Mary.

"Take the night off, Carlo," said Miriam. "This is a house-warming."

"She doesn't have to decide this minute," said Carlo, and as he spoke a nut and a washer fell from his artificial wrist and rolled under a daybed. "Looks like I'm falling to bits," he said. "Time to go home."

It rained hard that night after everyone on Neptune Street was asleep. Paul woke up and looked at his watch. He heard the soft insistent sound of Mary's walking around the house in rubber boots. Paul found her by the back window of the kitchen, with the rain driving down through the floodlight outside. Two days before, they had planted six flats of pachysandra in the back yard, and now they could see the unmoored plants floating slowly away. They put on raincoats and went out. The rain beat against their shoulders and ran into their boots as they sloshed around collecting runaway ground cover in buckets. The bathtub seemed the only place to put the rescued plants, and after three or four trips apiece Mary and Paul sat down on the edge of the tub for a breather. Then they heard faint cries from the kitchen, where the cat had finally emerged from under the stove. It was a black and gray tiger with spindly legs and white markings on its feet. Mary gave it a saucer of milk and lined a wicker basket with a blanket, and the cat drank the milk, scratched Mary's hand, and crawled back under the stove.

Mary pressed her thumb on the scratch, making blood bead along its length. "Maybe I will do some of those paintings," she said.

They lived in the house on Neptune Street for five years, and hardly a month would pass without Paul's remembering the pachysandra in the bathtub, which seemed to represent the temporary or reversible quality of many of their efforts.

They were always looking over their shoulders, and nothing done was done for good. An old couple had owned the house before Paul and Mary, and one of their crime-prevention measures had been to cut all the sash cords, as if a burglar would say, "These windows are too heavy, let's try some other house." All the cutting of the sash cords had done was to make the windows impossible to keep open without propping books, cooking tongs, or hedge clippers in the frames, so one day when Paul was feeling constructive he replaced all the sash cords. It was tedious work, threading the cords through the window frames, but when it was done the windows slid up and down in their tracks and stayed wherever they left them. That night, though, one of the windows fell with a noise like a shotgun going off, which sent the cat spinning like lightning through the house. The booming sound did not surprise Paul, somehow; on the edge of dreams he often found himself expecting big night noises. He remembered the thing his mother had heard in the trees down in Verona, and he wondered if he would also hear the cry of the banshee or the disenfranchised raccoon or whatever it was. Paul imagined the solid and cumulative lives of others, plotted lives, lives making some kind of sense, where if you did one thing, then you could reasonably expect another beneficial thing to follow. What he did not realize for a long time was that even people who live their lives as if this were the case could not refer to any proof. It's just faith, and there's nothing to be done about it.

The big noise he must have been waiting for came in the form of violent pounding at three o'clock on the morning of October 11, 1989. Paul vaulted cleanly over Mary and landed on his feet beside the bed. The walls shook but Mary did not wake. Paul grabbed a baseball bat that he had kept handy, leaning against his dresser, and moved slowly to the front door. White waves swept the walls of the front rooms, lighting a clothesline painting, a window, and a line of model horses that seemed ready to bolt from the mantel. Then he opened the door and police swarmed in. They had the baseball bat out of his hands before he even remembered he had it. The cops stomped around the house collecting paintings and brushes.

The United States built a racketeering case and its prosecution took two years. The government's attorneys lost interest in the forged paintings once they understood that Paul could and would describe the money laundering of the Record syndicate. When the trial ended, Mary and Paul were moved to Spokane, which never did work out. They could not find decent jobs and could not get a feel for the city. The truth is they probably would not have liked wherever they moved to. When a protected witness finishes testifying and moves to a safe place, his or her sense of purpose, if any, falls to zero overnight. And then Mary was driving along one day in Spokane when a Sunbird came out of a side street and spun her car twice. This was not gangland retribution but only a careless dental assistant named Sylvia. When Paul got to the hospital, Mary lay on a rolling bed with an orange brace on her neck and tears running down her temples and into her ears. She faced the ceiling and looked at him from the corner of her eyes. "Oh Mary," he said. "What's happened to you? Who did this?" The accident confirmed their feelings about Spokane, although they knew that accidents happened everywhere. When they left the United States, Scratch, the cat that Carlo and Miriam had given them, went to live with Paul's parents.

7

The inn that Mary and Paul ran in the Forest of the Ardennes stood, and still stands, outside the town of Vertige, on the former site of a religious society that had been established in the thirteenth century by the Mangeurs d'Herbes Folles, or Weed-

Eaters, a group of radical monks whose desire for maximum austerity had led them to shun even the crudest forms of agriculture. The Weed-Eaters had broken off from the Premonstratensians (who themselves had agreed to disagree with the Augustinians) and built a stone campus that lasted almost seven hundred years, only to be shelled to the ground on Christmas Eve, 1944, during the Battle of the Ardennes.

The present hotel was a whitewashed brick house with a red tiled roof, red shutters, and a balcony on two sides of the second floor. It was called Auberge des Moines, or Inn of the Monks, and sat crooked on the wooded lip of the deep and narrow valley of the Torchon River. A barn sheltered cows, goats, and chickens. Vertige had a pharmacy, a tavern, a florist, St. Cecilia's Cave, a Porsche dealership, a Catholic church, and two dusty museums — one for artifacts of the wars and one for the composer Henri Poilvache (1899–1961), a native who had moved to Paris and written the ballroom standards "Quelle Bêtise" and "Faute de Mieux" — but there was no train station and the Torchon was too rocky for excursion boats, and so when tourists came to Vertige, they tended to be lost or after something very specific.

Mary's cousin Gustave had run the inn before Paul and Mary took over, and he now held a note on which they made monthly payments. Everyone but Gustave himself agreed that the inn had done badly under his direction. For some reason, he had concentrated almost solely on the flower beds that rose in terraces to the meadows behind the house, had concentrated on them to the neglect of the inn when, after all, as Rosine Boclinville, the housekeeper, had observed, no one was paying to sleep in the flower beds. Gustave had evidently decided that the inn would become famous for the gardens, that the gardens of the monks would draw crowds from all over Europe — and perhaps this dream might have come true if at the same time that Gustave had been planting the elaborate beds he had also been building a railroad to Vertige or dredging the Torchon River for excursion boats.

Now the gardens had gone to seed and Gustave was a partner in a spring-water distributorship in Liège. He and his clients would come down to the inn for free and stand around as if the place were still Gustave's. Paul wanted to have this out with Gustave, but Mary disagreed. She said that her cousin had suffered depressions all his life and that he had once smashed up the kitchen of the inn with a hoe because a bottle of soda that he liked had disappeared from the refrigerator and no one would admit to having taken it. Now, said Mary — just as Gustave was getting somewhere finally with this mineral-water thing in Liège, to the relief of his family — now was no time to make him feel unwanted.

Languages were all mixed up at Auberge des Moines. Paul and Mary spoke English. Mary and Rosine spoke French. Gustave spoke French, Flemish, and English. Rosine would speak English to guests but only French to Paul, who did not understand French unless it was spoken very slowly, and even then he had trouble, and she seemed to enjoy the fact that he could not fathom much of what she said. Paul had tried to learn French from an elementary phrase book but could not master the verb forms or the gargled *r*. He had got sidetracked by the melancholy poetry of the sentences to be used in times of trouble.

> Help!
> It's an emergency!
> There's been an accident!
> Call a doctor!
> Call an ambulance!
> I've been raped.
> I've been robbed!
> Call the police!
> Where is the police station?
> Go away!
> Thief!
> I am ill.
> My friend is ill.

I am lost.
Where are the toilets?
Could you help me, please?
Could I please use the telephone?
I'm sorry. I apologize.
I didn't realize I was doing anything wrong.
I didn't do it.
I wish to contact my embassy/consulate.
I speak English.

As linguistically disabled as Paul felt for never getting more than a phrase or two of French, it was the availability of English speakers that gave the inn such popularity as it had. The only guidebook to list the Auberge des Moines had given it a B for food, a B- for furnishings, and a C+ for prices, but had also noted that the owners had come from the States, and so American and English tourists would arrive with the gratitude of those who had found a haven, albeit one with food that was just all right and with high room rates. And those residents of Vertige and the surrounding towns who wished to learn or maintain their English would come for supper.

Sometimes people from the former Allied countries came to see where their ancestors or they themselves had fought in the wars. The English who wound up in Vertige seemed in a hurry to leave when their memorial duties were done. One summer an old man from Battersea named Geoffrey stood at supper and denounced some of the kings of Belgium. He was a large and jowly man who had little good to say about Leopolds II and III, although he admired Albert I, who had toughed it out in West Flanders during the German occupation in the First World War. Paul knew some of the history but could hear only fragments of the analysis as he carried in plates of beef carbonnade.

"There have been few leaders to compare with the soldier-king Albert," said Geoffrey. "I remember when he fell off the mountain. A great tragedy, really."

There were seven others in the dining room: a party of four

from Vertige, a young French schoolteacher, and a middle-aged couple named Bob and Michelle from Kansas City.

"Where was this?" said Michelle, who wore coral bracelets and had the fierce and friendly aspect of someone who was going to have a good time no matter what.

"Why, in Belgium," said Geoffrey.

"I mean, where he fell off the mountain," said Michelle. "Was it around here?"

"That's a good question. It just may have been."

Mary came into the dining room with a wooden bowl of asparagus and onions. "Up by Namur. The Rocher du Roi."

"But then, as I say," said Geoffrey, "Leopold III surrendered to Germany in the Second World War, after which his own country became suspicious of him."

"Let the debate begin," said René Avaloze in a bored voice. This was a common phrase in the town and meant the opposite of what it appeared to mean. René ran the pharmacy in Vertige and enjoyed playing the part of the contrarian.

"Well, from what I understand, the English monarchy was not a very smooth operation either," said Michelle. "Bob and I saw a production of *Richard III* in Kansas City and the whole thing seemed to be stabbing and lying from start to finish."

The Englishman laughed loudly. "Very good," he said. "You've snared me in my own hoop."

"England used to matter, but no more," said René Avaloze. "England is an empty glass left on the night table of Europe."

"He says that about all the countries," said Paul.

"Let's eat," said Bob from Kansas City.

The dining room was narrow, with a single long table that lent itself to moments of silence and self-conscious conversation, and on this particular evening the discussion turned to the differences between the English spoken in the States and that of the United Kingdom.

"When you say 'quite good,'" said Geoffrey to Bob and Michelle, "you mean 'unusually good,' whereas I take it to mean 'try again.'"

After supper Geoffrey lit a cigar, which drove everyone except Paul, Michelle, and Bob from the dining room.

"What do you do in Kansas City?" said Paul.

"Run a screw company," said Bob. "One of the things I'm hoping to accomplish this year is to identify some concessions to demand from our workers. All the companies in the States are demanding concessions from their workers and I'm under a lot of pressure. The problem is our workers don't make much and their benefits aren't generous to begin with. There's not a lot for them to concede. So partly we're a victim of our own success, but try telling that to the board of directors."

"Make them work in the dark," said Paul. "In the winter try turning off the heat."

"We have turned the heat down before, but never off. We're already perceived as fairly rigid. One time, in the middle of negotiations the newspaper in Kansas City ran a story — and I had no qualms with the story, the story itself was fair — but the headline said, 'Management Makes Offer to Screw Company Workers.'"

"An unfortunate choice of words," said Paul.

"Bring back child labor," said Geoffrey. "That would be quite a concession. Sir, could we get something to drink?"

"What would you like?" said Paul. "We have Stella Artois, Diekirch, Loborg, Tuborg, Kriek, Framboise, Rochefort, Chimay, St. Sixtus, Blanche en Hoegarden, Grand Cru de Hoegarden . . ."

"Chimay."

Paul fetched bottles from the kitchen.

"I'm not sure how we ended up in Vertige," said Michelle. "We thought we were going to Dinant, but I seem to have misread the map or the traffic signs or something."

"The highway numbers have changed," said Paul.

"That must be it," said Bob.

Geoffrey pressed his belly and the heels of his hands to the edge of the table. "I came to see the cemetery," he said. "In London everyone said, 'Oh, don't go to Belgium, it's so dull. It's so remarkably dull in Belgium.' I said, 'But this is the Ardennes,' and they said, 'Oh, that's the dullest region of all.' But I have friends in the cemetery. I was in the Second Army. We wore white so as not to be seen against the snow."

Later, in the parlor, the Englishman recited "Gunga Din" and wept:

> *". . . But when it comes to slaughter*
> *You will do your work on water,*
> *An' you'll lick the bloomin' boots of 'im that's got it. . . ."*

Gustave arrived the next morning, to spend the weekend. By now Paul and Gustave could barely stand being in the same room. Paul thought the rate of the note was too high; Gustave thought that Mary and Paul's trips to the United States were wasteful and nostalgic. Gustave thought Paul should spend time tending the gardens; Paul considered it better to let the milkweed run wild. Gustave had found a mounted boar's head for seven thousand francs that Paul refused to hang in the dining room. And so on. Gustave did not live at the inn anymore but he could not find it in himself to let go of it. Like many houses, the inn always had something that needed fixing, and Gustave seemed to take pleasure in seeking out and reporting these problems. "The toaster is shot," he would say. "The floor shakes in this area."

That morning he complained about the washing machine. "Something's gone wrong," he said. "It is making a noise like a gun."

"What were you doing in the laundry room?" said Paul.

"I don't go near the laundry room," said Gustave. "The washing machine is making such a noise that it can be heard from any point in the house."

"The floor of the laundry room slants," said Paul. "It was built badly."

"M. Duprix built the laundry room," said Gustave. "He was the best carpenter in Vertige for many years."

"Mary said he drank."

"What did he drink?"

"What difference does that make?"

"Americans understand nothing about drinking. If he is drunk on whiskey, he could still be an able carpenter. On wine, however, he could not be persuaded to pick up a hammer. Nothing can be wrong with that floor."

"Take a level and check it," said Paul.

"How can I check the floor of the laundry room when it is off limits to me?"

Paul went upstairs. Mary lay on their bed with a washcloth on her forehead.

"Man, that Gustave," said Paul. "I could shoot him sometimes."

"You can't know what it's like to be Gustave," said Mary. "He was such an unpopular boy, and even when he was older, he started a cycling club and no one would join. He ordered red and white jerseys with little bicycles on them and they just sat, week after week, in a box in the front hall. That box of shirts was the saddest thing I've ever seen."

It was later that season that a young woman named Lisa Prendergast came from Virginia to walk in the footsteps of her grandfather, who had died in the Battle of the Ardennes. She wore orange hiking boots and a big nylon backpack that made her arms hang in front of her body like the arms of Frankenstein. What happened between Paul and Lisa Prendergast seemed harmless enough on its surface, but it pushed Paul and Mary farther apart than they had ever been.

It all began one night when Paul saw Lisa walking back from Vertige. Paul sat on the porch of the inn, listening to a portable radio playing softly. Lisa Prendergast slipped off her pack and leaned it against the wall. She sat beside Paul and began unlacing her boots. The sun had fallen below the far side of the valley, leaving red light in the air. The chickens ate with quiet intensity in the yard as the cows stepped slowly down the hill.

"You missed supper," said Paul.

"What was it?"

"Eel chowder."

"I ate in town."

"Did you get to the war museum today?"

"It's very superficial," said Lisa.

Paul shrugged. "I get a kick out of the wax figures."

"There are no maps and no mention of economics. All wars are about economics. My God, that's just elementary."

"Have you been to Grenier?"

"Grenier has some interesting exhibits. They're not first class, but they're better than what's in Vertige."

"You ought to go down to Bouillon. They've got an incredible *son et lumière* at the castle."

"This trip is not panning out," Lisa said. "Here's my grandfather's picture." She handed him a small photograph in a thick and tarnished metal frame. A smiling soldier, his uniform cap set at an angle, leaned toward the camera as he held an apple. The picture had been fixed in its frame by means of a scrap of newspaper from 1943, folded and taped to the back of the frame.

"Where did he die?" said Paul.

"In a cave," said Lisa. "All we know is he died with two other American soldiers in a cave. Only they didn't die, and they weren't American soldiers."

"I don't get it."

"Well, it turns out that German soldiers would come into the Ardennes dressed in the uniforms of the Allies."

"Sneaky," said Paul.

"It was a desperate measure," said Lisa Prendergast. "I've been to St. Cecilia's, but it doesn't feel like the place."

"You have to be careful in there."

"I mean, it just gets smaller and smaller and darker and darker. I was following along and I said, Wait a minute. Let's think this through. This is how people get lost."

"And they do," said Paul.

"So I'm not getting anywhere."

"There is another cave," said Paul. "It doesn't get the attention that St. Cecilia's gets, because it's harder to get to, and it's more of a geological formation than a real cave. Kids go up there to drink and smoke."

"Where is it?"

"I could take you."

"Yes, why don't you."

It rained for two days straight, and on the third day the rain held off long enough for Paul and Lisa to hike off in search of the cave or geological formation where her grandfather might have died. They rode in the inn's pickup truck to a clearing along the highway. Across the road a cow lay chewing grass beneath the branches of a tree. They followed a path that climbed steeply among blueberry thickets and fanning ferns and mica flecks glittering in the rocks. Their boots thudded on the packed path as if the ground were hollow. Twice they emerged from the forest onto high smooth ledges from which they could see the surrounding country, the highway that went into Vertige, and the curve of the ridge along which they were traveling. The sun broke through the clouds and a steady breeze pushed against their faces.

"What do you do in Virginia?" said Paul.

"I work for the Office of Monetary Allocation Studies," said Lisa. "But don't ask how the economy is going. That's what everyone asks me, but I don't know any more about it than what's in the newspapers. We're having a conference in Vienna next year, so I'm going to run over and do some advance work after I get done here."

"Are you part of the Fed?"

"We're totally independent," said Lisa. She took a pair of sunglasses from a pocket on the side of her pack and put them on. "Our board is composed of twelve influential people who fly all over the world holding conferences. After Vienna, I go to Stockholm and then on to Reykjavík."

"I've always wondered what Iceland would be like," said

Paul. "Once I saw a picture of kids riding bicycles on hot water pipes in a strange glacial valley. They wore gloves and scarves."

"Reykjavík is interesting. I like it. It's nothing to rave about. Luxembourg City is nice."

They made it to the rocks over the cave by noon. Red hawks wheeled under gray clouds joining slowly in the air. Paul led Lisa down a path that curled around the rocks. The path narrowed and they turned sideways to squeeze through the mouth of the cave. Broken slabs tilted in the ceiling, and gray daylight slipped through the cracks. A circle of rocks formed a fireplace, with brown Orval bottles nested in black ridged cinders. "What do you think?" said Paul.

"This *could* be it," said Lisa. She dropped her pack and stretched her arms above her head. "But I just don't know." Her underarms looked cool and pale blue. "I want to feel something. I want to be sure. If my grandfather appeared right now, he wouldn't know who I was."

"Give it a minute," said Paul.

"He would say, 'Who are you?'"

"This is what he would do." He removed her sunglasses, cupped the back of her neck in his hands, and pressed his forehead to hers. Her rounded forehead pushed back.

"Now I feel something," said Lisa. "I feel you crunching my head."

Mist became rain on the way back, and Paul turned on the windshield wipers. Mary had hung the banner for the "Magic Carpet Ride" dance party they threw every Friday night. One way that English speakers could feel at home in Belgium was by turning on the radio, for many of the songs were from the States, although in most instances they were not especially good songs. Paul had never heard the song "In the Year 2525" as often as he did while living in Belgium.

"I showed Lisa Prendergast the cave where her grandfather died in the fighting," said Paul. "Well, it might have been the place. She wasn't sure."

"Oh, right," said Mary. She stood in the parlor with a tomato tin full of sawdust for the dance floor.

"What part don't you believe?" said Paul. Mary stared into the can of dust.

"Did you kiss her?"

"We went up, we came down."

"You kissed her as plain as the look on your face."

"We butted heads."

Mary sifted sawdust onto the floor. "You sicken me."

"You sicken too easily," said Paul. "You need a vaccination."

"Whose name's on all the papers?" said Mary.

"Your name."

"My name is right."

There was a knock on the kitchen door and Paul opened it. A lodger from Hertogenbosch reported that the automatic shoe polisher in the hallway was broken and that the sink in his room emptied very slowly. Paul got a bottle of drain opener and went upstairs.

II

MATCHES

8

The day after seeing the strange dog trapped in the car in New Hampshire, Paul and Mary drove down to Boston to catch the afternoon plane for Brussels. They flew Ailleurs because of its favorable rates. The ramp did not quite reach the airplane, and sunlight flared on the silver cylinder.

Mary fanned her face with airline papers. "It's hot," she said.

"Do you have the tickets?" said Paul.

"I have the boarding passes."

"I have the itinerary."

"I have the baggage stubs," said Mary. She looked through her papers. "I have the boarding passes," she said again.

"I can't hear you," said Paul.

"What's got into you?"

Paul thumped his ear with the heel of his fist. "I have unequal pressure in my head."

Paul and Mary found seats in the loud section over the wings. At least they would not have to worry about hearing unusual snapping noises that might be the first faint signal of a deadly fall. They sat observing the boarding styles of other passengers, who got on in a sideways and vaguely despairing way. Something about overhead bins seemed to bring out a ruthless territorial streak.

Then the pilot announced a delay of forty-five minutes to an hour. Soon a man and woman in white blouses came down the aisle pushing and pulling a chrome cart.

"Something to drink on the ground?" said the woman. "Something to drink on the ground?" said the man. The cart might have carried gold bars for the effort required to move it.

Paul had red wine and Mary white, poured from small green bottles with screw tops.

"We forgot to get my magazine," said Mary.

She did not like to fly without a magazine called *Gone Hollywood*. She liked movies, liked nothing so much as going alone to a theater with a book to read until the lights went out. Her favorite movie was *Don't Look Now*, with Donald Sutherland, Julie Christie, and a bloodthirsty troll in a red hood. But there was another reason she wanted *Gone Hollywood*: its content meant so little that she felt the airplane could not crash or break apart in the air while she was reading it; a natural law would bar that much irony.

It seemed to Paul that people who on the ground would read most any magazine that happened to be lying around became suddenly inflexible when flying. Once he had watched a young couple waiting for takeoff at JFK. The woman threw down her magazine and said, "I didn't want *Elle*."

"What do you expect of me?" said the young man.

"You imbecile — I specifically asked for *Marie Claire*."

"I'll go get your magazine," Paul said now to Mary.

"Remember, it's *Gone Hollywood*."

"I remember."

The plane was vast and crowded, and Paul moved through it with the halting step that comes from drinking watery wine aboard a grounded airplane with afternoon light drifting flat through clouded windows — a waste of time preceding a bending of time. The stewardess who had given them their wine stood by the door looking disturbed. Paul guessed that she was adding the time it would take to fix the plane to the time she normally got home. Maybe she had cats. She looked like someone worrying about cats in an apartment in a faraway city.

"Do I have time to leave?" said Paul.

"Technically, no," said the stewardess. "But really, yes, because between the two of us, this airplane ain't going anywhere for a good long while. The wine tells you that. We don't bring out preflight wine unless we're assured of ample time for drinking and collecting the cups. It only makes sense. Passengers think it's good news when actually it's bad. Meanwhile, there's a hundred and forty Caesar salads sitting back there that we can't refrigerate and we can't send back. I don't know what's going to happen with them. There's a kind of Big Brother mentality this whole company suffers from. If I could get an opportunity to hook on with another airline, I tell you I would be gone like a shot. Just give me a chance, just talk to me and see what I can do."

"How are the pilots?" said Paul.

"They're a mixed bag."

Paul walked stealthily down the empty ramp, where an overhead sign said THE EMPLOYEES OF AILLEURS WOULD LIKE TO THANK YOU FOR CHOOSING THIS AIRLINE AND NOT SOME OTHER AIRLINE. WE KNOW THERE'S COMPETITION OUT THERE — WE WEREN'T BORN YESTERDAY. So as a lone person moving against the tide of airport humanity, he received the usual quick and yearning glances. Airports are so bound up with the idea of reunion that people visiting them — even people who have come only to retrieve a package — automatically scan faces for friends and relatives long lost. Paul passed the checkpoint of the metal detectors, where guards who were trained to find guns, knives, and explosives were once again barely concealing their boredom at finding only belt buckles and key rings and Saint Christopher medals.

Paul came to a store in a concourse with the magazine Mary wanted. An actress on the cover held masks of tragedy and comedy over her breasts. So many magazine covers tried to catch the eye with breasts. Even needlecraft magazines showed seamstresses with open shirts. Paul paid for the magazine. He admired the dark green austerity of U.S. dollars. Then he went across the concourse to a lounge, where he stood and ordered a gin martini. Just in front of him was a woman sitting at the bar in a red dress with veined white leaves on it. Cars raced around an oval track on a television set.

"Who's winning?" said Paul.

"Rusty Wallace," said the bartender.

The woman in the red and white dress turned around. "Excuse me," she said. Her eyes were red too.

"Don't listen," said the bartender.

"You keep out of this," said the woman. "Sir, I wonder if you might help me. I'm from Switzerland, and it seems I have missed my flight. It all began last night, when my friends and I quarreled. I hope you never quarrel with your friends, for there is nothing quite so upsetting. I was staying at their townhouse near the Public Garden when they confronted me over the sink. I was trying to wash my things on my last night in America when suddenly they are tired of me. 'Get out,' they said. 'Get out of our townhouse.' So I packed my suitcase and dragged it down to the street. Some of my belongings were wet from the faucet."

She stepped down from her barstool, lifted a red vinyl suitcase onto the seat, and snapped open the lid. "Touch my belongings and see if they're not damp."

Paul pressed a soft tangle of pale clothes — straps and borders and buttons. "O.K., they're damp."

"I raised my hand to engage what I believed to be an authorized taxicab driver," she said. "But I was mistaken. 'Take me to the airport,' I said. Because I had decided I would simply stay the night in one of the small chairs. You see, I'm really resourceful and do not require special treatment as some would have it. I can easily sleep in a chair and wake up ready to go. To my surprise, the driver said the charge would be ninety dollars. I knew this was unusually high but consented anyway, a big mistake, for the driver drove directly to a dark street, parked by an empty building with the windows all broken apart and lying in glass particles on the sidewalk, and he said, 'Everybody out.' And I said, 'What do you mean?' and he said, 'This is the airport.' And I said, 'I may be from Switzerland, but this is no airport — why, there are no windows.' And he said, 'It's the back entrance, closest to the Swiss planes.' He said, 'You can get out on your own steam or I will throw you on the ground, it's up to you, this is America.' And he was a large man, capable of managing his promises. And when I got out of the cab and opened my handbag to pay, he wrestled it from me and drove away. You see, it was nothing more than a sophisticated form of robbery. Well, sophisticated is not the word I mean."

"Convoluted," said Paul.

"Yes! Convoluted, I like that," said the woman. "You do understand."

"So anyway, there you were," said Paul.

"Well, I was fortunate enough to locate some police, but when I explained my situation they took me to a homeless shelter. The beds were so close together with the other homeless that I was afraid to shut my eyes or move. People screamed and cried all night long, it was a living nightmare, and in the morning I hitchhiked to the airport. You don't understand how laughable this is. Back at home, why, everyone knows me. Not in all of Switzerland, of course, I'm not making that claim, but certainly in my canton. I once ran for public office and am the president of a whist club called . . . perhaps the nearest transla-tion would be the Jolly Jokers. But right now I haven't eaten anything in many hours."

The bartender pushed a phone down the bar. "Why don't you call up these friends I keep hearing about?"

"I tried to call them," she said. "Believe me I did. But they have an answering machine. As they told me themselves, 'We love our answering machine, for it saves us from ever picking up the phone. Every now and then we listen to the messages, out of curiosity, I suppose, but for the most part it's like having no phone at all.'"

The bartender wiped his hands on a towel. "What's their number? I'll give them a buzz."

"You keep out of this."

"We don't give free pizza," said the bartender. "Pizza is six dollars a slice. That's the way we work it. There's a system we adhere to. If I give you one free, they'll all want one free. Did you ever think of that?"

Paul gave the woman twenty dollars.

"She's no more Swiss than this towel," said the bartender.

"It's nothing to you," said Paul.

"I'll have a slice of mushroom pizza," said the woman, "and a bottle of Samuel Adams."

Paul returned to the airplane, where the haze of thwarted travel hung heavily in the air. People slept, paced the aisles, twisted air jets in their aluminum sockets.

"I'm going to get off the plane now," said Paul.

"Where have you been if not off?" said Mary.

He handed her the magazine. "What I mean is I'm not going back to Vertige."

"I guess I'm supposed to fly now," said Mary. "I have my magazine and I will fly."

"Sell the hotel, Mary."

She opened the magazine. "There's no equity in the hotel."

"There should be some."

She closed the magazine again and looked out the window of the airplane. "Once I was going to be a doctor," she said. "Why did I not go ahead with that?"

Paul took the subway to South Station, where he bought a ticket on a southbound train. He found an empty car, but before long it had filled up with college students. American youth was supposed to be morose and fussy these days, but these kids talked about their summer in Madagascar and sang folksongs.

The lumberman goes on, till his money's spent and gone.
Goodbye, little Annie, I'm off for Cheyenne.

The train broke down along the shore and sat all night on the tracks. Moonlight slid down a trough of ocean toward houses leaning on stilts. The students played Hearts and drank themselves into hilarity and then quiet sadness. Paul got to sleep but he did not sleep well. When he opened his eyes or wrenched his legs around on the seat, his forehead beaded hot or cold. He dreamed that he had left the train for a walk in the sand. Someone called him back to the tracks but a light flared orange and white down the curve of the beach. On inspection the light turned out to be that of a soda machine, and Paul put a coin in the slot — this was all in the dream — and as he did so, a jet skidded across the sky and snuffed out in the water, sending hot waves of air, plastic, and skin blowing across the surface.

When he awoke a student leaned over the seat in front of him. Three silver brads perforated the shell of her left ear, and stubby pigtails rose from the top of her head. "You've been talking in your sleep," she said.

9

Paul called his parents' house from a pay phone outside the locked station in Verona, Rhode Island. His father came to pick him up in a red Cadillac with polished chrome.

"Why have you come back?" said Maurice. He drove with great satisfaction. One hand cradled the wheel and the other rested on his knee. He wore aviator sunglasses. The ride was soft and springy, and when they got to the railroad tracks it felt as if the Cadillac were being lifted by an uncoordinated team. "Did you forget something?"

"I need my car."

Maurice tapped the turn-signal lever with the edge of his hand. "It'll never run, though it's in the barn."

"I drove it in there."

"But how many years ago, Paul? Think of the years. Things happen to an internal combustion engine sitting idle."

"I don't expect to jump in and drive away. I know it will take work. Mary's going home and I'm staying here. I'm not asking for miracles."

"Is this for good?"

"I don't know. I don't know how long it's for."

"On the other hand, somebody could shoot out of a building and hit you on the head."

Paul shrugged. "That's all over."

"If they say it is."

"Yeah, they decide, but I think they have decided."

"You were never a fighter. Remember when all the other kids would fight at noon? Remember when they would throw sticks at each other? And I would say, 'Go and mix it up.'"

"I was afraid," said Paul. "Well, I wasn't afraid of losing, but I was afraid of being seen to lose."

"And now when you have something to be afraid of —"

"Right, and it makes no sense, but nonetheless."

They drove past the Shell station where Paul and his siblings used to hang around after closing. They would wire the lever down on the air hose and jam the nozzle into the bucket of window-washing fluid, causing the fluid to bubble into strange shapes and evaporate.

"You made marriage vows," said Maurice. "You were married by a bailiff or something, but still there must have been vows."

"A justice of the peace."

"And just like that you give up on them."

"It's been in the works."

"There are things I don't know and don't want to know," said Maurice. "But people do change when they fail in something. Maybe they end up reminding each other of whatever they might have done differently. So that when you look at the person, instead of seeing who she is, you're seeing the thing in the past that failed."

"Maybe that's it."

"Just don't tell your mother what's going on. She doesn't need to know about the gritty details."

Maurice nosed the Cadillac under a willow tree and they walked toward the house through the hanging leaves. It was one of those unplumbed New England farmhouses that appear to have fallen into place from a height of three feet or so.

Paul and Maurice went into the kitchen, where rotary-saw blades painted with landscapes hung above the sink. On the counter by the waffle iron stood an old metal clock under the face of which a boy and girl rocked on swings. Paul's parents had each devised new interests over the past several years — Diana worked for the Animal Rescue League and Maurice invented board games — and there were animal cages and sketch pads scattered about the kitchen.

Diana looked through a magnifying glass into a mirror above a sideboard.

"I think this contact lens must be on the back side of the eye," she said. "I just got off the phone with Carmen. She's all excited because her theater group is doing a musical based on Frank Lloyd Wright. It's called *Wax*, and it's about the building of the Johnson's Wax building in Racine. I can't imagine such a thing, I don't see how you'd stage it or what the lyrics would be, but she's very excited and she asked after you."

Carmen was Paul's older sister.

"They split up," said Maurice. "Paul and Mary have split up and he intends to live in the States."

"Promise me something," Diana said to Paul. "I want you to take that cat Scratch with you. She's become a real problem case. The idea is keeping the animals alive, but all she wants to do is kill."

"She always hunted," said Paul.

"Oh, that cat is a bad son of a bitch at night," said Maurice. "One time it killed a mole I swear to God the size of a football."

"A cat did this?" said Paul.

"She's worse than a cat."

93

"Take your sunglasses off," Diana told Maurice. "You're in the house now." To Paul, Diana said, "She sleeps during the day. Burrows into the insulation of the house, where you couldn't get her out with a shovel."

"They're basically nocturnal creatures," said Maurice.

Paul took a red metal toolbox out to the barn. Light streamed through gaps in the siding, and the fenders of the car shone dull green beneath a sheen of dust. The hubcaps were long gone, the tires flat. The faded no-handguns sticker that had added an off note to Leonard Dalton's funeral still anchored the corner of the windshield. The door hinge shrieked. He turned the key, but the only sound was a scratching in the fabric of the roof.

Paul got out of the car and lifted the hood, revealing a tangle of straw and spider webs and sunflower seeds. He found an old broom and swept the engine block. Then he pulled the battery, set it on the earthen floor, wrenched the spark plugs, and spun the wing nut from the air cleaner.

Mice poured over the sides of the air cleaner when he lifted the cover. The honeycombed paper had been chewed to lace and powder.

"Nature abhors a filter," Paul said.

Maurice opened the big sliding door at the end of the alley-way, letting light in. He pulled a metal cart with oxyacetylene tanks strapped on.

"The car is full of mice," said Paul.

"Well, I'm not surprised." Maurice fired up the torch and burned the gum off the spark plugs. He wore safety glasses and held the plugs in long-handled pliers before the knifelike flame.

"You used to light our sparklers with that," said Paul.

"I did a lot of things," said Maurice. He laid the spark plugs in a row on the fender and then opened a can of engine oil and poured some into the holes where the plugs had been. His hands trembled. He had hurt his back working for the railroad and now his hands shook when he lifted them.

"What's that for?" said Paul.

"Lube the rings."

"That's good, and I wouldn't have thought of it."

"Oh hell, Paul, this is basic," said Maurice. "There's nothing fancy in what we're doing now."

After supper Paul walked out to the grove beside the barn where he and his brothers and sisters used to play. Pale summer light shone on the ragged branches of the evergreens, and the needled ground gave just that much beneath his feet. A circle of rocks marked their old fire ring, but moss covered the rocks and some of them had been turned out of their places. He imagined the faces of his brothers and sisters in firelight and shadow. He pictured the rising orange sparks that he had once pretended were spaceships leaving a burning planet. Verona as he remembered it had been a fair place to grow up, although he had sometimes felt extraneous — not extraneous to the family or the town, but to the universe generally. He had especially felt this way on humid, unmoving afternoons when locusts hummed like power lines in the grass and the sky could not be looked at because it was too hot and too densely blue. Then he and some of his brothers and sisters would ride their bikes over by the Great Swamp, where the wicked soldiers had massacred the neutral Narragansetts.

Oldest to youngest, the Nash kids had been Fred, Carmen, Paul, Lily, Aaron, and Fletcher. Aaron died the winter he was about to turn eleven. His sickness had crept up on the family, and afterward the doctors said nothing could have been done. But doctors always say that, what else would doctors say? Once Paul had tackled Aaron viciously when they were playing football in the yard. The tackle had been uncalled for, and Paul knew it. He had even ordered Fletcher to hold Aaron up, keep him from falling, until he, Paul, could get over there and lay that savage hit on him. Could a doctor say with certainty that the sickness had not begun from a small point of damage such as might have been inflicted in a gutless tackle, especially when so much is not known?

Aaron had been thin and fair and given to fevers all his life, but he had always been competitive. When bruises had appeared on his legs, he theorized that he had banged his shins on the metal rails of his bed while jumping in. Really, the blood was springing up inside him wherever it could. On the day Aaron died, Paul and Lily had come home from school to an empty and unlighted house and found a yellow bucket in the bathtub with blood in it. He remembered the blood as filling the bucket, but that seemed unlikely. Slick and dark and deep and still, a lake of blood, a bucket of blood. Wasn't that a pirate phrase: Yo-ho-ho and a bucket of blood? No. That was a bottle of rum. Paul wished that he had a bottle of rum right now. The bucket had seemed to mock them, had seemed to say, This is all humans are, transient blood, whereas yellow plastic will last for centuries. Later they would find out that Diana had stayed with Aaron all that day, first at the house and then at the hospital, where he was dead by the middle of the evening. Paul imagined his mother kneeling with Aaron as the life flowed out of him and into a bucket. What kind of thing would that be for a mother? What would it do to her? He imagined her gliding through the house, her feet barely touching the floor, running to call the doctor, running back to Aaron, running like mad, convincing herself by the comfort of vigorous action that this illness would break as all the others had, would break and fade into the march of family memory. *Remember when Aaron was so sick? My God but he was sick. He himself doesn't remember it. You were so sick, Aaron, it's just as well you don't remember it.* He imagined Aaron's last thought. It still amazed Paul that every brain would have one thought at the end, followed by nothing but some distant humming sound. He expected that Aaron's thought might have had to do with the outdoors. He had been the only one of the kids who liked being outside more than he liked watching television. Even in the bad winters he would hike around the grove in a white stocking cap and blue plaid coat. He would cover bottles with argyle socks, call them birds, and plant them among the trees where he would pretend to hunt them. His hands were always cold. He would press them to the other kids' faces to demonstrate.

After the funeral, people had told Aaron's siblings that God's ways were a mystery, as if God had woken up one day and decided that it would be a good thing to make Aaron throw up blood until he died — in which case, Paul thought, "mystery" would not tell the story. Eventually, and this took years, Paul came to believe that God did not give the word on individual cases, did not say, "Kill Aaron Nash, and have that gray horse I like win the Preakness." Long ago in Verona there was an old man who had made a habit of sitting on a chair in front of the grocery store and memorizing the license plates of everyone in town who drove past. This was more like what God did, Paul thought: maintained a numerical system that accounted for everyone, seemed arbitrary, and could not have been devised by anyone else. God was not love, God was math, but math that gave the appearance of love because it added up.

If I could walk outside — this might have been Aaron's last thought — *if I could walk outside I would rough up my hands on the bark of trees and in this way get back to myself . . .*

The sun had gone down, and the day's heat was sinking into the ground. Paul took from his shirt pocket the flight itinerary. Mary would be over the ocean now, reading for the third or fourth time about Meg Ryan. He tore the paper into strips and burned them in the center of the fire ring.

Paul and Maurice got the Plymouth running and the next morning took it into Verona.

"How does it feel?" said Maurice.

"It feels all right," said Paul.

"Is there play in the wheel?"

"You know, there is, but there always was."

They motored by the house of Lars Lamb, Paul's old friend, and found him sitting in a webbed lawn chair and holding a portable phone in the shade of a huge black pickup.

"Pull over there and see Lars," said Maurice.

Lars got up and walked to the car. His shoulders rolled like those of the wrestler he used to be, although he had gained weight. "Here's a car that brings back memory."

"Tell you what I remember," said Maurice. "Springing two kids out of the state police barracks for possession of beer as a minor."

"That's right," said Lars. "The trooper called us illiterate woodcutters."

"There was no need for such remarks," said Maurice.

"Twenty years," said Paul.

"A good twenty," said Maurice. "The state cops have always disliked Verona."

Paul got out of the car and went around to shake Lars's hand. "What are you doing?" said Paul.

"Life insurance," said Lars. "There's more to it, but that would be the short answer."

"What else is there to it?" said Maurice.

"We consider insurance not as an end in itself but as one tool among many."

"Write out a policy for Paul."

"I could use the business," said Lars.

The running board of the black truck stood shoulder high, and a row of yellow lights crowned the cab. The fat and ridged tires seemed like something from a cartoon.

"She's on the market," said Lars.

"What's your asking price?" said Maurice. He sat in the car with his arms hanging youthfully over the side.

"Fourteen-five or best offer," said Lars. "That doesn't even recoup my investment, but at this point just take the thing off my property."

"How do you get in?" said Paul.

"Jump," said Lars. "Use a stepladder. Pull it up to the front porch and just walk in. Any number of ways. Millie and I bought it together. We both decided."

"Lars married Millie," said Maurice.

"We both knew about the payments. We weren't children. We went into this thing with our eyes open." He swung his arms so that his fists tapped together. "We're divorced now."

"Sorry to hear it," said Paul.

"That's all right," said Lars. "I remember when we first got the truck, why, the next morning I woke up and ran to the window just to see it in the driveway. We would put the baby on the seat between us."

"Not a baby anymore," said Maurice.

"He's in the armed forces," said Lars. "He began in the army and switched over to the air force."

"How's he like it?" said Paul.

"He doesn't tell me anything," said Lars. "You know, there was a time when monster trucks were so popular that if one came out in the *Shopper* it would be gone overnight. Now it's a buyer's market. You see them all over, big old trucks, nobody wants them. Would you believe I've had people tell me they like it but it's too tall?"

"It does ride high," said Paul.

"But that's my point," said Lars. "It's a monster truck."

Two of Diana's animal-rescue colleagues came to the farm that afternoon with an injured owl. Their names were Mercy and Kevin.

The owl was in a small cage, which Mercy held at arm's length. It was a little saw-whet owl with brown and white feathers, a fan-shaped head, and gold-ringed eyes that conveyed dignity and alarm.

"We call him Milk Toast, because that's what he likes," said Kevin. "He's friendly and inquisitive."

"Saw-whets tend to be," said Mercy. "That's what gets them into trouble."

"What happened?" said Paul.

"He got hit by a car," said Diana.

"Luckily the driver had the presence of mind to stop," said Mercy. "He was a pediatrician, and he picked the owl up from the breakdown lane and put him in the glove compartment of his car."

"Crammed in there with the pens and cigarettes," said Kevin. "I was on duty that day."

They were all quiet for a moment, picturing the owl in the glove compartment.

"Really, though, it probably wasn't a bad idea," said Diana. "Nice and dark and quiet."

"He did the right thing for the wrong reasons," said Mercy.

That night Paul drove the Fury out of the barn into darkness and down the winding driveway to the road. The air was cool and carried the humid smell of cut hay. He crossed the new bridge while looking at the steel ghost of the old bridge. He wondered if the plan was for the old bridge to fall of its own accord into the new bridge, resulting in big construction contracts all around. In Newport he took Thames Street to the Clam Barn, a warehouse of a restaurant where lobster traps hung from the rafters and garage doors had been thrown open to the harbor. Paul went up to the counter and ordered clam cakes and a plastic cup of Double Diamond, and the waitress gave him a little wooden stand with a number on it.

"Are you over twenty-one?" she asked.

"I'm over thirty-one," said Paul.

"I have to ask."

"It won't be long before I'm forty-one."

"It's pro forma."

He walked to his seat thinking that he could become a janitor in a small town near the Canadian border. Maybe he could read the classics and learn the piano. A man with a simple broom could be a king living near the Canadian border. What do we need money for? Food, clothing, shelter. What else? A movie on the weekend. *The Joy Luck Club* would be in for a long run. The waitress brought his food and he began to eat. And yet months would go by when he could not pick up any book. Once he had tried and failed to read *Bleak House,* and it was not long before the police came smashing on the door. Harbor lights drifted in black water. Two men sitting at the next table talked anxiously. Paul gathered that they had been sailing and wracked up a borrowed boat.

"Wait, wait, wait," said one of the men, who had a white sweater tied around his neck. "It's true that the hull is leaking, but I'm not sure that it is a hole. It might be some sort of rupture. I would just think very carefully before calling and saying, 'Duane, it's a hole, there's a hole —'"

"A what? A rupture?" said his companion, a heavy man holding a fork in his fist. "Of course it's a hole. Water's coming in. That's all the proof I need. We have to tell him. I have his number on Prince Edward Island."

"Listen to me and see if this doesn't make sense," said the man with the sweater. "At one end of the spectrum you have emergencies. You have disasters. The best example would be the boat sinks. That case, no question, you call him up. But on the other end you have minor things. A bit of chrome breaks off. You wouldn't call him on P.E.I. to say a bit of chrome had broken off. It would certainly seem strange if you did. So our job is to figure out where on the spectrum our running aground, or whatever we ran into, lies."

"I wish I'd never seen that boat," said the heavy man. "He's going to hate us for the rest of his days. I never should have gone below to make sandwiches."

"A seam. That's what I was trying to say. Maybe a seam has come unglued."

Paul returned to the house, where his father was sitting at the kitchen table, drinking orange juice and staring at a wire cage in which the injured saw-whet stood preening on a perch.

"Your mother asked me to watch the owl," he said.

"What does he do?"

Maurice poured a glass of orange juice and set it before Paul.

"Not a hell of a lot." He nodded at the cage. "He does *that* with some frequency. I've been trying to draw him out in conversation. I asked him what flying was like."

"And?"

"He didn't want to talk about it."

"You can't blame him."

"Listen, I've been thinking. You shouldn't stay here, Paul. It's not good for you, it's not good for us. It's not that I'm scared so much as . . . well, yes, it is. It is that I'm scared."

"I'll leave tomorrow."

"Do you need money?"

"No."

Maurice put the orange juice back in the refrigerator. "That's good, because I don't have any." From the top of the refrigerator he brought down a backgammon board set up with chess pieces.

"I call this chessgammon," he said.

The owl sighed deeply, and a feather floated out of the cage. Paul caught the owl feather in his hand. "Why don't you knock off early?" he asked the owl.

He went upstairs to his old room. The hallway was lined with built-in cabinets, and he recalled hiding in one of them with his sister Carmen. He remembered hot black air and the corrosive smell of mothballs. Her breath whispered in his ear and toy handcuffs dug into their wrists. Maybe he would go to Racine and surprise her on opening night of this wax play. It was hard to believe that any two people could have been that small.

He opened the cabinet door as if expecting to find Carmen and himself. Instead, there were towels and candlesticks and a book called *The Beginner's Handbook of Amateur Radio*.

Paul undressed and got into his childhood bed, which stood wooden and cinnamon-colored in a corner of the room. Anything could happen from now on. He had been in over his head, but the meaning of lost things was that they could be regained. For what was America but a place where those who had crossed the laws and customs of a given community could go some-where else and blend in? He had been called amoral by the lawyers of gangsters and had been glad that they said "amoral" rather than "immoral." To be amoral was not to be evil but merely to march to a different drum. When he and Mary had set out their garbage in Providence, Scratch the cat would cock her head warily on seeing the garbage bags — "What are these?" she seemed to be saying with that look. "I don't recall such things before" — and Paul thought the amoral person re-sponded to the concept of goodness the same way Scratch did to garbage bags, as something foreign but worthy of considera-tion. Even the judge had called him a selfish witness. Her stern remark was supposed to offset or justify her approval of the plea agreement, yet it was true that he had always felt chosen without any particular evidence. But he imagined that everyone felt chosen, and why wouldn't they? Nature is full of chaos that appears to be ordination.

He turned on a gooseneck lamp and leafed through the radio book. Quizzes followed chapters:

38. What may happen to body tissues that are exposed to large amounts of rf energy?
   A. The tissue may be damaged because of the heat pro-duced
   B. The tissue may suddenly be frozen
   C. The tissue may be immediately destroyed because of the Maxwell effect
   D. The tissue may become less resistant to cosmic radiation.

Some time later he woke thinking he had heard voices. In his heart there still existed that old nighttime anticipation. But it was only his mother cursing the cat. Paul pulled on jeans and a shirt and went downstairs. The cat had wrestled a rabbit into the mud room. Beside a Kiwi shoeshine kit the rabbit had turned into a statue. Its ears quivered and its black eyes shone. Meanwhile, the cat hugged the floor in a killing trance.

"Is this one of yours?" said Paul.

"Not yet, anyhow," said Diana.

Paul nudged the cat aside with his foot, took the rabbit by the neck, and carried it outside. Detecting motion, the porch lamp flooded the yard with stark light. Paul released the rabbit and watched it hop tentatively down the walk.

"Run away," he said.

Diana came outside carrying the cat and two cans of beer. She let the cat go. The light went out after a while and they sat in the dark on the back steps drinking the beers.

"I was so proud when you were a special witness," said Diana. "Isn't that strange?"

"I'd say it was wicked strange."

"I honestly believe I was prouder of you than I was of Fred when he was named Realtor of the Year."

"Don't tell Fred that."

"I can't account for it," said Diana. "I find that the older I get, the less I can account for."

The next afternoon Paul said goodbye to his mother and father, took the cat and a woven rug for it to ride on, and drove west. There was no good way to cut across Rhode Island and Connecticut. There were quiet, empty towns and churches with onion domes but no divided highways. It was hot and the sunlight shone sharp as a spike. A skunk had been hit near a Bible camp, and picking up the scent, Scratch sat up and opened her mouth, revealing the bone needles of her teeth.

"Don't do that," said Paul. "Close your mouth."

10

The revived Fury floated into Ashland, Connecticut, where a faded orange billboard called the town the Former Match Capital of the World. Padded black and yellow bumpers guarded the loading docks of flesh-colored corrugated warehouses. A bright and empty Chinese restaurant stood among dim stores that would never sell many of their inspirational books, their golden-oak chairs, their tiny prisms hung by threads.

Then came a series of identical brick buildings on a hill with zigzag rooflines and a row of windows glowing with green light. This was Ashland Fastener and Binder, the factory of Loom's family, the Hanovers.

Nearer the center of town he passed a row of big houses with steep blue lawns and multipaned windows reflecting the leaves of trees. On the porch of one of the houses a woman stood dressed in white, gripping a croquet mallet with the head tucked under her chin. In the fading light of afternoon the mysterious woman seemed to represent to Paul the possibility that things could begin to happen in a new town.

He drove along a dark lake bordered by a park, where a bronze statue of an ancient Greek stood with his back to the water, arms out, palms up, as if to say, "I can't find the lake."

Light towers rose over a rust-red stadium called Paraffin Park. Paul eased his car into the lot and walked into the stadium. He found a baseball game in progress between the Ashland Matches and the Tigers of Roscoe, Ontario. He bought a paper cup full of beer and a pretzel with large salt granules on it and took a seat on the third-base line.

A home run could land in the lake — that was part of the fun. The Tigers stole bases recklessly, without regard to the likelihood of being thrown out. Their third baseman was a massive lefty named Billy Trautbeck, who during the course of the game banged two line drives to right, both hauled in, and threw himself on grounders with abandon.

There were hundreds of fans on weathered green benches. Paul had not been to a baseball game in ten years, but he had no trouble placing the voices of the crowd: the man who had played a little ball himself once upon a time; the woman who kept a scorecard and constantly asked her neighbors, "What happened — did he strike out — what just happened?"; the retiree who knew all the rules and shouted lots of rule-based advice.

Then Paul heard another voice, one he could not place, a boy's voice that wove the usual encouragements with the names of players into an eerie and songlike lament that reminded him of the prayer call of the muezzin, which he and Mary had heard once on a television special about the Saudi Arabian city of Medina.

A foul ball arced into the stands; Paul retrieved it from under a bench. In a moment, a girl in a Matches uniform climbed the bleachers and took it back.

During the seventh-inning stretch Paul found the boy with the unusual cheer. He sat in a wheelchair at the end of an aisle, attended by a woman with a headband and a flower-print dress. The boy leaned forward, blond hair jutting from his forehead, wrists resting on the red railing. He had a direct and canted gaze like that of the young Orson Welles and wore a baseball glove on his left hand. Now a dozen children stepped onto the field to take part in a promotion sponsored by a car dealership. The crippled boy watched as the kids ran across the outfield grass.

What had been a close game dissolved in errors and pitching changes in the eighth inning, and Paul left the stands to walk through Paraffin Park, where three boys slouched at the base of the Greek statue. "Tourists, tourists, they suck. Bring your daughters so we can fuck," one of the boys chanted. He wore a Yale sweatshirt over camouflage pants with such vivid markings that it was hard to imagine the foliage among which they would blend in.

"You've got your pronouns mixed up," Paul said. "You refer to tourists as 'they,' right, so you can't be addressing them directly. But then you get to the 'Bring your daughters' part, and it all breaks down. We don't know whose daughters you're talking about."

"Of the tourists."

"Yeah, but that's not clear."

"The stranger's right," said a second boy, who sat cross-legged on the grass with metallic bands encircling his upper arms. "It doesn't make sense."

"How about this?" said the first boy. "Tourists, tourists, et cetera. If they bring their daughters, then we can fuck."

"Better," said Paul, "but it lacks impact. '*If* they bring their daughters' — see what I mean? You're just sort of musing about the pros and cons of tourists. Like, if they bring a net, you can play volleyball."

"Tourists, tourists . . . Now I forgot what I was going to say."

"Work on it," said Paul. "I'm looking for a guy named Loom Hanover."

"Hanovers are murderers," said the boy on the grass.

"How's that?" said Paul.

"Match mouth," said the boy.

"Match mouth?"

"Ask him."

"Where does he live?" said Paul.

"You can see it from here." The boy stood, moved around the statue, and pointed across the water. "Well, not the house. You can see the dock anyway. They live across String Lake, up in the trees. What you want to do is drive into town and around the lake. Look for the invisible-fence sign. They don't want anything to do with the rest of us."

"How do you know him?" said the boy who had made the tourist rhyme.

"We went to college together," said Paul. "Once Loom and I went out to kick a football in a lightning storm in Canada."

"We don't care about that," said the one with iron vines growing on his biceps.

String Lake twisted narrowly into the center of Ashland, and the road followed the shore only at intervals, so that what had sounded like a short drive took a long time. The town gave the impression of being a stage set for a play that had closed nineteen years before. Old mannequins wore sequined gowns in the brightly lit window of an otherwise dark store.

Loom lived in the country. A paved driveway climbed from the road to a large and many-gabled house covered with silver shakes. Round pillars rose from a stone porch, rafters jutted from the edges of the roof, and thick supporting beams crossed beneath the peak of the gables. There were three stories, counting the cupola, with an arbored courtyard beside.

Paul parked and let the cat out. He knocked on the front door but no one answered, so he walked around the house and down the grass to the lake. A wooden rowboat floated beneath a dock light. He untied the boat, rowed out in the lake, and let the boat drift. He found fishing tackle beneath the seats and cast a treble-hooked spoon with an old Johnson reel the color of shiny green flies. He was not much of a fisherman but he did like casting, letting the lure's weight do its work.

The lights of Ashland ringed the northern end of String Lake, and the southern end receded in darkness. After a while the rod bent and line raced out and Paul messed with the drag and the line broke. He rigged the line again, caught a fish and let it go, then worked his way slowly back to Loom's dock. A dark and overgrown cottage stood north of the Hanovers' house, but because of the treeline Loom and Alice would never have to look at it.

The night manager of the Coltsfoot Motel was an old man in a maroon sweatshirt. It encouraged Paul for no good reason when old people wore sweatshirts. He imagined them rising before dawn and lifting carefully folded sweatshirts from modest dressers.

Another customer came in, carrying a videotape and dressed in a red western shirt with white piping and black shoulders. Paul wondered what the man could be planning, short of an actual rodeo appearance, that would call for such a shirt.

"The TV doesn't work in room sixteen," said the customer.

"What's it doing?" said the night manager.

"It isn't doing anything, it's broken," said the man in the cowboy shirt. "I've rented a video. It's supposed to be an erotic thriller."

"Try room twenty-seven," said the night manager. To Paul, he said, "Are you here for the Lager Festival?"

"I'm looking for work," said Paul.

"I just came from the drinking contest," said the man in the red shirt.

"How did that go?" said the night manager.

"Fun." The man went out with a different key.

"The Lager Festival evolved from Old Bobbin Days," said the night manager, "which evolved in turn from Old Match Days."

"Do you know what match mouth is?" said Paul.

"Certainly," said the night manager. He straightened. "The workers in the factory were breathing straight phosphorus. Quite right. My grandfather died of match mouth."

"Sounds awful."

"I don't really remember him. They say he was quick with a joke."

The night manager raised a hinged slab of counter and led Paul down a hallway lit with sconces. He pointed to old photographs on the wall.

"That's the train station," he said. "That's when they used to race across the lake on skates. That's my father and me; I'm on the sled. That's the opera house after the flood." They came finally to a small silver and white console. The night manager opened the lid. "This is the ice," he said.

"Listen, I have a cat," said Paul.

"I have no way of knowing that."

Paul's room was on the second floor of the motel. He turned on the television, got into bed, and fell asleep. When he woke up, an old movie was playing. Two men in naval uniforms stood on either side of a table with a terrier on it. Paul wondered why black-and-white movies always seemed louder than color movies. Then he heard a key turning in the lock. The cat jumped from the top of the television and ran into the bathroom. The door opened and a woman flopped into a chair. "He's asleep. He's finally asleep, Billy."

"You have the wrong room," said Paul.

"Billy?"

Paul turned on a lamp beside the bed.

The woman seemed fascinated. "My mistake."

"What does 'pedigree' mean, anyway?" said one of the men on the TV. "Does it stem from the root word 'pet'?"

"Can I turn this down?" said the woman.

"By all means."

"I'm looking for Billy Trautbeck. Are you on the team? You're the second baseman."

"No, but I was at the game tonight."

"Well, I'm at the game every night," said the woman. She closed her eyes and folded her hands between her knees. "I'm from Ontario, and I really want to go home. But Billy keeps saying 'One more game.' It's all because of my son. My name is Barbara and my son's name is Keith. He can't walk, but he loves baseball."

"I think I saw you. Do you have a wheelchair?"

"Keith does." Barbara sighed. "It all started when he met Billy Trautbeck at a souvenir show at the shopping center in Roscoe. This was ten days ago. I don't know what was said exactly, but evidently Billy promised to hit a home run for Keith at the game that night. But it didn't happen. In fact, he didn't hit anything out of the infield. He chose just that moment to go into a slump. In the last couple days he's started to make contact again, but it's killing him to have let Keith down. I keep telling him it doesn't matter, but he insists that we follow him on the road until he hits one out. We've been to Kankakee and Lafayette and now here."

"Maybe you could just read the sports page."

"I think I could have called it off, early on," said Barbara. "But now he's too deep in the slump. I'm wasting my vacation time and my sick time, it's almost gone, all of it, and for what? Although today he hit some that seemed sure to go out. I grabbed Keith and said, 'Watch, honey, we're going home.'"

"But they stayed in."

"Yes."

A loud sound came from outside the room. Paul dressed quickly and he and Barbara stepped out onto the motel terrace. Down in the parking lot a man sat in the open door of a car lighting firecrackers and flipping them on the pavement, where they went off around his feet.

"This place is like a cheap circus," said Barbara.

"What do you know about dreams?" said Paul.

"I have them."

"I get off a train and go for a walk on the beach," said Paul. "There is a soda machine, but when I put money in it a plane passes overhead and crashes in the sea."

"Anxiety dream," she said. "Classic anxiety dream."

Barbara went to check on her son — they had a room nearby — and then returned to Paul's room to watch TV. Turning the channels, they found *Close Encounters of the Third Kind*.

"That's François Truffaut," said Paul. "The great French director."

"What's he doing in there?" said Barbara.

"I've never been able to figure that out."

"Oh look, a cat. I love cats," said Barbara. "They smell so clean. Come here, cat."

"She's called Scratch."

"Come here, you big old Scratch. Let me smell how clean you smell."

The next morning Paul woke up early and looked through a drawer in the bedside table for something to read. He found a Band-Aid, an ammonia capsule wrapped in clear plastic, and a pamphlet entitled "My Ashland" by someone named Alma Warfield. He shaved, cutting himself in many places, and sat on the bed holding a towel to his neck and reading:

Ashland is a New England city below Red Mountain and above String Lake. As a rule, the weather is harsher in Ashland than in surrounding towns. Winter rain in Tableville means heavy snow here, and when the wind blows briskly in Damascus, branches or whole trees can be expected to fall on Ashland. The elevation is eleven hundred feet above sea level and the architecture is Grecian, but the pediments are cracked and the Ionic columns wrapped in vines.

A clever man named Daniel Hanover must be given the credit for Ashland's appearance. He has been dead for one hundred and fifty years, but in 1828, acting on a hunch, he had the center of Ashland torn down and rebuilt to resemble the ancient Ionian city of Miletus. Thus the band shell is in a park on the shore of String Lake and the shopping district, or "Agora," is up the hill past the Temple of Hephaestus. A bronze statue of the Milesian philosopher Thales stands in the park. Thales believed that water was the mother of elements and that magnets had souls. Daniel Hanover spent his last years trying to change the town name to New Miletus, but this met with no success locally, and when he turned to state officials in Hartford and New Haven without the backing of his own city, he became the object of derision.

Still, the Hanovers have always held much of the influence in Ashland. Historically speaking, they were of that class which might be called Painting Industrialists. In a different time than our own swift era, the whole family would sail overseas in early summer and return before the first snowfall with their minds full of images. They executed Etruscan landscapes and Moroccan street scenes, not from love of land or paint but as a way to share what they had seen with the company workers. Over time, however, the paintings became less tied to place. The abstract expressionist and chairman of the board Gilbert Hanover (1921–1992) was the last artist in the family and once sold a series of lithographs to the American Psychiatric Association for distribution to its affiliated offices at reasonable prices.

Like all American merchants of the first brigade, the Hanovers have made money with one eye on their given industry and another eye on industries that might do them better. They never remained faithful to a single product: kettles, glass, matches, sewing-machine parts, and fasteners have taken their turn in the parade of goods from the workshops of the Hanovers. (Contrary to logical assumption, Ashland's name has no connection with the match trade. Moses Ash was a seller of dry goods who died in 1721 after rolling down Turpentine Hill.) The match company, known as Hanover Strike-Anywhere, prospered mightily in the years following the Civil War, doubling the population of Ashland, which came to be known as "The Match City." But a problem developed around the turn of the century as workers began to sicken and die of necrosis of the jaw. The disease killed terribly, and Ashlanders began to wonder whether the capitalist impulse had led them down the garden path.

The Phosphorus Tax of 1910 nearly bankrupted the company, forcing the transition to bobbin production, which was conducted under the name of the Ashland Bobbin Works. By omitting their family name from this new venture, the Hanovers seemed to be expressing contrition as well as deflecting blame for the necrosis epidemic. The bobbin works lasted a generation before Gilbert Hanover scrapped it in favor of plastic industrial fasteners. Gilbert was a thoughtful and enigmatic figure who in the 1960s realized that the profound postwar expansion would soon have everyone too busy buying new textiles to worry about mending the old. Bankers from Boston to Poughkeepsie admired Gilbert Hanover's strategy and let him write his own check. Only the workers, with sentiment and superstition, mourned the demise of the bobbin works. This feeling faded, as feelings will, and today the workers are happily too young to remember anything. All they know is that every parachute harness in the world contains components made in Ashland, Connecticut, and that whenever world peace is threatened, AF&B stock rises.

Today Ashland has thirty-three thousand residents, seven houses of worship, nineteen taverns, four schools, three fire engines, and twenty-two gas stations, run mostly by hollow-eyed teenagers who could not change the oil in your car if their lives depended on it; they don't even know where to look for the oil cap. Crime keeps hidden. Drug dealers, burglars, and embezzlers walk among us, but not so many. If headlines in the *Ashland Sun* suggest that sports betting has taken off in the past several years, we may console ourselves with the certainty that this problem is not only Ashland's, as the nation has become so antagonistic and simple-minded that even the confirmation of Supreme Court justices is conducted as a corrupt weekend marathon . . .

11

Paul would need a driver's license and he would need a job. He walked down the hill into Ashland feeling as intrepid as Richard Dreyfuss heading off to the planet of the saintly aliens in the movie he had watched with Barbara. It was an August day without a cloud in the sky. He crossed a bridge over a river. At the courthouse across the street from the Salvation Army, Paul passed through a metal detector with a handwritten notice saying NO KNIVES IN COURT.

The driver's license bureau shared a hallway with the state's attorney's office, and to get to the former you had to stand in line with those bound for the latter. Voices came from behind him.

"What did they get you for?"

"Disturbing the peace. And you?"

"Assault third."

"Domestic?"

"As it happens."

"Is she here?"

"She had to work."

"That's a stroke of luck."

"Except I'm on probation for something last year."

"Doesn't matter."

"I'm only hoping they won't violate me."

"They don't for domestic."

"Really. I never heard that."

"No, it's a funny thing. They do not violate for domestic."

Paul opened an oak door and found a woman sitting at a desk wrapping orange yarn around a clothespin.

"Are you looking for a license?" she said. "This is a wishing doll I'm making for a benefit for the hospital. Do you have a valid license currently? If it isn't a renewal, there could be a problem."

Paul handed over his licenses. "I have one for Belgium and one for Washington."

"D.C. or state?"

"State."

"Let's take a look." She put the yarn figure down on the desk and studied the licenses, one in each hand. Then she raised them to either side of her lightly glossed forehead. She had a narrow face and broad shoulders. "Were these revoked for cause, or did they only expire?"

"The Belgian one is still good."

She looked at the licenses again. "Fair enough. Why don't we go ahead and get you legal? My name is Carrie Wheeler."

"Is there a test?"

"This is the licensing bureau. If you want a test, go to the testing bureau, right? Come around behind the desk and have a seat by the camera."

Carrie Wheeler stood and stared into a gleaming metal camera on a white tripod; it looked like a camera in a Broadway musical about photography. She clicked the shutter once, and again. She looked up, tall and narrow-hipped in a red skirt and pin-striped shirt, and crossed her eyes in comically exaggerated frustration. "O.K., this isn't working."

"The camera?"

Carrie came toward him and scratched the back of her head. "I'm not getting what I'm after." She took his left arm in both hands as if she wanted to remove it and put it aside for the time being.

"What are you after?"

"Well, I don't know, that's the thing."

"It's just a license picture."

Carrie laid his forearm across his knee, which pulled his left shoulder down. She angled his face with both hands. She stepped away, leaned back, crossed her arms. "Not to say 'just,' Paul Emmons. Yeah. Let's go with this."

"Do you always put so much work into it?"

She shook her head slowly and with great concentration. "Do . . . not . . . move," she said. She stepped behind the camera and began taking pictures. "Good," she said. "That's right — be confused. I don't blame you. 'What's it all about? Who is this lady? Where is she coming from?'"

He left the office with a new license, hot from the laminating machine. The two men who had stood behind him in line were a bit closer to the door of the state's attorney's office.

"If you hurt anyone, I will find out," said Paul. "And it will work to your detriment."

"You're going to do this?" said one of the men. "You don't look like much."

"Don't you know me? I'm Paul Emmons, the outlaw accountant. I have cruel friends all over New England. You must have heard of the Record Family. It's a bad bunch and I wouldn't mess with them if I were you."

Later he got his hair cut at a barbershop with elaborate chairs and overheard a conversation about the hair found in wigs. It came about because a mother was overseeing the cutting of her daughter's long hair. Blond curls fell to the linoleum floor as it began to rain outside.

"You could do something with that," said the mother.

"When you get a wig, all the hair comes from Italy," said the barber. "The nuns in Italy grow their hair very long and cut it to sell for wigs."

Paul imagined a line of nuns making their way to vespers along a trail with the sun going down. Some of the nuns had hair falling down their habits and others were newly shorn, like Ingrid Bergman in *For Whom the Bell Tolls*. A windmill turned slowly in the background.

Hungry, he went to a health-food store to buy a sandwich. He stood in line for a long time as a clerk with a crocheted hat consulted a series of elaborate price lists in three-ring binders. Paul did not know why the purchases in American health-food stores had to be so complicated.

In the lobby of the Pail Hotel he ate the sandwich and read the *Ashland Sun*. A player piano played "Lara's Theme" with ghostly keys moving of their own accord. Paul decided not to try for an accounting job because he had been out of the business too long and the want ads listed acronyms he had not heard of. "Must have demonstrated experience in VINOS and FFLS." The newspaper itself sought someone called a swing reporter to write about the towns surrounding Ashland. The job title intrigued Paul with its echo of the Big Band era. He had no experience as a reporter but had written essays for *Québec Libre*, the literary magazine of Sherwood University. The magazine's name had appealed to Paul's youthful belief that whatever existed should be replaced by something new. Let Québec go free, let science roll back its oppressive findings, let capitalism crumble. When the magazine type did not fill the space, he would write little column enders: "The oppressed are moved to battle the oppressors, who are not anxious to be displaced." Paul also wrote about occult matters. One of his longer essays had told the story of "Mad" Anthony Wayne, a Revolutionary War major general who seemed to have left a trail of hauntings wherever he went. Nancy Coates's frail ghost appeared sometimes around Lake Champlain — she had drowned herself after becoming convinced that Mad Anthony loved another. The major general's own spirit had been known to cross Lake Memphremagog with eagles clutching his wrists.

Folding the newspaper, Paul rose to go. A plaque on the wall said the Pail family had been investors in the match trade.

Paul bought a three-piece wool suit from London for two dollars at the Salvation Army, put it on, and went to see about the job at the *Sun*. His old clothes were in a bag that he carried over his head to keep the rain off. The newspaper occupied the long white building known as the Temple of Hephaestus; the front door stood in a grove of columns. Paul filled out a true-false form in a small room in the basement that had coarse maroon fabric on the walls. The questions included:

T F When you get right down to it, I probably have the same hang-ups or anxieties as anyone else.

T F There is no shame in "ratting out" pen and paperclip thieves.

T F Charlie McCarthy was a senator from Wisconsin who accused subversive elements of infiltrating the government.

T F Most harassment cases could be resolved short of adjudication if people would simply "let their hair down" a little bit.

T F It upsets me terribly when I see that a possum has been hit by a car.

T F I take a drink now and then.

T F I am a social drinker, and what's the harm?

T F Sometimes I drink until I black out.

T F It upsets me terribly when I see that a deer has been hit by a car.

T F The meek shall inherit the earth.

Paul finished the test and gave it to the director of human resources, who sat for a moment scribbling on the questionnaire with a red marker and then rolled it up briskly and slid it into a cloudy plastic canister, which he then fitted into a vacuum tube that ran up the wall.

The canister rattled, lifted, and disappeared into the ceiling. "You'll be going up to see Pete in a moment," he said. "Pete sees all applicants."

"Who's Pete?" said Paul.

"Pete Lonborg," said the personnel man. "He's the editor and publisher."

Paul had to go up a flight of stairs to see Pete Lonborg. Rubber treads covered the metal stairs and printer's ink stained the walls. A sign counted the days since the last injury on the job. The publisher may have insisted on interviewing all applicants, but he did not seem personable or especially tolerant. His temples bulged — you could see the ridges of his skull where they disappeared into his hairline — and his mouth turned down at one corner. He had clear blue eyes, widely separated, that made Paul think of those animals (whales, for example) whose eyes come nowhere near each other. Who knows what their vision must be like?

"Call me Pete," he said. "Let me tell you how it works here. First, everybody calls me Pete. Second, we have a young staff. We get a lot of kids come through here straight out of school and wanting to make their mark. That's all right. Might only be here six months. Nothing wrong with that. We've got a woman right now, twenty-five years old, speaks four languages. Three of them happen to be languages nobody around here speaks. Still, it's a hell of a thing. But she'll be gone soon. In our minds we've already said goodbye to her."

Pete hitched up his cuffs, crossed his legs, picked up a pack of cigarettes upside down so that the cigarettes fell out, dropped to his knees, gathered the fallen cigarettes, stuffed them back in the pack. All the while he kept talking. ". . . Oh, the world is full of smart young people . . . they use us, we use them, and no one's the wiser . . . Then you come along, not really fitting the profile." He lifted Paul's application and tapped it with the back of his fingers. "You're thirty-nine years old and looking for your first reporting job. You're changing your career in midcareer. All right then. I don't know why, maybe you don't know why. *Comme ci, comme ça.*"

"I was an accountant for a number of years, and then I operated my own business in Belgium," said Paul.

Lonborg picked up a spray bottle and began dousing a bonsai tree on his desk. He did this for a good long time. Paul thought he would drown the plant if he did not stop. "That makes a certain amount of sense," he said. "You wanted to test your theories."

"Hmm?" said Paul.

"Your business theories," said Lonborg. He paused with the sprayer in his hand. "I'm suggesting you wanted to test them."

"That's true," said Paul. "I had a farmhouse-inn sort of thing called Auberge des Moines."

"People like Europe but they never love it," said Pete Lonborg. He set the spray bottle down and turned the branches of the bonsai this way and that. "Well, I take that back. People love Spain. I knew a guy went to Spain, and when he came back all he could talk about was *levantar el vuelo.* You would go to his house and it was *levantar el vuelo* this and *levantar el vuelo* that. I thought, Fine, you've been to Spain, next topic. I'll tell you what I like about your résumé, and it's the knowledge of finances. I write the editorials around here, that's my job, or a part of it at any rate, and from time to time I have to say something about the Fed. The Fed should pull back, the Fed should push forward, the Fed is charting a risky course. Fact is I have no idea what the Fed is. Like how many people or where they work."

"There are twelve banks around the country."

"And that's the kind of thing I need to know."

Pete Lonborg showed Paul the pressroom, quiet at this hour; the circulation room, where a dozen people were all talking on the phone; and the conference room, a long and track-lit space where a reporter labored, with graphs and charts, to explain his idea for a five-part series.

"Why five parts?" said Lonborg impatiently.

"I'm glad you asked, Pete," said the reporter. "One, what is eczema? Two, who gets it? Three, I'm not sure what three will be yet. Four, which medications are good and which are a ripoff. And five, hope for the future."

"Isn't it just a minor nuisance?" said Lonborg.

"That's what I thought until mine started acting up," said the reporter. "It's a million-dollar industry."

"Still, I don't know," said Pete.

A woman with braided brown hair looked up and shrugged. "I'm not wed to the five parts," she said.

"This is Jean Jones, our city editor," said Pete. "Paul has applied to be swing reporter and he needs to take the writing test. Paul, I'm handing you off now to Jean."

Jean took Paul's hand and led him into the newsroom, where a large brass sun hung on the wall above a row of clocks indicating the times in Tokyo, Moscow, Melbourne, Paris, Ashland, and Los Angeles. The writing test seemed so earnest or naive as to embarrass Jean Jones and the three other staff members required to administer it. "This is on the lame side, but it's what we do," she said.

Paul played the role of a reporter confined to the newsroom and piecing together the story of a disaster unfolding that moment at the airport. The newspaper was supposed to be right on deadline, so not only did people keep shouting tragic new developments at Paul, but others came over every few minutes to demand what he had written up to that point. Everyone smiled bashfully, and the test seemed like a party game based on an air traffic controller's nightmare.

A jetliner had crashed while trying to land. Then a gas truck, hit by flying metal, burst into flames. Then a fire truck speeding to the airport smashed into a city bus, killing two and injuring seven. Then it was discovered that a second plane had been involved in the initial collision, a small private plane bearing a woman who had once claimed to be the mistress of the mayor. Then three people from the bus crash arrived dead at the hospital, for a total of five dead. Then there was a rumor that the mayor had been on the small airplane with his mistress, along with a competing rumor that the mayor was safe at city hall, listening in horror and fascination to the police radio. On and on went the writing test, and by the time it was over Paul had produced two pages beginning, "ASHLAND — In what surely must rank as one of the worst days in aviation history . . ."

Paul walked back across the river and out to the Coltsfoot Motel eating a candy bar and carrying his bag of clothes. At the Salvation Army he had also bought a pair of black-soled canvas shoes reminiscent of the ones worn by Eiji Okada in *The Woman in the Dunes,* and these were on his feet. It had stopped raining and the water beaded in the grass. Everything had gone so smoothly that he felt he must be on the right track. The land behind the motel rose to a small swimming pool he had not seen before, surrounded by a wooden fence bearing red-lettered warnings about the dangers of swimming, including a diagram of a stick figure hitting its head on the bottom with jagged pain bolts shooting from its neck. Barbara, wearing a modest blue-and-white-striped bathing suit, played with her son Keith in the shallow end of the shimmering pool. Paul took off his shoes and socks, rolled up the cuffs of his wool pants, and dangled his feet in the cool water while Barbara pulled Keith firmly around by his arms. Paul told Barbara that he had taken a test at the newspaper, and Barbara told Paul that Billy Trautbeck had that very afternoon smacked a baseball over the wall of the stadium and into String Lake. Then the night manager came walking slowly over the grass and warned them not to dive.

After supper Paul tried the Hanover place again. Gravel snapped under his tires as he drove up the driveway, and two labradors, a black and a yellow, loped like horses around the corner of the house and struck a noble pose. He walked the dogs down to the dock, where Loom stood gazing across the water with binoculars.

"Are we ready to begin?" he said, then lowered the binoculars. "You're not the pest-control man."

"Try to remember," said Paul.

"Nash," said Loom. "I will be hit with a stick. Where did you come from?"

"The Coltsfoot Motel. And they don't call me Nash anymore."

Loom picked Paul up and swung him around. The dogs barked and jumped. "Who doesn't?"

"The Witness Security division of the U.S. Marshals," said Paul. "I'm Paul Emmons."

"You sad case!" Loom shouted. "Where did you get that name?"

"From Ragnar Emmons. He and Vilmö Frisch won the Caracas Prize for econometrics in 1987."

"Well, that means nothing to me," said Loom, "but they had a story about you years ago in the alumni magazine, and that's the last we heard. I just don't believe it. I am just standing here in total amazement."

"How's Alice? Where's Alice? Are you still together?"

Loom frowned pragmatically. "Oh yeah. She's wonderful. Works for the mayor's office. We have two kids, Faith and Chester. She is going to freak when she sees you."

"What did they say in the magazine?" said Paul.

"It was positive, for the most part," said Loom. "They said you brought down some crime figure."

"Not really," said Paul. "My testimony was so peripheral you wouldn't believe it."

"I'm trying to remember the guy's name."

"Carlo Record."

"Maybe," said Loom. "They gave his nickname."

"The Shepherd?"

"No . . ."

"The Pliers?"

Loom shook his head, then punched Paul hard in the shoulder. "You'll always be Nash to us."

They walked up to the house. The dogs danced on the slate floor of a courtyard and picked up tennis balls in their mouths. Paul threw a ball down the rolling yard and the dogs froze, then settled their haunches on the stone with great concentration.

"Clap your hands," said Loom, and Paul did so, sending the dogs galloping down the grass. Paul kept throwing the ball for the dogs, letting his arm unwind with harsh jolts.

"Their names are Mitzi and Bump," said Loom. "They're the reason we're having the house dusted for fleas. But come on in, I'll show you the place."

They walked into the house and down a cool wallpapered hallway to the library. The evening light fell on fumed wood, cracked leather, and blue glass. The books had the moss-green and maroon bindings and innocent titles of works written and last read by no one still living: *Here Comes Leona, The Mysterious Chamber, Jazz-Man from Kirghizstan.*

Stuffed animals and birds crouched on the bookcases and tables. A raccoon with frazzled wire whiskers rested its withered black paws on a stick. The animals looked cross-eyed and dizzy, as if they had been conked on the head and stars were orbiting their skulls.

"I'll be right back," said Loom.

Paul took an encyclopedia from a shelf and sat down in an armchair. The article on taxidermy seemed to warn people away from a career in it but admitted that the University of

Iowa taught the "complicated art." Paul thought that if all taxidermists had gone through the training offered by the University of Iowa, stuffed animals might look more alive and less insane. He returned the encyclopedia to the shelf, under a section that had evidently been reserved for books about children's behavior, including *What to Expect During the Winter Solstice* and *Raising the Mean-Spirited Child*.

Loom strode purposefully into the room with his old, pale red leg weights strapped to his ankles.

"Take them away," said Paul.

Loom laughed. "I never use them anymore," he said. "Instead, I'm into the martial arts."

"I read that your father died," said Paul. "It was in a pamphlet at the motel."

"The writer was biased against Dad, but she got his dates right," said Loom. "Basically, he dumped the company in my lap."

"I've never understood what you make."

"We do a lot of defense work," said Loom. "In missile guidance systems there is something called an Emery clip. It's kind of misleading, because it's not really a clip in the sense that you or I would think of a clip."

"How big is it?" said Paul.

"Just minuscule. Stick-of-gum size."

"And this is what you make."

"I wish we did. No, Emery clips come primarily from Texas, and some from England. What we make is the bracket that holds the Emery clip."

"Was your product used in —"

"The Gulf War?" said Loom. "Not much. Some. Hanover fasteners are mostly employed in submarine-launched missiles, meant to withstand the tremendous pressures of water."

"But at one time you made matches. The company, I mean."

"Yes, long ago."

"Some kid at the park told me to ask you about match mouth."

"They always bring that up," said Loom. "A town needs its bad characters."

They went for a drive then, down the western side of the lake. Loom had a fast blue car that was not much larger than a kitchen table. The lake raced blurred and broken through the boughs, and when the road opened they could see Red Mountain across the water. The car's engine trumpeted like an elephant during the downshifts. It dove eagerly into depressions in the road, drawing the riders' center of gravity below the pavement. Houses appeared every so often, log cabins with wind chimes and sagging ranches with power boats on trailers, or strings of laundry waving in the yard, and Paul had a vision of Mary trying to shove open the door of the laundry room back in Vertige. The door dragged, carving an ever-deeper arc into the red-painted floor. "You know," Mary had said one time, "I'm beginning to think that painted floors are bogus."

Why this should now seem such a disarming remark Paul could not say, but he suspected that it was a mistaken tactic to covet Mary now that they were apart. When he was a boy, his father had taken him and Fred on Saturdays to a park in Verona where there was a marble public bathroom next to the bocce court. The restroom was entirely underground save for its roof, which served as a modest grandstand. The Nashes did not waste time above ground, even on sunny days, but went directly down the stairway to the outer hall of the men's room. There the men of Verona rested in wooden chairs, tipped ashes into brass trays, played cards, and watched slow gray boxing matches on a television with iron legs. Paul remembered listening to the gripes and bidding, and watching the men draw coins from rubber squeeze pouches that seemed strangely out of place in their rough hands. Slit windows just above the grade of the park gave a low view of the world, and one afternoon a young lawyer stood by the windows commenting on the women passing by. If he saw a woman dressed in red, he would say, "I wish I was the color red"; if he saw a woman riding a bicycle, he would say, "I wish I was a bicycle," and once, by mistake, he wished to be "the color bicycle." After a while Paul's father said, "You're breathing a scab on your nose," which was his way of warning you that harm was headed your way.

Loom and Paul stopped at a bar called Hanrahan's, which stood at a lonely bend of String Lake next to a tangle of power lines and a pumping station that throbbed and clicked as they walked to the front door. Inside the bar, three men threw darts, and two men and a woman played pool, and the dart board and pool table were so close together that it seemed the darts might hit the pool players. Paul and Loom ordered drinks and sat at a wooden table near a window.

Paul explained the places he'd lived and the work he'd done. "The witness program is nothing like what people expect. It's all words on paper."

"That's all it ever is," said Loom.

"It has nothing to do with reality."

"That's all it ever has to do with." Loom pushed buttons on a watch with a leather band. "Guess what time it is in Burma."

"Time to get a new government."

"Breakfast time," said Loom.

Just then a man struggled into the bar carrying a large wooden dollhouse. He lugged the house around selling tickets to win it in a drawing.

"I will buy two chances," said Loom, "but if I win, I want you to give it to the March of Dimes."

The man set the house on a table and reached into one of its rooms for a roll of blue tickets. "Would the March of Dimes want a dollhouse?"

"You work out the details," said Loom. The man tore off the tickets and moved on.

"What is having kids like?" said Paul.

"Faith is wonderful," said Loom. "She rides horses and once had a poem printed in some magazine. Chester is a little bit of a trial. Do you have a family?"

"Well," said Paul. "Remember that professor who died? That professor who was supervising my internship in Boston, but he died."

"No."

"Well, anyway, he died," said Paul, "and I ended up marrying the woman he had been married to."

"Oh, come on. What was she, old?"

"Not at all," said Paul. "That's the thing. She was young. We met at his funeral. They had gotten married right after she graduated."

"Jesus, man," said Loom. "You have just made every mistake there is."

"No, that was good," said Paul.

"When do we meet her?"

"You don't. She's in Belgium. It's hard to explain. I remember one time I was on a ladder painting the barn at the inn, and hornets flew out of the eaves, so there was nothing to do but go down the ladder and wait. And I was sitting on the grass, you know, just doing nothing, just watching these mindless hornets, and there was this quiet sunshine, this dead-quiet sunshine, and I thought, There's got to be something else I can do."

"Chased across the Atlantic by hornets," said Loom. "There are sprays that would be much cheaper. Which reminds me — the exterminators."

They zoomed back to the house in the little blue car. Loom gestured toward the lake. "Right out there are a lot of people fishing in the dark that you can't even see."

Three silver vans sat in the driveway, and men milled about in gray overalls and orange rubber gloves with large rounded fingers.

"You can't go in," said one of the men. "Oh hi, Mr. Hanover. Sorry, but even you can't go in. We already started."

"Why do you work at night?" said Paul.

"Got to be at night, evidently," said Loom.

"The rays of the sun destabilize our fog," said the fumigator.

"It's much less toxic than other fogs, but it has to be applied at night. Some of our guys are in there already with tanks and such. Those fleas are well on their way to the magic kingdom."

"Has my wife been here?"

"They're all around back of the house."

Dense fog swirled behind bands of windows, and every now and then a beam of light would break free, sweep a pane, and disappear. Paul and Loom shifted their feet and kept a respectful silence in the presence of the unusual work.

Alice Miller Hanover had lit a kerosene lantern on a table, around which she and the children sat in wicker chairs.

"We have a visitor," said Loom. "Alice, you are going to fall over."

"Move to the lantern so I can see," said Alice.

"It's Nash," said Loom.

Alice stood with her black hair pulled back from her face. Paul hugged her and breathed in the smell of her hair, something of smoke and something of mint too. "Have you come to rescue us?" she said.

"From what?" said Paul. "From what, Alice?"

She stepped back and swept an arm toward the house. "From these *people*," she said. "These people in our house."

"Faith and Chester, say hello to Paul," said Loom. "He's an old friend from college days."

Faith shook Paul's hand. She had long arms and her mother's large and doubtful eyes. Chester crouched in a chair with his legs drawn up.

"Stand up, Chester," said Loom. "Stand up and be accounted for. Look Paul in the eye and shake his hand." Chester did so, then rolled himself up in the chair once more.

"Watch out for Chester," said Loom. "He steals."

"Like what?" said Paul.

"No, I don't," said Chester.

"What about that diamond ring?" said Loom. "Doesn't that mean anything?"

"We don't know how that got here," said Alice.

"I think it came from the jewelry store in town, but I'm not sure how to approach them," said Loom.

"I found that at school," said Chester. "I told you, Dad. I told you that I found that ring."

"Let's not argue," said Alice. "Can we just watch the red smoke in peace?"

"I thought we were going to Grandma's apartment," said Chester.

"When I say," said Loom.

"You're not the boss of me."

"Yes, though, I am."

"Faith," said Alice. "Take Chester around front to see how the workmen are doing."

"I will, Mother," said Faith. She pulled Chester away by the hand, and Loom sat in one of the chairs.

"But don't bother them," said Loom. "Just stand on the periphery. Who's got the dogs?"

"I kenneled them," said Alice. "I took the kids and the dogs and I drove all of us to the kennel."

"Bless you," said Loom. The children walked off into the darkness.

"Be careful," called Alice. To Paul she said, "I guess Loom told you we have fleas."

"It happens to the best of families."

"The other day I walked through the house in white ankle socks and I counted seven on one foot."

"Didn't there used to be a cartoon about a flea?" said Paul. "He was traveling over a dog and the hairs were as big as trees. And he carried a suitcase and kept singing about a home around the corner."

"I missed that one," said Alice.

"You could be him, if you had a suitcase," Loom said to Paul. He adjusted the wick on the lantern while giving, for Alice's benefit, a brief and confusing account of Paul's travels.

"Just don't go to Paris in August," said Alice.

"A home around the corner is sort of profound when you think about it," said Paul. "The *Odyssey* is all about a home around the corner."

"*The Searchers*," said Alice.

"*The Mill on the Floss*," said Loom.

"What happens in *The Mill on the Floss*?" said Alice.

"Hell, I don't know."

"Adam and Eve, after getting kicked out of Eden," said Paul. "Cain getting sent away."

Loom said, "Where did Cain go?"

"San Diego," said Paul.

"Cain slew Abel," said Alice. "And beyond that I'm a little hazy."

"Or did Abel slay Cain?" said Loom.

"No, Cain did the slaying," said Alice.

"There was always something weird about that," said Paul. "Here the mother and father have been thrown out of Eden and they're forced to scratch in dirt for their living. And so, when Cain murders Abel, what does God do? He makes Cain an outcast."

"Adam and Eve are Cain and Abel's parents?" said Loom. "I didn't know that."

"Yeah, who'd you think?" said Alice.

"My point is, outcast from what?" said Paul. But he felt as if he were talking too much, performing like a seal, for his old friends. "The whole family is outcast already. It's as if God can't keep his story straight."

"God was toying with the man," said Loom.

"'I shall be a fugitive and a vagabond in the earth; and it shall come to pass, that every one that findeth me shall slay me,'" said Paul.

"Good for you," said Alice. "But if I remember right, doesn't God do some favor for Cain?"

"I don't know how much of a favor it is," said Paul. "He marks him so everyone will know not to kill him."

"A small consolation prize," said Loom.

Alice sat back with one hand in her lap and the other holding on to the frame of the wicker chair. "The strange thing about God," she said, "when you think about it, is how quickly he lost control of his warped little experiment. From the moment people were created, they were lying and killing and running around on each other, and God was in the awkward position of having to say, 'Hey, cut that out. Stop that. Come back here.'"

"If you ask me, God set the bar too high," said Loom. "Anyone who flies into a rage over the eating of an apple is going to have a pretty long day."

12

Due to a last-minute shakeup at the *Sun,* Paul began not as the swing reporter but as a stuffer. The stuffers worked at galvanized metal tables at the opposite end of the pressroom from the presses: web-fed German offset machines that resembled a series of tractors without wheels. Rolls of uncut newsprint hurtled on jagged paths between ink-slick spinning cylinders, and the convergence of the webs from their humming and various levels into single newspapers seemed heroic and unlikely.

Proximity to the presses gave significance to the stuffers' jobs. If they had to work like machines, at least they had powerful ones to emulate, to draw rhythm and mission from. There were eleven stuffers, and each stood before three stacks of newspapers arrayed on the metal tables. They picked up inserts from the first stack, slid them into newspapers on the second stack, and moved the stuffed newspapers to the third stack. And then they did it again.

Like any simple job, stuffing could be executed with grace or clumsiness. It all came down to delivering the insert into the fold with enough force to slide the newspaper onto the third stack, and those who could not master this maneuver did not make their quota and were let go. By the end of August Paul could slam the inserts home like a veteran. The newspapers were warm from the presses, the ink smelled like licorice and fuel, and he found the stuffers to be a likable crew, driven by precision and a caustic sense of solidarity. Sometimes Pete Lonborg appeared in the pressroom, looking so anxious and distracted that the stuffers could not help feeling blessed and centered by comparison. At first Paul assumed that Pete's trips to the pressroom were intended to check on the wording of some controversial story, but it turned out that he worried about the quality of the *Sun*'s color printing.

"The readers want color," said Angela. Stuffers Angela, Ramona, and Paul were eating supper from lunch pails in the dark on the steps of the Temple of Hephaestus.

"They'll die if they don't get color," said Ramona. Her eyes seemed very moist, they always did, and Paul thought she looked like a woman waiting for her lover to return from the sea.

"That's what Pete thinks," said Angela.

"Look out for Pete," Ramona said to Paul. "Pete's a moody guy." She peeled a small oval label from a green apple and stuck it on Paul's forehead. "Look, it's Lent."

"I'm sick of your moister-than-thou attitude," said Paul.

"What do you have to say about it?" said Ramona. "You're the token male."

"The token has spoken," said Angela. She had an avid face with heart-shaped lips.

"Pete hates it when the grass in our photographs is blue, which it always is," said Ramona.

"Another thing the readers are supposedly dying for is to have all the news explained in little drawings," said Angela.

"Let them read comic books," said Paul.

"If you ask me, the readers are like anybody," said Ramona. "They don't know what they want."

"They want whatever we say they want," said Angela.

"And maybe what they want is not what they need," said Ramona. "They want *Andy Capp*."

"I don't fault Pete for being mad about the blue grass," said Angela. "Now, his cheapness — that I fault him for."

"Tell Paul about the Christmas editorial," said Ramona.

"You know," said Angela, "how they put a box in the post office for people to donate toys for poor children? So one Christmas Pete writes an editorial saying this is an improper use of federal territory."

"That's cold," said Paul.

"He said he was all for poor kids getting toys," said Ramona. "But he said federal property should not be used to favor one economic group to the exclusion of the others. He said once you start down that road, what would stop someone from using the post office to collect Rolex watches for the wealthy?"

"It was an idiotic argument," said Angela. "I know someone who had dinner at his home, and apparently he sliced the ham just compulsively thin."

"So what did the post office do?" said Paul.

"The editorial never ran," said Ramona. "Everyone thought it was too strong."

Another thing the stuffers did was to fold newspapers like paper boats and wear them as hats. The hats kept ink out of their hair, but they also added to the stuffers' sense of unity and esprit de corps. Even the pressmen, who alone could stop the newspaper from coming out, and who gave this power frequent and solemn consideration, seemed grasping and superficial next to the stuffers.

The *Sun* was a morning newspaper, and Paul's shift ran from three-thirty in the afternoon till midnight. Sometimes when they got off work a handful of stuffers would ride out to Hanrahan's for drinks. A burned state flag hung over the bar, and one night the bartender, who was bald on top and had long white hair on the sides, explained that the flag had come from the Tableville fire.

"It started at the old high school," he said. "The school was no longer used, but some filmmakers from Worcester had rented it to make sex movies. They used to come in every year and make a movie. There was an inquest, and it turned out that one of the cameramen left a cigarette burning. Ironically, the fire was the best thing that ever happened to Tableville, because the state came forward with a lot of rehab money. The *Sun* carried a big picture of the fireman rescuing the flag."

"I remember that photo," said Ramona.

"They finished the movie, though," said the bartender. "It was called *After-School Special,* starring Camille Livesey. The fire footage was incorporated in the movie. Those people made use of everything. Camille Livesey used to come in here all the time while the production company was in town. She loved the juke-box. Good dancer, too. Really good dancer."

The flag was blue with a white shield and three twisted grapevines that looked like dollar signs. "What does *Qui transtulit sustinet* mean?" said Paul.

"That which is transplanted sustains," said Angela.

Other nights Paul would walk the shining and empty streets of Ashland. Not far from the *Sun* was the evening-dress store, called The Good You, with the ancient mannequins. They seemed to squint, and all their hands were left hands. Farther along, he came upon the river that he had crossed on his first day in Ashland, a rocky river with old apartment buildings on either side. The lowest windows hovered near the water, and it seemed to Paul that these apartments would be romantic to live in, for though he could not swim well, he believed that bodies of water, even shabby rivers with old appliances littering their banks, had an erotic influence dating back to the beginning of time and the stirrings of evolution. Just as he was thinking this, a young woman with bare shoulders leaned from one of the windows and twisted a yellow cloth over the river. Then it began to rain, lightly but steadily, as if the woman had wrung the rain from her cloth.

Paul did his first reporting on Labor Day, when Jean Jones told him to contribute to the holiday roundup by going to see the Saberians' fireworks display at Adelphic School. For years the club had given its fireworks on the Fourth of July, like everyone else, and the shift several years ago to the end of summer amounted to an admission that the private club could not compete with the publicly funded fireworks in Damascus. "You can meet up with a photographer there," said Jean Jones.

Paul grabbed a notebook and pen and drove over to the Adelphic School, a series of burrowing buildings that had been designed by a cousin of a famous architect. A Marshall Tucker tribute band played for a while and then the show began, with the townspeople lying on the grass in the dark watching the orange fires overhead. Some had brought their dogs, an action that Paul could explain only in terms of that peculiar form of displaced narcissism that finds expression, for example, in the tying of red bandannas on golden retrievers. Certainly the dogs did not have fun, alternately bolting and cowering under lawn chairs. The spectators spoke longingly of "the grand finale" from the moment the fireworks began, and Paul wondered why such displays did not begin with the grand finale, thus greatly reducing the traffic jam at the end of the night. Ashes drifted down, and sometimes live sparks, which looked as if they would land far away but didn't, and spectators received small, pinch-like burns. "Get back, you people, get back," someone said in a hollow amplified voice. "You are way too close. Every year we have people coming closer and closer. If we are to continue having fireworks in Ashland, you must get back, and by that I mean behind the soccer bleachers."

Finally the blasting and smoke subsided, and people gathered their weary children and relieved dogs for the trek home. Paul saw a slender woman with long curly hair and black-bodied cameras hanging from straps around her neck. "I'm glad you found me," she said. "I'm Nina Berry. I took some pictures earlier and you have to get the people's names."

Paul looked around. "Where?"

"They were by the rock band a half hour ago."

"Well, what did they look like?"

Nina dropped her jaw and widened her eyes, mimicking Paul's confusion. "It was some fat guy and his fat kids," she said. "How would I know? Just find them. You're the reporter."

Instead, Paul interviewed Commander Smith, the Saberian in charge of the fireworks, who stood by the jungle gym with a bullhorn. "I'm from the *Sun*," said Paul. "How would you characterize this year's show?"

"Very good this year," said Commander Smith, a ravaged man wearing stiff blue jeans with the cuffs tucked into bulky white socks.

"How much did the display cost?"

"We don't give that out. It isn't about money."

"Do fireworks ever remind veterans of combat? Do they bring to mind certain battles?"

"For me they don't," said Commander Smith. "Maybe a little. That's a good question. I never thought of that. You'd have to ask around."

"Is next year's display really in jeopardy?"

"Oh, no. We say that, but we don't mean it. There will always be fireworks. But I do wish people would stay back better."

Paul wrote the story on a computer in the center of the newsroom. It was a slow night for news, but you would not have known it by the hustling figures of the dozen people whose junior status or lack of a social life had qualified them to work on Labor Day night. They hurried back and forth among the upturned screens and snaking cords of the newsroom carrying half-eaten sandwiches and wielding pica poles like silver daggers. Paul had borrowed the computer of the court reporter, who had gone to Castine, Maine, for the weekend, and as he flipped through his notebook, he listened to the staccato typing of the police reporter, Carolyn Wheat, who was working at the adjacent terminal.

"What's new with the cops?" said Paul.

"A red Ford Tempo heading eastbound on Route 283 crossed over the line and struck a westbound Pontiac Trans Am," said

Carolyn. "The drivers were treated and released at Red Mountain Infirmary. The bludgeoned body of a carnie was discovered behind the band shell at Thales Park, name withheld pending notification of kin. And the cab driver Herman Marx got stiffed and chased the fare-skipper to the corner of Walnut Street and Scrimshaw Avenue, where a roving band of youths helped apprehend the suspect. But forget the news. When I get off tonight I'm going to go home and make myself a root beer float. I put a tall glass in the freezer this morning, and I can almost hear it calling my name."

After Paul finished his story, he had to wait for the county editor to read it and sign off.

"What's this bullshit about people with dogs being narcissistic?" said the editor. His name was Chris Bait, and he was known for two things: eating celery in the newsroom and working himself into a panic over minor issues. "I have a dog. What are you, Nicholas von Hoffman?"

"Not if they *have* a dog," said Paul. "I'm saying if they *bring* a dog to a fireworks display. You know, it's just kind of strange. Think about it."

"I'm cutting all that," said Chris. "Do you hear me? Cutting it. And I still need an ID on some kids in a photograph."

"I don't have the names," said Paul. "The photographer didn't even know what they looked like."

"That's wonderful," said Chris. He scanned the room grimly. "Don't worry, Emmons. You're brand-new here, and this doesn't happen to be your fault. No, I'm afraid it's Nina Berry. She's on probation you know."

"Am I done?" said Paul.

"Yeah, go have a few pops," said Chris Bait. Then he stormed off to find Nina.

The trees turned color nearly a month early in Ashland due to the elevation, and the sky seemed to come down nearer to the earth. The days would dawn clear, but by afternoon smoky clouds would move in, gray and blue, and the late sun would be left to slide sideways beneath the clouds. Paul decided that it was the purple clouds that gave the red and yellow leaves their most powerful definition. Only rain could hurt the foliage. In the rain, the bright colors became a little pathetic. Leaves no longer whirled like twisters across the roadways but clumped glumly in the ditches. Those that had not yet fallen seemed finally to do so in embarrassment.

Yet people loved the leaves. No one worried about how they would look in the rain. Tour buses clogged the streets of the town. The tree everyone had to see was a basswood on the eastern ascent of Red Mountain called the Spirit Tree, after a poem written by the nineteenth-century diarist Cyril Sawtelle of Tableville. Leaves from this tree were said to grant wishes, and wishful visitors had usually picked its branches clean by the time of the Rake Parade, which was held on the second weekend in September. Ashlanders regarded the foliage season with ambivalence. On the one hand, it meant several weeks of hindered driving and no access to restaurants, and on the other, the leaf industry provided the town's third-largest source of income, after Ashland Fastener and Binder and the milk-processing plant. Bowing to the financial power of the leaves, and trying to demonstrate that he was one of the people, Pete Lonborg made a kind of ceremony out of raking the leaves that fell from the ash tree in a small park next to the newspaper. The resulting leaf pile would stand for several weeks, giving *Sun* readers a chance to guess at the number of leaves, which would be counted just as the bottom ones were losing their individuality, in order to win cash prizes.

One night between the Rake Parade and the counting of the leaves, Paul Emmons left work to find Alice Hanover waiting for him outside the Temple of Hephaestus. She sat listening to country music on the radio of a big station wagon with wood panels. Her back pressed against the door and her legs rested on the seat.

"You're up late," said Paul.

"I'm a night person," she said. "I like the house after every-one has gone to sleep. I sit at the kitchen table writing letters or paying bills. I drive around. There's always something to do if you're a night person."

Ashland's taxicab drifted by, with the vigilante Herman Marx at the wheel.

Alice got out of the station wagon, and she and Paul sat down on a wooden bench near the leaves that Pete Lonborg had raked.

"Where are you staying?"

"At the motel," said Paul. "They gave me a weekly rate."

"Do you like it?" said Alice.

"It isn't bad, but you can't cook. I'm going to start looking for an apartment."

"What about our house?"

"But you live there."

"No, listen." Alice got up from the bench, walked to Pete's leaves, and took a clump of them in her hands. "Now just think this over. We own the house next to ours, but it's been empty as long as I've lived here. I gather there used to be a family in it, but their circumstances changed, and Loom's father bought the place as a buffer. All this would be years ago. We've never done anything with it, and for a long time I've wanted to rent it out, but every tenant I could dig up, Loom didn't want living next to him. Loom has a funny relationship with this town. It gets better, and it doesn't get better."

"I think I saw that house when I went out in your boat."

"When was that?"

"The night I got here," said Paul. "You weren't home."

"You bold spider," said Alice. She threw the leaves at Paul. "It's pretty rundown. And the windows are small and high. How do you feel about small windows?"

"Well, how small?"

She held her hands perhaps a foot and a half apart.

"I have no problem with that."

"There's moss growing on the walls. And I just feel like if we don't do something with it soon, it'll fall down."

"I'm definitely interested."

He brushed the leaves from his collar, picked up Alice with one arm under her back and the other slung into the crook of her knees, carried her to the leaves, and dropped her in.

"Hey!" she said.

"You started it."

"You sound like Faith and Chester." She stood, knee-deep in leaves, laced her fingers in his, and tried to bend his hands back. They wrestled and fell, and Alice climbed on top of Paul. Leaves clung to her hair and shoulders, and the seam of her jeans pressed taut across his bones.

"Does Chester really steal?" said Paul.

"He doesn't think of it in those terms," said Alice. "In his mind, it's all his to begin with. He's got a pack-rat sensibility." Paul raised his hands and she grabbed his wrists. "Do you give up?"

"I'm just getting started," said Paul.

Alice's eyes gleamed in the darkness, and her shoulders rose and fell. "You have no business here," she said.

"I'm the swing reporter," said Paul.

Alice picked him up at the motel the next morning. She drove the station wagon with her fists touching at the top of the wheel, and an emerald ring on one of her fingers arced back and forth like a jewel on the wheel of trouble. It was a gray and windy day. Alice pulled off the road and onto a dirt lane that curved between birch trees with leaves spilling to the ground. The car bounced up the lane to where a tree lay across the path. Alice stopped and got out carrying a small suitcase. They walked up over a rise between the trees and through a gate made of vine-covered branches that had a peaked hood like an arrow pointing at the sky. The house lay hidden by dead morning

glories that had climbed the porch columns and stitched themselves together along the roof's edge. It was a small clapboard
house with patches of the foretold moss. A square stone chimney climbed the side of the house by an attic window. Scraps of
paint moved restlessly in the wind.

"This is like a place where trolls live," said Paul.

Alice stood on the front porch. "It's in worse shape than I
thought." She worked a skeleton key in the lock of a wide and
windowless front door and pushed it open. "See what I mean
about how dark it is?"

Furniture lurked in the gloom of the big front room: leather
trunks, claw-foot tables, heavy wooden chairs that didn't match.
An odd wall jutted three feet into the room, the beginning of a
partition that was never finished. When Alice's keys hit the
surface of a table, the sound sent squirrels running across the
roof. She lifted the receiver of a black telephone. "That's
strange," she said, and held the phone in the air. Paul went over
and listened to faint voices:

"So what did you say?"

*"Well, I told him he had to make a choice, frankly, and if that means we
don't go to the barbecue, then, by God, we don't go."*

"Wow, you really laid it down."

"Hello? Hello?" said Paul. "They can't hear me."

"To tell you the truth, I don't even know whose name this
phone would be under," said Alice.

"Are these things yours?" said Paul.

"I guess they are," said Alice. "Just reclaim it. Get the vines
off and do some painting. And that can be your rent, to make it
good again."

Paul and Alice walked methodically through the house as if
expecting to find someone. The setup was unusual in that the
rooms you would normally find on the first floor — the kitchen,
dining room, and bathroom — were in the basement, which,
because of the slope of the land, opened onto the back yard
through a door in the kitchen. They ended up in a long, narrow

workshop. Paint-spatter hieroglyphs studded the benches. Carving tools hung on pegboards with their outlines drawn behind them.

"I feel like I've been here before," said Paul.

"Maybe you have. Did you ever come to Ashland when we were in college?"

"I always meant to."

"It takes some getting used to."

Paul reached up and took a wicker-handled chisel from one of the tool racks. It had a blue blade with a V-shaped tip and Japanese characters inscribed on the metal.

"The man was a carpenter," said Alice. "I don't know very much. Loom has always shrugged it off. The woman was one of his teachers."

Paul put the chisel back. "I could live here."

"I haven't really told Loom," said Alice. "I want to present it as a fait accompli."

They went out of the house and into the back yard. Alice opened her suitcase, which turned out to be a portable tape player. She put in a cassette. A violin played a lonely string of notes that slowly took the form of "Greensleeves."

"This is Vaughan Williams," said Alice.

The music played over the bent grass. It reminded Paul of the time in Verona Elementary School when two girls — one with dark hair and a clarinet, the other with light hair and a flute — had played "Greensleeves" at an assembly. They both wore black skirts and white blouses, and after the song was finished the dark-haired girl tightened the screws on her reed with gentleness and respect.

Alice smiled and rubbed her black eyebrows. "I've been so unhappy," she said.

"Yeah, recently?"

"For years. It just seems like years."

He touched her arm. "Let's go into town for a matinee."

13

Paul took the cottage by the lake. He and Loom carried the furniture from the front room into the basement, leaving only a trestle table, chairs, and trunks upstairs. Green wallpaper with purple flowers covered the walls.

Paul's bedroom was a small room on the first floor whose door opened next to the fireplace in the living room. The electricity worked, and once the propane company had come and filled a rusted tank beside the house, so did the stove.

On his first night, having returned home from the newspaper, he sat at the trestle table listening to a radio and writing a letter to Mary. "All is well here and hope you are the same. I have a house by a lake in a town called Ashland, Connecticut. The country is wooded and steep. Some old friends from college live here. I picked up Scratch at my parents' house and she is as mean as ever she was. My address is West Shore Road and I hope you write . . ."

"Ever she was" — Jesus Christ, he thought, what is wrong with me?

He put his pen down and began stripping wallpaper, using a serrated blade he had found in the shop. This worked perfectly for the outer walls, which had shifted and flexed with the seasons, weakening the glue and making the paper brittle. All he had to do was slash the paper, put aside the blade, take hold of the torn part, and back away from the wall. The paper made a satisfying rasping sound as it gave up the surface, and glue dust coated his arms and clothes.

A little bit each night was the way the work went, an hour or two after his shift at the *Sun*, but the work got harder as the nights went on. The wallpaper clung stubbornly to the inside walls, and Paul ended up renting an iron steamer from a rental warehouse in Ashland that had a wedding tent pitched inside.

Electrical coils in the base of the steamer heated water in a tank, forcing steam though a rubber hose and into a plate the size of a clipboard. This plate Paul would clap to the wall and hold there while applying the steam with a metal trigger on the back of the plate. It was hot work in a cool season. Even with steaming he had to slash and scrape the inside walls, and often he gouged the plaster, revealing tufts of dark and wiry horsehair.

One Saturday night all the lights went out and the steamer died, and he went outside to sit on the back steps of the dark house. His wet shirt cooled in the night air and an outboard motor droned somewhere on the lake. Then he climbed into his car and drove into town for a bottle of club soda. His hands were dry and dusty and he stood scratching his palm in front of the woman who ran the convenience store.

"That means you'll be coming into money," said the woman.

"I'll be waiting." Like many of his unfinished generation, Paul gave reflexive credence to most superstitions.

"Take it easy," she said. "Or go crazy. Those are your options."

Driving back to the house by the lake, Paul got stuck behind a charter bus that lurched and huffed along the twisting road. He decided not to pass. He did not trust his depth perception, and the penalty for miscalculation seemed excessive. Instead, he turned on the radio and listened to a song called "I Can't Tell You Why" by the Eagles.

This reminded him of a winter years ago when he and Mary had spent a weekend in Williamstown, and they had gone down to Pittsfield to see a movie with "I Can't Tell You Why" on the soundtrack. In the movie, Diane Keaton and Albert Finney split up, Finney falls in with the crazy-eyed Karen Allen, and eventually he crashes his car into a tennis court, whereupon Diane Keaton's studly new boyfriend stomps him viciously into the court. Afterward, somber from the violent ending, Paul and Mary headed back to Williamstown.

On the way, they stopped at a ski lodge, where they drank

Irish coffee while sitting by a fire and watching the skiers gliding down the mountain under the lights.

Now, stuck behind the bus with nothing to do, Paul had a certain hunger for this version of themselves. Why could they not have spent their lives in the spirit of that moment between Pittsfield and Williamstown, with hot whiskey in their cups and brightly dressed skiers shooting down the mountain?

The next day they had gone to a museum called the Clark Institute, where Mary stood close to the paintings to study brush strokes and where Paul walked through the galleries considering the essential horniness of artists. So many seemed to dress up their hubba-hubba natures with an elaborate layer of allegorical interest. In *The Women of Amphissa* nine or ten women lay in flimsy gowns on animal skins spread on the stones of a market-place among tables laden with honeycombs and avocados. And Renoir's girl with a cat slept in a red chair with her peasant blouse fallen from one shoulder, as if Renoir himself had tip-toed forward to slide the strap off, which maybe he had . . .

Now a lone headlight danced in the rear-view mirror of Paul's car. The light darted and charged, up and back, left and right, conveying the impatience of a motorcycle driver.

"What would you have me do?" said Paul aloud. "Drive over the top of it?"

Exhaust fumes flowed steadily from the bus, and when the thin smoke paused for the shifting of gears the bus seemed in danger of losing momentum and rolling backward. Paul checked the mirror again, which reflected only darkness, and he wondered where the motorcycle had gone. Sometimes it seemed to him that vehicles simply disappeared with no expla-nation, or perhaps a sports car that had been behind him would be suddenly ahead of him, just like that. This was especially true in Belgium, where the motorists drove with that sense of high-velocity order that he associated with the highways of every country he had ever been in, save the United States and Canada — and even in Canada, around Montreal. Then the motorcycle headlight blinked on the edge of his vision; it flickered and climbed through the trees along the road. The rider had evidently found a parallel trail on which he would overtake them all. The light stayed even with Paul's car for a moment and then rose and disappeared in the trees. Soon the red bus lights flared and the bus stopped cold in the road and Paul stopped too, which was no trick, slow as he had been going. He pulled off onto the soft shoulder of the road, got out, and walked up beside the bus. The motorcycle had come to rest on its side in the other lane, and the rider sat somewhere else entirely, with his back to a pine tree and his head tilted away from the road. The bus's headlights flooded the corpse. The eyes were open, and Paul knelt down and shut them as he had seen done in movies.

The bus driver stood near the door of the bus with his arms spread wide as if to contain his passengers, for they seemed to be mindlessly moving into the darkness. One man clutched a duffel bag to his chest and shouted at the motorcyclist as if he were still alive.

"You cut it too close," he said.

"He can't hear you," said the bus driver.

A short woman put her arm around the driver. "It wasn't your fault," she said. "Don't take it on yourself."

"Please get back on the bus," said the driver.

Paul fetched his notepad and pen from the car and began taking notes. The police arrived, followed by an ambulance and a fire truck, and soon the trees shivered in waves of red light. Then another motorcycle came idling up, and a tall couple dismounted and walked toward the tree where the dead rider reclined as if resting in the cool of the evening. The man and woman knew the rider, and comprehension seemed to hit them very specifically in the shins, so they made halting progress. The man wore all denim, but instead of making him look rugged or hearty, his outfit gave him the appearance of a denim stick figure.

The EMTs covered the fallen rider with a sheet or shroud.

The couple took off their helmets and nestled them against their hips. The woman's long, thin face seemed familiar, but Paul could not place her. The police would not let the man and woman near the covered figure, so they walked over to the motorcycle, where it lay in the road, and hunkered down, set their helmets on the pavement, and looked through a saddlebag. Paul told them that he worked for the *Sun,* and if they didn't want to talk he would understand, but if they did want to talk, he would be there to listen, because he wanted to give some sense of the man for the people who would read the story but did not know him.

"We were going to play cards," said the woman. She sat back with her hands on the asphalt surface. "We were going to play poker at our house. Is that what you want to know? A game of cards? Happy now? His name is Mike Snowe. I'm Carrie, this is Lonnie, and that's Mike."

"You work at the courthouse," said Paul. "You gave me my driver's license. Remember? I thought there was going to be a hassle, but you just gave it to me."

"She has tremendous power no one knows about," said Lonnie.

"Poor Mike," she said. "What happened?"

"He tried to pass the bus on the side trail," said Paul.

"I mean, to our lives," said the woman. "I mean, what happened to our lives that we would wind up this way? On the side of the road talking to a reporter like some angel of death. 'We had no idea.' 'We didn't expect it.' How did it come to happen this way?"

"Is the poker game a regular thing?" said Paul.

"No, not really," said Lonnie.

"It was a regular thing for a while," said Carrie. "We were trying to start it back up."

"Where did Mike work?"

"At the hospital," said Carrie. "He and Lonnie both work at the hospital."

Lonnie took out a light blue pack of French cigarettes and lit one up. The match glowed between the fingers of his hands. They were all huddled by the motorcycle. "Mike was kind and gentle," said Lonnie. "That's the thing to remember about Mike. You would never hear a word out of him. If somebody couldn't make their shift, it was always, 'Call Mike.' If somebody needed help moving, it was always, 'Call Mike.' 'Mike'll be right over to carry things.'"

Paul wrote breathlessly, in a large and careless script. He filled pages and flipped them. He wrote like a fiend.

"He was good and understanding, and a lot of people treated him like their personal slave," said Carrie. "That's how I feel, anyway. He read everything he could find. He was a constant reader. I remember one time he picked up a bottle of shampoo and just read out all the ingredients. He had this wonderful curiosity, and he also cared for tropical fish."

Lonnie laughed quietly. "That's for sure."

"He had two tanks," said Carrie.

"That's a lot, I guess," said Paul.

"It was a lot for Mike, but he never complained," said Carrie. "I don't know what will become of the fish now. He wasn't from here. I don't know where he was from. We should call someone. His parents were in the service, so he traveled around a lot. He was an army brat."

"How old was he?"

"I don't know. I don't know how old he was. Lonnie, how old would Mike have been? Twenty-eight?"

"I don't know," said Lonnie. "He loved racquetball, and I'll tell you what, he was good at it." He reached down and flipped the saddlebag open. "Look, here's his racquet."

"Move away from the motorcycle, please," said a policeman with slick black hair. Lonnie, Carrie, and Paul stood up. "And put that cigarette out."

Someone began singing from a window of the bus. "Lead, kindly light, amid the encircling gloom; lead thou me on, the night is dark, and I am far from home . . ."

"We knew him," said Lonnie.

"Will you bring charges?" said Carrie.

"Unlikely," said the policeman. "I'm not sure what the bus driver could have done differently. And the other one gets out of charges the hard way. We've all made our mistakes. There's no joy in this job."

"What's your name, officer?" said Paul. "I'm Paul Emmons from the *Sun*."

"I hate that rag," said the policeman.

The emergency workers lifted the rider onto a stretcher as Paul slid the notebook into his back pocket. Leaving the accident, he picked up a clublike police flashlight that someone had left on the trunk of a cruiser. Then he got into his car, drove to the newspaper, and wrote up his notes for the police reporter Carolyn Wheat to find in the morning.

It was after three o'clock when he got home. He turned on the flashlight and went down to the basement. The fuse box was in the kitchen, and he unscrewed the blown fuse and replaced it with a penny. The electricity surged, sending thin rays of light down through the cracks in the flooring. He turned the kitchen light on, and Scratch came bleating down the stairs. Paul opened a can of cat food and ran her a fresh bowl of water.

The steamer was hissing and spitting when he went up to the living room, and he shut it down. Then he thought he heard something. Now, his hearing had never been good. At the trial of Carlo Record and the hotel thief Eddie Leblanc, he had had to cup his hand behind his ear to hear the soft-spoken judge, Clementine Darrigan. As a child he had been taken to a radical ear, nose, and throat doctor in Newport. This man, who on at least one occasion had worn thin black socks with a hole over the bone of one ankle, would place a rubber tube in one of Paul's nostrils, give him a drink of water from a pleated white paper cup, and direct him not to swallow the water but to hold it in his mouth while rapidly repeating the consonant k. Then the doctor would squeeze an air bulb connected to the rubber tube, blasting Paul's young brain right out of his head — that's what it felt like anyway. It all had to do with his eustachian tubes.

Today Paul wondered whether this treatment had done more harm than good. One of the manifestations of his hearing loss was an inability to tell where sounds came from or from how far away. This was especially true at night, due to the lack of visual clues.

"What's that?" he used to ask Mary. "Is there a moth in the room?"

And she would roll onto her back and say, in a midnight murmur, "It's only a truck, only a truck on the highway."

The noise he heard now was some sort of whistle that would go off and on. At first he thought it must be the steamer, that the steamer might be "dieseling" or winding down into silence. But it wasn't that — the sound varied in pitch, almost like singing. He checked the radio. Then he thought of the attic, where he'd never been. You entered the attic by way of a fold-down ladder, nested between ceiling joists. A cotton rope hung from the ladder, with a wooden knob on the end, and Paul pulled on the rope. Springs squealed and the attic smell drifted down: canvas, linen, and tar paper.

He climbed the ladder carrying the police flashlight and stood in the opening, shining the beam all around. Light fell on books and clothes and cardboard boxes and eccentric wooden chairs. Paul found a stamp album with pages labeled, in careful handwriting, *Animals, Birds, Trains and Tramways;* but whoever had kept the album had only managed to affix two or three stamps to each labeled page, and after seven pages even the writing stopped, giving the blank brittle pages the mocking poignance of all intended hobbies that come to nothing.

The flashlight's beam crossed the attic and lit up a shrouded figure near the small window by the chimney. Paul made his way through boxes and clothes. Whatever it was stood beneath a faded tarp edged with brass grommets. Paul gathered the heavy canvas and pulled it slowly away, revealing a statue of a woman. She had a long, delicate nose, blank eyes as in statues of Homer, and hair swept back from her face in carved waves. She knelt holding a candle in gloved hands. Even the flame had been carefully carved, with an inner and outer fire. Bare wooden toes emerged from the braided hem of a long and deeply folded gown. Her shoulders were unnaturally narrow, and the gown had a hood or cowl that began in a V at the base of her throat and rested on her back. Her right hand, set on her raised knee, supported the base of the candle, and her left hand held the upper part near the flame.

He touched her long fingers, the knuckles and the seams on the back of her glove. The wood was cool and smooth. He imagined the precise incisions, the setting of the chisel, the patient tapping of the hammer. Near the statue a soft felt hat hung from a hook on a rack of wool coats, and he placed the hat on the thick twisting strands of her hair, but this seemed the wrong thing to do, so he put the hat on his own head and looked at her blank eyes for a long time before going downstairs.

14

The story of the motorcyclist's death made the *Sun*'s front page because of the quotes and observations Paul had gathered, and he was happy to see that he had earned second billing in a double byline with Carolyn Wheat. The next story he wrote concerned the cost of houses in Ashland and took the headline AMERICAN DREAM OVER, which seemed to overstate the problem by quite a bit, but Paul already understood the hit-and-miss nature of writing headlines, which sometimes dissolved into jargon (PANEL SLATED TO MULL WOES), or encouraged mayhem in the guise of warning against it (VIOLENCE FEARED AS MARTIAL ARTISTS CONVENE), or adopted the loudmouth tactics of those being written about (MAYOR CALLS FOE BIG LIAR). Even the story about the motorcyclist had carried a misleading headline — CYCLIST DEAD IN LAKE TRAGEDY — which made it seem, first, that the lake had been a factor in the accident, and second, that the lake was named Tragedy.

Nonetheless, Paul had witnessed a fatality, and it gave him the unearned reputation of someone news happens for.

"Come over to my apartment," said Jean Jones, the city editor.

She lived in the building by the river, where he had seen the woman twisting water out of a cloth. Jean and Paul sat on paisley pillows in the front hall and drank iced tea and smoked marijuana from a pipe.

"At bottom it's another sad story, but it illuminates something," said Jean. She tipped her head back and exhaled. "There are two people I know of who have come into this organization and scored a big fatality right away. You're one, and the other is me. To see the broken body is one thing, and to look at it quite another."

Paul glanced into the apartment. Worn olive velvet covered a davenport and two chairs. "It wasn't anything intentional. I happened to get behind the bus. I don't want to make it look like something it wasn't."

She gave him a flat look that, with her dark eyes and full lower lip, created an impression of wistful superiority; she did not want to be wiser than he was, but there it was, a fact that she could do nothing about.

"There are no coincidences," she said. "If you hadn't come along, that story would have ended up being two inches back by the funnies. How stories are played is not an exact science. One time I did a series on the usury rate because I liked the sound of the word 'usury.' It turned out to be very boring, but by then it was too late."

"Tell me about your big fatality," he said.

"I was walking by a house one Friday night when all these kids came running out," said Jean Jones. "I didn't hear the shot. People said I must have heard the shot, but it was not so. A man at a party in the house had taken his life. 'Sometimes I cheat myself' were his words, then *boom*. Everyone ran. They said the gun sounded like a small firecracker."

"Why did he do it?" said Paul.

"Maybe it was a party joke gone awry. That's what I wrote in the story," she said, "a party joke gone awry. People who didn't like the piece said, 'What's the point of this?' But others knew I was on to something."

"What's the rest of the apartment like?"

Jean Jones took a pair of surgical scissors and scratched the burned grass from the bowl of the pipe into an ashtray. "We'll see that another time," she said. "It's a sweet little apartment. People say, 'Don't you want to go to Boston? Don't you want to go to New York?' I say, 'Why would I want to do something like that?' I've lived all my life here. I know the names of the roads. Chopmist ends in a T-intersection with Dark Entry. Dark Entry goes over Red Mountain and splits into Knife Shop and Hairbow. What would I have in Manhattan that I don't have here?"

"Better plays," said Paul.

"True," said Jean Jones.

"Better food."

She refilled the pipe and passed it to Paul. "Say, that reminds me. The Lipizzan stallions are coming to town. Would you care to review them?"

The marijuana had got into his mind, and he raised his arms, which felt big as timbers. "How can I," he said, "when I don't even know what they look like?"

"Where do you think this dope comes from?" she said.

"The past," said Paul.

"Just outside of Ashland."

The stallions performed one night in October at the hockey rink, and Paul got to sit in the penalty box by showing his press pass. White horses with great round bellies and deep necks floated the length of the rink accompanied by waltz music from Vienna. The horses walked on their hind legs, kicked, exhaled clouds of steam, formed parallel lines that drifted closer and then passed through one another like the wandering threads of a dream. The riders wore brown coats and tight white pants and high black boots. An announcer explained that the horses' maneuvers were derived from military enterprises.

Paul drove back to the newspaper after the show and sat down to write his review. He had his notebook, he had a cup of coffee, he had a plastic pack of nearly fluorescent orange crackers with peanut butter. He sat before a black screen at a small metal desk. He had not yet been given his own desk, and he wondered why not. Perhaps they were trying to tell him something by withholding a desk. The time passed but he could think of no words to start with to describe the horses. He decided to look at the national news. With a few clicks of the keys he summoned to his screen the *New York Times* wire service. There was conflict in the Balkans, idiotic bickering in Washington, something amusing in Tucson, and then the service signed off with the words GOODNIGHT ALL POINTS. Chris Bait came over. He had hairy wrists beneath frayed cuffs and was said to have wives and children in two different towns. "Time's up," he said. "What do you have on this Lipizzan thing?"

"Nothing," said Paul.

"We'll fill the hole with wire," said the editor. "I'm not making the pressmen mad over a team of horses that come to town every year."

The writers and editors of the *Sun* regarded deadlines as almost a natural force, fixed and mysterious, and they feared the pressmen, as if proximity to rolling metal had made them severe and magical; as if all a pressman had to do was snap his fingers and a reporter or copyeditor would turn to ink and run down a drain. Back-shop people were unionized, whereas the reporters never would be. There had been discussion of an editorial union several years back, and management had sat down with influential members of the staff and fired them.

Pete Lonborg's dislike of unions was philosophical and rigid.

He saw America as a nation of independent wheeler-dealers, and the idea that someone would need help or contrive to help anyone else just didn't register with him. When churches were burned, when floods wiped out farms — whenever some widely publicized event made people want to make contributions — he would write editorials calling for caution. How, he would write, did helping people prepare them to make their own way? Poorly, at best. He liked the phrase "at best." That and "patently absurd" were said to be his favorites. Something else he liked was predicting that a given phenomenon would end in chaos. (When he spoke this sentiment aloud, as opposed to writing it into an editorial, everyone worked hard to keep from laughing, for Pete had managed to live fifty or sixty years without anyone ever explaining to him that the *ch* in "chaos" was not pronounced like the *ch* in "chair.") He hated the president, despised the senators, loathed the congressmen, and sneered at the state representatives, with some exceptions.

On the night that Paul saw the Lipizzan stallions but failed to think of a word to write about them, Pete Lonborg was working late in his office, standing over a large scale model of Ashland. He called Paul in as Paul was about to punch his time card and leave the building. The model was very detailed. String Lake twisted like an actual string dropped into the landscape, and a windmill stood on top of Red Mountain. The model had cardboard buildings, plaster sidewalks, and plastic trees.

Pete, who was wearing a thalo-green lab coat, dragged strips of newsprint through a bowl of white batter and laid them one on another to build the ridge between Ashland and Damascus.

"This will go in the lobby when I finish it," said Pete.

"You should get a train to run through it," said Paul.

"It's not a toy," said Pete. He looked at Paul sternly — the creases beside his mouth deepened, and a shade seemed to fall over his eyes — and wiped his hands on a towel. "Listen, you did a good job with the motorcycle crash. I have to admit I liked the racquet in the saddlebag. It's the sort of offhand detail that stays in the memory. It's like when my sister drowned. It's now been many years. Her name was Linda, and she was a teacher at the Adelphic School. She'd gone for a swim, and I was a young reporter. 'It's something to do with Linda, Pete,' they told me. 'Something to do with Linda.' Well, I knew it couldn't be good. It's never good news when they preface their remarks like that. I remember I was wearing corduroy, and now I can never see green corduroy without thinking of her. She was a vibrant and loving person, although, to be sure, we had our differences. All her students came to the funeral. What a sight those students made, crowding the street outside the church. It was after she died that I started gathering the capital to buy this newspaper. She had wanted to sing, and she taught science instead, so I vowed I would do what I wanted."

Paul spun the little blades of the windmill. "Where did she live?"

Pete took from his shirt pocket what appeared to be a pen but turned out to be a pointing device that cast a blue dot of light some distance. The light moved across the model of Ashland and stopped on the shore of the lake, opposite Paraffin Park.

"I miss her," he said.

"The Hanover house is over there."

"Right next door. And I've debated with myself whether to put it in the model. My general rule is no private residences, because where do you stop with that? But it's so large that I may make an exception. Are you all right?"

"I drew a total blank on a story tonight."

Pete turned off the blue light by pressing it to the flat of his hand. "You'll get 'em tomorrow, champ."

Loom and Paul sat at a card table in the cupola, shuffling cards printed with obscure questions. The butler, Mr. Freel, brought up a bottle of Lagavulin with two glasses on a tray, then bid them good night and retreated down the stairs. The kerosene lantern burned on the wooden table and the lights of Ashland shone from across the lake.

"There's no mystery," said Loom. "Women die. The cemeteries are full of women, as well as men. Who put you up to asking?"

"No one," said Paul.

"It was Lonborg, wasn't it?" said Loom. "I know it was. Let me tell you something about Peter Lonborg. Let me tell you a little story. Once upon a time he came to me, dead drunk in the dead of the night, and asked me to serve on the board of his newspaper. He begged me, if you want to know. Got down on his knees and followed me around the library like a little short man. And I said, 'Let me tell you a secret, Pete. There are but two or three people in this town who could do that job. And Pete,' I said, 'none of us would take it.'"

"She was his sister," said Paul.

"Who?"

"I'm saying that the woman who lived in my house was Pete's sister."

"And she drowned," said Loom. "She was his sister and by drowning became his meal ticket. And you see this is why I hate this topic. Just talking about it makes me speak meanly. Answer a question. 'At the funeral of Governor Jonathan Belcher of Massachusetts, in 1757, his widow gave away one thousand pairs of . . .'"

"Gloves," guessed Paul.

"Gloves is correct," said Loom. "Now you ask."

"I go again, since I got the answer," said Paul.

"Oh, of course you do," said Loom. "'On Sunday, the twenty-second of January, 1905, seventy workers died when troops fired on a procession led by Father Gapon in St. Petersburg, Russia. This bloody day would come to be known as . . .'"

"Bloody Sunday," said Paul.

"You get all the easy ones."

"Maybe you're reading the wrong side."

"They tend to be either impossible or very easy. Oh — I

know what I was going to ask you. What did you do, exactly, when you broke the law? I never heard the whole story."

"It's pretty boring," said Paul.

"Sketch the highlights."

"I want to hear about Pete's sister."

"I want to hear the crimes."

Paul shuffled the question cards. "Using a middleman in Geneva, I made it look as if a lot of money had been earned by a silk-screening company in Rhode Island."

"What was in it for the Geneva people?" said Loom.

"Six percent. Same as realtors."

"I've never understood money laundering."

"If you can't show an income trail, the IRS plays knick-knack on your head," said Paul.

"And that's all you did?" said Loom. "That's not very much. I thought there was something about forged paintings."

"The media loved the painting angle, but all those charges were dropped. But the paintings were fun, I'll say that. They started out as something to do on the weekend. We'd add the signature 'Fitz Hugh Lane' to old paintings of the shore. We could have done that all the livelong day. Then it got complicated, because we began forging not only signatures but whole paintings."

"Students."

"I'll say what I said then," said Paul. "There were three painters. Two were graduates. One had an MFA."

"From the Rhode Island School of Design."

"Two were graduates, one had an MFA."

"Keep your secrets, I don't blame you."

"I never have gone beyond that. That was the issue once they charged me. The investigators wanted to know who made the pictures and who made the money, and I wouldn't tell. Although finally I told who made the money."

"Doesn't sound like you did anything terrible."

"The law hates forgery. It undermines everything."

"But you didn't tell on the painters."

"I did not."

"Something to hang on to. What kind of things did they paint?"

"We had a guy in Cleveland interested in all Arab subjects painted before the Depression. I mean anything. All he had to see was a photograph, or sometimes just to hear a description. Very terse phone manner. 'Yes.' 'No.' What he did with them I don't know. I think he may have sold them in London."

"When you say Arab subjects . . ."

"Street scenes," said Paul. "A wall, a woman, shadows, a clay vessel. We worked from source books. I would say, 'Do this one.' 'Try combining these two.'"

"My grandparents painted things like that," said Loom. "In Tunis."

"There's a market."

"What gave it away?"

Paul tilted his chair back and planted his knees against the table. The ceiling was painted white, with black gaps between the boards. "Some of the guys in the syndicate never liked the paintings. There was no secret about this. It wasn't what they were used to. They would go out of their way to make disparaging remarks when I came into the room."

"The syndicate? That's what they called it."

"Yeah."

"I like that."

"Now, what about the woman who drowned?"

"She taught science and biology at Adelphic," said Loom. "Her desk was made of black marble that had a curved silver faucet and a gas jet on top. Her name was Linda Tallis."

"But her maiden name was Lonborg."

"That's right," said Loom. "I don't know how old she was. Early thirties would be my guess. Pale face and pale lips and coarse red hair that she wore over her shoulders. There was a photograph of her one year in the annual, wearing a sweater and holding a skull. Everyone liked that picture. My sister and I thought it was great living next door to a teacher, as if it gave us special leverage. Once I went over to the house — your house — and she wasn't home, and her husband gave me my first beer, but I couldn't stand the taste."

"I found carvings in the attic."

"There would be," said Loom. "She drowned in the summer. She died in the lake and they buried her up on Red Mountain. There's nothing else to say about it. My family has always played the villain in Ashland. Some of it's founded and some isn't. I will say this: my father was never anything other than generous with us kids. Now ask me one of those questions."

"'In 1866,'" said Paul, "'the Austrian monk Gregor Mendel laid the groundwork for the theory of heredity with his cross-breeding of . . .'"

"I know this," said Loom. "Chickens?"

"Peas," said Paul.

A lush blue darkness blanketed the meadow as Paul walked home. The constellations of fall turned on their slow wheel — Andromeda in chains, her mother sitting in a chair, Perseus zooming to the rescue. Looking up, he stumbled over a stone bank that had once been the foundation of something.

Paul had a plan. He often had a plan while appearing to play things by luck and accident. Sometimes he had plans that even he did not know about.

He had noticed, as had everyone else, that banks all across the United States were tripping over their own feet to hook new credit-card customers. The operative principle was that of loan-sharking: comically profitable rates in exchange for ready cash and no questions asked. Just by taking the job at the *Ashland Sun*, he had somehow managed to attract the attention of banks in Lincoln, Newark, Fort Lauderdale, and Mexico City, all eager to shoot a little plastic his way.

This shotgun approach not only suggested a reckless lack of safeguards but confirmed Paul's belief that the banks and credit-card companies richly deserved to have a slice of their teeming money diverted to a struggling inn in Belgium, and he knew a retired federal agent in Hammerlea, Vermont, who was said to sell the names and social security numbers of the dead. The agent's name was Shumway, and he had spent so many years monitoring who stood closest to the Cincinnati kingpin Julius Siscovitch that his superiors began to suspect that Shumway himself stood closest to Julius Siscovitch. Paul had met Shumway after the latter had fallen from favor with Washington and been relegated to a supporting role with the President's Organized Crime and Fisheries Task Force, which had become a partner in the Record Family investigation due to its interest in the outrageous manipulations of the shad market of the late eighties. Paul decided to pay Shumway a visit.

He lived outside of Hammerlea, on a road that ran along a ridge with a long valley dropping away to the east. Paul approached the house, which was built in the international style and resembled a junior high school. Shumway's wife said he was out in the field shooting his bow and arrow. Paul walked down behind the house and found Shumway pulling target points from a bobcat poster bound by twin bands of twine to a bale of straw set against a stone wall.

"The arrow breaks if I miss the bale and hit the stone," said Shumway. "My theory is that the cost of new arrows will subconsciously force me to shoot better."

Paul explained who he was, but Shumway did not remember him and had to be reminded.

"I didn't find your situation engaging," said Shumway. He had a gold tooth that flashed in the sun. "You didn't even carry a gun. Pencils and numbers, they're not where it's at. Give me a case with guns, then I'll sit up and take notice."

"I thought you guys didn't care for shootouts."

"Some don't. I happen to."

"Larry Zumwald had a gun."

"I said *carry* a gun, not have a gun. Big difference."

"I threw it away for him," said Paul.

"Why did you do that?"

"He asked me to."

"Larry Zumwald. A third of the people associated with Record were halfwits. Zumwald, Ivan Montgomery, Stevie Shakes."

"But the other two thirds —"

"Well, I'll tell you who I respected, because there were some. Tommy Maynard. Eddie Leblanc. Vito Carmona."

"Line-Item Vito," said Paul. "What about Randall Cochrane, who had been a boxer?"

"He was lost in his scrapbook."

"The gun I threw away was a blue Llama pistol with plastic grips," said Paul. "I put it in a duffel bag and took it on the Block Island ferry. When no one was looking I opened the duffel bag and dropped the gun in the ocean. Then I got out to the island, rented a moped, and took a ride to the Palatine graves."

"You are going counterclockwise in a clockwise world."

Paul hoisted himself up onto the stone wall. "My alumni magazine thinks I brought down Carlo Record."

"Brought down? You couldn't bring down the venetian blinds. What hurt Carlo Record was the same thing that hurts all of them, to wit: they put a bug on everything he ever touched. They even wired his golf cart."

"He's a good golfer for a guy with one arm."

"Not much call for golfing in prison."

"Who's running the thing? Bobby?"

"Nominally. Bobby is weak. Look out for Bobby. A classic fear biter."

"Let me shoot the bow," said Paul.

"I don't want you to break my arrows."

Paul and Shumway walked up and away from the target. Paul strapped the leather guard to the inside of his left forearm and pulled on the three-fingered shooting glove. The bow was an old Shakespeare laminate. Paul lay an arrow across the rest, nocked it to the bowstring, and drew the bow until the tip of his index finger touched the corner of his mouth. He looked neither at the bow nor at the arrow but at the picture of the bobcat.

He put two arrows in the target, and on the third shot his drawing wrist bent, the string slapped the arm guard, and the arrow missed not only the bobcat but the bale and the stone wall. Shumway and Paul climbed over the wall to look for the arrow.

"Where did you learn to shoot?" said Shumway.

"Baptist camp," said Paul. "I'm looking for numbers."

"How many digits?"

"Nine," said Paul. "I need money to take piano lessons."

"It's true that with a few simple tunes under your belt, you might be more fun at parties instead of a wallflower," said Shumway.

"It's time," said Paul. "Because the gang is getting tired of my shadow puppets."

Driving south to Connecticut, he stopped for lunch in a town lined with antique stores, in one of which he found a large cabinet radio with a round and cleverly constructed tuning apparatus. At first glance the tuner seemed to consist solely of a red metal ring marked with the AM frequencies, which could be selected by turning a knob that rotated a needle extending from a central hub. In fact, the red ring was composed of linked segments that opened like a shutter and disappeared into the periphery to reveal a green FM dial, which in turn opened to reveal a blue marine-band dial, and so on.

It was an unusual radio, and he would have bought it right then except that it would not fit in his car.

He got back to Ashland with time to spare before work, so he rented a post office box and then had caraway soup and *túrós délkli* at a Hungarian place in town. That night he covered the school board in Damascus. This was an organization whose devotion to secrecy made meeting coverage a snap. They decided everything beforehand over drinks at the Arandell Tennis

Club and met only to vote without discussion. They fired an English teacher, approved a bid to dredge the pond at the elementary school, and directed the corporate counsel to take depositions for their libel suit against the high school newspaper, all in less than twenty minutes.

Paul wrote the story and made the police and fire calls. There were eleven police stations and three fire departments in the *Sun*'s territory. Calling them usually did not yield much, as the dispatchers had long ago learned to say "All quiet," no matter if town hall was burning and a tiger was on the loose. The more important the development, the less likely a dispatcher would be to give it to a reporter over the phone. Tonight there was a fender bender in Lignum Vitae and strange lights in the sky over Tableville. Paul would have ignored the lights but, as he was getting ready to leave, Chris Bait told him to take a call from a distraught woman. She said a brightly lit craft had hovered over her back yard as she unpinned the wash from her clothesline. Paul took notes but told the woman that he could not make it a story unless she gave her name. She declined, maintaining that people would laugh at her. Paul wrote the story anyway, as it had two sources, the Tableville police and the unnamed woman.

He went home thinking about the old radio he had seen. He had a table model that would have to do for now. He found himself fascinated with American radio, in which the invisible hand of the marketplace had landed its big dumb finger on forceful opinion. Public radio was still reassuringly measured — he got caught up listening to *Cardboard Box Journal,* a series about a family living in a cardboard box — but on the AM dial, whether you were right or wrong did not seem to matter so much as delivering your pronouncements with sneering indifference to the subtleties of existence. He thought of starting his own radio station, with the slogan "All forceful opinion, all the time." He even liked sports radio, although he had little idea who the players under discussion might be; he liked the way the hosts punctuated every third opinion with the phrase "you know what," as in "If I'm Dutch Perez, you know what, I don't love Joey Robineau. I like him, but I do not love him." The commercials were for hospitals and hair treatments, suggesting a listenership of bald men with medical troubles.

When he was ready to sleep he turned the dial to a deejay in Mount Kisco, New York, who droned like narcotics in the grand old FM style. The patter threaded in and out of Paul's dreams, but with such bad hearing he did not like waking up to a quiet house. ". . . We are in the two-thirty hour of a Friday morning . . . wheel turning round and round . . . this is the nighttime voice of the tristate gateway, where the frost is on the passport . . . I don't know about you, but very frankly I've got these strange coarse hairs growing out of my eyebrows . . . they're almost like steel wool, I'm completely mystified . . . driving in tonight, I took a wrong turn and spun completely around . . . it is three-nineteen on some Friday in the October month . . . up next, Kristin Hersh, coming at you in a blazing nightgown . . ."

Scratch the cat slept on Paul whenever possible — in the flat of his back, in the hollow behind his ear, in the sag of blanket over his legs. The bed stood in the corner of the room, and the cat clung to the edge of a marble-topped bureau like a ragged rain cloud, waiting for him to fade into sleep. Paul shoved her away eight or nine times some nights. The cat snarled, gargled, tripped away, lumbered back. She had figured out a way of leaving the house, through a hole in the bathroom floor, for all the great prey outside. But with the cold coming on, she stayed more and more inside and engaged in deluded scuffles with nothing. Paul got used to odd racing sounds and thumping paws. So one night he had the strangest dream. It must have been a dream, although he felt as if he were awake. Outside the window a full moon burned through black branches. The cat was sleeping on Paul's legs, and when Paul turned to wave her away, he saw the hand of a woman standing by the bed in a long white shirt, with two great falls of red hair fanning on either side of a pale and curving forehead.

Her hands pulled at the collar of the shirt. Studs pelted the blanket. Paul sat up in bed and picked up one of the studs. "Men's shirts will wear longer and look better if you repair rips and tears immediately," she said in a low and papery voice. "Why not number each shirt inside the neckband to help keep track?"

Her shoulders twisted free of the shirt, beneath which she wore a dark swimming suit, and with the white shirt drawn like a shawl across her forearms, she took one of his hands in her own. "It's no trick at all to button a stiff tab collar if you wet the tabs slightly," she said.

He eased down the straps of the suit. Her breasts shone softly blue in the dark, and he touched the cold skin of her shoulders. Her eyes sparkled like black stones, round and distant and not looking quite in the same direction. She peeled down the suit, stepped free of it, swung it by a finger, and circled the room slowly, brushing her palm over the marble slab of the bureau. She sat naked on a trunk with her hands folded in her lap. A mirror on the wall above her head gathered the room's shadows. The moon laid strips of light across her knees and toes.

"Who are you?" said Paul. "Are you always here?"

"Is the farm in the sort of community you like?" she said. "Will it be a good place to raise your family?"

III

GLOVES

15

Out in the country west of Tableville, a naturalist in a red wool coat stood in an earthen trough, surrounded by nine neighbors, and swing reporter Paul Emmons, on a road called Whiskers Lane. It was a cold morning and the wind had been blowing hard for days. Paul wore a pair of gloves and the felt hat that he had found in the attic.

"This is where it was?" asked the naturalist.

"And where you're going to make it be again," said a woman named Suzie Turner. She pulled her hands into the cuffs of her coat. "Am I right?"

"Calm down," he said. "I'm a naturalist."

"And I'm an engineer," said his partner.

"We're on your side," said the naturalist.

"We don't take sides," his partner quickly added.

The naturalist dropped to his knees in the bed of the missing river. "What we have here is opportunity as well as misfortune. With the water gone, the vegetation seizes the opportunity to migrate. You can see this happening. This maidenhair fern is making its move."

"That's all academic," said a man named Richard Legros. "Nine months out of every twelve, the last sound we hear at night is the water running over the stones. We want our stream back. A ditch full of ferns won't make us happy. Our children play in that river. Our dogs wade in that river. We have inner tubes. We have canoes. The science of it, we could care less."

"The state of Connecticut is not fighting you on this," said the engineer. "You want to restore the stream. We want to restore the stream."

"Do it, then, right?" said Suzie Turner.

"What my partner and I have to do now," said the engineer, "is go back and study the USGS maps to figure out where this brook came from."

"It's not a brook, it's a river," said Richard Legros. "It courses and rushes."

"You called it a stream," said the engineer. "I'm only going by what you said."

"Semantic arguments will get us nowhere," said the naturalist. "Until we know where the waterway came from, it's wild speculation to say where it's gone. One possibility, the obvious one, is that the river has dried up, in the course of natural events."

The neighbors rolled their eyes and clicked their tongues derisively. "Our weather hasn't been dry," one said. "We've had lots of rain. There's water everywhere. I have water in my basement as we speak."

"Rain and snow are only part of what determines the incidence of surface water," said the naturalist.

"A big part, though," said Suzie Turner.

The naturalist shrugged. "Anybody know what time it is?"

"A quarter to eleven," someone said.

"That's right," said Richard Legros. "Run off to some other site."

"Patience, Rich," said Suzie.

"It's development," he said. "Some developer has blocked our river, and because it's only Tableville, because it's just a pack of disgruntled nobodies in Tableville —"

"The last one on board requests permission to draw up the gangplank," said the engineer.

"I was born here," said Richard Legros. "That house right over there — that is my house. What sort of engineering have you done?"

172

"Coffer dams," said the engineer.

"Oh boy. Here we go."

The engineer dismantled his transit and began packing it back into its aluminum case. "There's only so much abuse I'll stand and take. I work too hard —"

"You do that," said Richard Legros.

The engineer glanced at the forked boughs overhead and walked up the bank and through someone's yard to a blue car with the state seal on the door.

The naturalist looked from the car to the neighbors and back. He started after his partner, but turned at a plastic swing hanging from the branch of a tree. "Has the river ever dried up?" he said. "Even in summer?"

"No," everyone shouted. "Never."

"All right. That is a piece of the puzzle."

After the meeting broke up, Suzie Turner asked Paul into her house. Richard Legros joined them. The three sat in the dining room on wooden chairs with calico cushions tied to the spindles.

"Did we come on too strong?" said Richard.

"You badgered them," said Paul.

"A lot of us did grow up here," he said. "We played in the stream as children, and more than likely when we got our first kiss it was over in the woods across the footbridge. That's where Suzie and I first kissed, although now we are happily married, knock on wood, to other spouses. Right, Suzie? I don't know. Maybe one stream doesn't make a difference in the world, but take it away and you better believe you'll hear a howl from up on Whiskers Lane."

Paul wrote on his notepad. "What did you say? Hear a yell?"

"A howl. Is that too strong?"

"No, 'howl' is good."

"There was even a family called the Crandalls who would baptize people in the stream," said Suzie.

Richard laughed. "God, the Crandalls, that's right! I had forgotten about them. To be honest, though, most people were not fond of the baptisms."

"There was a petition," said Suzie.

"And then the Crandalls moved," said Richard. "It seemed like once they couldn't baptize, the life went out of them. It was sad, in a way, seeing the moving trucks come and go. But you know what they got for that place? A hundred and forty-nine five."

"It's waterfront," said Suzie.

"It *was* waterfront."

"It wouldn't have been such a big deal if they hadn't lived upstream from most of the houses."

Richard took a marbled rubber ball from his pocket and began to squeeze it in his hands. "Maybe we figured their sins would wash down to us."

"It's not that," said Suzie. "But they used oils and so forth. That's my understanding, anyway — that there was anointment going on."

Paul drove away from Whiskers Lane remembering his own baptism. He had been twelve years old. His mother had told him it was important that a person choose baptism and not just have it done routinely at birth, as in other denominations. A gangly minister with bare feet dipped him into a pool of water beneath a false floor behind the altar of a church in Crystal City, near Verona. Bubbles rose around Paul's eyes and he expected that from then on, his prayers would travel first class and win him what he wanted.

The night of his baptism he prayed, for example, that he would be allowed to stay up late and watch *The War of the Worlds* on television. Instead, he had to go to bed at the regular hour. And then two or three years later he sat on the threadbare davenport in the living room in Verona praying that his brother Aaron would not die. In exchange for the favor of Aaron's continued existence, Paul would take the money he had saved from chopping wood and buy a rifle that Aaron had admired in the hardware store in town. Promising the dying boy a gun seemed like a novel approach that might catch God's attention,

174

but as it turned out, God could not be swayed, as Aaron would have been, by the unselfish gift.

"This is yours because I was worried about you," Paul would have said. "You don't even have to let anyone else shoot it. It's all yours."

From the site of the missing river Paul drove up Red Mountain to see Linda Tallis's grave. A small and overgrown cemetery ran parallel to the gravel road between a reservoir and a gray and weathered cluster of summer houses. The cemetery lay open to the road. Frost-canted stones leaned left and right, some with military markers, stars and stakes temporary in appearance. MOTHER read one granite block, surrounded by smaller stones into which one letter each was carved. Evidently this mother had named her children "R," "L," "S," and so on. In another part of the cemetery, the carving on a tapered white tower summarized the life of an old-time couple:

MR. & MRS. HADLIME WERE
NATIVES OF DUTCHESS COU-
NTY NEW YORK, AND REMOVED
TO THIS PLACE SOON AFTER
THEIR MARRIAGE; WHICH
TOOK PLACE MAY 7, 1799;
AND ENGAGED IN THE GLASS
BUSINESS HERE, AND WHERE
THEY BOTH LIVED UNTILL
THEIR DECEASE.

Paul walked over rigid and star-shaped moss through the uneven rows of stones. He felt hindered not by any presence of the dead but by his suspicion that they had all worked hard and led earnest lives of a kind unheard of these days. Liars and losers must have gone around in these bones too, but still, he seemed to move through the dust of a bitterly earned disapproval. In another section he saw the little old man who was the night manager of the motel clipping dead vines from the face of a stone. Precise clicks came from his garden shears. Paul did not disturb him.

Linda had a white stone with the inscription SISTER THOU WAST WILD AND LOVELY. She had been born in December 1939 and had died in August 1967. Dead flowers marked the grave, along with a light blue cigarette pack with a stone inside. The cigarettes had been Gauloises; a winged helmet tilted in flight on the front. Paul brushed the inlaid letters of the gravestone and tried to remember who in Ashland had smoked such cigarettes. Terry? Larry? . . . Lonnie. Lonnie Wheeler, the tall motorcyclist who worked at the hospital. That's right. Having recaptured the name, he tried with less success to imagine the funeral crowd gathered restlessly around the fresh grave of the drowned science teacher.

Paul received three pieces of mail that day: two were credit cards, one silver and one gold, and the third was a letter from Mary in Vertige. He drove up to the house and sat at the table reading the letter, which was typed on onionskin paper with the characters hammered in:

Dear Paul,

A German couple visiting for the weekend went down the river by kayak and into the caves yesterday. They have yet to be found. All of their belongings are upstairs, and the police keep coming by and eating whatever I have just baked. I feel somewhat responsible because when the couple asked me about the caves I said what we always have said — they are safe for people with cave experience [Paul pictured her serious brow and her tongue between her teeth as she backspaced to underline the words] — and of course I gave them a map and warned them about the waterfall. I did everything we always did. I guess the problem is that no one will admit to not having cave experience, at least no one I have ever spoken to. Apparently the couple are of some importance, as journalists from Köln have taken over the third floor in order to follow the search. They are not bad guests but very loud and very agitating to old Rosine. She has been such a help with you gone, but this morning she thoughtlessly dropped a tray of breakfast dishes down the laundry chute. So finally I asked her if something was wrong, and we sat down in the kitchen and she told me a story.

It seems that Rosine's name was Esther until she was six years old. This was in 1942. At that time her parents, in order to save her life, gave her up to the underground, which stipulated that they could not be told where she would be taken. It would be too dangerous if they knew. Esther was given the name Rosine and placed in a convent in Brussels, and when the war ended she waited for her parents to find her, but they never came. It was presumed that they were dead, and that turned out to be true. Her father had simply disappeared, and her mother had died of pneumonia in Charleroi. Rosine's mother had to hide from the Germans in a wet haystack. Can you picture it? After the war ended, Rosine was told that she could be Esther once again and go to live with relatives, but no relatives could be found, and she did not want to be Esther anymore, as being Esther had brought her only trouble. She told me that to this day she is angry at her parents for letting her go. It would have been better for all of them to live or die together, in her view. She apologized for putting the dishes in the laundry but said that she could not stand the sound of the German reporters and their shoes on the stairs. Well, I didn't know what to do. Giving her the day off seemed like a paltry response. So I went outside and found one of the cameramen from Köln smoking by the barn, and I dragged him into the kitchen and told him to sit down opposite Rosine. "Tell him," I said. "Listen to her."

The cameraman had no idea what was coming his way. Rosine repeated the story while he took to walking back and forth the length of the table with his hands fumbling with a light meter he wore on a strap around his neck. He said he had come to find a professor and her husband lost in a cave. That's all he had come for. He said if he could give her back her name, he would do so this moment. Rosine said she wanted more than her name; she wanted her parents. She got up and looked at him across the table. He offered her his hand, but she said a handshake would not bring honor to either of them. So he went out. Then I told her that I would give her the day off, but it would have to wait until tomorrow because I had to run to the doctor in Namur. I am two months pregnant. Please do not interpret this as me wanting you to come back. Cousin Gustave arrived this morning to help deal with the lost Germans. Stay right where you are, thank you, on your doubtful errand. But this is something you are entitled to know, and now you do.

Paul folded the letter and put it back in its airmail envelope. He had no response adequate to the news. He thought of Rosine's mother in hiding, tried to imagine her pushing the hay aside, digging out from under, peering across a quiet barnyard. It is nighttime. Maybe a light is burning. She is wet and hungry and wants only to come out into the air and stand on the ground beneath her feet. Her mouth is dry, her forehead fiercely hot. She breathes deeply, drawing bits of straw into her mouth. Then she tunnels out, pulling hard with her elbows. She rises and pulls her coat tight around her.

Paul's radio was broken, so he turned on the television. A drowsy afternoon movie was on. He turned off the television. He went down to the basement and brought up a green and white bucket. It was quite heavy and he almost lost his balance at the top of the stairway. Then he pried off the lid and began applying skim-coat to the rough walls.

The Ashland police had a mounted brigade that they maintained mostly for show, and they had gathered the schoolchildren of the town to demonstrate the usefulness of horses in police work. A cop in riding boots spoke into a microphone so that the hollow tones of his voice flared over the dead grass and tiered bleachers of Paraffin Park. "Now let's imagine an infant has been born," he said. "The first infant of the new year, here in our hypothetical city. And the mayor wishes to deliver a small gift to the hospital to welcome the child. But here's the catch. A long and bitter strike has divided the hospital food service, and informants have informed police that a small group of union troublemakers plans to block the hospital doors in order to upstage the mayor's visit. Our job is keeping the strikers from the door while allowing the mayor unobstructed access. Again, the solution is equine."

A group of volunteers moved in from the outfield, yelling and waving signs. Meanwhile, three large chestnut horses, each with braided mane, each bearing an officer, trotted sideways out from the third base line to meet them. The officers wore black gloves and snugged their heels smartly against the horses' flanks. Then someone in a blue suit got out of a Lincoln Continental and walked in from shallow right field with a red package in his hands.

Alice Hanover folded down a ballpark seat and sat beside Paul. She had come in a Chris-Craft parka as a representative of the mayor's office.

"This seems like so much propaganda," said Paul.

"I know what you mean."

"My wife is having a baby. She wrote and told me in a letter. Very complicated."

"What's she like? I picture someone with long fingers."

"She has normal fingers," said Paul.

"Where is she again? British Columbia?"

"Belgium."

"Are you going back?"

"I think we're getting divorced."

"You can't leave everything to her," said Alice.

"I just got the letter. It doesn't seem real yet."

"Loom and I have had our times," said Alice. "He was in Looking Glass a couple years ago."

"What's that?"

"A rehab place. He was drinking way too much, but we decided to stay together. My parents were divorced, and I just think it robs the self-confidence of the kids. I wouldn't do that to Faith and Chester. My father used to get plastered and come back and bang on the door. It sounded like he was hitting it with a battering ram. Loom is more moderate these days."

Students behind them chanted, "The people, united, will never be defeated!" and Alice stood and turned around. "Here, stop that," she said. "These are good issues but we'll discuss them later."

"The people, united, would like to see a menu!"

"O.K., very funny, but that's enough, please."

She sat down again.

"You have confidence," said Paul.

"It's all been acquired since."

"The green wallpaper's gone from the house."

"I can't tell you how much better I feel having that place lit up."

"Can you see the lights?"

"From the cupola. What do you do at night?"

"Not much since my radio broke."

"You can get another."

"I've got my eye on one up in Vermont."

Although the police-demonstration story, like the Lipizzaner story, concerned a public display of horsemanship, Paul had no trouble writing it, and he wondered if this was because he had respected the artistry of the Austrians but held the cops in casual disregard, based on the right-wing framework in which they had couched their dressage. Or maybe he was just gaining experience.

There was little time to consider the question, however, because he had to hurry up and write the story of the dry stream of Whiskers Lane. He did so, devising what he considered a catchy beginning ("TABLEVILLE — Once you had a river, now it's gone . . ."), but Chris Bait returned the story for revision with an electronic note saying, "I DON'T LIKE 'YOU' LEDES," which Paul shortened to "I DON'T LIKE 'YOU'" and sent back to Chris Bait.

Then he revised the story and went to see the librarian who ran the newspaper's morgue. She had a chair with casters and she would glide around all day, from her desk to the big black books in which the newspapers were collected to the gray banks of file drawers, pushing along with her feet in red tasseled shoes. The filing seemed inconsistent, and some people thought she threw away stories she did not like, either because of the subject or because of the reporters who had written them. She'd had a nervous breakdown and was often absent. She had introduced Paul to her filing system back when he started, and she had seemed stable enough, but then he did not suppose that such people were always "on."

Now Paul asked to see the newspapers for August of 1967. The librarian pivoted in her chair, rolled to a window, gazed at the cars driving by. "That may be a problem," she said. "We used to have those years on microfiche, but now everything is microfilm."

"I don't mind if it's microfilm," said Paul.

"People don't understand what a good format microfiche was," she said.

A dark hooded console for microfilm viewing stood on a table in a corner of the morgue. Paul threaded the smoky film through terraced axles and beveled glass plates. He turned a crank that made the days and weeks blur past. On Sundays the river of text ran narrow, indicating the fragile passage of the small-format TV magazine. The librarian kept talking while he worked. Evidently the city of Ashland had just given out a press release saying that too much surface water was entering the sewer system, and that a company had been hired to test the sewers by blowing smoke through them. What exactly this smoke would reveal had not been adequately explained, but this was not the librarian's objection. No, what she found annoying was that by the town's own admission, smoke might enter people's houses and cause irritation to their nasal passages. The release said experts would be on hand to distinguish the smoke blown into the sewers from the smoke, for example, of a burning house.

"To think that our elected representatives would arrange to have smoke blown into our houses," she said.

"'Back out of all this now too much for us,'" said Paul.

He found the story where it should have been, and this surprised him. Memory offered one version of the past, gravestones a second, and newspapers a third, and for all the versions to agree seemed a suspicious coincidence.

FORMER TEACHER IS DEAD IN STRING LAKE;
TEAM OF DIVERS LOCATE BODY OF SWIMMER

Linda Tallis had picked mint that day, had supper, gone for a swim at twilight. Divers brought her up near dawn from eleven feet of water a hundred yards from shore. Eleven feet did not seem like a great depth, and yet, Paul had to concede, it was about six too many. Her family, the Lonborgs, had worked in the match factory and then the bobbin factory. She had been the first of them to go to college. A photograph showed her smiling in a striped dress. Another photo showed the glassy murderous surface of the lake. Linda had left parents, a husband (Roman), a brother (Peter Lonborg), and a daughter three years old (Kim). Roman Tallis told police he had been flying a model airplane when the accident happened.

Other stories on the front page told of Yugoslav farmers who were counting on the Lim and Uvac rivers to "stop a horde of large, aggressive mice," of fourteen sky divers who had plunged into Lake Erie and could not be found, and of the release of H. Rap Brown on a gun charge. Paul cranked forward in time. The movies in Ashland included *Dr. Zhivago* ("Zhivago lived only for his exquisite wife Tonya . . . until the moment he saw the enchanting Lara!") and *Africa — Texas Style!* ("He came to tame a bucking bronc called Africa!"), and the fashion news included a trend toward "British-type boots that zip up side and back, or sport wide gored insets." Several days after Linda Tallis's death, Paul found a report of students reading Shelley for her at a memorial service:

> *Oh, there are spirits of the air,*
> *And genii of the evening breeze,*
> *And gentle ghosts, with eyes as fair*
> *As star-beams among twilight trees!*

There were student poems as well:

> *We're sorry, barn*
> *We're sorry, leaves*
> *We're sorry to the humming bees.*

16

November brought its cold sense of important work to do, but the swing reporter had no organized mission. He worked at different hours every day, rarely followed a story to completion, never wore the paper hats of the stuffers anymore, never went down to the pressroom at all, and he used whatever stray computer screen no one else was using. He had still not been given a desk. Most anyone could tell him to relocate and make it stick. One afternoon, while he was working on a story about the misuse of public funds, the arts reviewer, Will Kiwi, bumped him from a terminal. Kiwi disproved occult claims when he was not reviewing the *Fantasticks.* Debunking was his hobby, but he had the bad luck to be in a place where few people made occult claims.

So he upbraided the supermarket tabloids sarcastically, as if anyone in the supermarket believed a word they printed. His column, "Debunker's Corner," appeared on Saturdays. Statues did not cry, saucers did not fly, ghosts did not take off their swimming suits. Nothing walked among us but ourselves. Everything that could be known was known already. And this terminal was his to control. Will and Paul had got off on the wrong foot when Will debunked Paul's credulous report of the UFO buzzing the woman taking her laundry from the line in Tableville. STRANGE LIGHTS MAKE FOR STRANGE JOURNALISM, said the smug headline.

"I'm working here," said Paul.

"Beat it, spaceman," said Will Kiwi.

Paul pointed across the newsroom. "Look! It's the cast of *Camelot*."

"I would buy a whole new pair of shoes just to kick you out of your job," said Kiwi.

Paul closed his notebook, gathered his chewed pencils, and set off to find another computer. He walked past the town reporters, where the prettiest woman in the office sat with her small green galoshes up on her desk, entertaining her comrades with a story from the Tableville weekly in which the same name had been spelled three different ways: "Pocock," "Bocock," and "Pecock." The sports staff ate coffee cake and watched a track meet on television. The morgue librarian conferred with the agriculture reporter, and in so doing she had rolled her chair some fifteen feet into the newsroom, the farthest she could go without it seeming ridiculous that she was still in her own chair.

The librarian and the farm reporter were rumored to be in the middle of an obsessive affair. In an attempt to avoid litigation, the *Sun* allowed no dating or sexual contact between anyone except couples who were already together, and thus "grandfathered in," when the rule went into effect, but this ban had had the contrary effect of making everyone promiscuous.

Paul settled finally into the empty office of the executive managing editor for administration. Few people had a precise understanding of what this person did, and as it was past four o'clock, it was a safe bet she would not be back. The walls of her office were decorated with yellowing cartoons about comical office situations and with pictures of her children in which the flash had often bounced off the children's eyes, making them look like Satan's brood.

Paul called up the story that he was working on and stared at the pulsing letters. This might have been his first exposé but he didn't really have the goods, so he had to word it carefully. "Proviso funds" existed in most town budgets as a place to lay aside money for unforeseen events such as excessive snowfall and water-main breaks, and while seeming sensible enough, these funds in practice amounted to tempting piles of cash whose uses were understood by very few.

It was as if the towns were saying, "These taxes will pay for the fire department, these taxes will pay for education, and these taxes, well, we just don't know *what* we're going to do with these taxes." So if a public safety commissioner in Damascus wanted to buy a rare copy of *Ontwa, Son of the Forest*, by Henry Whiting, or a public works director in Badger Falls decided one slow Friday afternoon to order a Bose Wave radio to find out what all the excitement was about, or if the Homunculus parks department wanted to fly down to St. Lucia, only conscience would have prevented each from saying, "Hey, what about the proviso fund?" And then there was the woodstove. When Paul confronted the city manager of Ashland about a woodstove that had been purchased out of the proviso fund, the city manager drove Paul out to a stick house in the unincorporated village of Dufresne. Upon knocking and entering, they found a small white-haired lady who sat on a couch with an afghan drawn around her shoulders and her left hand groping for a three-legged metal cane that stood, as it happened, on her right side.

"This is my mother," said the city manager. "She can't shake hands with you because of the arthritis. Mother, this is a reporter who wants to know about the woodstove."

"Well, I can too shake hands," she said. She found the cane and rose slowly. She had a good strong grip. "The stove is a hundred percent effective. It accepts the little logs that I can carry myself. You know, I grew up in the Depression, in Parma, Ohio — such a long way off, it seems now — and I can remember my father saying, 'Janey, why don't you take your red wagon down to the depot and see if you can find some coal?' And that's exactly what I would do."

The book, the stove, the Caribbean junket, and the radio all seemed dubious enough purchases, but Pete Lonborg worried about the proviso fund story, for his scorn of elected officials stopped at the borders of the towns in which the *Sun* sold copies. Often when Paul opened the file he would find that Pete had been messing around in it, leaving comments such as "??? — PETE" or "WE CAN'T SAY THIS" scattered throughout the text in the highlighted and nonprinting font known as notes-face. (At least it wasn't supposed to print; some notes-face remarks had got into the newspaper, including, famously, Jean Jones's sensible "HMM . . . SOMEBODY'S LYING," which appeared in a story about Christmas trees stolen from town property.) Lately, Pete had come to the conclusion that the proviso fund story could only mention expenditures that were explicitly barred by town charter. Thus Paul had to read many town charters, which were printed in small type and made him wish that he had never undertaken to write about proviso funds in the first place. Telling the story of the city manager's mother would undermine the enterprise anyway, shifting the reader's sympathy to the corrupt. It certainly shifted Paul's sympathy to the corrupt. For that matter, he was corrupt himself. What business did an unclean accountant have making accusations? All in all, the investigative enthusiasm that he had experienced upon hearing about the parks department looking for rare birds in the rain forest of St. Lucia had evaporated like rain itself.

The story of Linda Tallis, by contrast, remained vivid and strange to his mind. Maybe it fascinated him because he did not have to prove or write it. It had not become a chore in the way that all journalism, no matter how exciting at first, becomes a chore, and quickly, such that a hollow-eyed reporter might respond to the compliment "Good story" by saying, "I hate it." Also, it had the tragic seal of approval, with the angel wings of the dead teacher spreading over the remote chain of events. And all he had to do was find those events and remember them, as he remembered, for example, a pear tree from his youth that had been gauzed over by tent caterpillars, or as he remembered a sickly yellow salve that he had once seen on his older brother Fred's arm after Fred had managed to burn himself with a soldering iron. Paul had mistaken the salve for the burn itself. He had thought for a while that Fred would have to live forever with a wide and glistening scar on his arm.

The next place Paul had to go was Red Mountain Infirmary, where Lonnie Wheeler, the Gauloise smoker, worked. The infirmary — a hospital, really, with an old-fashioned name — stood on a hill beyond the industrial flats of Ashland, where a broken and slat-sided wooden tower leaned dangerously, having long ago spent its usefulness as some component of a rock-crushing business, and where, farther on, a scrap-radiator concern displayed suits of armor on either side of its front door. The connection was not obvious, as the armor did not appear to have been made from scrap-radiator parts.

Paul waited for Lonnie Wheeler in the lobby of the hospital. Small birds hopped from branch to branch in a glass enclosure built into the wall. He watched them until he'd had enough and then began reading old news magazines with nothing of interest in them except the starlet cleavage in the personality roundup. A young child wandered, sighing loudly, among the plastic chairs. A television on the wall played a talk show featuring people who had made big mistakes. A couple sat arguing near Paul. Stop arguing, he thought.

"Well, I can't pull the plug," said the man.

"And I suppose you think I can," said the woman. With her

hands she smoothed a coat — glossy plastic, Mondrian squares — that lay across her lap. "I suppose you think I can march in there and pull the plug like a seasoned professional."

"Of course you realize there probably is no plug, per se," said the man. "In all likelihood neither of us has to literally pull a physical object from, you know, the wall. Maybe just sign a document or two."

"Even signing will be difficult for me," said the woman. "We never should have let him put up the storms."

Paul turned his attention to a poster on the wall for National Ear Week. The auditory canal was too complicated, with all those coils and frail bones that seemed like beach detritus. It was amazing that anyone could hear anything.

Lonnie worked in Housekeeping, and when his shift ended he pushed through double doors carrying a pack of vacuum-cleaner filters. He worked a palm brush over his hair and listened intently to Paul's rambling question.

"They're my cigarettes," he said. "But I didn't know her very well. Mostly the one I knew was her husband. You might say Roman Tallis was my mentor."

"In what?"

"Lots of things. I'm from Tennessee originally. I was just a kid when I came to Ashland."

"And when would that have been?"

"Why do you ask?"

"I'm renting their old house. No reason, really. It's just curiosity."

"Why don't you follow me home?"

As Lonnie drove his motorcycle his coat billowed, making him look like the Michelin man. The Wheelers lived in a Dutch colonial house out past the landfill. Blackbirds paced the spine of the garage and Carrie stood in the wide concrete driveway casting with a fishing pole.

"This isn't broken," she said as Paul got out of his car. "Lonnie, hon, this isn't broken."

"I wasn't having any luck with it," Lonnie said. It was an old bait-casting rig with line as thick as twine.

"You have to feather it. You have to feather it with your thumb. That's the whole trick. Watch me. Watch what I do with my thumb." She drew the rod back with both hands and slowly swung it forward. The shining lure on the line sailed across the grass and landed in a white birdbath.

"How'd you do that?" said Lonnie.

"Here comes supper."

Lonnie tried to cast, but the silver minnow slapped the pavement at his feet and line snarled around the reel. "This is what happened before."

"You're not feathering it, lamb."

They all went into the house, where thick linen curtains covered the windows and stacks of magazines and videocassettes leaned in dim corners. It was one of those extra-warm houses with cooking smells and soft yellow lighting into which you could sink and never be heard from again.

"I was visiting my cousin up here when I met Roman at a construction site," Lonnie told Paul. Lonnie slouched in a chair with his legs propped on a horse-print footstool so that his feet and head were on about the same level. "I remember Roman stepped on a nail that was sticking out of a board. We could see the point had come up right in the middle of his shoe, but when he got free and took off the shoe, the nail had somehow missed him. It was a weird deal. His foot must have been jammed way back in the shoe, I guess. That was the spring of 1966."

"Where was I?" said Carrie. "I wasn't on the scene yet."

"Yeah, you were," said Lonnie. "Because don't you remember? We used to have parties up at the windmill, and Roman would bring the keg."

"Roman liked kids," said Carrie.

"And vice versa," said Lonnie.

Carrie looked at her watch, shook it, and held it to her ear. "Not me."

"You forget."

"I never liked Roman."

"You were in the Glove Club."

"Wait," said Paul.

"Yeah," said Carrie. "You're getting ahead."

"O.K., you're right," said Lonnie. "Let me try again. Let me try again."

"I'm going to start supper," said Carrie. "Why don't we move this party?"

The kitchen had the shadowy and labyrinthine quality of the rest of the house. When Carrie turned the lights on, they were under shelves or recessed so that the light angled and cast shadows. Carrie ran water into an aluminum pot as Lonnie opened the pantry and came out with a glass jar of pasta.

"Roman Tallis carved wood and made stairways," said Lonnie. "He had a liking for young people. He got along better with them than he did with adults. And I don't think this is that unusual among the trades. When we first knew him, he was probably, I don't know, forty-five, and I was nineteen."

"And I was eighteen," said Carrie.

"You get the idea," said Lonnie. "His wife, Linda, was younger than he was, too. I didn't know that much about her background, although I'd heard there'd been some kind of trouble in Montreal when she was a kid. But Roman and Linda, as a family, were . . ."

"Cool," said Carrie. "I think that's fair to say." She turned a burner on under the pot of water.

"How so?" said Paul.

Lonnie dumped the pasta out on a breadboard and began sorting linguine. "They dressed in muslin."

"And they had Slim Harpo records."

"And with their daughter, you know —"

"Kim."

"With Kim there was some concern, because she hadn't learned to walk very well. But they didn't care."

"Couldn't walk," said Paul.

"Well, no, she could walk," said Lonnie. "But she walked you would almost say sideways. It was like one leg wouldn't unbend completely."

"They said she would walk as she needed to walk," said Carrie. "That's what Roman said."

"They wouldn't take her to doctors," said Paul.

"What do you mean?" said Lonnie.

"I'm just guessing."

"They took her to doctors."

"Oh, O.K."

"When the state removed her —" said Carrie.

"But that was later," said Lonnie. "That was not while Linda was alive, Carrie."

"No," said Carrie. "That was later."

"Roman had a gun collection," said Lonnie. "But he didn't have any shells. Nowhere in the house. And he said he had no interest in shooting. He had been in the war and he said he had no interest."

"What war?" said Paul.

"World War Two," said Lonnie. "In the Philippines."

"What did he look like?"

"He had deep creases in his forehead."

"He had huge nostrils," said Carrie. "When he got angry it seemed like he might just inhale everybody in the room." She was slicing tomatoes, and she pointed at Lonnie with the broad-bladed knife. "Tell him about when the cop came. The cop and the cop's gun."

"Go ahead."

"No, you tell it."

"One time a cop came to tell them to turn down the music — 'Baby, Scratch My Back' was playing — and Roman, don't ask me how, but he got the shells out of the guy's gun."

"And then when he left — which is the good part," said Carrie.

"Well, as the cop was leaving, Roman said, 'Don't forget your shells.' And he gave them to him."

"And you saw this," said Paul.

"Oh yes, we both did."

The water boiled, and Carrie dumped Lonnie's breadboard full of pasta into it. "I didn't," she said. "You have me in there all those times I wasn't there. But tell him who called the cops in the first place. Don't forget Gilbert."

"This is where it becomes interesting," said Lonnie. "Roman and Linda happened to live next door to some people named Gilbert and Evelyn Hanover."

"Yes," said Paul. "Them I met."

"Where? She's still alive, you know."

"At Loom and Alice's wedding. Do you know them?"

"We know of them."

"I was the best man."

"Loom thinks highly of himself."

Paul tried to remember where they were in the story. "But you're saying Gilbert called the police about the music."

"Well, we don't know that," said Lonnie.

"Who else, though," said Carrie.

"The real trouble, if you ask me, began when Gilbert decided to paint Linda."

"Well, clearly that was it," said Carrie. "And that's a delicate phrase for what he wanted to do with Linda. He just wanted to get her in his house."

Lonnie poured oil into a frying pan and set the pan on the stove. "It was about paint, and it was also about fucking," he said. "I mean, he did paint her. The portrait hangs in the Saberians Guild, which you can go see."

Carrie chopped garlic with a rapid clatter of the knife. "That could be anybody with hips and knockers."

"It's blurry and violent," said Lonnie. "Gilbert made no claim to realism. But all that summer Gilbert and Linda would be up on the sleeping porch, painting away."

"When you say 'that summer,'" said Paul.

"That she killed herself," said Lonnie.

"If she did," said Carrie.

"Come on," said Lonnie. "There was a note."

"A letter to her daughter."

Lonnie gathered the garlic on the knife blade and put it in the hot oil. "Who could hardly walk, let alone read."

They soon sat down to plates of linguine with garlic and tomatoes. Lonnie uncorked a bottle of red wine and filled three blue tumblers halfway to the top. Carrie tore a loaf of French bread and passed around the pieces.

"So *you're* saying it was a suicide, and *you're* saying it wasn't a suicide," said Paul.

"People considered it as such," said Lonnie.

"Agreed," said Carrie. "And what I'm saying is there is no way to know."

"What reason would she have?"

"That she was sad," said Lonnie. "That she had always been kind of sad. That she was married to Roman. That summer ended, the painting was done."

"And they canned her at Adelphic School," said Carrie.

"Right, that's the other thing."

"Which Evelyn had a hand in," said Carrie.

"Very possibly," said Lonnie.

"Gilbert had embarrassed her, but she couldn't get rid of him, so that only left Linda."

"And all this time you were, what, 'disciples' of Roman?"

"More his friends," said Lonnie. "He didn't really have disciples per se until after the . . . well, and you don't know about this either, I guess, or do you? About the duel."

"The duel," said Paul. "No."

Carrie poured wine into Paul's glass. "After Linda died, Roman got all fixated on having a duel with Gilbert. Isn't that right?"

Lonnie speared pasta with his fork. "He changed his mind at

the last minute, but, yeah, there's no denying he issued the challenge. 'The satisfaction of a gentleman.'"

"I don't remember him changing his mind," said Carrie.

"When the pistols were handed out," said Lonnie. "You don't remember Roman crying? And then we had to give him whiskey from a flask?"

"Maybe you're right."

"I am right," said Lonnie. "I gave him the whiskey because I was his second. I held the pistols. Roman shot first and missed, and then Gilbert got him in the leg."

"Where was this?"

"Up at the windmill," said Carrie. "Linda Tallis was dead, and they should have left it at that. They'd done enough damage. But Roman had to keep pushing and pushing."

"Did it make the newspaper?"

Lonnie shook his head with a weary smile.

"They hushed it up," said Carrie.

Paul washed the supper dishes and Lonnie dried, and then they drove over to the cottage. Loom's dogs trotted around in the weeds with heads held high. They had figured out a way through the invisible fence. Their jaws snapped mechanically in the dark. Once in the house, Paul pulled down the ladder and they brought the statue down into the living room.

"That's Linda," said Carrie. "God almighty."

"But you haven't seen this?" said Paul.

Lonnie knelt to touch the wooden hand that supported the candle. "Gloves," he said.

"What about them?"

"Gloves," said Carrie.

Lonnie took a chair at the trestle table. "The thing you have to remember about that time is how fast everything happened for Roman. His wife died, he found out she'd been sleeping with Gilbert —"

"He knew that," said Carrie. "Everyone did."

"Let's say that it was dramatically underscored," said Lonnie. "And then Gilbert ups and puts a bullet in his leg. It was all just bing bing bing. And finally the state came and took the daughter away because they thought Roman was unfit."

"He *was* unfit, if you ask me," said Carrie. "The state was on to something there."

"He let Kim get grubby," said Lonnie. "And then there was the way she walked. But it almost killed him, and in fact he went out into the woods to die, but instead of dying he had the glove vision. He dreamed of a giant glove that would fit over the five people and protect them."

"Which five?" said Paul.

"Well, let's see," said Lonnie. "He was one, obviously, and Linda was the second, and Kim, and — and — how many have I said?"

"Three," said Paul.

Lonnie counted on his fingers. "Maybe there weren't five . . . because Gilbert would not have been one . . ."

"Maybe it was you and me," said Carrie.

"Or maybe the thumb was empty," said Lonnie. "It matters not. Roman came back from the woods and explained what he had seen. And kids of that time — and I fault myself as much as anyone — were searching for ideas with such a passion that they didn't have to be especially good ideas. If you had an idea and *you* seemed convinced, that's about all it took. I don't know how old you are, but —"

"I just turned forty," said Paul.

"You would have missed it," said Carrie.

"But I mean it," said Lonnie. "People would flock to any new theory. I can remember looking out these windows and seeing nothing but tents and barbecue grills all the way to the water. We called ourselves the Glove Club. Roman would speak on Wednesdays and Sundays. I'm sure that what he said, that his remarks, would seem naive by today's standards, because the country has changed. But I knew people who came here from New Mexico. They stayed through winters they could not believe."

"How long did this go on?"

"Well, let's see." He propped his elbows on his knees and his chin on his fists. "Two years?"

"More or less," said Carrie.

"Eventually some Gurdjieff types moved into Ashland and they were super-aggressive, and the Glove Club lost a lot of members," said Lonnie. "Roman retired to Florida. He wanted to give me this house. But the place gave me the creeps with everyone gone. Still does, really. I could see why Linda might have felt isolated."

"We were criticized for glossing over Linda," said Carrie.

"Criticized by whom?" said Paul.

"Mostly self-criticism."

"We did not gloss her over," said Lonnie. "That was the problem with that group. We should have glossed over a lot more than we did. Linda was gone. Roman was here. I'm sure her life could not have been fun at times. Once, I remember, Roman hit me so hard with an open hand that I went right down on the floor."

Carrie said, "Why, honey?"

"I don't remember," said Lonnie. "Probably I had been using his tools and put them back in the wrong place."

"'Superman, you can be a real prick sometimes,'" said Carrie.

"What's that?" Paul said.

"A punch line."

"But not at the time, you didn't think that of him," said Lonnie. "That's what I'm saying."

"People think the philosophy back then was all love and tranquility, but they forget," said Carrie. "There was a lot of coldness. People sleeping with everybody left and right. Faithfulness was a thing of the past."

"The glove protects the fingers but keeps them from touching," said Lonnie. "Really, Roman was lucky they didn't try to put *him* away. In town, when anybody saw him coming they would cross the street."

"Did he collect stamps?" said Paul.

"Not that I know of," said Lonnie.

"There's an album upstairs, why I ask."

"That was probably Linda's," said Lonnie. "The little girl liked stamps for some reason. I'm just remembering. That Kim loved stamps."

"Where did she go?"

"A foster home?" said Lonnie. "A group home? Wherever they go."

Carrie got up and put her hand on the statue's shoulder. "Let's head out," she said. "I feel like going home and watching some TV."

"What's on?" said Lonnie.

"PBS has that special on the history of the banjo."

They left, and Paul sat wondering what would have become of the story if some snoopy bastard such as himself had not come along to track it down. Then he went down to the workshop for a crowbar. Based on his limited understanding of construction, he did not think that the house would fall if he removed the half-wall in the living room.

He took the crowbar in both hands and broke through the plaster. Strips of horizontal lath banded the space behind it, and Paul found that by hooking the bar under the lath and pulling sharply, he could spring the strips from the studs with sudden jolts that cracked the wall wide open. Shards of plaster bearing the striped imprint of lath crashed around his feet. Dust fogged the room. He knotted a red bandanna at the back of his neck so that its inverted triangle covered his mouth and nose like a bandit's disguise. It thrilled him how little there was to a wall. He imagined taking the house down strip by strip and piece by piece until the events that had gone on within it could float up through the crown of trees and into the blue-black air at the edge of the world.

While Paul was watching the eleven o'clock news he heard a knock at the door. It was the man who had run the raffle at

Hanrahan's, months before. The wooden dollhouse stood beside him on the porch.

"Loom Hanover won this," he said, "but I don't find them home. Can I leave it with you?"

17

Paul's assignment for the next day was to try out some device that the highway department had brought to the Civic Center to persuade people to wear seat belts. Leaving the cottage, he saw the dollhouse and decided to take it over to Loom and Alice's.

The house was heavier than it looked and wired with tiny lights such that an electrical cord kept falling and tangling around his legs as he made his way across the meadow and through the grove.

Alice came to the front door wearing a white T-shirt and a long towel tied at the waist.

"I thought you'd be at work," said Paul.

"They don't need me till later," she said. "I'm ironing my dress."

"Loom won this dollhouse. He said he wanted to donate it to the March of Dimes."

"What?"

"I don't know, I didn't get it."

"Bring it in," said Alice. "The kids will like it."

She had set up her ironing board in the kitchen. Ornette Coleman played on the sound system. Alice glided the iron over a black dress. On the floor, the Labs gagged, first one and then the other, as if holding a conversation.

"I'm glad I caught you in," said Paul.

Alice smiled shyly and pressed a button on the iron that steamed the dress. "I've been wondering when you would."

"And it's good we can talk about it," said Paul.

"We're talking about it this moment."

"Not that we necessarily act on it."

"That's why we talk about it," said Alice. "So we don't act on it."

"It's nature. It's not something you control."

"Nature is a riot."

"It's a stitch," said Paul.

Alice bore down with the prow of the iron. Ornette Coleman played the saxophone like someone applying sandpaper to a ray of light.

She took her dress by the shoulders and swept it away from the ironing board. "There, all ironed," she said.

"Maybe we should dance," said Paul.

"I make my own hours."

The knot of the towel pressed against his hip as they moved to the music. Her damp hair brushed his face. Holding her hand felt very good. It was hard to believe that holding a hand could have so much meaning after all this time.

They went to the bedroom. The bed was old and had spiraling wooden posts. They got undressed and under a bedspread with a compass pattern as a cold and cloudy light filtered through trees and windows. He was ready, she was ready, and then he wasn't ready, and then he was far from ready.

"I'm apprehensive," he said.

"Me too."

"I'm listening for cars."

But that wasn't all. He was afraid of Alice herself, set back by the evident unity of her life, which he had admired for years and years.

He dressed and apologized. She apologized too. Their apologies went back and forth and they both wanted the same thing, which was for him to be out of the house and far away.

The Civic Center was a large steel barn between Ashland and Damascus. Inside, a man from the highway department tended a trailer-mounted device called the Convincer. A caged cockpit with a black vinyl seat and shoulder harness stood at the top of steeply slanted metal rails.

"Have you had many customers?" said Paul.

"Some," said the man. "A lot of them had the spit knocked right out of their mouths."

Paul climbed a metal ladder into the cage and fastened the seat belt and shoulder harness. The Home Show was coming up, and he could see refrigerators in the distance.

"Are you ready up there?" said the man. "You don't have to do this if you don't want to. It's a lot worse than anyone expects."

"Let's go," said Paul.

"Do you have a heart condition?"

"Heart's fine."

"Any pens or pencils in your pocket?"

Paul shook his head with his mouth clamped shut to keep the spit inside.

The man from the highway department gripped a red-handled lever and drew it back. The cage screamed down the rails and slammed into a metal wall. Paul's mind left him momentarily. He couldn't remember what day it was or why he had come. Nothing hurt especially, but everything seemed to shake. He staggered down from the contraption and heard the ratcheting sound of the chain drawing the cage back up.

"That's the equivalent of five miles an hour," said the man. "So just imagine if it were thirty-five or, you know, eighty."

"I know," said Paul. "Can I go again?"

The next time Paul and Alice were alone was on a Sunday in December. A drinking session the night before had produced a hazy plan in which Paul, Loom, and Alice would drive up to Vermont in Loom and Alice's station wagon to pick up the radio that had intrigued Paul. But an emergency arose on Sunday morning and Loom would have to fly down to Buenos Aires, where the construction of a bearing factory for Ashland

Fastener and Binder had been stopped due to a shipment of faulty reenforcement rods from Pennsylvania. The rods were coated in epoxy, but in transit the epoxy had chipped off and the building officials in Buenos Aires were refusing to approve their use, while the project manager insisted the chips and dents would do nothing to undermine the stability of the concrete. It was a standoff.

Loom flew to JFK in a Cessna operating out of the airfield in Ashland, and Paul and Alice departed for Vermont in the wood-paneled station wagon. Faith and Chester were staying with a friend who, according to Alice, looked like Patti Smith, and all her children looked like Patti Smith.

"I like Patti Smith," said Paul.

"So do I," said Alice. "Why 'Summer Cannibals' did not become a hit is beyond my understanding. It was the perfect beach song."

The winter sun swept like spokes across the windshield. It had snowed days before, and the snow lay in crested banks along the highway. Paul and Alice were both hung over and a little unwound.

The store in Vermont sold vintage clothing and radios. Soft white slips dangled on ribbon straps above flesh-colored Bake-lite radios. It was one of those fussy antique stores with hostile warnings posted every few yards.

WOULD YOU TAKE A TEN PERCENT PAY CUT?
THEN <u>WHY</u> ASK ME TO
DON'T TOUCH IT UNLESS YOU MEAN BUSINESS

The consumer who has decided to buy something he does not remotely need might have one of two extreme reactions on arriving at some later date to make the purchase. Either the item in question will seem shabby and overpriced, and the trip itself a fool's errand bordering on the fraudulent, or the item will seem even finer and more ingenious than the consumer had remembered it being. Paul's reaction to the radio fell into the second category. The oak cabinet gleamed, the round tuner seemed as wittily deceitful as a false panel in an old house, and the marine band, whatever it might bring in, struck Paul as an especially exhilarating band. He pictured himself and Alice in the radio's green glow, listening to a clipped and suspenseful report of an icy sea rescue in which not everyone would be saved. The correspondent's voice in this daydream was British, for some reason. Alice would tug anxiously on the strap of a thin, soft garment like the ones hanging from pegs in the antique store.

"Does it work?" said Paul.

The owner of the store plugged in the radio and found a music station on which Kenny Rogers and Dolly Parton sang that song the chorus of which had always sounded to Paul like "island dentistry."

"I hate to let it go," said the owner, a middle-aged man in a chamois-cloth shirt. "I've got one just like it at home."

"Can you do anything with the price?" said Paul.

"Why'd you have to ask that? Now I don't feel like selling it to you."

"You're the owner."

"I'll pretend you never said it."

Paul paid with one of his credit cards, and the owner helped carry the radio out to the car. An old couple in scarves and overcoats were looking at a butter churn on the sidewalk.

"It's a nice churn," said the man.

It was late afternoon. Alice and Paul stopped at a lighted rink outside the town of Wetsell and rented ice skates. "We're closing pretty soon," said a boy in a purple stocking cap pulled down to his eyes. Alice and Paul raced over the ice holding gloved hands as wind burned their faces. Eventually the boy wobbled out onto the ice and said they were closing. When Paul and Alice got back in the car, it would not start. Paul lifted the hood and tugged on a web of rubbery black wires until his knuckles scraped the engine block. He closed the hood. The boy in the stocking cap was drawing a wooden shutter over the counter where they had rented the skates.

"I can't help you," he said. He looked not at Paul but above him. "We don't have a telephone. My brother doesn't want one. He's got a phobia about people making calls."

"We're stranded," said Paul.

"I'm closing now," said the boy. "Probably I'll see my brother back in town. Maybe he can help you."

"Why don't you give us a ride?"

"My brother wouldn't go for that."

The boy locked up and drove off. The sun was almost down and the hills were dark and deeply wooded. Paul swore and hit the hood of the station wagon with his fist.

"Don't hit the car," said Alice. "There's nothing to be gained by that."

They sat in the front seat eating pretzels from a bag. The radio lay heavily in the gloom of the back. Just as they were setting off to walk into town a tow truck arrived. A man with a crew cut and wire-rim glasses rolled the window down.

"I'm Leif," he said. "I believe you and my brother Toby are acquainted."

The brothers got out of the truck. Leif started a generator on the back and pulled red and black cables from a reel. Toby opened the hood of the car and shined a flashlight inside. Leif handed Toby the toothed clamps on the ends of the cables and Toby squeezed them open and attached one to a battery terminal and one to the frame of the car.

"We'll let them get to know each other," said Leif. "What do you think, Toby?"

"Alternator looks like to me."

"Yes," said Leif. He walked around the station wagon with his hands clasped behind his back. "Could be the alternator, could be the generator, could be a host of things." He looked in the back window. "What's this, an old casket of some sort?"

"A radio," said Paul.

"What do you do with a radio like that?"

"Play it," said Paul.

"Where you folks from?" said Leif.

"Connecticut."

"We're lucky you came along," said Alice.

"Everybody breaks down on Sunday night," said Leif.

"Leif owns the gas station and the skating," said Toby.

Paul got into the station wagon and turned the key. The engine started, but a needle on a gauge showed that the battery was not charging.

"What did I tell you," said Toby.

"Can we get home?" said Alice. "Can we make it back to Connecticut?"

"Unlikely, yet not impossible," said Leif. "But listen to me. Now that it's going, you cannot let it idle down and stop. And it's not like it's idling well."

"It's idling rough," said Toby.

"What happens if we do stop?" said Paul.

"Will get real quiet," said Leif.

The trip home proved arduous and brittle, with Alice taking obsessive care to keep the car running. Before touching the brake, she would push the transmission into neutral and step on the gas. They talked very little, the better to monitor the idle.

"I have land over in New Hampshire," said Paul after they had been driving half an hour.

"Is there a cabin?"

"We talked about one."

The car rolled through empty towns in the dark. Outside Brattleboro, a deer broke from the black trees into the cones of headlight where they could see the whites of its eyes and the muscles of its flanks. Alice kicked the brake pedal. The station wagon racked and skidded. Time slowed way down. They could have counted the burrs in the golden coat. The deer's waxy black hooves cleared the fender of the car and Alice turned into the skid, as one is supposed to. The deer stood staring from an avenue of tree trunks.

In Ashland again, Alice parked the car at the porch of Paul's house and they walked with vibrating legs across the snow and away from the radio. It was one-thirty in the morning. In the house, Paul had left lights on in odd places, which seemed to damage his credibility.

"Who's this?" said Alice. She stood undoing her coat before the statue in the corner of the living room.

"Linda Tallis," said Paul. "She lived in this house before Loom's family bought it."

Alice stroked the face of the statue. "I've heard bits and pieces," she said. "She overdosed on pills."

"She drowned in the lake."

"Why was I thinking pills? I guess I associate the sixties with pills."

Paul led Alice into the bedroom, where he opened the trunk that the woman in his dream had used as a bench.

"I think these are her clothes," he said.

There seems to be something identifiable about clothes that have been put away because someone died. Light touches them a certain way, imparting a dull blue sheen, and the folded edges are frail with the years.

Alice took a lavender dress from the trunk. "Turn your back," she said.

"I'll get us something to drink." Paul went downstairs to the kitchen, where, after a moment, he heard Alice's belt buckle crack against the floorboards.

When he returned she had put on the dress and was looking into the mirror on the wall above the trunk. He buttoned her up and she turned toward him. The neckline of the gown was low, in a modest way, and trimmed with a ruff of gauzy linen. The dress of the science teacher appeared to free Alice from the tension of the long drive and from the rules and history she had known. Her eyes held longing and sadness and seemed to offer passage through time. A wide ribbon circled her waist and Paul pulled it tight and tied it. He kissed her face while holding her shoulders. Her hair, redolent of the ice rink's cold wind, fell long and black and thick over his hands. She reached behind, feeling for the trunk's leather lid, faltering, finding it, lowering the lid slowly so that it closed with no sound, or none that he could hear. She sat down on the rounded surface, drew up her left leg so that her heel rested on the edge of the trunk, and wrapped her hands around her knee. Her right leg extended, relaxed and open, foot to the floor, and the fullness of the lavender dress covered everything above her shins. She smiled, said it was cold in the house, and he knelt before her, and she let go her knee and pulled him close. She whispered something in his ear that he could not understand. He asked her to repeat what she had said, but he still could not make it out. She said it over and over until he began to love the sound itself, the roll and hiss of her breath.

In the morning he made coffee and toasted thick slices of bread on the gas stove. He brought the food to the bed. They ate and talked above the radio and then they got up and put away the lavender dress. They put on their clothes and went outside, where it was cold and where the broken-down car sat like a lump in the driveway.

"It's the Mir station wagon," said Paul.

Alice let down the tailgate. "You know what I felt like?" she said. "Like one of those storm fronts."

Paul slid the radio over the gap between the bed of the station wagon and the tailgate. "Like on a map."

"Yeah," said Alice. "Over Canada."

They set the radio against the living room wall near the fireplace. Paul turned it on and dialed in a station from Manhattan on which an orchestra played "The Celery Stalks at Midnight." They danced to that and left each other in a state of ardent confusion. In late morning a wrecker came to take away the station wagon.

18

Because the egotist habitually perceives himself at the hub of the functioning world, it is hard for him to know when he has truly fallen into something. He may even ignore the evidence out of some false or compensatory attempt at modesty. So Paul expected nothing but a good time when, in January, Ashland Fastener and Binder threw a party in a stone church for the twenty-fifth anniversary of the factory's conversion to the manufacture of fasteners.

Loom wore a tuxedo and seemed to forget or disregard whatever tendency toward abstinence he had learned at the Looking Glass clinic, but then, it was an easy night on which to drink. Caterers offered whiskey and champagne and deviled eggs, and nostalgia hung like an oily film in the vault of the church. To avoid drinking in this setting, you would have needed the determination of Theognis, a Greek poet whom Paul had read long ago and whose insistent verses about when to drink from the wine bowl and when to stop drinking from the wine bowl suggested a writer with a big bad habit.

At a table beneath stained-glass windows, Paul sat with Loom and two veterans of the fastener trade — Ernie Warwick and Lester Cranston — and a manager in the Switch-Barter division named Mimi Austin, who wore a red sequined dress and drank her champagne through a straw.

Loom introduced Paul to his colleagues. "He wrote about that stream that went away in Tableville."

"Whatever happened with that?" said Mimi Austin.

"They don't know," said Paul. "Where's Alice?"

"Home," said Loom.

"Let me tell you about this kid Loom," said Ernie Warwick. "From the time he came into this company, he made the most of a difficult situation. He could have done whatever he wanted, but he never let that stop him."

"I don't follow you," said Mimi. Her blunt finger stoppered the straw as beads of champagne fell slowly into her glass.

"Money was never the issue," Ernie said. "He came into this company green as a blade of grass, and his old father told him, 'Take any job you want. Hell, take my job.' And what do you think he chose?"

"You have it all wrong," said Loom.

"Night watchman," said Ernie. "And don't be shy about it. You said, 'Father, make me a night watchman.'"

"Wrong," said Loom.

"I believe I heard it with my very ears," said Ernie.

"He told *me*," said Loom.

"It amounts to the same thing," said Lester Cranston. "You did become the night watchman."

"Which put us in a dilemma," said Ernie, "because at the Hanover plant, night watchmen get initiated."

"I admit we try to rattle them a little bit," said Lester. "It's just the way it's always been done, and I expect always will."

"Hazing," said Paul.

"Hazing, sure, though we call it initiation," said Ernie.

"Let's have a drink," said Mimi. "Here's to twenty-five years of hard labor."

"So we asked ourselves, Should we initiate the boss's son?" said Ernie. "Maybe we'd get fired. Or should we forget what we had always done?"

"Our theory was, skip what we had done," said Lester Cranston.

"Sure, to save our jobs," said Ernie. "But then Loom came to us, and this you can't deny, and he said, 'Boys, we all put our pants on the same way.'"

"Meaning . . . ," said Mimi.

"The feet go out the holes," said Paul.

"So then," said Ernie, "we thought, 'Hell, that being the case, we have no choice but to initiate him.' So first we told him the story of Bitter Charles."

"How does that go?" said Paul.

"Lay off," said Loom.

"The story will fall flat without it," said Ernie Warwick.

"Don't tell it."

"Very quickly, then," said Ernie. "A summary. A long time ago in the bobbin works there was a young man named Charles, who one day came down with a fever and asked to be excused from the lathe shop. But Ambrose Hanover — this would be Loom's great-uncle or something, right, Loomis?"

"Stop, Ernie."

"Just one little bit, then I'm done," said Ernie. "Ambrose Hanover said that if Charles left, he could just keep going. So he didn't leave, and the fever got worse, and, long story short, Charles fell into his lathe and lost a hand. After that, they didn't know what to do with him, so they made him night watchman, and the legend goes that he still haunts the plant, looking for the bloody remains of his hand."

"I never heard that," said Mimi.

"It's a myth," said Loom.

"Not entirely," said Lester Cranston. "There's a shred of truth in it."

"And then what we do," said Ernie, "we put a rubber hand in the guy's lunch pail for him to find later, when everybody's gone."

"Where do you get the hand?" said Paul.

"Mail-order house."

"What did you do, Loom?" said Mimi.

"I didn't want you to tell that," said Loom.

"Why not?" said Ernie Warwick.

"It's a free party," said Lester Cranston.

"He took French leave," said Ernie.

"I left the plant," said Loom. "I went over to a fortuneteller who had a storefront on Harp Street where she sold beer and told fortunes."

"Madame Fleming," said Lester.

"I ducked into her place and sat on a bench in the front of the house until eventually she came out and read my fortune for five bucks."

"I'll bet it was just really general," said Mimi Austin.

"She looked at my palm and said I had a great sorrow in my life. And then she said for five more dollars she would pray for the sorrowful thing to pack up and move along."

"Did you pay the extra five?" said Paul.

"I didn't," said Loom. "I mean, it could have applied to anybody. So I went back to the plant, but unfortunately I had let the door lock behind me. So I had to jump up on a barrel and break a window to get in. But it worked out all right, since I was able to report the broken window as if I had happened on it instead of causing it."

Ernie Warwick stood and hugged Loom's head to his chest. "We forgive you," he said.

"Let go of me," said Loom. "Mimi, would you take Paul and show him the carvings on the chancel? I want a word with Ernie and Lester."

Mimi stood unsteadily with a bottle of champagne and two glasses. She led Paul up a side corridor of the church and into a little room with a picture of Jesus raising his left index finger as if something had just occurred to him.

"I thought we were going to the chancel," said Paul.

"What is a chancel?" said Mimi.

"I don't know."

"Well, I don't either. And one thing you find out about Loom over the years is that when you don't know what he means, you shouldn't ask."

They sat on carpeting in the corner of the room. Mimi poured champagne and then shook a vial of powder over the glasses.

"It's a buffered pain reliever," she said. "Keeps the hang-over away."

They drained the glasses.

"What do you do in the Switch-Barter division?"

"I'm a troubleshooter," said Mimi.

She opened a handbag, took out a tube of lipstick, and twisted it.

"Here goes," she said.

She began drawing on his forehead with the lipstick. He tried to raise his hands, but his arms seemed to be under water.

"Happy new year," she said.

Mimi left. A swarm of images moved through Paul's mind. The gouge with the wicker handle, the lavender dress that Alice had worn, the bathtub full of groundcover in Providence. "Get me out of this," he said to the picture of Jesus, and it seemed to speak.

"You'll be all right," it said. "You're the actor James Mason."

"This has been a magical day," said Paul.

He got up slowly and made his way down the hallway and back to the party lights. "Club soda, please," he said to an impassive bartender.

"You're shut off. You have writing on your head."

"I'm James Mason."

The bartender wiped his hands on the edge of a tablecloth and proceeded to hustle James Mason down the center aisle of the old church. Everyone cheered. When they got to the front doors the bartender kicked one open and pitched him off the steps and onto the sharp cold stones of the parking lot.

Paul got up and went for a walk. He was confused about the direction in which he was going. The skin of his hands stung. He ended up near a dumpster at the back of the church. It was a large dumpster with an 800 number to call to have it taken away. He did not know what to do next.

"Hell, I'm losing my mind," he said.

Mimi Austin found him and drove him home in her car. Paul

sat in the passenger seat with the ghost dress swaying before his eyes. "What did you put in my drink?"

She smiled sympathetically as they waited for the light in the center of Ashland. "Tranquilizer," she said. "Were you really a member of organized crime?"

"I went to an induction ceremony once, but it wasn't me being inducted," said Paul. "The tent kept flapping in the wind, and the orchestra played the Canon in D Major."

"That happens to be one of my favorite songs," said Mimi. "Loom is agitated. You have to leave Alice alone."

"Did he say that?"

"He didn't have to," said Mimi. "It's written all over your face." She flipped down the passenger-side visor, which had an oval mirror attached. He could see the red letters on his forehead.

"Having fun?" said Paul.

Mimi turned a corner and let the steering wheel roll back on its own. "I've had better times." Her hands hovered inches from the wheel with fingers spread. "Once I even rode a ferris wheel."

Paul woke up in the morning without any memory of arriving home and went into the bathroom to scrub the words ASK ALICE off his forehead. He felt so lousy even his feet felt lousy. His head ached, in waves. Carrie Wheeler came by while he was eating breakfast in the kitchen.

"What happened?" she said. "You look bad."

"I went to the Fastener and Binder party," said Paul. "I got hooked up with some woman named Mimi."

"Mmm," said Carrie. He poured some coffee for her, and she got up to find the milk. "Mimi Austin, probably," she said, with her head in the refrigerator.

"That's right," said Paul.

Carrie brought milk to the table and poured it into her coffee until it was very light. "The fasteners are a pretty wet crowd."

"She spiked my drink," said Paul.

"I did a great license photo one time of Mimi. She's pretty in a hard sort of way."

"Loom set me up."

"I thought you were friends."

"He has his reasons."

"We all have reasons. Listen, I found out something about Linda Tallis. Do you remember when we talked about the letter she wrote?"

Paul held his coffee cup to his forehead. "Not really."

"Sure you do," she said. She got up, ran a dishtowel under the faucet, and rubbed it gently over his wrists. "The letter that Roman found after she died. Well, there's a lawyer in town who might have a copy. He's very old, and it's hard to keep him on the subject. The letter to the daughter, Kim."

"On the other hand, the hell with it," said Paul. "What is Ashland to me?"

"It's only a town."

"It's twisted."

She opened her handbag and took out a pen and a notebook. "I'm just going to jot down that lawyer's name on a piece of paper. Then, if you want it, it will be there."

"You could leave tomorrow. You could go to California. You could go to New Orleans."

"Too shaky for one, too hot for the other. Don't you read about California? People kill each other for no reason on their complicated freeway system."

"You could go to New Hampshire. I have property there, which I would let go for a bag of shells."

"You're confusing your interests and mine."

"I think you're right."

He walked her outside, and they stood on the porch listening to the wind coming down from the head of the lake. Tree limbs bent and gritty snow struck their faces.

"They're calling for a nor'easter," said Carrie.

By evening it was snowing hard and the wind pressed steadily against the cottage. Paul built a fire, drank tea, and listened to the old radio. He worked on a jigsaw puzzle he had found in a musty box in the attic: a deer standing in a swamp. The pieces were thick and they locked together with quiet snapping sounds. He found the corners and set them where he estimated they would be when the puzzle was finished. The radio's dial glowed softly in the corner by the fireplace, and twisters of snow moved past the windows.

It was very pleasant to be recovering from a hangover in a snowstorm. His head did not ache anymore, and the cold sweat had evaporated from his skin. He sat at the hearth watching the fire. How amazing fire was, when looked at carefully. The logs that had burned first had crumbled into a bed of a hundred distinct coals across which heat shuddered as if they were still joined. The coals flashed from orange to black to orange again, faster than he could follow. Someone should study this, if they hadn't already. He had a fleeting understanding that even the uglier events could be redeemed via humble activities. He put on boots and a coat and went out into the weather. The wind roared with a steady sound as if it would never stop. Fallen branches lay half buried in blue-white snow.

Back inside, he yanked the door shut, and hung his coat on the statue of Linda Tallis. When he turned to the table she was sitting there in a long flannel shirt and thick gray socks.

"I find it interesting that you can change clothes," he said. He took the coat from the statue and threw it on the davenport. "This is you, you know."

"Lipstick or rouge," she said, "rub with lard or vaseline. Wash in hot suds. Do not use soap first; it may set the stain."

"Too late," he said. "Do you speak other than in housekeeping lingo?"

"Empty tin cans also make attractive flowerpots," she said. "Paint the top and base a bright, child's-favorite color. Paint the sides in stripes. Glue the seat of a doll onto the center of the top and presto! That youngster of yours owns a very dream of a toy chest."

"I could get a Ouija board," said Paul.

"Why spend money on expensive new things to achieve effects that new colors can give you?"

Her eyes met his impersonally, in the way that the eyes of photographs sometimes seem to.

"What color?" he said.

"Child's-favorite color," she said.

"Your child."

"Presto."

"Where is she?"

"Off for the weekend?" she said.

"It's been longer than that."

"Men like sweater girls," said Linda. "That's what is meant by the 'stitch in time.'"

"I'll look for her," said Paul. "I don't know that I can find her, but I'll try."

She went to the fireplace and rubbed her hands before the flames. "Even rain-soaked veils will regain their look of newness with this treatment."

"Can I ask you a question?" said Paul.

She nodded.

"Did you want to die?"

She stared into the fire. "'If your basement runs a fever,' warns a leading furnace company, 'your furnace is sick.'"

"Well, I understand. I think I do. Come to bed."

In the bedroom, Paul brushed her hair. It was long and dry and pale red. The brush was hers. He fell asleep with his arm around her waist, but when he woke up in the middle of the night there was no one there. He went out to the living room to turn the radio off. The puzzle was finished but for one piece, which he pressed into place.

Loom and Paul repaired their friendship in wary increments. They played racquetball at the Y, they hiked on Red Mountain, they toured the Fastener and Binder plant. This was a deafening place, with signs printed in two colors and three languages reminding everyone to wear their earplugs and take their salt pills from strategically located dispensers. Loom had a discount arrangement with the Big Man clothing company, and everyone, even the women, wore Big Man pants and shirts, of dark primary colors, as they stood wearing goggles before laser cutters or glided around behind steel carts stacked with pallets of insectile components. A large tent of fogged plastic stood in the center of the floor, where a construction crew was preparing to install a punch press that in theory would allow the company to shoulder its way into the coveted Emery clip trade. Paul and Loom stood by an air compressor inside the tent and watched the workers jackhammering the floor. Chisel placement seemed an art or science. The floor fell away in jagged pieces under the bell-like striking of the hammers. Then one of the thick green air hoses that fed the jackhammers broke at a brass coupling and rose like a cobra before the hypnotized workers. It slashed the plastic tent and turned its attention toward the humans, but Paul quickly reached down and shut off the compressor.

This thoughtless but useful act seemed to dissolve their enmity entirely, and one Sunday in March Loom took Paul to see the birthplace of Nathan Hale. Loom's blue car traveled the back roads of Coventry before arriving at a dark red house with nine windows in the front. Dead leaves blew across the lane. There were gardens and fields and a large stone pyramid marking the graves of a horse and a dog that had belonged to someone named George Dudley Seymour. Seymour had been the New Haven lawyer and Hale devotee who bought the house in 1914 and who finally persuaded the U.S. Post Office to issue a half-cent Hale stamp in 1925.

"Take away Seymour, and Hale would be less known," said Loom. "Seymour did a lot of good, and I'll be the first to say that, but I resent all this Seymourabilia. That's the term I've coined for it. The man's horse died, but the connection with Nathan Hale seems tenuous."

A woman named Debbie Wyoming, of Johnstown, Pennsylvania, led their tour. She was president of Nathan Hale International and the honorary guide for the weekend.

"He never lived in this house," she said as they stood in the hallway outside the room where Nathan Hale's father, as justice of the peace, had once rendered judgment on his fellow citizens. "This house would have been nearing completion when the British hanged Nathan Hale as a spy, at what is now Sixty-sixth Street and Third Avenue in Manhattan. He had gone to Long Island disguised as a Dutch teacher, all dressed in brown. Hale's last words — 'I regret that I have only one life,' and so forth — may have been borrowed from Addison's verse tragedy about the Roman statesman Cato, which the patriot may have read at Yale. He believed strongly in the education of the female. He was a lively young man who liked to jump into hogsheads and then jump out of them. This portrait here is of one of his nieces, who served as a missionary in China. She is believed to be the lady in white who can sometimes be seen in the rooms upstairs. Back then, even young girls were expected to girdle their bodies."

"What is a hogshead?" Loom asked.

"A barrel or cask holding anywhere from sixty-three to one hundred and forty gallons."

Later she showed them Hale's Bible, his deerskin trunk, a tracing of his silhouette on a door, and the silver shoe buckles that he gave to a comrade for safekeeping before going on his spy journey.

"In Johnstown we call our annual pageant Silver Buckles," said the woman. "Nathan Hale had his Yale diploma with him when he was captured. They left him hanging many days."

"I'm related to him," said Loom.

"What's your name?"

"Hanover."

"Hanover . . . Well, I won't say you're *not* related to him, but much research remains to be done."

On the way back to Ashland, Loom told Paul that he was sorry about what happened at the fastener party. "Mimi went overboard. She's a great manager, but sometimes she shows poor judgment."

"I've already forgotten it."

"You can't bring back the past. There's nothing there. It's only trouble. And I don't mean with Alice. It's bad enough with Alice. But it's just as bad with this woman who died so long ago that no one even remembers."

"I've seen her."

"You worry me."

"I've talked to her."

"You worry the living fuck out of me. When you begin talking to statues it's time to think of getting your own place."

"She wants me to find her daughter. I don't know. Could this be? Maybe I'm dreaming."

"Yeah, maybe."

"Where is the daughter?"

"No one knows. That's what foster homes are for. They foster disappearance. I've learned two things from running the company, and they are, one, any decision is better than no decision, and two, once you've decided something, close your ear even to the best counterargument. Nietzsche knew this well. He said even the will to stupidity is better than constant rehashing."

"What did you mean when you said that Linda Tallis became her brother's meal ticket?"

"Pete Lonborg sued my parents. That's all I meant."

"On what grounds?"

"I don't know. Wrongful dismissal?"

Loom swung by the Red Mountain windmill on the way back to Ashland. Paul had not seen it before except in Pete's model. Fieldstones formed a round tower and four blades curved to cup the wind. A padlock secured the wooden door. Loom and Paul climbed onto a ledge from which Loom pulled himself up and through a window in the stone. Paul took the edge of a blade in both hands and pushed. The blades moved and the hub turned, silver and black; the windmill must have been taken care of by someone, or perhaps a committee. Loom called from overhead. Paul walked around the ledge to find him. He had got up inside the windmill and stood now in a high opening on the side of the tower opposite the blades.

Without warning, Loom jumped from the tower, sailing down with the red plaid lining of his hunting jacket streaming at his sides. His glasses and white hair flashed in orange sunlight. The blue shadow of a blade crawled across the round rough stones mortared into the tower. Loom cleared the ledge on which Paul stood, but he fell back against it after landing in the weeds.

Paul climbed down and stood over him. "Are you all right?" he said.

"I've been drinking less and finding that I have tremendous energy."

19

The man who selected the *Sun*'s letters to the editor took two months' leave to have his hips replaced, and Paul assumed his duties. Those who wrote to the editor seemed to fall into two categories: people who either did not understand or else ignored the traditional purpose of letters to the editor, and people so given to scornful, know-it-all language that they had a hard time specifying what it was they were scorning. An example of the first category would be a letter from a Brenda Forest in Lignum Vitae, who wrote, "Where and when did the practice of putting candles on birthday cakes originate? It seems like this would have resulted in a lot of needless fires in earlier times before flame-retardant building materials. Don't you think?" Instances of the second category were more common and used such similar language that they might have all been written by the same person. "Once again the *Sun* betrays its socialist agenda with a rank cornucopia of broad claims. One is tempted to conclude that the privileges of the media monopoly have befuddled your brains such that you can no longer discern between reasoned reportage and character assassination, while predictably championing the unholy triptych of Mayor Clifton 'Moscow on Line Two' Trammell, Hamlet Counsel Marjorie 'Hearts and Flowers' Wessels, and Fire Warden Steve 'No Nickname' Plum. If you would take the time to study the severance clause of the United States Constitution, which clearly you have not, you would understand that, in a federal republic, fiduciary authority resides EXCLUSIVELY in the so-called third tier, and that your arguments ring hollow indeed."

One of the best parts of letters duty was writing the headlines, which, as his bad-hipped predecessor had emphasized, must reflect the content and spirit of the letters no matter how derogatory that content or spirit might be to the newspaper itself.

SUN IS FULL OF BEANS

LANDFILL EDITORIAL EXAMPLE OF BIG-LIE TECHNIQUE

HOME PLANET OF MONA CHAREN IS QUESTIONED

READER SEEKS ORIGIN OF CANDLE TRADITION

The working conditions were also better compared with those of the reporters. Editorial-page employees worked on the top floor of the Temple of Hephaestus and came in at nine or nine-thirty, or ten or ten-thirty. It didn't really matter when they came in, as long as they were present for the eleven o'clock conference, during which they ate crullers, drank coffee, and engaged in wistful discussions of what it must be like to live in other countries. They took long lunches, followed by a quiet time. Sometimes they made brainstorming field trips to a religious shrine called the Embers. Paul thought that the letter writers who accused the *Sun* of satanic opposition to gun proliferation would have had their eyes opened if they could have seen the editorial-page department discussing the flat tax in a sun-streaked alcove full of biblical icons, but he also liked the department's principled refusal to cite these meditative trips in its favor.

One Thursday, after completing the letters layout for the next day, Paul went to see the lawyer whose name Carrie Wheeler had written on a piece of paper. Rudolph Bonner had an office in a Queen Anne–style house between a car wash and the unemployment office.

"I'm glad you came in," he told Paul. "I think I can find the information you seek, but I wonder if you would first witness some signatures for me. Normally I would call on my paralegal, Helen, but she's having an operation."

"What kind of signatures?"

"Well, I have a man and woman in the other room who are signing over their house and assets to their son," said the lawyer. "It's a routine maneuver, for tax purposes. The boy won't really control anything."

The family sat at a long glass table in a conference room. The man and woman stood as the boy scribbled in a coloring book.

"This is Paul Emmons," said the lawyer. "He has come to the office on other matters but has kindly agreed to serve as a witness."

The couple signed some papers and the boy wrote his name in big block letters. "Things are going to be very different from here on out," he said.

After the strange ceremony ended and the family had gone, Rudolph Bonner asked Paul to come by the Saberians Guild sometime and give a luncheon talk. "I've heard that you're in the Witness Security program," he said. "Everyone is curious about how that works. You must have some interesting anecdotes."

"Not really," said Paul. "See, no one is supposed to know about that."

"Oh, I'm sorry," said the lawyer. "But don't worry. The Saberians Guild is a secret society."

"I don't think so," said Paul.

"Can't twist your arm then?"

"It's an honor to be asked."

The court papers in Pete Lonborg's suit against the Hanovers had been sealed for twenty-one years, but those years had elapsed, and so Rudolph Bonner allowed Paul to look through a red folder in a small room with law books and a bumper-pool table. Paul spread the documents on the green felt between the rubber-ringed bumpers. The estate of Linda Tallis, with Pete Lonborg as its executor, had charged Gilbert and Evelyn Hanover and the board of the Adelphic School with conspiring to remove Linda Tallis from her position as teacher of the biological and chemical sciences, resulting in a projected loss of salary and pension equaling $348,312.92. The lawsuit said the school board had fired Mrs. Tallis "at the behest of Gilbert Hanover, whose bodily relationship with Mrs. Tallis, as documented in Appendix D, had in the bracing light of day caused him second thoughts, leading to a desire on his part to have Mrs. Tallis dismissed from the school."

Paul found Linda's letter to her daughter beneath a receipt for a dozen white roses.

August 11, 1967

Dear Kim:

Your father was born in 1922 in a house with high windows. The reason the windows were high was because your father's people were servants, and the family they worked for did not want them to be able to look out the windows and see anything that was going on in the big house. They worked for the Pail family. The Pails had once been partners with the Hanovers in the match factory and with good luck had sold out handsomely to the Hanovers before the necrosis scandal kicked the stock price down to nothing. Old Man Pail invested most of the money with the Cicada Trust Company, on 17th Street in New York City, but Cicada failed in the Panic of 1907, and the testimony of Stephen and Everett Pail would help pass the Aldrich-Vreeland Act. The family was also mentioned in a folk waltz of the time, whose chorus went, "If I fall out of New York City / I will land on soft moss." This is because the Pails had hedged their bets by buying stock in an obscure maker of vacuum tubes called the Moss Transfer Company, whose orders soared out of sight after the saving of the SS *Republic* via radio messages in 1909. Then the Depression wiped the Pails out and the big house burned. Your father was seven years old. The last Pail man left Ashland many years ago, signing the land and remaining house on String Lake over to his servants' family. You come from worker stock, which may help you in the uncertain years ahead.

Your father returned home from World War Two at the age of twenty-three and went to work as a carpenter. He had an artistic touch, and to have a staircase finished by Roman Tallis became a point of status around Ashland. He was lanky and arrogant, I am told, with dark skin and small and indifferent eyes that were yet very piercing. I first saw Roman in 1955 when I was a junior in high school. The debate team was debating in the high school auditorium one afternoon when he appeared in the doorway to bid on the carving of the Spartan's head that still resides today over the stage. (Roman was not happy with the way the carving came out, but then, he was never happy with the way things turned out.) I was on that debate team. I even remember the question: "Resolved: Hunger is unavoidable."

I knew two things only about Roman: that he had been in the war and that he was "the staircase man." Someone said he worked without shoes, unless it was too cold, and though still young, we understood this to be a hopeless affectation. Yet high school no longer held my attention. I had the bad luck of being born with good looks, and I write this neither with pride nor with feeling sorry for myself. Maybe a little of feeling sorry for myself. Just by looking at people I could transport them to a blurry dreamland that made it impossible for them to talk to me. You will see someday that I am right, because it will happen to you. I could not blink or hum or whistle a popular song without creating waves of anxiety. I had done nothing to earn anyone's love or terror, but neither was there anything I could do to stop it. Even Mr. Tremlow had gone crazy. He had been the voice coach, and once after a chorus recital in Amherst during my sophomore year he stole me away to Montreal. I went along, foolishly, because he was a handsome man and always carried a walking stick. We slept together in the Excelsior Hotel in Montreal, where on the third night he was so crazed that he struck me with the walking stick hard enough to break the blood vessels in my leg. The house detective heard my screams and Mr. Tremlow went to jail for one year and I came home to Ashland on a bus. No one blamed me, but really they did, they blamed my body and my face and the wicked city of Montreal. My parents — your grandparents — then took me out of the chorus and put me in the debate team.

Roman and I dated off and on during my senior year in high school, and later when I went to teachers' college in Waterbury. I liked the fact that he was older, because he did not stand around with his hands in his pockets like the kids my own age. We were married in 1961 at St. Polycarp of Smyrna's in Ashland. Your Uncle Pete served as best man, for Roman had no friends then, just as he has no friends today. That's what the model airplanes are about, being friendless. We moved into the house with high windows in which I stand writing this letter. Roman had been charming at first and he convinced me (how? I have often wondered) that he was carefree, but his charm was the charm of the selfish, bound to turn cold when I proved myself to be an insufficient mirror of his own self.

I enjoyed teaching but found myself with nothing to do all summer, and I could not accept the fact that I was supposed to lock myself away in the woods in this bizarre damp house, scrubbing and cooking and being the maid of a self-obsessed woodcarver. I felt like Snow White but without the peasant dresses and helpful animals. Nothing had prepared me for this. The housewife scandal will be found out one day. No one sees it for what it is. Roman's mother would come over and write lists of things I had done wrong with the house. She gave me a little book called *A Treasury of Household Hints,* which I found to be such a vicious joke that one endless morning I decided to tear the pages out and burn them one by one in the fireplace. The only reason I didn't go ahead with this plan was because of the drawings in the book, of a slender housewife with thin dresses and a small, heart-shaped face. I suppose I saw myself in that incompetent mascot. In one illustration she had accidentally sewn the hem of her dress to the slipcover of an upholstered chair, so that, as she backed away from the chair, the dress was pulled away from her in front and drawn tight behind. She was knock-kneed in high heels, material had unfurled on the floor around her, and this illustration made me very restless. I am looking at it right now and I feel some of the old restlessness. Maybe it has to do with the hint on the opposite page: "For smooth running and lightning speed, *oil that typewriter.* First, the bearings at each end of the cylinder; then, the little roller that engages the ratchet wheel to lock the lines in position; finally, all ribbon-spool shafts and gear shafts . . ." Anyway, I did not burn the book, and later I was standing barefoot at the kitchen counter and grinding carrots for you, my little one, when Gil Hanover came from next door with ink on his hands looking for Roman. He said he was thinking about an easel that would fold out of the wall somehow. I showed him in the little book how seltzer could be used to remove ink, and I showed him the picture of the woman who had sewn herself to the arm of the chair. He said that the only solution would be for her to take the dress off, and then he got embarrassed, he even blushed, the blood rose wonderfully to his ears, and I gave him one very small kiss, and he asked if I would like to pose for a painting. So you see that it was my mistake, and whatever you hear about the way things happened, from whomever you hear it, you must know, my love, the mistake belongs to me. The Hanover family has taken too much grief from this town, and if I leave no other impression, let me say they are people like any other who have been bestowed by the accident of God with all sorts of cash.

You may ask where your father was when all this was happening. Florida, sometimes. One of his clients was putting up an enormous house on the island of Captiva. The trim alone took a year because the client insisted that the woodwork depict scenes from Florida history and that these carvings be rendered by Roman and no one else. This was fine with Roman. In his mind, he had been gone from Ashland for a long time, and to make the withdrawal physical while also having his artistry recognized was just the thing he was after. He knew that the client considered him a backwoods craftsman, and he had to make his style cruder, but that was a small price to pay for the project at hand. The house was finished last year, and Roman came home looking very old to me. With him he brought model airplanes, money, and a suitcase full of marijuana, which he sold for a good profit, using the money to cut down trees for air space to fly his planes in. He did not care about Gilbert's paintings of me. Or if he did, he didn't say so. Our relationship lasted one year, stopping only when Gilbert's wife threatened to pull her money from the bobbin company as it stood poised for conversion to a maker of modern fasteners instead of the futureless sewing machine parts. "People don't sew the way they used to," Gilbert would say, "but there will always be a need for fasteners." I felt bad for Gilbert's children, and I knew that I was eroding my credibility as a teacher. I knew it very well. But the summers are so hot and still here. Sometimes the lake sits for hours with nothing moving on the surface. You get to wishing even a leaf would fall on the water.

The letter did not seem to be over — it ended at the bottom of a page and there was no closing — but Paul could not find more pages. As he thumbed through the worn and yellowed papers, Rudolph Bonner came in and suggested a game of bumper pool. Paul played with an empty feeling that made his game much better than it would have been otherwise. He could not think of anything that remained to be found out except the whereabouts of the daughter, and his shooting was instinctive and true. But the old lawyer was very good. After all, it was his table, and he was a master of the carom.

"Where would I find Kim Tallis?" said Paul.

Rudolph Bonner peered down the length of the cue. "I'll ask around."

Paul and Alice's affair might have been over. It would have been a natural time for it to end. Instead, in April, they went away for a weekend on the New Hampshire coast. Alice had told Loom that she was going to a conference of municipalities.

Paul parked his car, and he and Alice walked through the rain to a hotel across the road from the ocean. The hotel was a modern concrete building with brass lanterns on either side of the front door. A staircase climbed to the lobby, and at the top of the stairs there was a small bar where they ordered grass-flavored vodka and talked about whether to go ahead with what they were clearly going to go ahead with. Soon they were kissing in full view of half a dozen jaded but interested customers. Then they realized that they had forgot protection, and they went out to a vast supermarket with a pharmacy, a bookstore, a coffee bar, and a travel agency. It was seven o'clock, dark, and still raining, and a neon light blinked off and on in no evident rhythm above the bright and colorful condom display. Speakers played music, announced discounts, and relayed obviously counterfeit messages summoning security guards to the main floor of what was obviously a one-story building. Paul considered the talismanic power of condoms. If they bought them, he and Alice would make love; if not, not; and he had the strange impression that the latex prophylactics were calling the shots. Meanwhile, the music playing in the supermarket changed from an instrumental version of "Smoke on the Water" to an instrumental version of "Stop! In the Name of Love." That this song should be playing at this moment seemed incredible to Paul, but he knew that they were not going to stop — not for love, not for any reason.

If anything, he thought, love was a reason not to stop, and maybe he had known this all along.

They returned to the hotel, where the clerk gave them a key to a room on the seventh floor. Paul turned the key in the lock and pushed the door open, but someone had already taken possession of the room and left it an impressive mess. Clothes and newspapers covered the furniture, suitcases lay open-mouthed on the floor, and a pair of pants that looked big enough for both of them sprawled across the bed. The large pants had an obscene and elusive quality. It was as if the room contained the ugly mechanics of the lies they would tell, and the lies were large, with large pants.

They laughed nervously and went back down in the elevator. "Someone's already taken that room," said Alice.

"An obese man," said Paul.

"I apologize on behalf of the hotel," said the clerk. He glanced about and brought from under the counter a red velvet box from which he produced a golden key. "This," he said quietly, "will open what is surely the finest room in the hotel, with perhaps the most comprehensive view of the sea."

"I like this hotel," said Paul.

"Do I know you?" said the clerk.

Paul said he didn't.

The second room was on the corner of the ninth floor. Six windows looked out on the ocean, each in a narrow alcove above a bench seat, and through streaks of rain they could see the lighted shoreline. They put their bags down and Alice called the desk. "Please send up candles, extra pillows, and something good to drink," she said.

"You order well," said Paul.

"It's my hobby."

"I always think I should be serving them."

"What kind of hotel would that be?"

"It would be different," said Paul. "I guess it's because I've been on the other side of the desk, and I know what the staff thinks."

"Which is what?"

"Oh, you know. That the customers are frivolous deviants. That they're wastrels."

"I don't think I should like going to your hotel."

Paul smiled, for with this mild argument their relationship seemed to be moving on to the next plane. "We're not usually overbooked," he said.

They lit the candles and drank from narrow glasses. Alice wore a soft faded nightgown and slouched charmingly in a window seat with her black hair falling down her back.

"We might have ended up together," said Paul.

"You don't have to say that."

20

The water looked rough and green as glass in the morning. Alice drew her knees under her nightgown and rested her forehead on her hands. "I woke up and cried," she said. "I felt awfully alone last night about three. I replayed everything I've done wrong to the kids. I've been mean to Chester. I let Faith go outside when she was only two years old and it was too cold. I've neglected them by being here with you. This weekend they're with Loom's mother, who hates them. She braids Faith's hair so tight it pulls her eyes back."

They left the hotel around eleven o'clock and found two men in tan trenchcoats waiting on the sidewalk. Paul knew one of the men, Ivan Montgomery, but not the other.

"Go back inside," he said to Alice.

The men steered him toward a big white Oldsmobile parked by a lobster restaurant. Paul broke from their grip and ran into the restaurant. He entered the kitchen, where he found a maze of silver cooking machines and two cooks in T-shirts and white hats. "Where is the back way?" he said.

"What?" said one of the cooks.

"I'm being chased. Where's the back way?"

"Do you mean the pantry?"

"The back way, for Christ's sake, the — the back door."

"I don't know that there is a back door," said the cook. "But who you should ask is Alf. Because I've only been here two weeks. Alfie, Alfie, this guy is looking for the back door. Says somebody's after him."

Alf stirred a big bowl of dough. He glanced at Paul. "We're not really open," he said. "There used to be a back door, but they bricked it up when they redid the place."

"A closet," said Paul. "A crawl space." Then Ivan Montgomery and the unknown man found their way into the kitchen. One took Paul by the arm and swung him into the side of a refrigerator. The cooks picked up their spatulas and moved away from the violence. The two men brought Paul out through the empty restaurant and shoved him into the back seat of the Olds.

Ivan did the driving. He was a short, thick-chested man with a birthmark over his eye. The other man leaned his head back and went to sleep.

"Who's your friend, Ivan?" said Paul.

"A young guy, name of Bodoni," said Ivan. "He's got an interesting style which people mistake for him being slow-witted. But actually I think he's going to be very good one day. He'll go farther than I have, and that's all right. I'm not looking for the high-pressure situations anymore. Just collecting doomed losers like you is fine with me. Me and Cathy got a kid now. It rearranges your point of view."

"Oh, I'm sure," said Paul. "So what's going to happen?"

"You mean with schools?" said Ivan. "My mother's really pushing for Sacred Heart, but there's supposed to be an excellent Montessori nearby. So we'll see. I mean, there's no rush, the boy's only three. Still, they say you have to plan far in advance. That's how come you can't get out back there. Child-lock doors."

"Where are we going?"

Ivan yawned. "Well, I think we're supposed to kill you," he said. He picked up a clipboard and read it. "Let's see. Yeah. Says right here: 'Kill Nash.' But first we're going to switch cars, because your wife probably called the cops."

"She's not my wife," said Paul.

"Oh really."

"How'd you know where I was?"

"We know where everybody is," said Ivan. "You should have done your time like a brave scout. Accountants don't go to bad prisons. Then you wouldn't be in this trap. Did you hear Carlo got out? He's real sick, Paul. They don't think he has that long left in him."

"What about Leblanc?"

"Jail."

Paul named some others and Ivan said, "Jail also."

"Carlo got out because he's sick?"

"That's not unheard of," said Ivan. "They don't do it for an earache or something. But they do it. The court has to be convinced that something is really wrong."

"Let me talk to him," said Paul. "How sick is he?"

"I'm not his physician," said Ivan. "And you can't talk to him. Your days of talking are over."

Ivan got off the interstate south of Boston. Bodoni woke up and gave him directions to a warehouse in the woods. They pulled up to a building with no windows and the younger hood got out, unlocked a bay door, and pushed it open. Ivan let off the brake and the car coasted into the building, where a dozen men worked on cars in various stages of disassembly. Bodoni closed the door and came up to the driver's window.

"Paul wants to talk to the Pliers," said Ivan. "What do you say, should we let him?"

"I thought he was going to," said Bodoni.

"You have to learn how to play along," said Ivan. "That's one thing you haven't learned yet. What Bodoni's saying, Paul, is that while you're requesting to see the boss, ironically, the boss wants to see you."

"Why?"

"Maybe he's still mad about that time he bounced those checks," said Ivan. "Remember that?"

"That was bank error, if you'll think back."

"Oh, it's never you, is it? It's never Paul Nash. *Im*possible. But the Shepherd sure thought it was you. He said, 'Where is that accountant? I'm going to grind his elbows.'" Ivan laughed hard, although neither Paul nor Bodoni laughed at all. "Shoot . . . ," said Ivan.

"And I told him not to write checks," said Paul. "There were stacks of cash lying around, on top of which he could have walked into any store and come out with what he wanted."

"He wouldn't, though," said Ivan. "Too proud."

"Wait a minute," said Bodoni. "Are you telling me that Carlo Record writes a check, and somehow there ain't enough funds, and the bank returns it?"

"You've been going to night school," said Ivan.

"I know what he means," said Paul. "He's asking why a bank would risk making the Shepherd mad."

"Don't paraphrase me, cadaver," said Bodoni. "But basically, yeah, that is my question."

"Well, hell, it's all computers, isn't it?" said Ivan.

"A lot of it is," said Paul.

"That's all it is anymore," said Ivan. "A computer can't tell Carlo Record from Johnny Two-Bit."

"There are even computers in use here," said Bodoni.

"Where are we?" said Paul.

"This is what is known as a chop shop," said Bodoni. "But that doesn't do it justice."

Ivan and Paul got out of the car, and Bodoni gave them hard hats to wear. Then the three of them walked among the bays.

"Vehicles make their way here from all over the eastern seaboard," said Bodoni. "My job has two parts, evaluation and assignment. Let's say for the sake of argument a red Mercedes comes down from Beacon Hill. The first question I have to ask myself is if the car has any value in one piece. Let's say down in Florida they're dying for red Mercedeses. Which is true. Pretty car, looks great in the sun, all the elements are there. But then, when I look closely, maybe the car's not in such good shape as I thought. Maybe it's rusted out. Maybe they had to fuck up the interior too bad when they stole it. In other words, just because a car might be a sophisticated marque, you can't assume it won't get chopped. Give you an example — and this happens routinely — a kid comes in a couple months ago with a 'ninety-two Rolls. He's all excited. All he has to do is put out his hand to get the big money. But the car had body dents all over, the bumper was hanging down, the master cylinder was finished. Really, I've seen better-looking Subarus. So I said, 'I don't know how you got this car here, over mountains perhaps, but the most I can offer you is two hundred bucks, and that's mainly to send you on your way.' And you know where that Rolls is now? Everywhere. Minnesota, New York, Utah, Pennsylvania. So even the best brands might get broken up. That's when I turn to somebody like Jim Gordon. Excuse me, James, what do we have going today?"

"It's a Volkswagen Passat, Mr. Bodoni," said an earnest mechanic with an earring. "Until recently it belonged to a Viveca Belgeddes in Albany, New York. She took care of it, too, which is always nice to see. Right now what I'm doing is removing the body panels."

"They'll go to Europe, am I right?"

"Yes."

"And how's it going?"

"Well, it isn't easy, but I feel that I'm learning as I go," said James. "Volkswagen's got their own way of doing everything, that's for sure."

"Good, good," said Bodoni, as a big Chrysler wheeled across the clean cement floor. "Well, here you are, Paul. I won't be going on the next leg of your journey. My place is here. Good luck to you in hell. They say it ain't so bad once you get used to the climate. Now give me back the hard hat."

Ivan let Paul drive. The car glided across the coastal plain. Ivan used the armrest and sighed.

Carlo had closed up the house in South County and now lived with his son, Bobby, to be close to the hospital. At first the plan had been for Paul and Ivan to drive straight down to Bobby's house. But Ivan kept getting calls on his cell phone, and just outside of Providence the meeting was postponed. Ivan and Paul were told to go back to Boston and get a room at the King Philip Hotel.

"What are we doing that for?" said Paul.

"The King Philip is the only place Bobby can remember the name of," explained Ivan.

This was an old hotel with murals of stag hunting, but it was less fun than it might have been, given the circumstances. Then there was some mix-up that led the hotel staff to believe that the room had been taken by Ivan and his son. Bellhops kept turning up with child gifts — a toy lobster, a Little Mermaid coloring book — and although Ivan explained each time that there was no child, the message never seemed to filter through the system.

"I guess the Shepherd had to go to the hospital for his treatment today," said Ivan while playing solitaire by the window. "Well, actually, he's not getting treatments. The terms of his release specify treatments, but he doesn't believe in them, so he just goes to the hospital and hangs around."

"Doing what?" said Paul.

"Reads magazines," said Ivan. "The fact is he's not in his right mind. I wouldn't expect too much when you see him tomorrow. If tomorrow it is."

That evening they went out to dinner at a restaurant in Chelsea, where big-screen televisions showed horse races from across the country, and afterward they drove back downtown and sat on a bench in the Public Garden drinking beer. "Want to go back to the room?" said Ivan. "What do you want to do? Play cards? Watch the TV?"

"Sure, I'll play cards with you," said Paul.

The game that Ivan liked was California Jack. Paul could not stop reorganizing his cards, sometimes by suit and sometimes by rank. He was all nerves. Around ten o'clock a bellhop knocked on the door, set a tray of milk and cookies on a desk, and left with a puzzled expression.

"My wife is pregnant," said Paul.

"Congratulations," said Ivan, "but I wish you hadn't told me. What if I have to shoot you? I mean, I'd do it, but it would not be pleasant . . . Aren't these mini-bars great? They're just so goddamned convenient. You want something?"

"Scotch," said Paul. "I can't decide what's going to happen. He wouldn't want to talk to me if he just wanted me dead. He wouldn't put me up in this hotel."

"Well, you just don't know," said Ivan. "With Carlo anymore you just do not know. I don't mean he's going to put a cigarette out in your eye or anything. He's got more class than that. So where is your wife? Why are you running around with stray skirt when you got a pregnant wife of your own?"

"Mary and I split up," said Paul. "She went back to Spokane before we knew she was pregnant."

"We know where she is."

"You might be omniscient, but you don't know anything about cards," said Paul.

"I always wanted to be a croupier."

"Mary deserves better than I've given her."

"Lynette Fromme deserves better than you've given Mary."

"Who?"

"That Manson follower who tried to kill Gerald Ford," said Ivan. "Christ, there's no common base of knowledge anymore. Why don't you call her? Why don't you call Mary? Let the Shepherd pay the toll. This is your night."

Paul called the next morning, reaching Mary's cousin Gustave, who said that the pregnancy was going well — she was in her seventh month — and that a diamond merchant from up north had taken an interest in the inn. Gustave said that Mary and the diamond man had gone out for a drive just now. Then Paul called Carrie and Lonnie Wheeler and asked them to feed the cat until he got back.

On the way to Providence, Ivan Montgomery explained Bobby Record's career. Some years before, Bobby had been made overseer of the unruly Boston branch of the Record syndicate, which included Tommy "Mirage" Maynard, who once killed a schnauzer with his hands; and Bobby's mission had, it could now be said, never gone well. Most people sympathized with his situation without necessarily having much fondness for Bobby himself. It had been inevitable that sooner or later the Boston affiliates would take a look around, realize how much bigger a territory they were working ("Say, Jerry, take a look at these figures . . ."), and cast aside their historical and artificial allegiance to quaint little Providence. It so happened that this shift happened on Bobby's watch. With Carlo in prison, the Boston gangsters started doing whatever they felt like doing without giving a thought to Bobby Record. Or if they did give him a thought, it was only to devise some interesting way to needle him. For example, there was a guy named Yancy Delessandro from Buffalo whom Bobby had never got along with, and Tommy Mirage would get Bobby on the phone and go on at great length about what a swell guy Yancy Delessandro was. Another time, some of the Bostonians went ahead and killed a diamond swallower whose fate Bobby had wanted to ponder over the weekend. The upshot was that Bobby was left with not much to do in his big house in Providence, and real estate was flat, so the only way he could have sold the place was by taking a big loss. And then his wife, Karen, was killed in a plane crash, a sad and mysterious event that was said to have ruined Bobby, for he had loved her in his way.

"Karen came to our house once," said Paul. "She was just a kid. She didn't like our music."

"She's not a kid anymore."

"They all came over and gave us a cat."

"Funny story about that cat," said Ivan. "Bobby wanted to kill it. He wanted us to hire some guys to go and kill your cat. This was last winter. But a bunch of us convinced him that it was stupid."

"It was Bobby, Karen, Carlo, and Miriam."

"Let me ask you something. Give me your honest opinion of Miriam's singing."

"I don't know," said Paul. "I guess I think of it the same way I think of pole-vaulting. It's interesting that it can be done, but it doesn't engage me."

"That's kind of what I think too."

Part of Bobby's problem within the organization, according to Ivan, was that while he had taken an advanced business degree from UCLA and hoped to complement Carlo's authority with sound management practices, this had never worked out. It was not surprising that Carlo had assigned Bobby to monitor Boston, the importance of which Carlo had never quite understood. Sometimes when small and not particularly profitable activities were mentioned, Carlo would say, in Bobby's presence, "Let's give that to Bobby," or "Let's give Bobby a crack at that." This was hardly a direct putdown, and yet Bobby was subtly undercut. The same thing had happened when Carlo invited Paul into what was called "the circle around the circle." At the time, Bobby had been lobbying for the syndicate to fire Clovis, Luken & Pitch, and he had spent months comparing the brochures of other accounting firms; so when Carlo invited Paul to the Terrapin in Madrid, all of Bobby's work went down the drain overnight. Paul suspected, in fact, that it was Bobby who had tipped the cops to the forged paintings, figuring that Paul would be too afraid to talk. When Carlo was convicted, Bobby was said to be especially furious at Paul, although it was clear that, as the shady agent Shumway had said, tapes obtained through wiretaps and eavesdropping had carried the day. And who had been responsible for keeping the offices of New England Amusements swept for listening devices? Of course it was Bobby.

Paul and Ivan arrived in Providence around noon. Bobby let them into the house, where some of the boys were watching a movie in the living room.

"The rat comes home," said Tommy Mirage.

"Shh, Ray Liotta's coming on," said Max "Lionel" Ricci.

"Tommy, how are you?" said Paul.

"I consider you the lowest form of human garbage."

"Well, you look good."

"Shut up, everybody," said Bobby. "We're not here to spar each other with insults."

In the dining room Carlo's wife, Lillian, and Miriam Lentine were drinking coffee and playing Yahtzee. They had poked their pencils through the face of the little professor in the corner of the score sheets.

Bobby folded his hands and bowed. "We were hoping to use this room."

"Well, you can't," said Miriam Lentine. "Don't you see we're in the middle of a game?"

Lillian Record shook a velvet cup and spilled dice on the table. She stared at the dice. "Bobby, honey, what would you do?"

Bobby went to the base of a stairway. "About what?"

"With this roll."

He came back to the table and nervously chewed the skin of his left thumb. "Go for your large straight. But I mean it, we need this room."

"Why do you want to do it down here?" said Miriam.

"This is where he wants to do it."

"Then you've got to bring Carlo all the way down the stairs and all the way back up," said Lillian. "We go through this every three minutes."

"He likes this room."

Lillian gathered the dice. "I know what I'll do. Roll again."

Miriam and Lillian carefully picked up their game and went into another room, and Bobby directed Paul and Ivan to take seats at the table.

"Do you dance anymore, Bobby?" said Paul.

Bobby paused in the stairwell. "I've prepared a number for your unmarked grave," he said.

Some time later, Bobby came down the stairs carrying his father in his arms. Carlo wore white pajamas, black corduroy slippers, and a dark red robe with an empty sleeve. The specter of the decrepit boss brought home to Paul how long he himself had been in exile. The same years that had been taken from Carlo had been taken from him and Mary. They had grown nearer and nearer to middle age, all the while thinking that nothing in particular was happening.

Bobby settled Carlo into a chair and then went to a sideboard from which he produced a green leather folder. He sat down and placed the folder on the table. Tommy Mirage and Max Ricci appeared in the open doorway between the dining and living rooms. Carlo frowned in recognition and spoke in a voice that was dry and soft but not difficult to hear.

"Everyone is in pain because you put your friends in the boneyard," Carlo said to Paul. "You let me down, you let Spiro down, you let Cochrane and Nicky and Jimmy down. Who else? Stevie Shakes is another one I can think of. Who else, boys?"

"Larry Zumwald," said Bobby.

"Hatpin Henry," said Max Ricci. "Also Ed Leblanc."

"I knew I was leaving someone out," said Carlo.

"How is Stevie Shakes?" said Paul.

"The same."

"Eddie Leblanc," said Bobby. "I've been trying to think of his name all week long."

"'Flipper,'" said Max.

"What?" said Carlo.

"They called him 'Flipper' at the pool, Shepherd."

"Who calls him that?" said Carlo. "I never heard it."

"His pals," said Max. "They used to go to the Y and they called Eddie Leblanc 'Flipper,' 'cause he didn't like shooting hoops, he liked swimming. Like that porpoise that used to be on TV."

"Jesus help me," said Carlo. "Do you remember the cemetery in Madrid, Paul? I used to walk there every night after supper, if it wasn't raining. You must remember. Max remembers. He would drive me over and he would walk along. Remember, Max? Later I began walking at the mall, but before the mall it was the cemetery. In prison there was no cemetery and no mall, only a yard. I tried walking in the yard, but one evening I saw some young men injecting dope into their bloodstream and I realized this was no place to walk. And so I stopped walking, reluctantly, and I would spend my evenings in the prison library looking at books. One that I liked in particular was a collection of paintings, and of all the paintings in that book, my favorite was by John Singer Sargent. And in the picture that I liked by John Singer Sargent a young woman sat by a stream, half in shade and half in light. Her expression was not happy or inviting but preoccupied, or even . . . even —"

"Pensive," said Tommy "Mirage" Maynard.

"Yes," said Carlo. "Thank you, Tommy. Tommy has found the right word. Paul, as you know, I spoke up for you many times in our monthly meetings, and against considerable opposition. And you probably don't know how painful it is for me to concede now that if you were half the man Tommy Maynard is, you would be twice the man that you are."

"Let me get my calculator," said Paul.

"Someone hit him," said Carlo, and someone did, on the ear. "One night I even dreamed about her in my dreams. Together we walked on the sand in Little Compton, the woman in the painting and I. In this dream I was young, my legs were strong and limber. I was nineteen years old, with two strong arms, and we walked together like brother and sister. After that, I tore the page from the book and taped it on the wall of my cell. It seemed somehow that whatever was taking up her thoughts would be waiting for me when the doors opened and I walked into the light of freedom. And now, here is the picture. I brought it out with me."

Bobby pushed the leather folder across the table and Paul opened it. The print was worn around the edges and had been twice folded.

"This is good," said Paul.

"See the cloth of her skirt? Is it not amazing how you can almost feel it between your fingers?" Carlo raised his hand slowly and rubbed his thumb against his fingers. "And yet the girl could not care about that. Her mind is elsewhere. She is not looking at us. She is not thinking about the fine fabric of her skirt. We don't even see her eyes."

"Come to the point," said Bobby.

"Soon I will be dead, and you will have no more chance to learn manners," said Carlo. "The point is the title. For what would we call a portrait painting if we were, as we surely must be, lesser artists than John Singer Sargent?"

"I don't know," said Paul.

"Answer him," said Tommy Maynard.

Paul turned to look at him. "That is my answer. I don't know what he's getting at."

"We might call it, oh, 'A Picture of Dolores,' or, perhaps, 'Betsy by the Stream,'" said Carlo. "But is that what Sargent did?"

"No."

"What did he do, Nash?"

"He called it *The Black Brook.*"

"Yes," said Carlo. "Because the painting is not about the woman. Do you understand that? It's about that part of her that we cannot reach, no matter how many times we look at the painting. *The Black Brook* is the stream of her troubled thoughts."

"Well, your analysis is very good."

"Get me this painting."

"It wouldn't be hard to find who has it," Paul said. "But it would cost millions. And that's if the owner wanted to sell, which seems unlikely."

Carlo nodded. He took a cracker from the pocket of his robe and chewed it slowly. Everyone could hear the sound of his teeth breaking the cracker. Finally he said, "The painting is owned by the Tate Gallery in London. I have spoken to the people there, and they want to keep it."

"As I say."

"Well, the Tate Gallery is not invincible. I had Bobby do some research. There are people who could do it. Their price is on the high side, and Bobby doesn't think the end justifies the means. And if I wanted to steal the painting, or for that matter if I wanted to buy the painting, I would not be talking to you."

"Because you would be dead as a clam," said Bobby.

"Oh," said Paul. "I get it."

"How soon can it be done?" said Carlo.

"God, I don't know." Now he began to really look at the

painting. The rendering of the woman's hands seemed inordinately complicated, and the water was composed of planes of black and purple and brown. "End of summer."

"Do you know what Tommy has in the trunk of his car?" said Carlo. "I will give you a clue. He has a shotgun in the trunk of his car."

"And, I just cleaned it," said Tommy.

"Labor Day is not as unreasonable as it may sound," Paul said.

"You have until the end of May," Carlo said.

"July first."

"This is not your last chance, but your only chance. We know all about your little hotel in Australia."

"Belgium," said Ivan.

"Now give him the insurance and let him go," said Carlo.

Tommy Maynard and Ivan drove Paul to a self-storage place near a row of black oil tanks.

"What's the insurance?" said Paul.

"You're a big brain," said Tommy. "Ask yourself what would become of the slender thread of credibility this organization still has if we found you and got nothing out of the encounter but a painting."

Ivan nodded with a thoughtful expression. "We have become somewhat laughable."

"I retire in September," said Tommy. "Otherwise I would not stay."

In a room full of dusty mountain bicycles Tommy unrolled an orange cloth, took out an aluminum X-acto knife, and fitted a blade into it. Ivan crunched Paul's arms behind him and said, "Don't get his eyes."

"I've done this a thousand times," said Tommy. He took a pair of glasses from the pocket of his jacket, put them on, and tilted his head back patiently to see through the lenses. He began singing under his breath. "Call John the Boatman, call, call again . . ." Then he pushed the tip of the blade into the skin beside the bridge of Paul's nose and flicked the knife diagonally across his face.

"O.K., that's done," said Tommy.

Ivan let go and Paul staggered back into a row of bicycles. He tried to catch the falling blood in his hands.

"Be careful," said Tommy. "Those bikes belong to Brown students." He tossed Paul the orange cloth. "Use it as a compress. Get blood in my car and I'll be angry."

They let Paul off at Anne Hutchinson Hospital. In the emergency room, lying on a wheeled cot, Paul explained that he had broken a glass while doing the dishes, and a doctor prepared a needle and injected novocaine in the skin under his eye. The needle hurt more than the knife had, and a nurse let him squeeze her hand all during the stitching. Paul felt as if his face had turned to leather and someone tugged on it with hooks.

When the stitches were in, Paul thanked the nurse and she pointed to his clothes on the floor. "You'll be needing new sneakers," she said.

Once released from the hospital, Paul took a cab into Providence and got a room in an old hotel. He looked in the cloudy mirror above a sink. The doctor who did the stitching had said the cut would result in a scar that might fade over the years. He brushed his finger against the transparent stitches. That hurt a great deal. Then he lay down on the bed and fell into an unmoving sleep, dreaming of bicycles.

The next day he put a Band-Aid over the stitches and went looking for the house of one of his former painters. The painter and his wife had lived on Morris Avenue. Maybe he would not want to paint copies again but could be drawn in by the challenge of recreating Sargent. A man he had never seen answered the door and kept the chain on.

"Don't know them," he said. "Never heard of them. They must have moved away long ago."

Paul walked back downtown. The stitches pounded and it began to rain. His separateness from others always seemed insurmountable on rainy Saturdays. He crossed new bridges, passed the park, skirted City Hall, and started up Hellespont Avenue to the hotel. Halfway between the park and the hotel a woman descended a set of steps and spoke to him.

"What is your religion?"

Paul thought a moment. "Well, if anything, I'm a Baptist. But I'm not really that, either."

"Good — would you do me a favor? Would you turn off the lights in the sanctuary?"

The woman led Paul up the steps into a tall building with a facade consisting of panels of polished stone. They walked along a hallway and into a softly lit room where she knelt at the base of an altar.

"These are the light switches," she said.

He knelt too, surprised by how many there were — nine, in a horizontal band — for the room's illumination did not seem elaborate. The lights went out one by one, but for an oil lamp in a glass case suspended from the ceiling.

"Did you just get done?" said Paul.

"About twenty minutes ago."

"How did it go?"

"Well, you know, we read, we prayed . . . we *sang*." She stroked her hair, which was silver, and seemed to search her mind. She smiled. "And you shut out the lights. Thank you."

"I'm glad to be of service," said Paul.

21

Back in Ashland, Paul found Scratch sitting forlornly in the rain on the black branch of a tree beside the cottage. He called her down, but she had rarely come when called and did not come now. He pointed quickly at the ground. "Look, it's a vole." No response. Then he went inside, opened a bag of cat food, poured some into a dish, and went back out. Scratch looked miserably at the food and then turned her face again to the sad rain. Her nose was the exact color of a pencil eraser.

Paul set the dish of food in the wet grass and climbed the tree. Rain dripped from the branches and ran in rivulets down the trunk. He gripped the big cat by the wet fur behind her ears, and when he lifted her from the branch she made no attempt to claw his arm. He called a veterinarian in Damascus and described the cat's behavior. The man he spoke to asked after the cat's temperature and described how it might be taken, and Paul said that instead he would bring her in.

But first he went into town to do his laundry. He always felt squalid doing his laundry until the moment when the first dryer load was done. Then a sense of warm and foldable industry took over, and the moral bankrupts slouching around the washers revealed themselves to be divinity students and honest clerks: his clothes were clean. There were not enough dryers, as there never are, and he wondered if this was a corporate strategy designed to force people to hang around looking at the obscure cleaning products in the vending machines.

The sun came out and kids began playing baseball in the street. Paul went outside and joined the game. They had a seamed plastic ball that broke wildly when pitched. He got hold of one and sent it arcing into the bed of a pickup, a ground-rule double. After a few innings he went back inside and finished his laundry and then drove home with baskets full of folded clothes. He left a towel in one of the baskets, put the cat in the basket, and drove to the veterinarian's.

Damascus sat on a plateau west of Ashland, and the road climbed to it. The vet's office was in a log cabin. Normally Scratch would have hissed and swatted at the curious dogs in the waiting room, but this time she scrambled up Paul's left arm and dug her claws through his slicker and into his shoulder. With the cat shivering beside his ear, Paul got up to talk to a woman behind the counter.

"Well, I don't know what's wrong," he said. "She's definitely not being herself."

The woman's fingers brushed across the side of her face. "Did she do that?"

"A glass broke when I was doing dishes," he said, and as he spoke, he heard the sound of water on plastic. A stream of cat urine ran down the front of his coat and into his pocket.

"Oh . . . she's scared," said the woman.

She came out from behind the counter with a paper towel and a bottle of disinfectant and scrubbed Paul's jacket. His heart filled with sorrow for the old cat.

The veterinarian waited with hands folded as Paul spoke, and she seemed about to break in at three or four points but never quite did, making Paul's description of Scratch's behavior seem halting and exaggerated. Then she made an expressive gesture with her hands, waited a moment, and said, "Yes, older cats are susceptible . . . ," and, later, "Some feel, though it's not a universal belief . . ." Her voice was high but dense, and her diplomas showed that she had taken her degrees in Kentucky. She took samples of Scratch's blood and gave Paul a vial of powder capsules to break open and sprinkle over the cat's food.

There were no meetings to cover that night, and Jean Jones told Paul to make the police and fire calls and play it by ear. "All quiet," said the dispatchers. He went out driving with a notepad and camera to see if anything newsworthy was going on, a random approach that had worked for him in the past, yielding curious stories such as New England's Tallest Man handing out golf balls at the ice cream parlor and the model-rocket fair in which one of the rockets veered into the crowd, injuring a babysitter. This time he drove all over town before turning onto Knife Shop Road and seeing a tank lurching toward him. He pulled over and got out of his car waving his arms. The tank stopped and the hatch lifted.

"Hello!" said a man. He was exhilarated and red-faced, as if there were not enough air in the tank.

"What are you doing?" said Paul.

"Driving my tank," said the man. "I have access to lots of scrap metal, so I thought, why not build a tank? My partner doesn't mind. He figures it will keep me busy."

"What kind of tank is it?"

"Just a generic tank," said the man. "I'm having the time of my life. I could have worked from pictures, but I thought that would be cheating."

"I've lived in Belgium," said Paul. "There's a tank in the square at Bastogne."

"I can imagine," said the man. "The Ardennes is one of the most evocative regions in history. I have a refrigerator in here. Want a beer or soda?"

"Do you have Royal Crown?"

"Well, I just might." The man disappeared in the turret and then looked out. "The refrigerator doesn't seem to be working."

Paul walked around the tank, stopping now and then to take pictures. "Have you gotten any flack from Public Works?"

"The secret is, the treads aren't real."

Paul looked under the prow of the tank. "This is very clever," he said.

"Thanks. Most people think I'm in the National Guard, but I'm not. I had a draft card for the Vietnam War, but it ended before I could be called up. Why are you writing when I talk?"

"I'm a reporter," said Paul.

"That's O.K."

Jean Jones removed the stitches from Paul's face. He sat on the velvet couch in her apartment and she cut the plastic threads with the surgical scissors she had used to scrape the bowl of her pipe on his last visit. She used tweezers to pull the stitches out, and they gave up his skin with a light breaking feeling.

"What happened?" she said.

"My real name is Paul Nash," said Paul. "Seven years ago I testified against some people, and they just now caught up with me."

"Hold still," she said. She pulled out a stitch and brushed the wound with a cotton ball soaked in rubbing alcohol. "I do know something about this. Rudy Bonner told me who you are. I had gone to see him about a lawsuit against the police. He asked me to give you something."

She pulled a briefcase from under the couch and took out a map of Scotland. Paul unfolded it and found a town on the southwest coast circled in red marker.

"Are you going here?" she said.

"Eventually. But I'll be leaving the paper any day."

"Well, O.K., because I need to talk to you about that," she said. "Pete wants your resignation. I fought him, but he's the boss. I said if witness protection is going to work, then our institutions have to learn to live with the witnesses."

"What'd he say?"

"That the *Sun* is a newspaper, not an institution."

"That's all right."

"What did you do in the first place?"

"Killed my brother by tackling him too hard," said Paul.

"I thought it was mob-related."

"That was in the second place."

"People don't die from hard tackles."

"I know."

"Are you going to the Revue?"

"What's that?"

Every year, she explained, the newspaper put on a Spring Revue at the Pail Hotel. This was a dinner and musical show that made light of current events in the town. Money raised went to charity, and this year it would help the hospital buy a CAT scanner.

The Revue took place two nights later. Paul and Jean bought tickets and sat near the stage. Paul thought this would be a good farewell to the life of Ashland and that it might distance him from strange recent developments, such as how the dead could talk to him. He wondered again if he was losing his mind, but at the same time he had never felt better. Since his meeting with

Carlo, his hearing had become keen. He could hear a clock ticking from across a room or hear the siren of an ambulance winding through Damascus. He could feel the blood going through his veins and arteries. And just before a phone rang, he would see waves in the air. He always knew. These phenomena seemed like personal enhancements but also took something out of him, and perhaps it was sentimental, but he felt that a night of drinking and obscure comedy in a provincial hotel might bring him back to the quiet existence that he had wanted when he came to Ashland — all that simplicity he had desired.

They shared a table with Will and Sharon Kiwi and Pete and Hope Lonborg. Across the room, Paul could see a table of stuffers and he wished that he had never left the stuffing floor. It took a lot of nerve to presume to tell other people's stories. But the food lifted his spirits, and he went back for seconds, and the people at the table seemed to approve of his big appetite. They nudged one another and nodded, as if to say, "He's right, of course. We should all eat more." Then blue spotlights raked the stage and the show began. The players danced and sang with the manic enthusiasm that can be seen in all small-town productions and seems to express a common desire to escape to the big city and become a star. Paul understood the point of a few of the numbers, such as a horn-driven rendition of "Cry Me a River," meant to commemorate the disappearance of the stream on Whiskers Lane.

As in any cross section of the population, a surprising number of people had voices that were strong and clear, and Paul drank glass after glass of red wine and laughed along with the crowd, although he often had only a vague sense of what was funny and there were many uproarious lines that he didn't get at all. Loom Hanover would close the show, as he always did, with a song linked to Ashland's industrial history. One year he'd done "Needles and Pins," and another "The Tighten Up." Tonight he strode onto the stage holding a shimmering green guitar by the neck.

"Thank you," he said, then tilted his head sidewise to make eye contact with the band. The song began. And as Loom sang about Romeo and Juliet, and Samson and Delilah, and their loves that couldn't be denied, the music faded in Paul's ears, faded to silence, and he seemed to hear other words from a long time ago, from Canada, from a lecture given on chalcedony by the treasured scholar Virginia Lovetree of Sherwood University. "Chalcedony was a type of quartz used by the ancient Egyptians to drive away ghosts, night visions, and sadness. Chalcedony is never crystalline, but translucent and waxy in appearance. It usually is a smoky blue, but it may also be yellow or a cloudy white. The Egyptians used it on their scarab seals."

The flashing lights he saw when he got home reminded him of the motorcycle crash that had been his break. He got his police flashlight out of the house and went into the back yard, where he could see tire tracks pressed into the grass. He jogged down through the trees. Spotlights glared along the shore. A young man in dark pants stood back from the water's edge, examining a white shirt. Paul tried to tell him that he was from the *Sun*, but the young man did not respond, as he was too busy studying the monogram on the shirt. An old ambulance sat crooked on the sand with an orange cross painted on the side and its back doors flung open. Paul moved up and down the rocky beach among small groups of men and women smoking cigarettes that turned intermittently bright orange and black. Then a diver walked up and out of the water carrying a woman in a black bathing suit. The diver lay the woman on the sand, removed his mask, knelt, and breathed into the woman's mouth. He tried filling her lungs for some time before looking up. Paul crouched by the body of Linda Tallis. Her eyes had swollen shut and her long reddish hair fanned about her head, entwined with lake weeds. Paul gripped her cold shoulders but could not shake her, could not move her, could not lift her into his arms.

Back in the house, a man stood at the kitchen counter wearing a broad red shirt with a coconut tree and monkey embroidered on the back. He held a thin wooden propeller in one hand and a strip of emery paper in the other. He would raise the propeller to the light, examine it with squinting eyes, and set to sanding with loud and rasping slashes. From time to time he dipped the sandpaper in a dish of water stationed at his elbow.

IV

KEYS

22

Usually he ignored the safety instructions, out of superstition, as if to prepare for disaster were to invite it, but this time — on the night flight from New York to Brussels, not long after takeoff — Paul examined the plastic card of colorful emergency pictographs and found it to be a work of clever satire. He especially liked the trio of illustrations directing passengers to refrain from smoking or collecting their suitcases or wearing high-heeled shoes in case of the airplane ditching in the ocean. He could not imagine the choice of footwear making a difference one way or the other as the icy water of the North Atlantic flooded the plane.

The man sitting behind him was one of those passengers who while away the hours by making direct observations to his seatmate. "The Concorde is actually a relatively small aircraft . . . All done with your yogurt, I see . . . Virgin planes are red . . ." Paul fell asleep listening to him discuss some problem he was having with his insurance company — "Given the fact that I was on doctor's orders, and told to stay on bed rest, I kind of assumed I was in compliance" — and woke up, at the end of the short night, to the spidery shock of sunlight on the world's rim.

He realized with a start that he did not know the name that Kim Tallis went by now. He hoped that the Scottish town he had been directed to was not a large town.

He rented a car at Zaventem airport and drove into Brussels, where he took a room in a clean and modern hotel around the corner from the Place St. Catherine. That night he sat on a scarred wooden bench by a long rectangular fountain with trees and cobblestones all around. Dark water spouted from the mouths of stone crocodiles, and neon tubes of green and orange outlined the facades of the bars and restaurants across the way. Listening to the trickling water and the low rumble of tires on the stones, he felt released from time. Later, he tried to order supper in a restaurant but the kitchen had closed, and he was befriended by an old couple, who sat nearby. The man was from Amsterdam originally but had driven Mack trucks back and forth across the United States in the forties.

"I jumped ship in New York," the man explained. "When I first arrived I was too young to drink beer, so I drank root beer. After a time I went down to South America. There I jumped ship also."

Every time he talked about jumping ship, he made a gesture of contempt, raising his right fist and slapping his left hand into the crook of his arm.

"He is hungry," said the woman. She wore a red dress with black beads sewn in.

"We will take you," said the man.

The couple paid their bill and led Paul down a street with music spilling from a café. It sounded like an accordion, but a woman with thick black glasses was playing an electronic keyboard in the front window.

"In there," said the former truck driver, "they have dancing for old people."

A piece of plywood covered a hole in the sidewalk and the man pointed it out as they went along. "Be careful," he said.

Near the old stock exchange the couple said goodbye to Paul. He crossed the street and went into an Irish bar, but the kitchen was closed there also. Paul drank a pint of Stella and read the *International Herald Tribune*, with "The Boys Are Back in Town" playing on the sound system.

～

The next morning Paul took the E411 and N4 into the Ardennes. Even out in the country the light stanchions huddled close together along the highways. The Belgians hated to let a road go unlighted.

A festival was under way in Vertige. Men in red felt jackets walked on stilts, leading a parade down the main street and forcing Paul to make his way through the narrow alleys that cut between stone buildings. He saw Guissard, who owned the grocery store, trying to break up a fight between two small dogs. He seemed to be having no success. Then the road lifted, leaving Vertige behind, passed a walled cemetery with a wrought-iron gate, and arrived at the inn. There a man in purple coveralls stood on a chair at the front door, hammering a trim board back into place as Mary watched with folded arms.

Paul leaned out of the car window. "Madame, can you direct me to the Festival of Stilts?"

She turned and looked at him without seeing him, the way that you do when you own a small business. Her belly was round and high, in a long blue dress worn over white leggings with bees printed on them. "You'll want to go back into town, and I'll tell you the way."

He got out of the car, took her hands in his. "Did we do this?"

"What happened to your face?"

"I ran into Tommy Maynard," said Paul.

She touched the scar. "Is it over?"

"Almost."

"Look at my hair," said Mary, lifting it with her hands. She wore a diamond on the ring finger of her left hand. "My hair was never like this. It's because of the protein."

Paul felt her hair, and it was very thick. "I don't know what to say, Mary. You just look so . . . full."

"I'm stinging with it," she said.

"I know nothing about diamonds," he said. "I couldn't tell a carat from a facet."

The man on the chair handed down the hammer, and she took it. "This is Axel," said Mary.

"Nice to meet you," said Paul. "I've been meaning to fix that for about three years."

"Now it's done," said Axel.

"Axel and Judy are my left and right hands," said Mary. "They came from Jardins du Saint-Hubert. Pierrick Gilloteaux took one look at the place and said we need a bigger family."

"And he would be . . ."

"Pierrick's my partner," said Mary. "He came down from Antwerp one weekend and fell in love with Vertige. He deals in diamonds and lace."

"That about covers it."

"You can try and get my goat," said Mary. "But it won't happen."

"How are the goats?" said Paul.

"Sheba had kids."

"Good for her," said Paul. "Where is Pierrick?"

"London."

"You work fast."

"That's rich," said Mary. "That's so rich I could smash you with this hammer."

"I can take it," said Paul.

"Judy," shouted Axel. He had come down from the chair and was examining the frayed weave of the seat.

A woman with red cheeks and wild gray hair looked out of a window. "What?"

"Make a snack tray," said Axel. *"M. Emmons est retour."*

"How about cheese?" said Judy.

"Oui, merci," said Paul.

When Judy brought out the food, she said she could tell that Mary was going to have a girl by the way she was carrying.

The guests at the inn included two birdwatchers from The Hague, a Canadian war buff, and a bicyclist named Clement from South Africa. After supper Paul went out to the barn and sat in the clean straw of the goat pen. Sheba and her kids — Jo-Jo, Pin-Pin, and Stanley — came tripping over to lick his face, and he patted the coarse hair on their necks.

Clement entered the barn tentatively and leaned his arms on the fence of the goat pen. He wore sharply creased khakis and a jacket of waxed cotton. The goats hurried over to the fence to greet the visitor.

"Good evening," said Clement. "I hear you're from America."

Paul rose from the goats and brushed straw from his jeans. "That's right. From Rhode Island."

Clement nodded. "I toured America when I was seventeen years old. We rode bicycles in Iowa, Montana, and California, but never in Rhode Island. In Iowa we dipped our wheels in the Mississippi and Missouri rivers — first in one and then in the other. Such a crowd of bicycles as one could scarcely fathom."

"What do you do when you're not riding?"

"I'm an engineer," said Clement. "A bicycle manufacturer in Durban sends me anywhere I want to go, testing not only our bicycles but those of our competitors. When I return, I go to my drafting table and make suggestions."

"What a great job," said Paul. "You must have won races and such."

"As a rider I am slightly better than average," said Clement. "What I do have is stamina. There are few mountains that would pose a great problem for me. And I have an understanding of the way that a bicycle works. But as for speed, I am only slightly better than average. The great cyclists of the Netherlands would leave me in their wake. But this makes a kind of sense, for how many of all the bicycles sold worldwide are purchased by top riders?"

"Very few," said Paul.

"Precisely," said Clement. "I wonder if you have kayaks to rent."

259

"You can get them in town," said Paul. "There's a shop next to the Catholic church with a sign that says 'Descente de la Torchon en Kayak.'"

Clement yawned. "Excuse me, but I find myself rather tired this evening."

"So do I," said Paul. "I flew back from the United States yesterday."

"My greatest memory of North America, do you know, has nothing to do with bicycling. It concerns a restaurant. I'm not even sure what city the restaurant was in, but it consisted of a turning disk at the top of a building."

"A lot of cities have them."

"Understandably," said Clement. "It was a clear night, and we could see the city lights as if a golden bowl had been inverted over the sky. There was a lake, I remember that, whatever city it was. We had drinks and sketched our itinerary on cocktail napkins. And then someone noticed that the restaurant seemed to be turning faster than it had been previously. The glasses trembled on the tables. The place was really spinning. At first it seemed comical, but gradually a panic set in. People did not know whether to go to the windows to watch the whirl of lights or to hurry down to the ground. A church choir who had pushed lots of tables together now began to sing. Their singing was most impressive but had no impact on the frightened crowd. I caught an elbow in the eye as I moved to the elevator. The fear was that the restaurant would lose its mooring and sail to the ground like a Frisbee. And when I finally made it through, the door slid open and out came a group of people in shining yellow suits."

"Who were they?"

"Firefighters," said Clement. "They had come to supervise the evacuation. And I must say they did a good job of it. I wish I could remember the city. No one died, though several were injured."

"Would you go in that kind of restaurant again?" said Paul.

"Oh, most probably I would," said Clement, "for the reasons

that drew me to it initially. I believe in the technology, for one. I believe in the material advancement of the society. I have no doubt that by the time my children are grown there will be a city on the moon, with all the advantages of reduced gravity. Manufacturing, for example, becomes exponentially less costly."

"How old are your children?"

"I'm not yet married," said Clement. "But certainly someday . . . after I've stopped traveling so much, I should say that I will have children. I look at your wife and I think, Someday, Clement, you will have children of your own, and you will bore them to distraction with stories of riding bicycles in the range of the Grand Teton."

"Are you kidding? They'll love it," said Paul.

Clement went back to the house, and Paul fed the animals and changed their straw-specked water. Then Rosine came into the barn. She walked heavily, carrying a bucket of scraps. Paul offered to take it but she held tight to the handle. She gave the scraps to the goats, then went around emptying the buckets of water that Paul had put out and refilling them from the hydrant in the center of the barn.

"I just did that," said Paul.

"J'entends un bruit," she said.

Mary gave Paul a sleeping bag, and he unrolled it on the floor of their room. It was a green sleeping bag with pheasants printed on the lining. They lay down — he on the floor and she on her bed. Mary, in her nightgown, settled on her back. "They're going to induce me on Monday if nothing happens."

"I'll go with you," said Paul.

"O.K."

"You can have Pierrick there too."

"He may not be back," said Mary. "Look, this is a friendship ring. Don't misunderstand. I'd like for you to misunderstand, but you shouldn't. It was returned because there was a flaw in the stone. So he let me wear it, he said he wanted me to wear it, and that's all there is to that."

"Diamond dealers don't give out diamonds on a whim. He could get good money for that stone. Let me see it."

"No."

"Obviously he's got your number."

"I already have a brother, and you're not him," said Mary. "You left me."

"You wanted me to leave," he said.

"Rub my back," she said.

She turned on her side and he knelt beside the bed, kneading the muscles on either side of her spine. He had always thought that, given the chance, he could make women feel less tense. They seemed sometimes to carry a mantle of everyday worry that he felt capable of lifting. This was not a calculated belief but more like a spontaneous illusion, and it was consistent with his amateur's theory of organic pragmatism in human behavior. Not that he considered the reproduction of his personal cells the point of living — far from it — but he would not have been surprised if his cells had a different take on the matter. He wondered if the physical and emotional rush of making love, that feeling of falling, could be accounted for by the enthusiasm of the cells — as if they were saying, in unison, "Hey, this is more like it" — and if, correspondingly, his sense of sexual mission resulted from a chemical imbalance.

However that question could be answered, he sensed that in his absence something had changed in Mary. Whether this was due to the pregnancy or to some resolution on her part, she now seemed less needful of whatever help he might offer. She appeared steady and full of purpose, and good for her. Good for her. She had offered to brain him with a hammer, but she had not seemed committed to the notion. Maybe the assertion of vengeful independence was a passport admitting her to a better world where the wind could be heard sighing in the branches. Not to be sarcastic about it. What really got to him was the likelihood that he could not hurt her anymore but only cause her some distant and bemused unrest. Hurting her was not his aim, but he did want to be flesh and blood in her life.

"I just remembered," he said. "I need you to make a painting."

"Forget it."

"It's Sargent," he said enticingly. "We'll talk about it tomorrow. This massaging would go better if we could lift your nightgown."

"Forget that too."

"We do this, Carlo leaves us alone."

"Carlo wants it?" said Mary. "God, Carlo Record . . . How is he?"

"Not very well."

Paul worked her shoulder muscles, lifting and squeezing. "And what's with Rosine? She just pretended I wasn't in the barn."

"Maybe she thought you hadn't been."

"I was in the barn at the time."

"She says, *'Il me tape sur les nerfs.'* That you get on her nerves. She's mad at you. We all are. We've learned to manage without you. The truth — and you should know this — is things are very good, right here, right now."

"Well, I'm glad."

Mary said nothing. He could feel the tidal rhythm of her breathing. How excellent are bodies, he thought. To get a machine to do all that they do would cost a fortune, and even then, the machine would be covered in steel or dull plastic instead of this warm, responsive skin.

"I'm drifting off," she said.

Paul went downstairs for a cup of tea. The Canadian, whose name was Glover, sat at a desk in the library, studying a map of the Battle of the Ardennes.

"This is where the Germans made their last great effort," he said. He opened a leather case full of sharp colored pencils. "They wanted to get back to Antwerp. Antwerp was the goal, but of course they came nowhere near it."

"They didn't even get Bastogne," said Paul.

"They were all around Bastogne."

263

"What did the American commander say? 'Nuts to you.'"

"No," said Glover. "What he said was 'Nuts!' That was Brigadier General Anthony McAuliffe."

"Our monastery 'fell to the Allied bombing.'"

"Some people today find the discipline of the Wehrmacht inviting," said Glover.

"Let them go live under it," said Paul.

"Or die under it," said Glover. "I've been to Dachau. *Arbeit Macht Frei* is written on the gate. 'Work makes you free.' It's hard to accept this was our century."

"What do you do for a living?" said Paul.

Glover sketched with a colored pencil on the map. "I'm a professor, but I'm on sabbatical," he said. "This is the famous bulge that we speak of. Here is where the Third Army came in, directed by the mighty Patton. Up here is where the Ninth and the First came in. And here the British Second."

"We had a guy here one time from the British Second," said Paul. "Geoffrey."

"How I would have liked to speak to him. Eisenhower saw the German push into the Ardennes not as the disaster that everyone else saw but as an opportunity."

In the kitchen, a taut bag of fresh goat cheese hung dripping slowly over the sink, and Paul pivoted the faucet away from the cheese to run the water into an electric kettle. Rosine sat in one of two chairs on either side of the empty fireplace reading the Vertige newspaper. "They're going to build that radio tower despite environmental concerns," she said in English. "The European Union has issued a commemorative pen and pencil."

Paul plugged the kettle in and pressed a button on the handle. He was thinking of Rosine's name, of Mary's letter. "Rosine, I'm going to have tea. Would you like to join me?"

"Yes, I think that I would."

He took two white porcelain mugs from the sideboard. "I'm going to have whiskey in my tea. This combination comes with my highest recommendation."

"Whiskey, yes," said Rosine.

Paul uncorked a bottle and poured Scotch over the tea bags in the cups. He sat down in the chair opposite Rosine's and put his feet on the woodbin. "What else is in the newspaper?"

"A chimney man fell, but he will be all right."

"A sweep."

"Yes, a chimney sweep, but he will be all right."

The boiling of the kettle came gradually to the foreground. "And here we are," said Paul.

The diamond merchant Pierrick Gilloteaux came back from London on Sunday. He and Paul and Axel and Judy spent the afternoon putting up first-cut hay in the barn. Axel and Judy unloaded the hay from a pickup onto an elevator, and Paul and Pierrick collected and stacked the bales in the loft of the barn. Pierrick slung the heavy bales with ease. He wore Carhartt jeans with big pockets and a gray work shirt.

"They put uncut diamonds in lots," he explained. He and Paul stood in the open doorway of the loft with the elevator canted between them and wind in their faces. "It's tricky how it's done. Sometimes, in order to get the stone you want, you have to buy other stones you are indifferent about."

"How do you feel about the stone you gave Mary?"

"I'm fond of it," he said. "I showed it to her one day to illustrate the story of its return. A woman had agreed to buy it but wanted it independently appraised. I encourage this. 'By all means,' I say. Then she came back saying there was a crack. Now, there is no crack, and that is out of the question. There is a blemish, but not a crack. We spent some time talking in an inconclusive way. So I took back the stone, and when Mary showed an interest, I had it set for her."

"The message you're sending is, Here's some debris I can't get rid of."

Pierrick shrugged. "She wears it, so she must like it. That's all I can say."

"How did you find our *estaminet*?"

"All day long I hunch over a desk, looking through a loupe," said Pierrick Gilloteaux. "That's not strictly true. Sometimes I walk a diamond around a bit. I believe natural light is critical, although some prefer filament. It would be a protracted discussion. Sometimes I walk to the zoo while tossing the diamond in my hand. If you have never seen the zoo in Antwerp, you should. The dolphinarium I find quite fascinating. I had come down to Vertige only a few times before Mary's condition became apparent." He pronounced her name the French way, *Marie.* "I happen to believe that Vertige has great potential. So one night we went to a film. English with French subtitles. Like all movies these days, this one had a scattering of suggestive scenarios, and I became very conscious of Mary, seated as she was at my side."

"She'll do that to you," said Paul.

"Now I divide my time between here and Antwerp," said Pierrick. "My apartment in Deurne has nine stark rooms. But I realize the situation is uncommon. Perhaps my generosity has been a charade. Perhaps a frank approach might not work with a woman who is going to have a child. My own mind is mysterious to me on this question."

That night Mary went into labor. Paul drove her to the hospital in Moeurs-de-Province, where she was given a room with a view of the Pont des Ardennes. The contractions were long and gradual and did not seem too painful at first. Then they seemed very painful. The doctors gave Mary an anesthetic that made her apologetic and loopy. "I'm sorry," she said. "I'm so sorry."

"You have nothing to be sorry for," said the doctor.

"I know, I'm sorry."

Near the end, she surprised Paul by murmuring the punch line of an ancient joke concerning Toulouse-Lautrec's tailor: "Is it too tight, Toulouse?"

The baby was a girl. She squalled with an exhilarating anger that split the wall of medical expertise separating the doctors from Paul and Mary. Everyone's eyes shone above their masks. Paul went along to an adjoining room where doctors suctioned the baby's lungs with a tube that seemed to have gone all the way down to her toes. The baby hated the suctioning. She glistened, scarlet and barrel-chested, with fists knotted and face reflecting nuances of pain and surprise. Paul carried her back to the delivery room. There she opened her dark eyes for the first time at the taste of the milk. Later a beautiful midwife stood over the baby and put silver nitrate in her eyes.

Pierrick Gilloteaux arrived at the hospital carrying a video camera with which he recorded the sight of the infant hiccuping and wailing soundlessly behind the glass of the nursery. Paul stood beside him.

"Now I go and film the mother," he said.

"You have a lot to learn about Mary."

"The record will not be complete."

"In our minds it will be."

Paul could not leave the glass wall. He stood on his toes watching the round red face. Sometimes he looked at the other babies as well. They would go on to be messed up, dressed up, proud and miserable. And this was happening in every hospital in every town in every country. He wondered at the sense of accomplishment a normal parent must feel, because his own sense of accomplishment was great, and all he had done was to sleep with Mary on a hillside in New Hampshire one afternoon at the end of a marriage.

Mary and Paul named the baby Françoise and brought her home to the Auberge des Moines three days after she was born. Glover, the Canadian, was the only guest, as Rosine had been turning people away in anticipation. Breast-feeding had become more and more difficult since that first time in the delivery room, and one evening when Mary, Paul, and Françoise were not getting anywhere a midwife came to the inn. This was not the one who had helped out in the delivery but another one, from Vertige, but also beautiful. The midwife placed a rubber nipple over the real one, and Françoise caught on to this unusual arrangement, and the midwife petted Mary's hair, saying, *"Mettez-vous l'esprit en repos."* Set your spirit at rest.

23

Paul found a portfolio of Sargent prints in the book-market town of Redu, and just as he had hoped, the beauty of the painting convinced Mary to remake *The Black Brook*. She wanted to know how the painter had captured such a subtle moment with such coarse strokes. And so they traveled to London in June to see the work firsthand at the Tate Gallery. The baby stayed with Rosine in Vertige while Paul and Mary took the Eurostar out of Midi Station in Brussels. The train sped across the countryside and through the Channel Tunnel, arriving at Waterloo Station in late afternoon. They walked across Waterloo Bridge, looped around Aldwych, and headed up Kingsway and Southampton Row to Bloomsbury, where they got a room on the fifth floor of the Russell Hotel. It was a small and comfortable room with a balcony, a huge bathroom, and a freestanding trouser press.

"You and Pierrick should get one of these for the inn," said Paul. "You could attract more of the trouser-press crowd."

Mary and Paul stepped out onto the wrought-iron balcony overlooking Russell Square.

"I miss Françoise," said Mary.

Paul watched a band of yelling students as they swarmed to a teller machine below. Then two bald men got into a cab in front of the hotel, holding their jackets to their stomachs with that little Napoleonic gesture. Then another cab pulled up, and a third bald man got out.

"Probably just a coincidence," said Paul.

In the morning they had breakfast in the hotel dining room, where the banquet offered biscuits, croissants, fruit in syrup, twiglike cereal, muesli, some sort of flakes, and, in a series of silver bins with rollback tops, damp tomatoes, beans, fish patties, scrambled eggs, mushrooms, fried eggs, sausage, and ham. They looked at all the food and went back to their table, where they drank coffee and ate toast from a silver rack.

Later they walked along the Thames on Victoria Embankment and stopped to examine Cleopatra's Needle, an obelisk flanked by sphinxes that had been damaged by a German bomb in September of 1917. Paul fitted his thumb into a hole in the left-rear paw of one of the sphinxes as Mary read from an inscription on the obelisk:

> Through the patriotic zeal of Erasmus Wilson F.R.S. this obelisk was brought from Alexandria encased in an iron cylinder. It was abandoned during a storm on the Bay of Biscay. Recovered and erected on this spot by John Dixon C.E. in the 42nd year of the Reign of Queen Victoria 1878.

"No one has patriotic zeal anymore," said Paul.

The Black Brook was not on display at the Tate. A woman at the information desk explained that there used to be a program through which works not on show could be seen privately, but this had been discontinued.

"She has to paint a copy for a gangster back in the States," said Paul. "Otherwise we'll be killed."

"I'm terribly sorry."

"We understand. You don't make the rules."

"I thought you called," Mary said to Paul.

"The line was busy."

They retreated to a large stone room, where they sat on the floor with their backs to the wall listening to the museum rumbling like a heart. A boy in a light blue shirt examined a sculpture by Henry Moore, a muted gray woman carved from

Armenian marble. The boy yawned and rubbed his eyes while circling the sculpture. The woman's left hand cupped her right elbow, and her right hand cupped her left breast. Her eyes and nostrils were just little holes in the marble.

"O.K., I'll work from the print," said Mary.

"Carlo will never see the original."

"Clearly, since it's not on view."

With new resolution they got up and went into the Hogarth Room, where they looked at a painting by Allan Ramsay, 1713–1784, in which Thomas, 2nd Baron Mansel of Margam, holds a shotgun and a dead grouse, or pigeon, while surrounded by his half-brothers and half-sister. These are the children of Anne, daughter of Admiral Sir Clowdisley Shovell. Thomas's half-sister wears a kerchief on her head and is resting her left hand on the pigeon, and Thomas glances at her with a friendly appraisal, as if to say, "You want the pigeon? It's yours."

They wandered from room to room. They looked at Turner's big and tragic *Parting of Hero and Leander* and George Stubbs's series of paintings of an unlucky horse happening on a lion beneath a ledge.

"'The setting for this violent encounter,'" Mary read from the wall, "'and for others in the series, is the harsh, rocky landscape of Creswell Crags in the Peak District.'"

They looked at Constables and Romneys and Giacomettis and at John William Waterhouse's *Lady of Shalott,* in which a woman in a thin white dress with a black sash drifted toward Camelot and her own death in an ornate black boat with three candles burning in the bow. Her head tilted back with red-lidded eyes, and her long sandy hair fanned in the breeze.

And then, in a room containing a bronze athlete wrestling with a python, they saw an honest-to-God Sargent: *Ena and Betty, Daughters of Asher and Mrs. Wertheimer.* Betty was the taller of the two, and light seemed to slide down her off-white gown. She had her arm around the waist of Ena, who wore a red velvet dress. Unless Paul had Ena and Betty confused.

"You really want to feel that velvet," said Paul.

"You can't touch the painting," said Mary, taking notes.

When they walked out of the Tate and into the river wind, they felt as if they had been through a trial; their bodies seemed lighter, out from under the oppression of so much genius. They laughed, fell into the back of a cab, and told the driver to take them anywhere a good meal could be had. They had been to London several times, and contrary to the prevailing opinion, they did not mind the food. The driver commented, as had Geoffrey before him, on the nuances separating British and American English. "Pavement here means 'sidewalk'; in the States it means 'not the sidewalk.'" The pub to which the cab driver delivered them had a welcoming dimness, worn brocade benches, and a tapestry commemorating the landing of a meteorite at the wedding of Elizabeth Sydenham in the sixteenth century.

Afterward Mary and Paul walked along the Serpentine and saw a large man in a tight electric blue suit feeding the animals. He stood by an iron fence while squirrels walked up and down his arms. Paul and Mary agreed that this was partly naturalistic and partly pathetic. That night in the hotel, they faced again the question of whether to make love.

They did. They almost had to, after seeing so many paintings. Paul kept running his hands over her face, her forehead, her ears, as if trying to make sure she was really there.

Pierrick Gilloteaux gave a picnic when Mary and Paul returned from England. He lofted a blanket over the grass of the meadow behind the inn and laid out black bread, smoked venison, cheese, pickled trout, and a bottle of wine called Clos de la Zolette. The sun broke through the clouds from time to time, and the baby, Françoise, lay on her back with a blanket over her feet. Cats had followed the scent of the food up from the barn and now lay hypnotized on the grass. Paul wondered how old Scratch was making out. He had entrusted her to Carrie and Lonnie Wheeler, who said they would feed her only fish, and by this means make her better.

After the food the clouds split open, leaving a fair blue sky over the valley of the Torchon, and everyone fell asleep. Paul dreamed that grass had grown in his bathtub and he could not find a scythe. Mary and Paul awoke to the sound of Pierrick Gilloteaux putting plates and empty wrappers back into a basket. Mary lay on her back with the baby on her chest while Pierrick told about a couple from New Mexico he had overheard arguing about the significance of the Brabo Fountain in Antwerp.

"The fountain is peculiar, and you really cannot blame them," he said. "A man is running and carrying a large severed hand. He is holding it by the index finger, as if he is about to throw it. The couple had no idea what they were looking at. The woman thought it was a fragment of a larger statue, and the man said it must be an allegory of European unity. They were both wrong, of course. The running man is the Roman soldier Sylvius Brabo, who is supposed to have chopped off the hand of a terrible giant and then thrown the hand into the Scheldt. So I told them this. The woman nodded, but the man did not want to abandon the allegorical interpretation he had worked out. He conceded that there might be a specific story behind the statue, but beyond that, the work must be about some larger idea. I said, 'Yes, the giant Druon Antigonus.' The woman said, 'See, baby, that's how come the hand that is cut off is way bigger than the man's hands.' But you know, this is what I love about American women, that even when their men are completely deluded, they will still help them out of a jam."

Just then, some children from Vertige came clanking up the dusty road with tin cans tied to their ankles, singing "Frère Jacques." But instead of the morning bells ringing "Bing bong bing," they rang "Bim bom bim."

"What's that all about?" said Pierrick.

"They're playing," said Rosine.

Mary worked on *The Black Brook* in a small room under the eaves on the third floor. She painted at night while Paul cleaned up in the kitchen, Rosine fed the animals, and Axel and Judy watched *Les Rues de San Francisco* on television. Axel had built Mary an easel from ash boards he had found in the barn, and Paul had helped her stretch and staple canvas to a wooden frame thirty-three by twenty-two centimeters. She primed the canvas with three coats of gesso, sanding between each coat. With a pestle she ground her paints on the glass top of an old dresser, adding, by eye dropper, *siccatif de cobalt* to make them dry faster. The attic room was often hot by the end of the day, and Paul brought up a large standing fan that whirred and oscillated as Mary worked in shorts and a T-shirt.

She decided to proceed from the lightest to the darkest parts of the portrait and so began with an underpainting of the figure of the seated woman, whose shoulders leaned one way and narrow forehead tilted another, and whose long and slender fingers were interlaced over her knees. Contrary to Carlo's description, the woman wore not a skirt but a loose golden dress, of which only the lower half and the voluminous cuffs of the sleeves were in the light. Her face, shaded, was a warm reddish color, and her hair was gathered behind her ear like a young woman's. One short strand had strayed over her forehead, and behind her lay the darkness of the stream.

Sometimes Françoise slept beside Mary as she worked, in a carrier on the broad planks of the floor, but if the infant was awake, Paul would look after her. Those evenings he walked around the house and grounds holding her like a sack of potatoes, balanced belly down on his left shoulder, with her arms hanging over his back. She seemed to like this mode of travel. He would not see her eyes but everyone said they were either wide and happy or half-closed and sleepy, depending on how long ago she had been fed. Paul and Françoise would cruise Mary's garret, checking out the debris that had been stored there over the years. He showed her, for example, the controversial boar's head. "This belongs to your Uncle Gustave," said Paul. "But if anyone tells you it *is* Uncle Gustave, don't listen, because this is an exaggeration." In a torn chair Paul read to her, Kipling stories or an illustrated book from 1914 called *The Forest of Arden* by George Wharton Edwards.

In the forest villages may still be found the true principle of marriage all unconsciously observed. In the large cities they say that love matches are becoming more and more rare, and it may be so; but in these simple villages the lover does not usually seek a mate because of her *dot*, which is rarely of great account, and the young people do not marry until the swain is well able, through his own thrift and industry, to support a wife and family.

"This is a fairy tale," said Paul.

Mary leaned toward the painting. She touched the fibers of a coarse brush to a smear of white on her palette and then transferred the paint to the canvas in subtle feints — pressing hard at first and then pulling quickly away. The brook came alive with these nervous marks.

"Françoise will not marry until she is famous," said Mary. "That's what Judy says."

Paul held the baby and looked into her eyes. "She's going to study at the Marine Biological Laboratory in Woods Hole."

"And she won't marry in this country."

Paul laughed. "Well, if she's going to be famous, it goes without saying that it won't be in this country."

Mary searched through a clay jar of brushes. They clicked peacefully together. Her diamond caught the light from the unshaded bulb over her head. "Tintin's famous. And where do you think oil painting was invented?"

"In Flanders," said Paul. "Van Eyck. *The Betrothal of the Arnolfini.*"

"Good for you," said Mary. "But they don't believe that anymore."

～

In the meantime, the professor named Glover had organized a club that on weekends engaged in war games in the forest. A number of Vertigians joined the club, following the lead of Cornet the locksmith, Guissard the grocer, and Avaloze the pharmacist. The plan was to restage the eighteen days between the German invasion of Belgium in May 1940 and the surrender of Leopold III, but they did not have nearly enough people to make this credible. So they imagined themselves as a crack squad of saboteurs, which at least made it possible for them to put on old clothes, shoot rifles, and wade stealthily in the river.

At the end of the day they would clean up and meet at the Auberge des Moines for a big supper. They drank beer and ate stewed rabbit and talked with straight faces of the bridges and railways they might destroy to hinder the German advance. Cornet, who in addition to fixing locks served as the mayor of Vertige, led the strategy sessions in his quietly authoritative way, but most of the others spoke loudly, as if to underscore their stubborn resistance, and Pierrick would tell them that if they did not pipe down their plans would be known to all of Germany. After dessert they would resume their real identities and play cards. The staff of the inn tolerated the make-believe while considering it foolish. Rosine pronounced the war club a sacrilege. Axel went out with them twice before slipping on loose gravel and twisting his knee.

Then one day Glover's rifle misfired and part of a blank cartridge lodged in his neck. His comrades carried the bleeding professor out of the woods and through the kitchen door of the inn. Rosine followed them with a mop, and Paul cleared a zinc table where Glover could be laid out.

"The professor is wounded by a sharpshooter," said Guissard.

"Stop that," said Paul. "I'll call the doctor."

"Don't call Andelot," said Avaloze. "He makes fun of us in the town."

Glover held a towel to his neck and sighed with a rasping in his throat.

"This is a pretty thing," said Rosine.

"We were firing blanks," said Henri Guissard. Charcoal striped his sweating face. "Our blanks have never malfunctioned before."

"He is shaking," said a retired butcher who held Glover's booted ankles.

Dr. Andelot had gone fishing, so Paul called the midwife who had come to the inn on the night the baby was desperately hungry. She removed the fragments of the blank with tweezers, applied antiseptic to the wound, and gave Glover a shot that would allow him to sleep. She asked to see Mary and the baby, but they were nowhere to be found. After the war gamers had cleared out with sheepish expressions, Paul went looking for Mary. She was neither in her room nor in the office nor in the barn. Finally he saw her up in the meadow with Françoise and Pierrick Gilloteaux. They were sitting on the grass where they had had the picnic after his and Mary's return from London.

That evening, Mary and Paul stood in the attic looking at the portrait of the woman by the stream. It was nearly finished, and Mary was not happy with it. Or she was *fairly* happy with it. It had not gone the way she wanted it to go. It had turned into something entirely different from what she had expected. She respected what it had become. She had given it her best and made something, whatever that might be.

"I love it," said Paul.

"There's a starchiness to the dress that eludes me," said Mary.

"I think her dress looks starchy."

"Do you?" said Mary.

"Oh, definitely. If it looked any starchier, she would seem uncomfortable," said Paul. "And I love her hands. I thought they would be really difficult, but you seem to have had an easier time with them than Sargent did."

"I do like her hands," said Mary. "I think the shadow is good, I think the redness of the fingertips is good. Well, she's almost done. I still have to lay the lavender light over her arm. You know, she's really kind of forlorn when you look at her."

"Pensive," said Paul. "That was Tommy Maynard's word."

"You talked to Tommy Maynard?"

"Yeah. He's the one that stabbed me in the face."

"Oh, that's right. You said. It's healing well."

"Thank you. How long will the painting take to dry?"

"If we ship it so that nothing touches the surface, you want to be on the safe side . . . two weeks."

"They're not going to say anything."

Mary wiped her hands on a rag. "What will you do when it's done?"

"Go to Scotland," Paul said. "I met a woman who wants me to check on her daughter."

"Let *her* go to Scotland."

"She can't get away."

"Spin those wheels," said Mary.

"What do you mean?"

"You know what I mean."

"Tell me."

"That you run around, and run around, and pretty soon you'll be old and you won't have anything."

"I don't need anything."

"Well, that's good, because that's exactly what you're going to have."

"I promised that I would go to Scotland."

"Well, go then. I'm not stopping you," said Mary. "I'm not stopping you, I'm only telling you. I'm only giving you a warning."

Within the week, Glover had packed for his return to Alberta. Paul drove him to the train station in Jemelle and carried his trunk to the siding. Glover boarded the train, and while Paul did not see him inside the car, he waved at the blank windows as the train pulled away.

Mary finished the painting in time for the local carnival commemorating the driving of the rats from the granary. Axel built a frame and Paul placed the painting on the mantel in the dining room of the inn. They ordered cases of beer and champagne and threw a party. Villagers gathered around the painting and celebrated Mary's reemergence as an artist. Their fingers reached for the rough texture of the paint but stopped short of touching it. The mayor, Cornet, asked Mary to paint his portrait, and she agreed. Rosine took Mary by the hands, kissed her, and said that the young woman by the river was more beautiful than anyone ever could be.

24

Paul had heard about the hard history of Scotland, and some of the people he met there seemed to project the bitterness of the recently conquered. In a grocery store in a southern town, a young girl asked her mother if she could have a sweetie, and the woman behind the counter said, "Where did she get that horrible English accent?" Then the mother and child left, and the grocer told Paul, "My husband's father has never spoken a word in his life, but I consider him lucky next to a Scot with an English accent." She said the English reputation for loyalty and discipline was a farce and that someday the Romans would return to Richborough.

"We'll see," said Paul.

He found the grocer's regional animosity antiquated and small until considering that regional animosity characterized every place he had ever heard of. Take the Flemings and the Walloons. Take Rhode Island and southeastern Massachusetts. Playing out your frustrations on the unknown other was one of the most consistent human traits. Take, for that matter, his own impressions of the Scottish character, about which he knew nothing, really.

Paul adapted to left-side driving by repeating the phrase "Lean left, wide right" like a prayer. The first part meant both stay to the left and take sharp or "lean" left turns; the second part reminded him to loop into the far lane when turning right. Bonner the lawyer's map lay beside him on the passenger seat with the town circled in red. Kirkmadrine was a port on the Irish Sea, and even on a map it looked bleak and romantic.

A plume of rain rose on the horizon but Paul's windshield remained dry. He stopped at a roadside restaurant where the special that day was a lettuce sandwich and tea. Thinking he had encountered some local shorthand, he asked the waitress what all was in the lettuce sandwich, and she said, "Lettuce and butter."

The paper mat beneath his plate had a timeline of Scottish history.

1513: Battle of Flodden. Defeat and death of James IV.
1542: Declaration of war on England at the request of France. Rout of the Scots at Solway Moss.
1544: Burning of Leith and ravaging of the Lothians.
1546: Beginning of the Religious Revolution; burning of George Wishart and murder of Cardinal Beaton.

It was raining when he left the restaurant, but the recent birth of his daughter had given him a resilience he could not shake. When parents perceive the world as it appears to a child, they realize both the beauty of paradise and how far they have strayed from it. It does not matter if this paradise cannot last, or if there are severe limitations on the child's exercise of free will. From the parents' perspective, the child's dependence is part of the appeal. For if the child is in paradise, and if the child is ruled by the parents, what does that make the parents but the king and queen of paradise? This suggests why parental doting can be so obnoxious. Paul had not found it hard to leave Mary and Françoise, and he wondered why. Maybe it was because he had nothing left to do in Vertige, or because he had been meant to go to Scotland, or because it was easier to love people from a distance. If that was true, he thought, then all of human society is a house of cards.

Paul took a room in Kirkmadrine, an overdecorated room in a light blue house facing the bay. There are uncannily specific elements to bad taste that make it seem deeply embedded in human nature, a pinwheel chain of DNA. Pastel colors repeat, as do techniques of textile manufacture that strive to emphasize the individual strands, and decorative covers for things that do not need covers. His long-dead grandmother from Woonsocket could have walked into this room across the ocean without missing a step. She would admire the sconces, the handmade dolls, the puppy photographs. He pictured a black-and-white documentary with stark narration: "And here, in a room where time had virtually stopped, the innkeepers conducted their bizarre experiments."

Actually the innkeepers seemed too meditative to conduct experiments. Their names were Catherine and Mike.

"How did you find us?" said Catherine. "Even the English don't find us."

Mike sat forward in a big chair in the parlor, pulled up his socks, and let his pant legs fall over them. "There's very little here beyond the golf course," he said.

"I'm looking for an American woman named Kim," said Paul. "She would be in her thirties."

"Try the golf course," said Mike.

Paul walked on the strand in the late afternoon. Kirkmadrine had black streets lined with granite houses and painted wooden doors. The town sloped down to the harbor. A sailboat heeled so hard in the driving wind that the sail threatened to take on water. Paul stood for a long time watching the sailors bring the boat around a stone breakwater and come up from the docks in yellow raincoats. The three men seemed tossed still by the motion of the waves.

"I'm looking for an American named Kim," Paul said.

"You would do better to be less particular," said one of the men. "We just came from Northern Ireland."

He kept walking. Where the houses ended, two wooden posts stood on either side of a trail that climbed steeply through hills of coarse grass. Paul followed the path as it wound along the cliff above the water. Packed gravel gave way to footbridges over deep gullies with pummeling waves far below. Clouds hid Northern Ireland and darkened the air. The trail arrived at last at a small castle. Invaders would have had a hard time attacking from the water; they would have had to land down the coast and loop around. The jagged holes of the lower windows gave no light. Everything in his childhood suggested that something waited in the castle to rip his heart out, and everything in his adulthood told him he would fall in a hole, break a leg, and starve to death, his calls for help heard only by the wheeling and indifferent terns. He stepped up into the doorway of a round tower. Moss blanketed the stone steps and the sky hung in a velvet circle far above. A crow cawed and flapped from a place that seemed right beside his ear, and then the black shadow lifted and disappeared against the soft gray disk of sky.

Paul climbed the turning steps to the second story and stepped into a long room with light in it. The roof of the castle had long since evaporated, and there seemed to have been another floor or two at some point, because the gable walls continued to climb, as did fragments of chimneys, forming black spikes against the sky. Paul walked on the long matted grass of the room, where narrow windows looked out on the sea and birds' nests clung to the windowsills.

The air seemed full of time. He wondered how many people had been here before him, all believing as he did that now was the only moment that mattered, that the past was a comic prelude and the future a disorganized rumor. Probably a lot of people — generations of royals and servants locked in their lopsided dependency. As a child he'd had a repeated nightmare involving some massive object from space descending on a ring of children mired within its growing shadow. Just then he realized that the falling body in his dream was only the earth, sweeping down to bury the dead.

Mike and Catherine carried bowls of water down the stairway of the hotel.

"We have a hole in the roof," said Mike.

"We call this kind of rain a haar," said Catherine.

"I found a castle outside of town."

"When I mentioned the golf course, I forgot to mention the castle," Mike said.

"The story goes that a terrible siege occurred there in 1317," said Catherine, "and was broken by a flock of corbies bearing the features of John Baliol."

"I don't put much stock in it," said Mike. "Tell him about the flung baby. I find that story more credible than the supernatural corbies."

"There's little to choose between the two," said Catherine. "But I will tell it. A servant girl dropped the heiress into the sea and then jumped herself, and this left the laird so shell-shocked that the Solemnists led by James Harper captured the castle in ten days."

That night, Paul lay beneath a crocheted bedspread, drinking ale and listening to a BBC radio show on which a host interviewed Rex Compton, who had once fronted a Blackpool band called Rex and the Freemasons, whose main hit had been a song called "Let's Have a Cigarette." Rex Compton drove a truck these days, and he told a long story about losing his dog.

"I went all about, you know, calling ''Ere, Tuffy . . . 'Ere, Tuffy.' Finally it occurred to me to look in me mum's garage."

"This is still in Blackpool?" said the interviewer quietly.

"No," said Rex Compton. "This would be many years later, in Mungrisdale."

"Mungrisdale in Cumbria?"

"Precisely."

"And, at the end of the day, did you find Tuffy?"

"I did. And very relieved I was to see that little dog."

In the morning, over a breakfast of tea and fried potatoes, Paul watched out the window of the dining room as the boat he had seen the night before headed back to Northern Ireland, still sailing at a slant, under a blue sky with brush-stroke clouds. Then he drove out to the golf course, which was called Dreighknowe. He knew nothing about golf, but this seemed like a difficult course, with fairways that angled between sand traps and swift-moving streams.

Paul asked after Kim in the clubhouse. "We don't have any Kim," said a man with thin black hair combed over his scalp. "Most probably you mean Robin Redding. She is an American. Grew up in Ohio, as the story goes, and won the Akron Invitational at a very young age. Robin came to Scotland to learn the history of her game, and to our good fortune she stayed. We have two pros, Robin and Kyle. We believe it's important that the apprentice golfer get on with the instructor, and what we like to say is, 'If you don't care for Kyle, you'll care for Robin.' Is it lessons you're after?"

"Yes," said Paul.

"Go down these stairs to my left," said the man. "It's thirty-seven pounds for an hour."

Robin sat on a bench sharpening her cleats with a small rasp. She was an angular woman who wore her ash-blond hair in a ponytail held by red elastic.

"Mostly, the game of golf is a game of balance," she said. "It's all about an awareness of your center and what it's doing." She stood up and planted her feet wide apart. She wore little white socks rolled once at the ankle. "You want this" — she thumped her sternum with a fist — "to line up with this" — she bent down and touched the floor between the tips of her toes. "When it doesn't, the golfer develops a lot of anxiety without knowing why. And though I know it sounds simple, it's really very hard."

"It doesn't sound simple," said Paul.

"Now let's go out and hit a few."

Paul drove the ball straight off the practice tee but extremely high. His second drive ripped viciously along the ground. His third did the same.

"Where did that go?"

"Doesn't matter," said Robin. "Have you ever golfed before?"

"No," said Paul.

"Try relaxing." She drove the heel of her hand into the middle of his back. "You've got a tension thing going on right here. Draw the club slowly. Don't bend your spine. Let the back of your neck rise as if drawn by a string. You have good arms, but your hands get in the way. They say if you could swing a club without hands, you'd be better off. Put all things from your mind. For now, just grab the club any old way."

Paul hit the next shot long. A boy gathering golf balls and putting them in a red bucket watched it go by.

"And that is what I'm talking about," said Robin.

"I came from Connecticut looking for you," said Paul.

"Well," said Robin. Her eyes struggled to maintain their bland and friendly gaze. "That's flattering."

She showed him the way to hold a club, with the index finger of the left hand hooked around the little finger of the right. He swung the club and missed entirely.

"Was your name ever Kim?"

"Once upon a time," she said. "But I hated it. It's so flat, don't you think?"

"Everyone's name sounds strange to that person."

"Kim," she said. "Kim. It just sits there. What sort of parents would call their child Kim?"

"I don't really want to learn golf."

"This is a golf course."

"I lived in a house on a lake," said Paul. "This was the house where you were born. I encountered your mother — I guess 'encounter' is the word — and she wanted to know that you were all right."

Robin sat on a bench next to a ball-washing stand. "You're not funny."

"I'm not trying to be."

"Who are you really? A lawyer? What's going on?"

Paul sat beside her on the bench. "A journalist."

"I have no quotes to give you."

"Don't want any," said Paul. "I've only come to find out how you are."

"I'm a golfer," she said despondently. They sat watching the boy wandering from ball to ball with his red bucket. "I don't know what else to say."

"And I don't know what else to ask."

"Some journalist you are."

"I'm a bad journalist. One of the very worst."

"In Ohio the reporters would dog me all over the locker room. 'I got my ass kicked,' I would say. 'My clubs are fucked.' And they would write, '"I took a drubbing,"' she said. "My clubs are nonsense."' It was crazy. I would never say 'drubbing' even if I had taken one."

"But you won big matches."

"It's true," she said. "My mother? My mother lives in Toledo. And if you mean my mother by birth, she's dead. She died younger than I am now."

"I have a letter she wrote you."

"I've already read it," said Robin. "She was a very messed-up person. I hate to say it, but what happened was probably lucky for me. Really, the whole ugly thing, in the long run. I had a beautiful childhood in Toledo. My parents loved me because they couldn't have kids of their own. I rode horses. We had an in-ground pool. My life was going from course to course, and everyone loved me. I never wondered about my real parents. I never had this anxiety everyone talks about. I loved the sun. I never wanted to go on some journey to find everything out."

"That's fair."

"What do we do now?"

"We could go on with the lesson," said Paul.

"Take the club."

He stood at the tee again with his fingers locked over the leather grip. "It's like I can't feel it."

"You'll get over that," said Robin. "Imagine a sheet of glass, a picture window, next to the ball. This helps a lot of people. And you want to get the club head as close to the glass as you can without breaking it."

Paul raised the club and stopped. "I don't get it," he said. "If there's glass in front of the ball, and I swing, how can I help but break it?"

"No," said Robin. "*Beside* the ball. Let me show you." She knelt on the far side of the tee and raised her hands with outstretched fingers. "If you imagine a line connecting your right foot and your left, and pointing in the direction you want the ball to go, the glass runs *parallel* to that line."

"Yeah?"

"This is the glass. O.K.? My hands are the glass."

The sailors from Northern Ireland returned to Kirkmadrine three days later. In a pub they invited Paul to join a card game. It had rained all night but now the sunlight came through the windows and across the copper surface of the bar. The sailors' names were Kern, Leland, and Jerry. Kern wore a flat cap, Leland had a beard, and Jerry was short. The game was closely played and took half the afternoon. Jerry could shuffle cards with either hand. Paul was up twenty-seven pounds when the men invited him on a sail down the Mull of Culloden.

The four of them motored from the dock in an orange

Zodiac inflatable. While boarding the sailboat Paul took care not to fall in the water lest he sink. The wind was a concern. There was hardly enough of it. While showing Paul how to use a cam cleat, Leland said he did not remember it being this calm in two fortnights. The cam cleat was a technologically satisfying device made of two toothed and teardrop jaws that secured the jib sheet and the kicking strap and other lines of significance. After seeing how the cam cleat operated, Paul worked his way around the boat looking for stray lines. "Want me to cleat this?" he would say.

The boat glided past the breakwater, and Paul looked back at the round harbor and the ring of houses hugging it. When the boat was farther along, he saw the cliffs and then the castle, with its black spires and grassy windows.

Leland pointed away from the coast, at a low outcropping of land with gnarled trees and white buildings. "Do you know those islands?" he said. "That's Tulloch and that's Kail."

"I see one," said Paul.

"There are two," said Kern, who worked the tiller with one hand while bracing the other against the gunnel. "Kail's behind Tulloch."

Leland tugged the beard beneath his chin. They were all seated in the cockpit. "Tulloch has a monastery. There's a healing spring, but for the most part they watch television."

"Never try to draw a monk away from a televised tennis match," said Kern. "It's like trying to take lamb chops from a tiger."

Jerry produced a tin of chewing tobacco, put some in his mouth, and squinted at the instrument panel on the cabin wall. He tapped one of four glass dials with a knuckle. "We should turn on the engine if this is all we can manage."

"I don't like turning on the engine," said Kern.

"We'll have trouble in the race," said Jerry.

"And if I wanted to, it's out of fuel."

"We're going to race?" said Paul.

"No, no," said Leland. "It's a point, right up there, where currents converge."

The wind moved drowsily, directionless, and the boat coasted into the rough water at the southern tip of Tulloch. The transition seemed to happen immediately, as if a line had been crossed. The waves churned, the sail luffed, and the boom lifted and fell, making the stays at one moment slack and the next taut to the point of breaking, or so it seemed. Meanwhile, the boat was turning gradually sideways.

Kern laughed and drew in the mainsheet, which threaded through a series of pulleys. "Paul," he said, "what wind there is, we can't catch, with the boom flying about."

"I understand that," said Paul.

"I want you to go up there."

"Where's that?"

"On the boom."

"Really?" said Paul. "Why?"

"For the weight," said Kern. "I need Jerry and Leland down here. There's no great trick involved. You sit with your back to the sail. It's just like a hammock or a comfortable chair."

"For how long?" said Paul.

"Until we get going."

Paul gripped a wooden handrail and climbed on top of the cabin. "Wait," said Jerry. He tossed a life jacket to Paul. "Don't forget your waistcoat," he said.

At the mast, where the foot of the mainsail drew nearest to the bulkhead, Paul placed two hands on the boom, hoisted himself as one would onto a balance beam, turned, and dropped back against the sail.

He looked at Kern, but Kern was staring now at the rocky shore of Tulloch, which seemed to be drawing closer. "Like this?" said Paul.

"What?" he said, looking up. "Move aft! Come back! You've no leverage there."

A sheet of water broke over the bow and rained down. Paul

worked his way back along the boom. With the cabin no longer beneath his feet, he rode well above the deck, looking down at the sailors. Jerry gave a silver handle to Leland, who fit it into a winch and began turning.

"What keeps me from swinging over the water?" Paul shouted.

Leland watched the currents. "Will of God," he said.

"Do you do this all the time?"

"No! Not really!"

Paul considered the situation, taking comfort in the fact that if he were thrown from the boom, it would be an open question whether he would be better off landing in the water or in the boat, where he might strike his head against some fitting.

"Look," called Jerry. "It's a monk." A figure moved among the houses on the island.

"Hello, Father!" yelled Leland.

"Are we getting anywhere?" said Paul.

"Making progress," said Kern. He stood at the tiller and peered down the length of the boat. "Paul, I think I want you to come down now."

"Meaning, to the deck?"

"I wouldn't wait, either."

Paul slid back toward the mast, and as his sneakers touched the cabin, the boat dropped away from him. By all evidence, they had sailed off the end of the sea. The bow, or perhaps the entire boat, fell for an amazingly long time. Then water slammed the hull and the boom or the mast or the stays or something cracked like a cannon. Paul felt as he sometimes did during the thunderous initial climb of flight: if he must die, then best to go in spectacle, leaving nothing but scraps.

Then he found himself beside the companion hatch and holding the wooden rail. The boat headed in a substantially different direction than it had been going, east instead of south, but at least it was still floating, and the wiry trees of the Tulloch coast receded over the rough water.

"I believe we'll go this way for a while," said Kern. "Your timing could not have been better, Paul. Any later and you would have been watching Martina Hingis with the monks."

"You should have warned me," said Paul.

"I did warn you."

"Is it something you would have wanted to know?" said Leland.

"I wouldn't have wanted to know that," said Jerry.

"And how to phrase it?" said Leland. "'Say, stranger, the boat is about to be shaken like a stick in the mouth of a huge dog.'"

"It would have alarmed you beyond what is warranted," said Jerry.

"Still, I take responsibility," said Kern.

Paul hired Robin to golf with him on the bank holiday in August. He liked carrying clubs, resting his arm on the bag, and judging when to pull the flag from the hole, but beyond these formal matters his play was fundamentally unsound. Robin used left-handed clubs, though she was right-handed, in an effort to make it more of a match. Still, by the time they had reached the fifth tee, she was eleven strokes up.

"Does it demoralize you to be losing to a woman golfing left-handed?" she said.

"It didn't until you mentioned it."

She cupped her jaw in her hands. "These wisdom teeth are bugging me," she said.

The fifth hole was a par three that fell sharply from the tee. Paul kept his head down, stayed mindful of the imaginary glass and the imaginary string and all of the other phantom junk she had planted in his mind, and socked the ball onto the green. Robin duplicated his shot, and they started down the path from the tee. They walked briskly and had already played through two foursomes who got to stand in severe witness of Paul's unpredictable tee shots. Now he hurried along watching as a man on a parallel fairway had the head of his club fly off on the follow-through.

The sporting mismatch seemed to reflect the absurdity of his mission to Kirkmadrine. He had expected to find Linda's daughter destitute, stick thin, a limping junkie, a morbid clerk with dark rings around her eyes. Instead, she stalked the fairways with strong bronze legs beneath a swinging green skirt, she drove the ball with force and ambidexterity, and she regarded her strange origin as a mild curiosity. After the solid tee shot, he four-putted the fifth hole.

"Many rats catch the cat," said Robin.

"Did you see that guy on the other hole?" said Paul. "His club came apart."

"Oh, Paul," she said. "I wouldn't tell that. In Scotland we don't repeat such stories."

25

Robin had two molars pulled by a dental surgeon named McTawse, whose office was in Ochterfail, about ten miles away. Paul drove her there and waited in a room with red wallpaper while the surgery took place. He went up to a window in the wall to ask the nurse if there would be plenty of painkillers for Robin when she was done. The nurse said sternly that he needn't worry, that Dr. McTawse would medicate her according to her needs. Seven diplomas hung on the wall — a defensively high number of diplomas, to Paul's way of thinking. A shoebox held free tickets to a play called *Pain of Youth*, and Paul took two. A children's corner of the waiting room offered the adventure books of the Skelmorlie Twins, Graham and Tana, and a battery-powered ice floe on which plastic penguins climbed an escalator and slid down a curved chute. This was a clever setup, and he watched the penguins tottering along in lock step for some time before switching them off and picking up the *Ochterfail Times*, the front page of which featured a review of the Lipizzan stallions' SRO appearance in Oban on Friday last. He wondered how many hundreds of stallions qualified as Lipiz-zans, or if, in addition to their undeniable jumping talents, which were richly described here, the horses had the ability to be in all places at all times. The story compared their graceful antics to those of the mythical kelpie or river horse — a nice touch that he had not had at his disposal back in Ashland, for he had never heard of kelpies until this moment.

When Robin returned to the waiting room, he saw her un-steady for the first time. She cried softly into a thick white towel, and Paul rose to put an arm around her shoulders. They moved slowly to the window, where the nurse stood waiting. Then Dr. McTawse came out; he had blood on the fringe of his smock. With slashing strokes he wrote a prescription on a clipboard. "She wouldn't take a general," said Dr. McTawse. "I told her everyone takes the general, but Miss Redding was disinclined to hear my advice. It was a bit of a tussle."

"We could've gone somewhere else," said Paul.

"It makes no difference to me," said Dr. McTawse. "I run people in and out of here all day."

"We'll need plenty of painkiller," said Paul.

"I'll give her two bottles of Percodan," said Dr. McTawse, "and that's treating her like my own daughter. They were difficult teeth which had grown sideways in the gum." He pulled down his lip to show where the teeth had lodged as Robin's eyes widened and her crying became audible through the towel.

Paul fed Robin pills and stopped to pick up lemon yogurt, bananas, and beer on the way to her house. She had what the lowland Scots call a but-and-ben, on the green ridge above Kirkmadrine. Red tiles roofed the cottage and ivy climbed the walls, and still it seemed a modest place to house someone of Robin Redding's stature. Paul dropped his keys into a bowl of blue marbles that stood on a table near the front door and helped Robin to her davenport. In the tiny bathroom he rinsed cold water over a washcloth. A box of tampons stood ripped open beneath the sink, and a wooden-handled back scrubber hung intimately on the tiled wall above the bathtub. He looked at his face in the mirror of the medicine chest. The scar was healing, but beyond that he looked older. His whiskers, which he had shaved only the night before, seemed less a sign of freedom from regimentation than proof of repetition and degradation. The black holes in the center of his eyes alone connected him to his youth, and it was good that they did, because when they clouded up, he figured, he would be dead. But that could take years, and, thus enlightened, Paul returned to the davenport with a detour to the kitchen, to fetch a spoon for the yogurt.

He cooled Robin's hot brow with the wet cloth and pulled up a chair to watch her eat. He had never seen her eat before and took encouragement from the scrape of the spoon against the curved wall of the plastic cup. He remembered the observant passenger on the plane. *All done with your yogurt, I see.* Ivy leaves crept along the sills of the windows. Paul said it was a pretty place and asked Robin if the pills had kicked in. She lay back on the couch, closed her eyes, and said she could feel the breeze through the window on every molecule of her face. When Paul had had his wisdom teeth removed, he had almost wished that they could grow back in, so he could get more Percodan, and he told her so.

"Where did you live then?" said Robin calmly. The gauze that the doctor had stuffed into her mouth made her voice a thick and distant buzz.

"Providence."

"You said that my mother wanted to know about me," said Robin. "What did you mean by that? You were only surmising."

"I mean I've seen her and talked to her."

With these words he remembered his bereft grandfather, standing aslant in a cemetery in Woonsocket and claiming to have seen Paul's grandmother and the young dead Aaron standing side by side; and he remembered what a deluded old man his grandfather had seemed, with bumblebees cruising heavily around his ears.

"But if you've read the letter," said Robin, "everything you know could have come from that, and the rest you could have imagined."

"That's occurred to me," said Paul. "But I don't think it went that way. Let me show you something." He went out to his car and fetched the stamp album from the trunk.

"This is yours." He held the album before her eyes and slowly turned the frail manila pages. "You and your mother did this together, because you liked stamps. Isn't that something?"

"We didn't follow through," said Robin. But she took the album, closed it, and held it to her chest. "Give us a beer, will you?"

Paul did so. "Now, I'm going to leave this yogurt cup on the chair," he said. "Do you know what for?" He leaned near her ear and whispered, "So you can spit blood if you need to."

"You are a trip," she said.

He put some Percodan tablets in his pocket and left Robin looking at the stamp album on the davenport.

The castle ruins looked safer in sunlight, and the low green profile of Northern Ireland hovered on the edge of the water. Paul explored the lower chambers that had been dark on the afternoon he arrived. Perhaps they had been used for torture, or more likely something mundane — the storage of wheat. In an underground room he took one Percodan and climbed the stairs to the long open room above. A centipede scuttled across his shoe as he sat at the hearth of the crumbled fireplace. It had enough legs for a host of regular insects, and he decided that this was what gave centipedes their creepy quality — the presence of many animals in one. He swallowed another pill. Dose calibration was paramount.

He remembered his student who had overdosed at the high school in Providence. Paul had gone to see him in the hospital.

"I was supposed to go to a party," said the student. "My friend Ned invited me to a party. The problem is that my other friends don't like Ned. One of my biggest conflicts in life is walking that line between my two sets of friends. Sometimes I dream that I'm standing in a supermarket between the soup cans and the crackers, and I have to choose. For some reason, in the dream I can't get both."

"You can't mess with needle drugs."

"If you could put needle drugs in a bottle, everyone would love them. Everyone would say, Let's have some more of those needle drugs."

Paul said nothing, for he found the student's logic persuasive.

"I don't shoot up lightly, Mr. Nash. You know me — only when the world crowds me in. I keep everything I need in a cigar box in the attic. So I shot up and everything felt simple again, just the way I like it. I came down from the attic and pulled on my coat and took a bus to the school. That's where everyone meets, in the parking lot, by the incinerator. When you see two cars full of kids stopped in the street, that's what they're saying, 'Go to the school,' which is very ironic, because no one likes the school. So I was walking through the weeds behind the incinerator when I realized that something was wrong. I fell on my knees and then over on my side. I could see the weeds, and through the weeds I could see a bicycle chained to the incinerator with its front wheel all twisted. Why is it that when you see a chained bicycle the wheel is always bent?"

"Good question. I don't know the answer."

"I'm not ashamed to die. I mean, I'm not afraid to die, but I am somewhat curious."

"You're not going to die."

"But eventually, I mean. In church they used to say heaven has angels with tinsel hats, but I never believed that. I guess I think it will be like the time I was doing handstands on my desk in study hall and somehow I lost my balance and fell. It made a terrible racket, and the teacher got furious and sent me up to the sickroom. I don't know if you've ever been in the sickroom, but it has a good view of the city. And I thought, Well, you can call

295

it punishment, but this seems pretty nice to me. Then no one came to get me all day. I guess they forgot where I was. Finally the sun went down and the lights started coming up all over town. And that would be my best guess of what heaven will be like . . . a little room with a good view where they never come to get you. What do you think of heaven? Or if not heaven, whatever you want to call it."

Paul sat back in a hospital chair, resting his heels on the frame of the bed. "My hearing isn't the best."

"We know."

"It works out well in class, because when kids mouth off I don't hear it, so pretty soon they stop."

"Not really."

"But even in perfect silence I hear something. It's like the noise the ocean makes, and sometimes it's very loud. It's like someone speaking a language I can't understand. And I think that when you die that's all you get — a sound."

"You have a shabby theory," said the student.

"You're younger and more optimistic."

When Robin's mouth felt better, Paul commissioned her to ride horses with him on trails near the golf course. Robin rode a former polo stallion named Carton, and Paul rode a towering and barrel-bellied mare. She was by far the widest horse he had ever ridden, with massive legs and a meter's swing in her gait. They walked or posted the horses down hills and cantered them up. Paul's horse seemed dismissive of his riding skills until he demonstrated that he had some; then her ears pricked and she began to work. When she overtook the polo horse on a hill, the stallion watched calmly and then extended his black and shining neck and pounded the sandy path. There is no beating a polo horse, except on another polo horse. Robin's hair streamed behind her in the wind. Eventually they left the trails through a wooden gate and meandered down a narrow road where a workman hammered the tin roof of a house going up by a bridge. Then they cantered along a soft needled path between evergreens, dipping their heads beneath the scratching boughs and arriving in a clearing over the sea.

"This is my place," said Robin. "I smoked when I first got to Scotland, and Carton and I would come up here and have a smoke. It was very peaceful."

"Smoke sinks right into my brain," said Paul. "I never buy cigarettes."

"I miss them sometimes," said Robin.

They watched a big barge moving through the water, followed by a cloud of birds. The barge made its way like a floating city block.

Robin fell on the way back. Her rein broke on the right side of the bit, and Carton bolted. Robin reached up to take the bit in her hand, and at the same moment the horse jumped something real or imagined in the path, and she tumbled off and landed on the ground. The horse kept running but stopped after a while to look behind. By the time Paul rode up, Robin was on her feet and holding the back of her head.

"You've jinxed me," she said. "I don't fall. I never fall."

"Are you O.K.?"

"I will be," she said. She circled her arms at her sides. "I will be if you'd give me some breathing space."

Carton trotted up but would not look at her, as if to spare her the embarrassment; instead, he gazed placidly across the hills.

"I have to give lessons this afternoon," said Robin. "I should have known better than to come out here with you."

After the accident Paul felt apprehensive about seeing her again, but he had those theater tickets and had given her a lot of business, so two nights later she agreed to see *Pain of Youth* in Ochterfail. It was performed by a traveling theater and told the story of decadent medical students in reckless Vienna at the turn of the century. After the play they had spaghetti at a restaurant called the Casino and then walked the nearly empty streets of Ochterfail. Robin had cigarettes, and they smoked, and Paul felt a peaceful and dark blue veil dropping over his mind.

Turning down an alley, they arrived at the dental surgeon's office, which was in a small house.

"What do you say, let's roll out the archbishop's doormat," said Robin.

Paul said he was not familiar with the phrase, and Robin produced a plastic bottle from her purse and splashed liquid onto the door of the house.

"What is that?" said Paul.

"Club cleaner," said Robin.

She lit a match and tossed it at the door, which began to burn in streaks of yellow-white flame. Paul kicked the door to douse the flames, and three men who happened to be coming around the corner of the alley shouted and gave chase. Robin and Paul ran, but Robin had got a head start, and Paul ducked behind a mobile home with two wheels on the curb and two on the pavement. The three men put out the fire and walked up the alley. And then something lucky happened: a man and a woman stepped out of the back of the mobile home. The three men chased them down the alley, shouting, and finally dragged the young man to the ground. He did not look much like Paul — he had long shaggy hair and glasses — and yet he and his companion had some explaining to do before the men could be convinced that they had the wrong couple. The man showed them the tag on the collar of his shirt, although how this might have established his innocence Paul did not know.

He found Robin waiting in her car by the theater. She drove south past Kirkmadrine and onto the narrow two-lane road that curved down the Mull of Culloden. It was a clear night with a moon bright as a drum. The farther they drove, the higher the land rose above the water. There was not much out here — knots of houses from time to time, and a caravan park with lighted trailers in which people could be seen moving past the windows.

"Burn many houses?" said Paul.

Robin worked her fists around the steering wheel. "A sport told me about it." That's what she called her golfing clients. "I couldn't teach the other day, by the way. Too much of a headache. I called in sick and just lay in my bed remembering things."

"Probably you had a little concussion," said Paul. "But you can go to jail for things like that."

The dashboard lights softly lit her face. "I even thought I remembered my mother," she said. "We were on the porch of a house and she was painting the floor. I want to say she was painting it green, if that's possible. Was the porch of the house that you lived in painted green?"

"I don't think so. But it could have been painted over."

"Yeah. Yeah. Sure it could. But anyway, as she was painting, some bug got stuck in the paint, and it seems to me she got really upset. She said, 'Cockeyed bug,' and I thought this was a literal reference, that the bug must have strange eyes. She was wearing a white shirt with the tails tied over her stomach."

"Do you want me to drive?"

"I'm fine," said Robin, and after another mile or so, she said, "Do you have everything you need? I don't really know what you came to find out, but maybe you've found it and could leave in good conscience. Because I don't think I want to see you anymore. You put some kind of spell on me. They say that golfers are superstitious, and it's true. Plus, we really have very little in common."

"Just give me the sign."

The road ended at a white wooden gate, beyond which a driveway led to a lighthouse with a blue-white beacon that swept over the headland. A sign on the gate said FREE CATS, and though it was late Robin insisted on going up to see about the cats. The gate was locked, and they climbed over it and walked to a small house at the base of the light.

"Come in, come in," said the lighthouse keeper. "I just made bean soup. It's very good. Come in."

"You have cats?"

"They're all gone. And I thank you for reminding me that the sign must come down. The mother is up in the tower. She is the best mouser we've ever had. I say 'we,' but out here it's just me, and I'm eager for the company."

Paul and Robin ate soup and biscuits with the lighthouse keeper. The soup was very good, just as he had said.

"Do you follow the news?" he said. "The Americans are trying to get Mars. With all they have, they now want Mars."

Robin touched a napkin to her mouth. "I did hear something about that."

Paul said, "I would go to Mars, get a little place and settle down."

"You don't really believe that," said the lighthouse keeper. "Who can figure out the way things are anymore?"

Paul and Robin agreed that no one could.

There was a piano in the parlor, and Robin played while the lighthouse keeper and Paul sat in overstuffed chairs and listened to the music. She played "Loch Lomond," "Bang a Gong," and "How Are Things in Glocca Mora?" Paul found himself in such a good mood that he sang along with "Glocca Mora," which he sort of knew because his sister Carmen had been a page turner for the piano player in a high school production of *Finian's Rainbow.* He remembered the curtain calls, the cast loaded down with roses, and he faked the words he'd forgotten. *Is that little brook still happening there?*

26

Paul made it back to Ashland one last time. He did not know why he was going or what would follow. The idea of returning to tell a ghost that her daughter was a golf pro in Scotland was so obviously nuts that it never occurred to him. In any case, he found a crew of workmen swarming over the Tallis house, carrying ladders, toolboxes, and buckets of skim-coat. A mason stood on a high ladder chiseling brittle mortar from the chimney while inside painters rolled white latex over the walls. The statue of Linda and a suitcase stood on the front porch as if the statue were waiting for a bus.

Paul walked over to Loom and Alice's house, but no one was home, so he went into the kitchen and heated up a can of lentil soup. While waiting for the soup to cook he found the address of Loom's mother in a phone book. Then he poured the soup into a bowl, broke Crown Pilot crackers over it, and ate. Afterward, he washed the dish and spoon in the sink, put them away, and climbed one set of stairs and then another to the cupola, where ledger books and a letter from an investment firm lay on the table. The letter said that the strategy that had been devised for Loom and Alice had become outmoded, what with blanket bonds sitting dead in the water. Paul looked out the window and saw Mr. Freel the butler lying on a rug in the trough of the roof over the sun porch. Paul raised a window and stepped carefully down the shingles.

"What's going on next door?"

"The house is being renovated in order that it might be sold," said Mr. Freel. "Your belongings have been packed for you. They could not find any luggage, so Alice picked up some Samsonite."

"What are you doing?"

"Taking sun," said Mr. Freel. He pointed at the crown of a tree beside the house. "Do you see that? It is going to come down."

Evelyn Hanover lived in a tall apartment building for retired people in Damascus. The doorman called ahead and sent Paul to the top floor.

The old lady led him into her apartment. Paintings of many sizes hung on the walls: ocean pictures, desert pictures, foggy abstract pictures. A bank of windows looked down on the hills and settlements of Damascus.

"I remember you," said Evelyn. "You read from the Song of Solomon at my son's wedding."

"'How beautiful are thy feet,'" said Paul.

She turned to the windows. "This is the best view in the county. I consider myself lucky to have lived in beautiful places all my life. I grew up in Philadelphia, and then we moved to Taormina and then Banff. It was in Banff that I met Gilbert. After I saw him ski, I told my father I would have him for my own. My father's name was Loomis."

"I always wondered where that came from."

"When my parents gave parties, we children would sit in our bedrooms reciting Keats. 'God of the golden bow, / And of the golden lyre, / And of the golden hair, / And of the golden fire —' I remember the chandelier in Taormina, with griffins and angels facing each other across the lights. But of all the views I ever had, none could top Banff."

They left the windows and sat down. "There was a teacher named Linda Tallis," said Paul. "She was a neighbor of yours who lost her job and drowned."

"It happened so long ago."

"You would remember."

"And what if I don't want to? And what business is it of yours?"

"I moved into their house," said Paul. "I found a statue, I found a scrapbook, I found a hat."

"And I'm glad you found a hat, Mr. Nash," said Evelyn Hanover. "I'm so glad that you found a hat for your head."

"You would remember if you had someone fired."

Her eyes contracted and glittered. "You concern yourself with unfairness," she said. "I can tell that you do. What if I told you of a man who left his wife and invaded the home of another family with the intention to disrupt and deceive and take that which he had no business even wanting."

"There was a teacher —"

"Let me finish. To the point where two little children would sit where you are sitting and ask, 'When is she coming home? When is my mother coming home?' What would you say about a man like that?"

"Just on the face of it?"

"How else?"

"I don't accept the premise. But I know what you want to hear. That he is 'without scruples.' Something like that. That he is 'not good.'"

"And the evidence would bear you out."

"Maybe the evidence would."

"Loom doesn't pay attention," said Evelyn. "But I pay a great deal of attention. My eyes are as keen as the day I was born. Why, look what I found on the ground today."

From a small table she took a woven grass pouch, cupping it gently in both hands. Dried grass ends trembled in the air. "This was once the nest of a Baltimore oriole. It must have blown down over the winter. I found it with my eyes."

She set the nest back on the table. "As for Linda Tallis, the school board giveth and the school board taketh away. Gilbert and I were not privileged to be on the school board. Did we know people who were? I'm sure that we must have. Mostly, I believe they talked about furnaces."

"It was not your concern."

"I wouldn't say that," said Evelyn. "No one wants to see a young woman die. I didn't. And Gilbert *really* didn't. He went up in the cupola and stayed there. For days at a time he kept the door locked, doing what, I could not tell you. Then one night — this would have been after the funeral — Roman Tallis came over to say that from his place he could see a fire burning at the top of our house. So Roman and I hurried upstairs and began pounding on the attic door. Fortunately Roman was wearing his tool belt, and he took a pair of pliers and removed the hinge pins in an instant. Roman Tallis was like that. Just when you thought he was useless, he would do something clever."

"Was the house on fire?"

"Not really," said Evelyn. "But it soon would have been. There were flames and soot and smoke everywhere. It turned out that Gil had carried the barbecue grill up there and built a fire. So I blasted away with a fire extinguisher, although it occurred to me later I might have just closed the lid of the grill. But it was too late. And I asked Gilbert why he had done this, and he said that he loved her. And I said I understood that, but burning the house I did not understand. Then Roman took a glove from his tool belt and dropped it at Gilbert's feet. It was a work glove with a flared cuff and looked just like a gauntlet from olden times."

Someone knocked on the door. Mrs. Hanover's physical therapist had arrived. "Don't mind me," he said. "My name is Roland. Go ahead with your talking."

The therapist stood by Evelyn's chair raising and lowering her arms, one at a time. "Once I was sick and Evie called me at home. She says, 'Roland, I need my routine.'"

"Mr. Nash has been asking after a Linda Tallis," said Evelyn.

The therapist shook his head. "Never heard of her."

"Well, you wouldn't have."

"And the glove . . . ," said Paul.

"Roman wanted a duel," said Evelyn. "And he got one."

"Sounds interesting, though." said the therapist. He smiled as her shoulder made a small cracking sound. "Easy, old bones."

The Lager Festival had come around again, and neither the Coltsfoot Motel nor the Pail Hotel had vacancies. Carrie and Lonnie Wheeler let Paul pitch a tent in their back yard next to the swimming pool. Scratch the cat walked around the cedar railing at the top of the round pool as Lonnie, Carrie, and Paul sorted ropes and stakes.

"I won't be in your way long," said Paul.

"Now where you going?" said Lonnie.

"Go, go, go," said Carrie.

"Rush, rush, rush."

"He said we should go, did you know that?" Carrie said. "To New Orleans or California."

"For what? This is the life."

"I'm taking my car into the shop tomorrow," said Paul. "They're going to tune it up and get it in road shape."

"Forget that beater," said Carrie. "Get a new car. The bank has very attractive rates."

"That's a good idea," said Paul.

"I would lease," said Lonnie.

"They want you to lease so bad it must not be in your favor," said Carrie.

They raised the tent and went over to a dealership on the south side of Ashland. A saleswoman with red bangs and transparent lipstick showed him a dark green sedan with a moonroof and six speakers.

"I'll take it."

"Decisive," said Carrie.

"He wants to lease," said Lonnie.

"Leasing is no mystery," said the saleswoman. "The up-front cost is about a thousand dollars. Anybody who tells you otherwise is giving you a line of bull. And a lot of places will. You better believe it. We used to here, but we don't anymore. What's the use? Now, is anyone hungry? We have ramen noodles in the rec room."

"We already ate," said Paul.

The saleswoman got out a calculator and punched in numbers with the eraser of a pencil. "The monthly charge is four hundred and ninety-nine dollars."

"I only want to pay four hundred and fifty," said Paul. He just said this to say it. What he paid made no difference.

"O.K."

The dealership took the Fury in lieu of the up-front charges. The saleswoman came out with a razor blade and scraped off the anti-handgun decal.

Paul parked the new car by the tent, and he, Lonnie, and Carrie sat in the deep seats listening to "Gypsy Woman" turned loud on the six speakers.

"There's bass in that song I never even knew about," said Lonnie.

Then he and Carrie went in to bed, and Paul unrolled a sleeping bag in the tent. It was a canvas umbrella tent that smelled of old grass clippings. He left the flap open for the cool night air to drift in. Scratch stood in the opening for a while but would not enter. Paul took the last of Robin Redding's Percodans and stretched out in the sleeping bag.

The tent reminded him of a camping trip his scout troop had gone on in a state forest in Massachusetts. The knot instructor had been reprimanded for hitting students with rope ends, and all of the scouts had been required to spend one night in the wilderness armed with nothing but a compass and a cigarette lighter. Paul had hiked beyond the forest boundaries and into someone's garage, where he found a refrigerator stocked with orange juice, vodka, and plastic cups. He drank a couple of screwdrivers and fell asleep on newspapers in the garage. Waking cold in the early morning, he put on a military-surplus coat and found a ring of keys in the pocket. One of the keys fit a Ford LTD in the garage, and around dawn he eased the car out of the garage and down the driveway. He was fifteen years old and had driven his parents' car three times. He cruised an empty highway and got on the Massachusetts Turnpike by mistake.

It was peaceful on the highway, with sparse headlights drifting along the road through the early light. When he came to a tollbooth, all he had in his pockets was the compass he had been given for his survival experience. Two state troopers took him to a café, where they all had scones and coffee on the house before returning to the scout camp. Paul and his parents went up to juvenile court in Worcester, where the judge told him never to try that again, and Paul said he wouldn't. In the car on the way home from court, his mother had cried and said that Aaron would not have wanted to live to see such shame on the family.

"Sure he would," said Paul.

His father twisted around in the driver's seat and swatted at Paul with his right hand. "I'm going to hit you when we get home."

Paul's father forgot to hit him when they got home, and the only thing that happened as a result of Paul's brush with car thievery was that Uncle Bernard took him on a tour of the Massachusetts state prison in Walpole.

Coincidentally, just as Paul was remembering all these things, Uncle Bernard appeared in the open flap of the tent. Paul shone a flashlight on his beret and coarsely lined face.

"What are you doing here?"

"Listen. Bobby Record's people are looking for you."

"What time is it?"

"Just after midnight."

"How did you find me?"

"Made some calls."

"I had a painting delivered to Carlo."

"Carlo's dead. It was in all the papers. You have to disappear. An FBI guy clued me in. They've got an informant."

"Who?"

"Is this your car out here?"

Paul yawned. "I just got it tonight."

"Nice."

"Who's the informant?"

"How should I know? You have to scram."

"It's Ivan, isn't it?" Paul turned off the flashlight. "I'll bet anything it's Ivan Montgomery. But I don't feel like scramming. I'm already turned in for the night. Go away. Let me be."

"I promised your mother I'd find you."

"Go away."

"Supposedly, you have until the twenty-eighth."

307

"When is that?"

"In three days. They're all out on the Vineyard, and they're going to scatter Carlo's ashes on Sunday."

"Poor Carlo."

"But I wouldn't trust that. Leave now."

"I'm sleepy."

"Then I'll pull you out of there."

And he tried, but couldn't. He stood in the opening of the tent breathing heavily. "You were always a stupid bastard."

"Stop the presses."

"I remember once I took you candlepin bowling. Of course candlepins are tough for even experienced bowlers, but you wanted to get them all down right away."

"I'm sorry."

"You stamped your feet and walked off in a huff into someone else's lane. It was just stupid."

"How will you go home?"

"Route 2 to 395."

"You don't want to drive at night."

"Sure I do. I like driving at night."

On the next morning, Paul went to a shop in Ashland that sold guns, canoes, and art supplies, and tried to buy a gun, but there was a waiting period for a computer scan, and God knows what roadblocks that would turn up. Leaving the store, he found Alice Hanover standing on the sidewalk admiring the canoes.

"Where have you been?"

He told her, skipping over Scotland, and, fascinated, she observed the scar. "You just never really know, do you?"

"I know some things," said Paul. "I came here because of you. And I'll miss you when I'm gone."

"Don't say that. Nothing has really changed. We've always been friends, haven't we? Listen — tonight is Loom's birthday party. Do you think he'd like a canoe?"

"You have the rowboat."

"That's true," said Alice. "I also have something you would

get a kick out of." They went to a diner by the railroad tracks, where Alice opened her briefcase and took out some papers.

"The mayor's office gives scholarships every year, and so we get application essays. You want to hear one?"

"Yes."

"'To Whom It May Concern: I want to be a constitutional lawyer and this episode explains why. As is our custom, my boyfriend and I rented a room in the hotel last October to watch the World Series of baseball. We were drinking a substantial amount of cherry sloe gin. Suddenly uniformed police officers broke into the room with no warrant. In the confusion I slipped into the bathroom and began vomiting cherry sloe gin. This was not due to the police presence but because of simply having drunk too much while watching the ballgame. Then a policeman came in to see if I was all right, and he saw that I was not all right, for given the coloring of the cherry sloe gin, he surmised that something was very wrong indeed.'"

"I don't want to hear this."

"Wait, it gets better. O.K. '. . . And the policeman said, "Hey, you're really sick." An ambulance was summoned, and soon I was admitted to the hospital for observation. My point concerns the motivation of the police. It seems there had been a robbery in the hotel, and they mistakenly guessed that my boyfriend and I were the culprits. Thus it was that they smashed in our door. It cannot be tolerated in America the so-called Beautiful that the state should override the constitutional rights of the citizenry for the mere possibility of some greater good. Now, I don't drink much, and that's the truth. In fact, as I have told my mother many times, were I more of a drinker I might not have reacted so violently to the cherry sloe gin. To sum up, I want to be a lawyer so that I can prevent other people from having their rights trodden upon as were the rights of my boyfriend and me that night when the police broke down the door of the hotel.'"

"Give her a scholarship," said Paul.

"Isn't that wild? I have another essay here, but I don't think I'll read it."

"I could listen or not listen."

"It's not as jazzy as the first one. This other kid goes on and on about an old carpenter named Huck he shingled with on summer vacation," said Alice. "It turns out the wise and simple laboring man had many lessons to teach the middle-class youth."

"'This is a shingle,'" said Paul.

"But then the young workers locked Huck inside a portable toilet," said Alice, "and the toilet fell over, and Huck chased everyone with a hammer."

"Give Huck a scholarship," said Paul.

He folded the tent, packed the car, and drove out to Loom's birthday party that night with a European Union pen set wrapped in newsprint. Approaching the house, he heard someone wailing, "I want an equal dose!"

Paul knocked on the door. "Hello? Anybody home?"

Loom appeared in the hallway wearing a red terry-cloth robe with tags hanging from the sleeves. "Chester thinks he didn't get as much ice cream as Faith."

"Mama, I want an equal dose," cried the child from somewhere inside the house. Lame as his complaint might have been, his voice sounded heart-rending in the big and echoing house.

"He's very sensitive, and we're all sick of it," said Loom. He turned. "Chester!" he shouted. "Eat what you *have*, and you will get *more*."

They went into the kitchen. Chester huddled under the table and Faith looked at a book of Robert Capa photographs.

She smiled at Paul. "I got this for Father," she said.

"Come out, Chester," said Loom. "Come out before I take you by the ear." But Chester only repeated his demand for an equal dose.

Alice sent the children upstairs and the adults ate cake and drank Courvoisier and listened to the fighting overhead. Then a painted grate broke out of the ceiling and swung perilously above the table. Loom put down his fork and ran upstairs.

Paul stood to stop the motion of the grate. "I shouldn't have come," he said. "This is too weird."

"It is weird. But Loom doesn't care."

Paul took a drink. "But here's what justifies it in my mind. And I believe this. That I asked you first."

"Asked me what?"

"To move in," said Paul. "I asked you to move into the house in Bell Station. Don't you remember? When we were in college."

"Oh, Jesus," said Alice. She leaned back in her chair and laced her fingers behind her head.

"Why do you think that was?" said Paul.

"That's right," said Alice. "You did, honey. You asked me first."

Loom came back downstairs with the children. He explained that Chester had grabbed on to a bedpost, and Faith had pulled Chester by the feet, dragging the post over and through the ceiling grate.

"Let's go outside," said Chester.

"Good idea, Ches," said Loom.

They all sat in the courtyard. Alice brought out a Martin D-45 Dreadnought with pearl inlays — her present for Loom.

"Play us a song, doc," she said.

The children zoomed over the grass while Loom strummed the rosewood guitar.

"I skinned my knees in a small town," he sang. "I waxed my skis in a small town. I lost my keys in a small town, oh, and that's all right with me . . ."

Later, he and Paul went over to the Tallis house to look at the changes. Loom turned a key in the new lock.

"Taking the wall out was good," he said, "although you might have removed the broken plaster."

The interior was blank and white, and red tiles covered the wooden floors. A woodstove stood anchored in the hearth, new and black and shining.

"I don't get this," said Loom.

He was looking at the floor. Framed photographs had been taken apart and left in four stacks: photographs, mats, frames, and glass.

"Are you going to hang these?" asked Paul.

"We did hang them. There's an open house next week. We put them on the wall yesterday."

"What are they photographs of?"

Loom looked through them. "Nothing in particular. Fence posts and all that. But why would the contractor take them down, let alone take them apart?"

"It's strange."

"I'm sure there's an explanation," said Loom. "No teacher's ghost did it."

"Her daughter is a professional athlete who lives in Kirkmadrine, Scotland," said Paul. "She wins tournaments and rides horses. She's as happy as anyone I've met. She had some wisdom teeth out, but she's over that."

"How do you know?"

"Found her."

"Tell me something. Who pays for all of this?"

"Plastic," said Paul.

"This is what is wrong with the economy," said Loom. "Debt is king. Stocks are headed for a fall and everything else is running down a French drain."

"That reminds me, I got a new car."

Loom and Paul put the photographs back together and hung them once again on the walls.

27

They finished their inspection of the Tallis house. The upstairs bedroom had become a kitchen, the downstairs kitchen a bedroom, the old wood shop an exercise room with a stationary bicycle. The only reminder of the room's old purpose was a rack of carving tools on the wall.

Paul took down the V-shaped gouge with the wicker handle. "These were Roman's."

"Yes, and I'm not sure I like the chisels."

They left through the basement door and walked up beside the house. Lights flooded their eyes and died away. Tommy Maynard and the car chopper named Bodoni stepped from the darkness. Tommy snapped his wrist, making a yo-yo spin down and back.

"Want to see me walk the dog?"

"I thought you were on Martha's Vineyard," Paul said.

"Can't vacation," said Tommy. "I get antsy or something. And yet I wish I could, but I can't. People reading books and walking on beaches, they only depress me. I'm just the wrong kind." He did some trick with the yo-yo requiring both hands. "I'm just a born worker."

"Who are these men?" Loom said to Paul.

"Introduce us to the guy you've killed," said Tommy.

"Send him back to his family," Paul said.

"They'll see him again. I understand there's a lake out there somewhere."

"Who are they?" said Loom.

"They're tools," said Paul.

"I like you, kid," said Tommy Maynard. "I'd like to kick your fucking head in. And I just may. I don't know what it is that I'm in such a good mood. I guess I've never worked by a lake before."

"Find that hard to believe," said Bodoni.

"I shot at some people by a pond once but I was only trying to scare them."

"You sat and listened to me make a deal with Carlo," said Paul.

"Carlo's dead and burned," said Tommy. "The doctors gave their all, but there was no hope."

"You should honor what was said."

"Tough," said Bodoni, "because we're not."

Tommy put the yo-yo away and took out a gun. "What about this lake I keep hearing so much about. Which way do we go?"

The lake lay in a series of striations under the moon. House lights glowed in the wooded ring of the shore.

"It's all extraneous," said Tommy. "Like the Vineyard in that respect. It's beyond my understanding. I'm too simple to get it. Just that it's so beautiful to the eye, I guess."

"That, and recreation," said Bodoni.

"Let him go," said Paul.

"'Golden lads and girls all must, / As chimney-sweepers, come to dust,'" said Tommy.

"Is that what this is?" said Loom.

"Any minute now," said Tommy.

"Let us have a cigarette," said Paul. "Or has that also fallen away?"

Tommy sighed, switched the gun from his left to his right hand, and found a pack in his coat. "'Smoke ye all of it, do this in remembrance of me.'"

"None for me, thanks," said Bodoni.

Paul and Loom and Tommy smoked the cigarettes and flicked their ashes on the sand. They were king-size cigarettes and seemed to take a long time burning down. Water lapped the shore and bats darted like rags among black branches. Paul raised the wicker-handled gouge slowly.

"What do you have?" said Tommy. He aimed the gun at Paul's heart and grabbed the gouge. "You could get hurt carrying a thing like that."

"Just what we don't need," said Bodoni, looking past all of them.

Someone was walking down the beach with a flashlight, a girl, wearing a long red coat over a white nightgown. It was Faith Hanover.

"Oh Father, there you are," said Faith. "Come home. Come

home and look at this book of Robert Capa photographs. We can look at them together."

"In a minute, Faith," said Loom.

"See, Father, here's a picture of a man with a cigarette, carrying his daughter in Sicily. Isn't it sad? Her leg is broken."

She handed the book to Tommy and aimed the flashlight on the pages. The man in the photograph stood with shadowed eyes and held his daughter so that her bandaged leg shone in bright sunlight.

"This whole time we should have done it at the house," said Bodoni. "We should have done it in the street."

"Hello again, Mr. Nash," said Faith. "Are these your friends? Good evening, men."

"Miss," said Tommy.

"Where do we go from here?" said Bodoni.

Tommy dropped the chisel on the sand. He laughed. They all laughed. The situation seemed funny. "Nowhere," he said. "The scene is too crowded."

"It is crowded," said Faith, touching the photograph with her fingers. "Who is this in the doorway? It must be the mother. The poor woman. War is so terrible."

"We'll catch you later, Mr. Nash," said Tommy.

He and Bodoni left, Loom and Faith went up the beach with the flashlight playing on the picture book, and Paul stood for a long time by the water before making his way up through the trees and around the house.

The side door of the *Sun's* office, in the Temple of Hephaestus, stood propped open by a bundle of newspapers, and Angela and Ramona sat on the grass near the ash tree. Paul had meant to drive on by, but seeing his former comrades, he pulled over.

"The token looks broken," said Angela.

"I'm leaving town," said Paul.

"I thought you already left."

"I'm leaving again."

Angela tore open a bag of licorice laces and passed it around. "Where to?"

"South."

"Well, we're done," Ramona said.

"Why don't we go out to the Embers?" said Angela. "We'll bless your trip."

"I'm tired," said the moist-eyed Ramona.

Angela slid into Paul's car and he angled it into the street. An orange neon sign said the palm reader's shop was open. A policeman walked unsteadily to his cruiser like a wind-up soldier. Ashland dropped away behind them. The road turned west and fell steeply.

FRIDAY OF EMBER WEEK IN LENT SHRINE, said a sign. NO TRESPASSING AFTER DUSK.

"Ignore that," said Angela.

A cinder lane led to a grotto in the side of a hill. There were iron benches, tiers of burning candles, and a raised slab of gray stone.

Angela led him to a dispenser of holy water. It was made of aluminum and looked like a coffee maker on wrought-iron legs. She ran water on her fingers and touched his forehead. They lit candles in smoky red jars and then retreated to the stone table.

"They serve communion on this, I think," said Angela. "But what I like to do is stretch out on it." She pulled herself up onto the table and lay down in her blue jeans and white polo shirt. "The stone is very cool."

Paul went back to the candles and began taking the glass jars from their tin holders. He arranged them around the resting Angela.

"This is so pleasant," she said.

He sat down on one of the benches, stretching his arms along the back, and watched Angela surrounded by the flickering red jars.

"Hey, token," she said. "I was just having the craziest dream. You know those dreams you have when you're not really asleep? I was having my car emissions tested and the guy said there was something wrong with the equipment. He said he wasn't getting a reading. So he opened a trap door and we went down metal stairs to a room full of dancing people. They had this underground place no one knows about. Everyone was dressed in tuxedos and long, beautiful gowns."

"Sounds good."

"It really was."

He walked to the stone table and looked at her, and she looked at him, and she breathed out slowly, through her nose, and the warm vapors of her breath moved past his face like the dancing civil servants of her dream.

He crossed the Delaware River into Pennsylvania in the middle of the night. It was a big night for car transports. *Tree of Life — on the Road to a Better America,* read the side of a truck. The clouded sun rose while he was following the Alleghenies.

It began to rain, and a detour sent him off the highway, where a state trooper stood by a gas station waving his arm. Later Paul stopped in a gravel clearing beneath a sheared rock face. Across the road there was a valley dotted with farm buildings and silos.

Paul fell asleep and did not wake until dark, when he got out of the car to walk around. Sparks flew — he could see them beyond trees — and he went on through. A half-moon and hundreds of stars lit the sky as a man in overalls with a propane torch went about cutting up large metal tanks laid on their sides.

"What are you doing?" said Paul.

"You could call it recycling," said the man, lifting the goggles from his eyes. "Taking the steel out of these fertilizer tanks and cutting them down to a size where they can be processed. They'll be shipped out to a foundry and melted down. They've got to be certain lengths to fit in the big foundries, or in their pots, I should say — their melting pots or whatever."

"Got a good night for it."

"Oh, it's a beautiful night out, it's beautiful. I'm trying to get them done fast before the damned grass turns brown. You know, I've had a lot of fires going."

"What kind of fuel do you use?"

"I'm using propane. You can use propane or acetylene. Some people prefer acetylene, which burns a lot hotter. I'll probably go until my oxygen runs out."

"I'm an accountant," said Paul.

"Well, the economy is doing real good," said the man. "People are buying and they're building. Here's what I would do if I were you. Stay on 80 until just short of Youngstown and take 79 south to Charleston, West Virginia."

Paul took 79 to Charleston, 64 to Louisville, 65 to Nashville, 40 to Memphis, and 55 to Jackson, Mississippi. By then he had had nothing to eat or drink for two days except soda from filling stations, and he felt so light of body and mind that, had he opened the moonroof, he might have floated up and out of the car. The streets of Jackson were broad and curiously empty in the light of noon. He parked near a diner and got a newspaper, which said that it was Saturday. The diner had a blue sailfish mounted on the wall. He ate stuffed red snapper and fried potatoes and drank bottled beer. It was the best food he'd had in his life. Leaving the diner, he heard a band practicing a blues number in an empty tavern.

> *My sister's got a home entertainment center,*
> *She bought it yesterday,*
> *She put a hundred dollars down*
> *With a hundred years to pay,*
> *And when she turns up the volume*
> *She's a thousand miles away.*

From Jackson he took 55 to New Orleans, where he got off the interstate and followed a series of ever-smaller blacktops down to the delta. Canals laced the marshes, and a forest of bleached and broken trees rose like fingers from a flooded plain.

He drove through a town where moss-draped branches sheltered the main street and where children were boarding a bus in front of an elementary school. Faith Hanover's voice came back to him: *Come home, Father, come home.* He kept on, wanting to see the Gulf of Mexico, and arrived at last in an outpost called St. Denis, which was composed mostly of fenced lots containing oil drums and drilling equipment.

The beach was shallow and separated from the settlement by a ridge of thorny grass. Paul walked on the oil-dark sand and watched a squadron of brown pelicans gliding low and parallel to the coastline. He skipped rocks, collected grains of sea glass. Occasionally helicopters flew overhead. Some were large and hollow-bellied cargo carriers and some were the more familiar passenger models, which cut through the air with an impatient, nose-down tilt. The day was hot and fairly dry.

Eventually a helicopter descended to the beach and landed. This was perhaps a quarter mile from where Paul stood, but the blades raised such a whirlwind of grit that he had to turn away. As he waited for the rotor to stop, he wondered what would make a pilot land so near the shore with the tide coming in. Or was the tide going out? Maybe the engine had failed. Paul walked closer to the helicopter, which was white with a red pinstripe and stood on sled runners. Sunlight flared on the curving windshield. The door, wherever it might be, did not open, but he had all the time he would ever need in which to hear the pilot's story. Water covered the toes of Paul's shoes, the small round rocks rolled underfoot.

ACKNOWLEDGMENTS

Linda Tallis's remarks come from *A Treasury of Household Hints*, edited by Michael Gore. The hauntings associated with Mad Anthony Wayne, as well as Virginia Lovetree's explanation of chalcedony, may be found in *The Encyclopedia of Ghosts and Spirits* by Rosemary Ellen Guiley. The *Western Europe Phrasebook* of Lonely Planet Publications supplied the sentences to be used by travelers in an emergency. Elements of Rosine Boclinville's story were inspired by an article in *Insight Guides: Belgium*.

Portions of this book have appeared in *The New Yorker* and *Granta*. The author wishes to thank the editors. Thanks also to BBC Radio 4, which broadcast chapter 1, to Pat Strachan, Larry Cooper, Dawn Seferian, and Camille Hykes, for their diligent editing, and, as always, to Sarah Chalfant.